he never knew what
   delights would await her
         in the bridal bed . . .

Closing his eyes, he breathed in the sweet jasmine scent of her skin.

He wished he could pull the rest of the pins from her hair so the thick mass would tumble like waves of dark silk over his chest.

Images flashed in his mind of her rising above him, her tresses falling forward to surround their faces while she kissed him and he kissed her back.

Stifling a groan, he struggled to force the fantasy away. Once he had himself firmly under control, he angled his head to study her, smiling again to see her so deeply asleep. Unable to resist, he brushed his lips against her cheek.

With a sigh, she burrowed closer against him.

Swallowing a fresh groan, he stared up at the sky and let her sleep.

By Tracy Anne Warren

WICKED DELIGHTS OF A BRIDAL BED
AT THE DUKE'S PLEASURE
SEDUCED BY HIS TOUCH
TEMPTED BY HIS KISS

TRACY ANNE WARREN

Wicked Delights OF A Bridal Bed

A V O N
An Imprint of HarperCollinsPublishers

AVON BOOKS
An Imprint of HarperCollins*Publishers*
10 East 53rd Street
New York, New York 10022–5299

Copyright © 2010 by Tracy Anne Warren
Untitled excerpt copyright © 2011 by Tracy Anne Warren
ISBN 978–0–06–167344–3
www.avonromance.com

First Avon Books paperback printing: September 2010

Avon Trademark Reg. U.S. Pat. Off. and in Other Countries, Marca Registrada, Hecho en U.S.A.
HarperCollins® is a registered trademark of HarperCollins Publishers.

Printed in the U.S.A.

10 9 8 7 6 5 4 3 2 1

Wicked Delights
OF A
Bridal Bed

Chapter 1

Braebourne House
Gloucestershire, England
August 1812

Seated in the elegantly comfortable surroundings of her bedchamber, Lady Mallory Byron stroked idle fingers over the cat in her lap, his soft, inky fur a nearly perfect match for the solemn black of her gown. Charlemagne, a pampered housecat, who had started life as a kitten in a quiet corner of the Braebourne stables, purred with clear contentment, his green eyes slitted with undisguised pleasure.

If only I could be so at peace, Mallory thought. *If only my existence could be as ordinary and untroubled as his.*

But try as she might, nothing had been right in her life since the devastating morning she'd received word that her beloved fiancé, Major Michael Hargreaves, had been killed in battle.

Her throat squeezed tight at the memory, but her eyes

remained dry. After more than a year, she'd become inured enough to the loss that she no longer cried, certainly not as she had during those first anguished weeks when she would be abruptly overcome with bouts of uncontrollable weeping and despair.

Only in her dreams did she still experience those same sorrowful depths: vivid nightmares that crept upon her without warning to bring her awake on a strangled gasp, tears flowing in a hot, damp wash over her cheeks.

Intellectually, she knew it was time to put aside her grief and get on with the task of living—as her well-intentioned family gently kept urging her to do. But emotionally she felt numb, unable to find a path back to the carefree, lighthearted girl she'd once been. It was as if she had no heart at all now, her world veiled in a shadowy fog that held the worst of the pain at bay but kept out the pleasure and vibrancy as well.

Sighing, she continued stroking the cat's soft fur while she stared out the window at the magnificent, precisely maintained grounds of her brother Edward's estate. Home to the Dukes of Clybourne for more than two centuries, Braebourne was one of the finest aristocratic houses in England, a property of rare beauty and grace. But she appreciated none of it. Nor did she pay more than scant attention to the activities of her maid, as the girl bustled around in the room behind her.

"The guests are startin' to arrive fer the festivities, miss," Penny said in a pointedly cheerful voice. "The house is fairly swarming with noise and goings-on. Shall I go ahead now and lay out yer evening frock for tonight? Which one would you prefer? There's the pink silk with the fancy lace on the bodice? You always look so pretty in that color, what with your dark hair and rosy complexion. It's certain sure you'd be the belle of the evening dressed in that."

The girl paused, obviously hoping to receive a response. When Mallory offered none, Penny continued. "Or maybe you'd like the blue one instead? Her Grace, your mother, was telling me just the other day that she can't think of any lady who wears that shade so well and how perfectly it complements your aquamarine eyes. Then, of course, you're beautiful in any color you wear. So which shall it be, miss? Pink or blue or something else?"

Mallory knew she should make some reply, even if it was only to give a noncommittal shrug. Instead, she stayed silent, taking comfort in Charlemagne's small, undemanding presence as she moved her hand slowly over his velvety coat.

He wasn't the only animal in the room; at least a couple of the multitude of Byron family pets were in the habit of wandering in each day for a visit. A tabby cat named Elizabeth—short for Queen Elizabeth—was asleep in a tight curl in the center of her bed, while Henry, a brindle spaniel, lay stretched out atop the plush Aubusson carpet near the unlighted fireplace hearth.

The trio of animals had her little sister Esme to thank for their regal names. They'd all been added to the fold the year Esme had been studying the lives of great rulers. And although she might only remember a portion of those lessons now, the pet names continued on. Recently, Esme had taken to naming new animals after famous composers. The latest additions so far were a cat named Mozart and two dogs she'd dubbed Haydn and Handel. Esme might be a rather indifferent musician, Mallory thought, but one couldn't help but be amused by the whimsical and irreverent nature of her imagination.

A faint smile curved Mallory's lips at the thought, her gaze wandering toward "King" Henry where he lay across the room. As if sensing her regard, the dog raised his head and thumped his tail twice before returning to his nap.

"Which gown shall it be then?" Penny persisted. "You have only to say, and I'll see it pressed and ready."

Mallory drew a breath and prepared to answer. As she did, she heard the sound of voices carrying from somewhere in the corridor beyond.

Guests, she thought with an inner weariness.

She knew Mama and Claire meant well, but she really wished they had decided against throwing the usual late-summer house party. The annual celebration was tradition, commencing with the Glorious Twelfth and the beginning of the hunting season. But Mallory had already broken once with tradition this year by not attending the Season, and she would much rather have continued in that vein and skipped the house party as well. Instead, Braebourne would be overrun with family and friends who all wished to make merry.

Well, she wasn't in a merry humor and didn't relish the prospect of being put to the trouble of pretending she was. Nor did it help matters knowing how much Michael had always enjoyed this time of year. "Shaking off the city," he used to call it, as he reveled in the slower pace and quiet surroundings of the countryside.

A heavy pang squeezed inside her. Shunting aside the emotion and the recollection, she finally answered Penny's question. "I shan't need a gown this evening," she announced. "I have decided to take dinner in my room tonight and will not be joining the party."

The maidservant's eyes widened. "But miss—"

"Pray be so good as to convey my wishes to my sister-in-law, Her Grace. That will be all for now, thank you, Penny."

For a moment, the girl looked as if she might argue.

Instead, she lowered her gaze and dipped a respectful curtsey. "Yes, Lady Mallory."

Her lady's maid left the room.

Only then did Mallory let her shoulders sag, the last bit of starch going out of her spine. Bending over, she pressed her cheek to the top of Charlemagne's head and closed her eyes.

"Welcome, my lord. May I say what a pleasure it is to have you with us again," the butler greeted, as Adam, third Earl of Gresham, made his way into Braebourne's grand entry hall.

"Thank you, Croft," Adam said, passing his hat and gloves to the longtime retainer. "Good to see you again as well."

Exactly as he had each time he visited Braebourne, Adam took a moment to appreciate the splendor and refinement of his surroundings. He could still recall his very first visit when he'd been no more than a raw, eighteen-year-old down from Oxford with his new school chum, Jack Byron.

It had been summertime then too, the entry hall flooded with the same warm, natural light that cascaded now from the windowed dome curved high overhead. On the surrounding yards of ceiling stretched a visually stunning depiction of the rise and fall of the Roman Empire—a masterwork painted alfresco. While on the far side of the large hall lay a wide, sweeping marble staircase with a set of elegant Corinthian columns that rose majestically upward on either side. The floors were fashioned of a matching marble whose variegated hues always put him in mind of cool cream and warm clover honey.

Just then, he heard a sibilant whisper of skirts off to his right and glanced across in time to see a beautiful blond woman dressed in peach silk emerge from one of the nearby drawing rooms.

"Adam, you're here at last!" Claire, Duchess of Clybourne, proclaimed in dulcet tones, a genuinely happy smile of greeting brightening her features.

Turning, he strode to meet her, his polished black Hessians ringing quietly against the tiles. Reaching out, he clasped the young duchess's outstretched hands, then made her a courtly bow, pausing to brush a kiss across each of her knuckles before releasing her. "Indeed, Your Grace, I have arrived despite the occasionally treacherous state of the highways."

"You had no trouble on Byron lands, I trust?" she inquired.

He smiled. "None at all. His Grace maintains only the highest quality thoroughfares, as well you know. But enough of such mundane talk. I would much rather discuss how radiant you are looking, even more beautiful than I recall."

She flashed him a pleased though self-deprecating smile. "Thinner, do you not mean?" she corrected. "When last you saw me at the holidays, I was as round and wide as a wine barrel and twice as heavy."

"You were nothing of the sort," he reassured. "You were in a family way and glowing with a charm only impending motherhood can bestow."

Claire chortled and threaded her arm through his to lead him to the main staircase. "What a great load of fiddle-faddle, my lord, but you do it so well a lady can't help but be charmed. I see you are the same as ever, acting the shameless flirt and inveterate flatterer without so much as an ounce of contrition. No wonder women swoon so easily at your feet."

He grinned, a teasing twinkle in his eyes. "Thankfully not all of them, else I'd have a deuced difficult time wading through the mass of insensible females I would find in my path."

Claire laughed again.

"Clearly, motherhood and marriage agree with you," he observed on a more serious note, as the pair of them strolled up the stairs at a leisurely pace.

Her expression turned inward, her lovely blue eyes taking on a dreamy cast. "You are right, both suit me extraordinarily well."

"And how is little Lady Hannah, the newest Byron addition?"

Claire's smile widened with obvious pride. "She is wonderful. A true angel of a baby, bright and happy, and she hardly ever cries or fusses. Edward claims she looks just like me despite her dark hair. But she has his eyes and mouth, and when she scowls . . . well, there's no telling the two of them apart."

Adam grinned, knowing exactly the look she was describing. Although since Edward Byron's marriage to Lady Claire last year, it was an expression that rarely appeared on the duke's face anymore. "And where is Clybourne? Busy in his study?"

"Actually, he's out riding the estate with his steward today. One of the tenants is having trouble with a sour well, and they've gone to consult on the matter. Which, of course, leaves me to greet everyone for the party."

"A task at which you naturally excel."

Claire sent him a little smile.

"So who, pray tell, is everyone?" he asked.

"The family, of course, including some of the cousins. A few friends and enough extra gentlemen to round out the numbers at table. Mallory's old friends, Miss Milbank and Miss Throckly, who recently became Lady Damson, were invited most especially in hopes of pleasing Mallory. But now, I'm not so sure it was a wise idea."

At the mention of Mallory, his mellow humor fell away. "How is she?"

"Refusing to come to dinner tonight, that is how she is. Her maid brought word only a few minutes ago that Mallory plans to dine in her room. I tried reasoning with her, but she would hear none of it." Claire sighed and brought them to a halt as they rounded the top of the stairs. "Ava and I were so hoping that a bit of relaxed, friendly company would help cheer her spirits, but our efforts won't do an iota of good if Mallory won't leave her room."

He frowned. "No, clearly not."

His chest grew tight to hear of Mallory's continued unhappiness. Of course, he'd known she was mourning, as she had every right to do under the circumstances. For that reason, he'd forced himself to stay away over the past few months, aware she needed the freedom to deal with her loss in her own way and time. He'd exchanged a few letters with her, unable to help but notice that her missives dealt with everyday events rather than any personal details or emotions. She hadn't wished to share, and he hadn't pressed her to do so.

But more than a year had passed now, and he didn't like what Claire was telling him. Mallory was only two-and-twenty years of age, far too young to bury herself away like some ancient widow. She wasn't a widow at all. She and Hargreaves hadn't even been wed. They'd scarcely been engaged before the major had left to join the fighting on the Peninsula. It was time for her to move on whether she did it of her own volition or needed a helpful push.

As if sensing the direction of his thoughts, Claire gave his arm a squeeze. "I am so glad you've come. You and Mallory have always been such dear friends. I know seeing you will be just the thing to shake her out of her doldrums. Say you shall cheer her up, Adam," the duchess encouraged. "Please tell me you think you can."

He met her steadfast gaze. "Of course, I can," he said with determined assurance. "I'll have her in spirits again before you know it."

. And he would.

If it's the last thing I do, he promised himself, *I'm going to make Mallory Byron happy again.*

Chapter 2

$\mathcal{M}$allory was in the process of deciding whether to read a book or take a nap when a knock came at her bedroom door. Charlemagne, who had long since abandoned her lap in favor of a sunny spot in another chair, cracked open his eyes and stared toward the door, clearly annoyed by the interruption.

"I don't blame you a bit," Mallory murmured to the cat in a low voice. The other feline, Elizabeth, stood up, stretched, then began grooming her fur, while Henry's damp black nose twitched with patient curiosity.

Inwardly, Mallory suppressed a sigh. Very likely the caller was Claire or Mama, come to give her arm another twist over the issue of dinner. But she'd already said everything she had to say on the subject and saw no point in being compelled to repeat the exercise.

"Whoever it is, tell them to come back later," she ordered her maid. "I wish to rest and not be disturbed."

Penny, who'd been busy putting away handkerchiefs and tidying up various other sundries on Mallory's dressing table, stared for a pronounced moment before dipping an obedient curtsey and walking to the door.

Without glancing around, Mallory listened to the discreet murmur of voices whose words she couldn't quite make out. She recognized Penny's high feminine tone, but the person who answered was clearly not another woman. The caller's voice was low and throaty and laced with a seductive warmth that hinted at all manner of forbidden delights. In fact, she'd heard tell of more than one girl who'd swooned in his presence since even his most innocent statements seemed imbued with a frisson of sin as the words rolled from his tongue.

"Come now," she heard Adam Gresham coax in a silvery tone that was loud enough to carry this time. "I am certain your mistress wasn't talking about me when she said she didn't wish to be disturbed. Why don't you go ask her again? I'm sure she'll change her mind, do you not think?"

From the corner of her eye, Mallory saw Penny sag, then straighten again, the servant giving a firm shake of her head as she made a valiant effort to resist his entreaty.

"Or mayhap I'll just see for myself," he said, pushing the door wider despite the maid's presence. "Mallory, you're not really sleeping, are you?" he called in a half whisper, as he peered around the frame.

"If I had been," she replied on a mildly acerbic note, "I would not be any longer. You're as inconsiderate as the twins."

"Oh, surely I'm not as bad as that pair of scoundrels," Adam remarked. "Though come to think, perhaps I am." Stepping around her maid, he walked into the room. "Anyway, I knew I wasn't disturbing you since I could see the tips of your shoes and realized you weren't abed."

"I might have been dozing in this chair," she countered.

"You might, except for the fact that in all the years I've known you, I've never once seen or heard of you slumbering in a chair. You've remarked on more than one occasion that you hate to sleep sitting up."

Halting in the center of the room, he made her an elegant bow before straightening to his full height of nearly six and a half feet. His mouth turned up as he flashed her a roguish smile, his teeth showing white against his swarthy complexion. He swept her with a fulsome look, his warm, chocolate brown eyes gleaming in obvious pleasure.

She noticed that he'd let his hair grow a little since last they'd met, the thick, dark sable strands now threatening to brush the top edge of his neatly tied cravat. But his casually styled locks only enhanced the undeniable beauty of his face, with its sculpted forehead, proud nose and an uncompromising jawline that no one would ever mistake as anything but pure stubborn male.

"Hello, Mal," he said.

She returned his gaze, but not his smile, despite the undeniable swell of warmth that rose in her breast at seeing him. "Hello, Adam. You oughtn't be in here, you know. It isn't proper."

"You're entirely right. It's not," he agreed, crossing to drop with negligent ease into the chair opposite her. His long, athletic frame was clothed in a dark green coat and trousers with a cream waistcoat and gold watch fobs. Leaning back, he lounged with the insouciant grace of some fabled prince—strong, confident, and possessed of a dark sensuality that elicited interest wherever he traveled, and from whomever he met.

"Then again," he continued, "I've never been any great hand at obeying the rules. Besides, what's going to happen with your brothers no more than a quick shout away? And considering the open door and your maid's presence in the room," he added on a devilish turn, "chances are rather slim that I'll sweep you off your feet and ravish you in your bed. Do you not agree, Penny?"

The servant's eyes grew round as marbles before a giggle escaped her lips. "I should certainly hope not, my lord."

He laughed and sent her a wink that turned the girl's cheeks a bright crimson.

"Quit tormenting my maid, Lord Gresham," Mallory said in a reproving tone that had no real heat behind the words. "Penny, you may go along now and leave us. I shall be completely safe with his lordship."

Her maid glanced between them before nodding. "Yes, miss."

"But leave the door open," Mallory called at her retreating back. "Wide open."

Adam grinned.

Henry, who'd been watching the tableau from his spot near the hearth, chose that moment to rise and amble toward Adam, the dog's tail wagging a cheerful greeting that bespoke of long acquaintance and old, dear friends. Reaching out, Adam stroked the dog's sleek head, earning Henry's complete adoration.

Mallory watched, realizing that she was another of Adam's old and dear friends. She'd known him more than half her life and in all the ways that counted, he was like one of her brothers. Well, not entirely like her brothers, she amended, since he was a man that even the most frigid of females would deem desirable.

In fact, years ago as a green girl of sixteen, she'd nursed a powerful, though short-lived infatuation for him. But when he'd been kindly dismissive of her naïve overtures, she'd quickly realized that her feelings were not returned and had worked to put out the nascent flame. Since then, she'd been satisfied, even happy, to be his friend, any notions of deeper intimacy between her and Adam Gresham gone forever.

And now he was here to act as her friend once more.

"Mama sent you along, I suppose," she said. "Or was it Claire?"

He studied her for a moment. "Neither, at least not directly, although I have been charged with the goal of lifting your spirits."

She grimaced. "Yes, that seems to be everyone's duty these days. See to Mallory's flagging spirits."

"Which is why I shall make no such attempt," he stated, steepling his fingers together on top of his lean stomach. "You have every right to feel miserable under the circumstances, and I shall do nothing to curb your despondency."

"Oh," she said, air flowing in a small puff from her lungs.

"What is the point in trying to jolly you when you clearly do not wish to be jollied?"

"That's very . . . good of you, Adam," she said, wondering why she felt even lower of a sudden.

"You are a grown woman, after all, and if you don't want to eat dinner, that should be up to you."

She frowned. "Who says I don't want dinner?"

"Oh, I just assumed as much when the duchess told me you would not be joining us this evening."

"No, I shall not, but that doesn't mean I plan to forgo dinner. I will sup here in my room."

"Of course, I understand." He paused in quiet contemplation. "Although I should think you could be every bit as unhappy among company as you would be alone here in your room. No one will expect you to do anything but sit quietly and take a bite from your plate every now and again. If you like, we can all of us ignore you completely."

"Adam!"

His dark eyes met her own. "*Mallory*."

"Don't be cruel."

"It is not my intention to be. But I believe you ought to consider the fact that you are hurting your family by hiding yourself away. Surely dinner is of little enough consequence that you could put in an appearance this evening."

When he said it that way, she realized how churlish her behavior sounded. "But Adam, all those people . . ." she whispered.

He reached over and covered her hand with his. "All those people are family and friends, each of whom loves you."

She lowered her head. "Yes, I suppose you are right."

"There is no 'suppose' about it. But if it would make you feel easier, what do you say to sitting between me and one of your brothers? Drake, perhaps? He's quiet, always busy figuring out something in his head. That way, if you don't wish to talk, you don't have to."

She looked up again. "I guess that might be acceptable."

Adam smiled.

"But I'm not joining everyone afterward for cards and games. And I don't want to play the pianoforte. I cannot bear the idea of being put on display and forced to perform. I simply haven't the heart for it since . . . well since."

Adam squeezed her hand in silent understanding. "Once dinner is finished, I'm sure no one would mind if you retired early. Although I hope you won't rush off the instant the last dessert fork is laid down."

She narrowed her eyes. "Why is it I feel as though I've just been thoroughly managed."

His wide shoulders rose on a shrug of supposed innocence.

"And you say you're not in league with Claire and Mama. Has anyone ever told you that you're diabolical, my lord?"

His smile turned into a slow grin. "Just one of my many and varied talents, sweetheart." His thumb stroked over the top of her hand for a long moment, her flesh tingling where he touched. Before she had time to think more on it, he let go and leaned back in his chair. "Now," he asked, "what are you planning to wear?"

Her eyebrows furrowed slightly. "I hardly see that it matters. My grey silk will do, I expect."

Adam's dark brows joined hers in a scowl. "Grey? Lord no, you can't wear grey."

"Why not?"

"For one, because it's long past time you were out of mourning attire. For another, because I absolutely detest grey, at least on women."

"Black then, though I do not believe I solicited your opinion on the selection of my wardrobe," she pronounced with a challenging tilt to her chin.

"You may not have sought my opinion, but you're going to get the benefit of it nonetheless."

Her lips parted. "You are completely outrageous, do you know that?"

"And you are pigheaded enough to appear tonight in widow's weeds despite the fact that you are not a widow."

She froze, stricken, as a tight band of pain squeezed her chest. Adam was right, of course, she wasn't a widow and had never been a wife. Still, she felt Michael's loss as keenly as if she'd been both. Her lower lip trembled, a tear sliding without warning down her cheek.

Leaning forward, Adam wiped the moisture away with the edge of his thumb. "*Shh,*" he murmured. "I didn't mean to make you sad. Don't cry."

"I'm not usually weepy," she defended. "Not any longer. I thought I'd already cried all my tears."

"Apparently there are still one or two left."

She said nothing further, her damp gaze meeting his as he caught her chin gently in his hand. She waited, expecting him to tell her what everyone else said.

That all would be well.

That time would heal her wounds and make her whole again.

That she was young and had so much living left to do.

And most importantly, that she had mourned Michael Hargreaves long and well, but that it was time to let him go.

Her family meant to be kind, she knew. She had their steadfast love and support, and she adored all of them for it. And yet, despite their best intentions, they didn't understand, and she couldn't seem to find either the words or the strength to explain.

And now Adam was here.

Now Adam would say it all again.

She glanced away.

"He wouldn't like you wearing grey and black any more than I do, you know," Adam said in his deep, resonant voice. "He wouldn't want you clinging to customs that serve no useful purpose. Wearing pretty colors doesn't mean you loved him any less."

She trembled and shed another tear, which he brushed away as well.

"Besides," he told her, withdrawing his hand, "we can't have you going to dinner looking like a crow."

Her lips parted on a mixture of outrage and amusement. "A crow!"

Leaning back again in his chair, he crossed his arms. "Most definitely, particularly if you decide to wear black feathers in your hair."

She gasped. "I ought to box your ears for such impertinence."

"Go ahead if you'd like. The right or left?" He turned his head to both sides. "Which one do you prefer?"

She huffed out a breath. "Fine. I'll wear a shade other than black or grey."

Adam praised her with a smile.

"You'll make Penny ecstatic, you know," Mallory informed him. "She's been pestering me for the past month to put off my mourning. Every day when she asks what I'd like to wear, she suggests some bright color."

"Good for Penny. Why don't we ring for her now, so you can choose." Without waiting, he rose and crossed to the bellpull.

She tossed him a look. "Surely you don't plan to remain here while I select a gown?"

"I don't see why not. That way you won't be tempted to recant your decision. Or pick lavender."

"What is wrong with lavender? It happens to be one of my favorite colors."

"It also happens to be a traditional color for half mourning. Starting tonight, you're officially out of mourning, at least when it comes to your clothing. I think you should begin with something bold. Green, perhaps. You're always especially striking in that hue."

A sound soon came at the open doorway, drawing his attention. "Ah, and here is your maid now. Penny, Lady

Mallory has decided to attend dinner tonight after all. I am going to help her choose a gown."

The maid's eyes grew round at his bold and decidedly improper statement. But she made no objection, clearly pleased that Adam had been able to convince her mistress to change her mind about attending the party.

Perturbed, Mallory laid her hands on the arm of her chair. "I didn't realize you took such a keen interest in fashion. Have you turned into a man milliner, Adam?"

Rather than taking offense, he tipped his head back on a laugh. "Not at all. I don't give a rap about men's attire. Now women, they are another matter entirely. I love dressing women."

And undressing them, she thought, fully aware of Adam's reputation when it came to the fairer sex. No doubt he knew his way around a woman's garments—and undergarments, come to think—with the skill of a master violinist playing a concerto.

Heat warmed her cheeks, and she found herself vaguely shocked by such musings. She swallowed, wondering if Adam had noticed. If he had, though, he gave no sign, his attention fixed on the pair of evening dresses Penny was holding up for his inspection.

Begrudgingly grateful for his interference, Mallory leaned back and let him choose.

Chapter 3

A few minutes past six o'clock that evening, Adam stood bare-chested in front of the washstand mirror. With confident precision, he drew the sharp edge of a straight razor across his cheek, coming away with a coating of soap and black stubble. Rinsing the blade clean in a basin of warm water, he repeated the routine action. Generally, he ended up having to shave twice a day since his beard grew fast and heavy.

After years of living a hairbreadth away from penury, he'd grown used to performing his own ablutions without the aid of a valet. And although his recent increase in wealth had afforded him the luxury of hiring a man to care for his clothes and other personal belongings, he still preferred to bathe and dress himself without assistance. God knows he didn't need anyone to hold his shirt and trousers for him. He could put them on himself, thank you very much.

Scraping away a last strip of whiskers, he rinsed the

razor, dumped the water and poured fresh. Using both hands, he splashed his cheeks clean, then reached for a nearby towel. With his face presentable enough now for company, he took up a pair of silver-backed brushes and ran them through his hair, smoothing the dark, wayward strands into place. As he did, his thoughts turned to Mallory, her beautiful countenance alive within his mind's eye.

I was hard on her, he realized. But had he been too hard? Had he been insensitive and unsympathetic to her needs and her grief?

His heart gave a painful beat to remember her tears, her distress having nearly proved his undoing. For the last thing in the world he would ever wish to do was hurt Mallory.

He remembered his first sight of her today and his shock at seeing her looking so thin and hollow-eyed. Her blue-green gaze had been as lonely as a distant sea, her cheekbones sharp beneath skin as pale as alabaster, her raven-dark tresses arranged into a severe chignon that exactly matched her doleful mood. The need to protect had risen inside him in an instant, making him long to snatch her up in his arms and hold her close.

Instead, he'd forced himself to sit and talk, determined to do what was best for her even if that best might not be what she wished at the moment. Because mourning or no, everyone could see she needed a push. She'd been walled up inside her grief for far too many months now, allowed to retreat so that she was a shadow of her former vibrant self.

Quite obviously, continuing to leave her to her own devises wasn't the answer. Nor was tiptoeing around and indulging her with kind words, attentive care and concern. What she needed was a bit of shaking up, a diversion that would draw her back into the life she used to lead. While it was true that nothing would ever be quite the same for her again, it didn't mean that her life was over.

He understood about grief, knew firsthand what it meant to lose someone so dear that the hole left behind yawned as wide and endless as a chasm. But he'd learned to go on, and so would Mallory.

From what he'd observed though, she was too entrenched in her pain right now to break free on her own. She needed someone else to help her escape.

She needed him.

After all, when you loved someone, that's what you did. You helped them.

And God knows, if there is anyone on this earth I love, it's Mallory Byron.

Even now, he could remember the day, the very instant, he'd recognized his feelings for her. The way the awareness had reverberated through his muscles and veins as though he'd taken a jolt from one of Drake's electricity machines.

"Come play a game, Adam," she'd entreated, her lilting voice filled with all the merry innocence of the sixteen-year-old schoolgirl she'd been then.

He hadn't wanted to play. He'd been a grown man of six-and-twenty. What use did he have for children's games? Especially since he'd stopped being a child long before his youth was even done. But somehow Mallory had drawn him in, she and her young female cousins and little brothers, the happy band frolicking with youthful abandon on the verdant grounds of Braebourne. The time of year hadn't been all that different than it was now, late summer, with its moist ripples of sunshine and heat, droning insects and blossoming honeysuckle bushes releasing clouds of succulent perfume into the air.

Mere seconds after he'd begrudgingly agreed to Mallory's scheme, the world went dark, the black cloth of the hoodman-blind thrust over his head. All of the participants squealed with excitement, hands spinning him in a circle before dancing backward to evade his pursuit. They laughed and prodded him as he turned and chased, their footsteps soft against the grassy lawn.

Then he caught someone, one of the older girls by the feel of her as she squirmed and struggled in his embrace. She was a delightful handful, her lithe young body brushing against his own in a most enticing way. Whirling her around, he held her fast, as he reached up to yank the hood from his head.

His gaze locked with Mallory's, her aquamarine eyes gleaming more brilliantly than the sky. Air rushed from his lungs, then stilled completely when she leaned up and kissed him, laughing all the while. Her touch was nothing more than a peck, an affectionate brushing of lips. But that simple touch sent his world spinning around him, and improbable as it seemed, he knew in that moment that he loved her. Stunned and uncomfortable, he pulled away, making some excuse that took him quickly back into the house.

He waited for the emotion to fade, telling himself he couldn't trust such irrational feelings. She was only sixteen, after all, far too young for him to consider in any adult sort of way. It was preposterous, mooning over a girl not even out of the schoolroom. And yet she was bright and sweet-natured and so unbearably lovely the sight of her made him ache.

Over the weeks to follow, he felt like some jaded roué coveting a tender young morsel and did his best to steer clear of her company. She was forbidden fruit, and he trembled with longing to pluck her from the vine. But he couldn't have her, and not simply because of her youth and the disparity in their ages.

For a start, she was his best friend's sister, the cherished daughter of a family he'd come in many ways to regard as his own. But as much as Jack and the other Byron brothers had welcomed him into their circle, he knew they'd take his head off if they so much as imagined he had designs on their little sister.

Yet even if that obstacle might have been overcome, and he waited a respectable amount of time for Mallory to come of age before courting her, she was still as far beyond his reach as the stars in the sky.

Galling as circumstances might be, he'd inherited a title that was all but worthless. His wastrel father had seen to that—gambling, drinking and whoring to the point where there'd been almost nothing left of the estate except a moldering house and lands so poorly utilized they barely provided the funds to pay the necessary taxes each year. His father would have sold those off as well if the entailment hadn't kept him from liquidating every last nail and brick. Nonetheless, the old devil had done a masterful job stripping the estate of its pride and possessions, so that pitifully little remained by the time the reaper came to carry the earl off to his final reward.

Or eternal damnation more like, Adam thought now, as he reached for his shirt and pulled it on over his head.

No, when it came to Mallory he'd had nothing to offer her back then, and he hadn't been so idealistic as to imagine that love would make up for a life of want and privation. Of course, she would have had the large dowry Clybourne settled on her, enough money to keep them both in reasonable comfort and style. But he had too much pride to be branded a fortune hunter and too much respect for Mallory to ever want her to question whether it had been her he'd wanted or her money.

And so, he'd given her up before he'd ever had her, burying his love for her as deep as he could force it to go. Instead, he'd settled for her friendship, a pale substitute for his real desires but a small salve nevertheless.

Or at least it had been until she'd met Michael Hargreaves and fallen in love. He'd died a little the day she'd announced her engagement to the other man, knowing he'd lost her forever.

Or so he had thought.

Hargreaves had been a fine man, and he would never have wished him ill. When he'd heard news of the major's death, he'd been saddened by the loss—especially for Mallory's sake. But he'd also experienced a secret sense of relief, along with a tiny spark of hope that flickered back to life inside him.

Mallory was free again and could be his, as he'd never before allowed himself to imagine she might be. Not only was she a grown woman now, he was no longer one step shy of the poorhouse.

Roughly two years ago, he'd scraped together enough money to make a couple of investments with Rafe Pendragon, a man reputed to be a financial wizard. Jack had mentioned his own decision to give the man's advice a try, and Adam had followed suit. Thank God he had, since the risk had more than paid off, garnering him what now amounted to a sizeable fortune.

With money to spare, he was finally starting to undertake the improvements to his estate that he'd always longed to make. Reclaiming the land was his first priority, large numbers of fallow acres having been allowed to turn wild over the past twenty years of disuse. Next, he planned to build new houses, repair many existing ones and give his tenants the means needed to profitably work the land. The rents alone would provide him with a good income, allowing him to concentrate the rest of his funds on repairing Gresham Park and seeing the grand old property returned to its former glory. Even more, he wanted to bring laughter and love back to a house that had known far too little of either. He wanted to bring Mallory there as his wife.

But first she would have to emerge from her grief, and while she did, he would have to continue being patient.

I've waited for her this long, he mused with stoic resignation, as he reached for one of the starched linen cravats his valet had laid out for his use. *I can wait a while longer. If necessary, I would wait an eternity to have Mallory as my own.*

Ignoring the ache of longing that settled in his chest and lower in his semiaroused groin, he turned to the mirror and began tying the cloth around his neck in an intricate knot.

Earlier, when he'd made his remark about ravishing Mallory on her bed, he hadn't entirely been joking. Oh, what he wouldn't give to have locked them alone inside her room so he could kiss and caress her until she couldn't think of anyone or anything but him. Stripping that black dress off her body would have been both a privilege and a pleasure. Yet another desire that would unfortunately have to wait.

Admonishing himself for his wayward thoughts, he fixed a final knot in his cravat, then reached for his white waistcoat with its long row of mother-of-pearl buttons. A black evening jacket came next. Last he added a few extras—a pocket handkerchief, a gold watch he'd carried since his days at university and an onyx signet ring that had belonged to his grandfather.

After a last glance in the mirror, he left the room to join the assembled company for dinner.

Mallory slipped into the drawing room on silent feet, hoping none of the others would take notice of her arrival. Her luck held for exactly thirty seconds before her mother turned and caught sight of her.

With a smile on her elegant oval face, Ava, Dowager Duchess of Clybourne, glided across the room, the bronze silk of her evening gown complementing her trim figure and soft chestnut hair. Were it not for the few, fine strands of silver in her tresses and the faint lines that fanned out near the corners of her clear green eyes, one might have imagined her to be a much younger woman. Even her own children agreed that she didn't look old enough to have borne all eight of them, the eldest of whom was now four-and-thirty years of age.

"Hallo, dear," Ava greeted in a quiet voice before leaning over to dust a kiss against Mallory's cheek. "I'm so glad you changed your mind about joining us tonight."

Mallory gave a murmur of assent, but said nothing more.

"And don't you look beautiful. That willow green gown is most becoming. I hope you won't take it amiss, but it's good to see you in something other than black."

Mallory held her tongue again, deciding not to mention the fact that she'd had help from an unexpected source in choosing tonight's attire. As if attuned to her thoughts, Adam turned from where he stood across the room in conversation with her brothers, Jack and Cade, and their friends, Niall Faversham and Lord Howland. A slight smile curved Adam's mouth, his rich brown eyes warm with approval as they swept over her.

And why should he not approve, she thought, _considering he's the one who picked out my dress?_ She shot him a look that drew a wider smile.

Glancing away, she focused her attention on her mother. Seconds later, they were joined by her sisters-in-law, Grace and Claire.

Claire smiled and leaned near. "I hope you're not cross with me for saying something to Adam this afternoon," she whispered.

Mallory gave a tiny shake of her head. "How can I be cross when I know you only mean well."

Claire relaxed. "I do, truly. Now come and speak to Meg. She's trapped on the sofa at present."

Her other sister-in-law, Cade's wife, was "trapped" because she was heavily pregnant with the couple's second child. Despite being due to deliver late that month, Meg had insisted on coming to Braebourne for the country party. Mallory knew that Cade had initially worried about the journey south but had given up arguing without much protest. He was glad Meg would be surrounded by family during her confinement and labor.

Apparently aware of the attention she was receiving, Meg waved them over, her lake blue eyes alive with a tranquil happiness Mallory could only envy. Meg and Cade were so completely in love, their bond was plain to see. The same could be said for all of Mallory's married brothers, each of them in turn doting on his wife with an open affection that was returned fully and without reservation.

Before Michael died, Mallory thought she would share that same kind of wedded bliss. Instead, he was cold in his grave, and she was alone. Not for an instant did she begrudge her family their happiness, but seeing them so content served only to highlight her own emptiness and loss.

Abruptly, she wished she could retreat back upstairs to her room. Instead, she forced herself to cross to the sofa and sink down next to Meg. She and Meg exchanged warm greetings, as Grace and Claire took up chairs on either side.

Their cousin India joined them moments later, her pert green eyes dancing with warmth and good humor. Two years ago, she'd married the Duke of Weybridge, a handsome devil who'd quite swept India off her feet. As Mallory watched, India glanced toward her husband, Quentin, who stood in conversation with Edward, Drake, Lord Damson, and Edward's personal secretary, Mr. Hughes. Their gazes met, India and Quentin sharing a brief, though thoroughly intimate, smile before glancing away again.

A new knot formed in Mallory's chest as memories swept through her of another occasion when she'd been in this room with India and Quentin and so many of the others. How happy she'd been then—Christmas three years ago, the day she and Michael announced their engagement. How long ago that seemed, the last time Michael had been with them all at Braebourne.

A chill went through her, her emotions drawing inward so that she scarcely noticed a new pair of ladies join the group gathered around the sofa. She made some perfunctory murmur of greeting to her old friends, Lady Damson and Miss Jessica Milbank, ignoring the small furrows of worry that marred their smooth foreheads.

Directing her attention elsewhere, Mallory gazed around the room. Her twin brothers, Leo and Lawrence, and India's brother, Spencer, lounged with negligent ease near one of the windows in the far corner. No doubt the three were trading stories about life at Oxford, Spencer having just graduated while the twins were on holiday awaiting the start of the next term.

In another corner sat thirteen-year-old Esme, along with India's younger sisters Anna, Jane and Poppy, and Claire's teenaged sisters Nan and Ella. Not yet of age, the girls would be taking their meals in the schoolroom rather than joining the adult company. But as Mallory knew, given that Esme had spoken of little else this past month, her sister was simply glad to have so many other young people in residence and didn't mind being relegated upstairs.

And arranged in a last, very elegant group, were those at the opposite end of the age spectrum. Among them were: kind, plump cousin Wilhelmina, who'd acted as London chaperone for her and Claire last year; Claire's parents, Lord and Lady Edgewater; the local vicar, Mr. Thoms; family friends, Lord and Lady Pettigrew; and her mother, Ava.

Being with them all should have put Mallory at ease. Yet as comfortably familiar as the assembled guests and relations might be, she no longer felt as though she belonged.

Why, she asked herself, *did I ever let Adam talk me into coming downstairs tonight?*

Suddenly Meg tensed for a moment before relaxing again. "Gracious, that was a hard one. Right under the ribs," she said, laying a hand on her rounded belly. "This baby certainly can kick. I keep telling Cade I'm carrying a boy again, but he says he wants a daughter this time. I suspect we're going to have to try for a third baby if he's to get his wish."

"Well, I'm sure you won't have any trouble talking Cade into helping you with that particular endeavor,"

Grace remarked with a saucy smile. "But perhaps you ought to give birth to *this* baby before you mention wanting the next."

Meg nodded. "You're right. Poor love, he nearly paced a hole in the drawing room last time I went into labor. I believe he was in more pain than I was."

All the ladies laughed, everyone except Mallory, who couldn't muster the requisite humor. After that, the conversation turned to babies and the third-floor nursery, which was full of nursemaids and little Byrons. India's firstborn son, Darius, was also there, a lively playmate for his other toddler cousins.

If she and Michael had married, Mallory realized, she might have a baby in the nursery now too.

Rubbing her icy fingers together in her lap, she wondered if she could find a way to slip out of the room unnoticed and make it back upstairs. She was considering her options when Adam suddenly appeared.

"Ladies," he said, sending them all a dimple-flashing smile. "Pardon the intrusion, but I wondered if I might borrow Lady Mallory for a moment or two?"

Feminine eyebrows arched with curiosity, but no one voiced an objection.

Less than a minute later, Mallory found herself off the sofa and halfway across the room, standing with Adam in the only quiet corner remaining.

She folded her arms at her waist. "So, what is so urgent that you had to drag me away?"

"Is that what I did?" he drawled. "And here I thought I was providing you with a much-needed rescue."

Her gaze shot to his before glancing away. "I had no such need," she dissembled, perversely refusing to acknowledge that he was right.

"So you weren't on the verge of bolting? Because from my vantage point, you looked as though you were contemplating mutiny."

Why does he always have to be so deuced observant? she thought. "I haven't the faintest idea what you mean."

A soft chuckle rumbled from his chest. "Of course you do not." Reaching over, he caught one of her hands in his and drew it over his arm.

"Now, what are you up to?" she asked.

"Dinner. If I'm not mistaken, Croft just informed the duchess that everyone may go in."

And so it would appear he had, Mallory realized, as Claire rose from the sofa and began circulating among the guests to share the news.

Mallory released a sigh. "You were right before, you know, when you said I wanted to mutiny. I do, so why don't I just slip out when no one's looking and go upstairs to my room?"

"Now now, none of that." He patted her hand. "Anyway, you're doing fine."

"Am I?" she said. "Well, I suppose we shall see just how fine I am by evening's end."

Chapter 4

"Have another spoonful of the cheese soufflé," Adam encouraged Mallory, as he directed one of the footmen to add more to her plate. "I know it's one of your favorites, and you need to eat something. You've scarcely touched your dinner so far."

Mallory waited until the servant moved away before she replied. "I'm saving room for dessert."

"Then you've plenty of room to spare. Now, eat that soufflé and a few bites of the duck as well. It's quite excellent, as you'd know had you done more than slide it around in the sauce."

Her thumb played over the elaborately scripted C engraved on the base of her silver fork. C for the ducal title Clybourne rather than for Claire as her sister-in-law sometimes liked to tease. "Strange," she remarked, "but I didn't realize I was in need of another mother. Obviously

I've been living under the mistaken impression that the one I have is sufficient."

A brief silence fell as Adam reached for his glass of Bordeaux and took a swallow. Carefully, he returned the glass to the table. "Oh, the dowager duchess is more than up to the task of being your mother. Unfortunately, though, she cannot be everywhere at once and perforce requires the occasional surrogate to act in her stead. So eat your dinner like a good girl and don't make me call for reinforcements."

On her other side, Drake let out a muffled guffaw, having clearly been eavesdropping on their conversation. Instantly realizing his mistake, he turned away to address a comment to Miss Milbank, who was seated on his left. Within seconds, the pair were engaged in conversation, Jessica Milbank appearing slightly dazed to suddenly find herself the focus of Lord Drake's undivided attention.

Mallory's mouth tightened as she swung back to confront Adam. "My lord Gresham," she stated in a voice too low to carry, "are you implying that I am behaving like a child? Because if you are—"

"No, not at all," he interrupted. "I am simply trying to make the point, however inexpertly, that you ought to take better care of yourself. As your friend, I feel it my duty to mention that you've become far too thin over the past year. The pretty roundness in your cheeks is gone, along with that extra curve to your hips that I've always admired. I'd like to see both of them return. So eat your dinner, Mallory. Please."

She swallowed and glanced away, begrudgingly aware that Adam was right. In her grief, food held scant interest for her. Over the past months, she'd eaten for reasons of necessity not enjoyment, finding it easy to skip a meal here and there without noticing the lack. But perhaps she'd skipped a few too many since he wasn't mistaken that she'd dropped several pounds. Her maid Penny could attest to that better than anyone, since the girl had taken in all of her dresses—some of them more than once.

She studied the offerings on her plate.

Please, Adam had said. And Adam almost never said please. A forceful man, he wasn't the sort to beg, not even in the most minor of ways. Yet he'd begged her over a meal.

Am I really such a hopeless case?

With an inward sigh, she acknowledged that perhaps she was. Taking up her fork again, she slid the tines into the airy mass of whipped eggs, cream and cheese. The bite melted on her tongue with a pleasant tang.

Suddenly intent on trying for Adam's sake if no other, she ate another forkful before picking up her knife to cut a piece of duck. She discovered Adam smiling at her as she chewed and swallowed the game, finding it flavorful despite its now-lukewarm temperature. She ate most of that course and the next, earning his unspoken approbation.

When dessert arrived, she really didn't have room, having consumed more tonight than she had in too long to recall. "Oh, I shall never manage," she said, casting a baleful eye at the delectable-looking fresh peach tart with vanilla-scented cream.

"Of course you can," Adam told her. "Two bites, then you may stop."

"One," she said.

Yet with her sense of taste reawakened, the first forkful of flaky crust, sweet fruit and cream proved irresistibly delicious. Giving way to the urge, she ate another bite, then another. Before she knew it, she was licking the last bit of crumbs and cream from her fork, wishing it wasn't considered gauche to do the same with her plate.

Glancing up, she met Adam's twinkling brown gaze. "Delicious, was it not?" he remarked.

She laid her fork across her empty plate, one of the footmen appearing with silent efficiency to clear it away. She waited until he left before replying. "It was . . . satisfactory," she said.

A laugh burst from Adam's lips. "If that was satisfactory, I'd love to see you eat something you really liked."

She didn't smile—she just didn't seem to have it in her to smile these days—but she enjoyed watching Adam's amusement. He was never handsomer than when he laughed or smiled, his cheeks creasing with long, sigh-inducing dimples, his even teeth flashing white against his swarthy complexion. Sometimes he looked almost boyish, a trace of mischief peeking from his dark eyes as though he were concealing a wicked secret he hadn't decided whether or not to share.

He was a complex man, she knew, his personality composed of an infinite variety of interests, intellect and desires. He was full of contradictions as well, his reputation shockingly wild on the one hand while his actions could be surprisingly sensible, even staid, on the other. There was a goodness in him that few people saw—or rather that he let people see. But he let her see, and she was grateful for his openness, his candor. She knew she owed it to him to be equally candid.

"When Claire asks the ladies to withdraw, I'm going upstairs to bed," she told him. "Please don't try to persuade me to do otherwise. I cannot bear the idea of returning to the drawing room to sip tea and make pleasant conversation. I can't pretend to be happy when I'm not."

"No one expects you to, Mallory."

"Don't they? It's been over a year. They all want me to be normal again." She stopped and drew a calming breath, knowing she should say no more on that subject. "I-I'll bid you a good night and hope your dreams are sweet."

"I shall wish you the same, but first I must ask a favor."

Her hand grew still in her lap. "Oh, what is that?"

"Come riding with me tomorrow. We can set out early before everyone else is stirring and make a morning of it."

"I-I'm not sure."

"Why not? You've always loved to ride."

"Yes, but—"

"But what? The exercise will do you good. Besides, if you're out of the house, you can't very well be expected to paint screens or embroider handkerchiefs."

"Claire hates painting screens, so I'm sure that won't be among the suggested activities. As for handkerchiefs, no one embroiders those in company any longer."

"Mayhap not, but there's certain to be something in the offing. Or maybe I mistake the matter, and you'd rather spend the morning in one of the salons arranging flowers and trading bons mots with the ladies."

"What time do we leave?" she asked.

He grinned. "Seven, if that's agreeable. It's full light by then but still too early for most of the guests to be awake and dressed."

She wasn't used to rising that early either, but it would be worth the agony in order to escape the party guests. "Seven it is. I'll meet you in the stables."

"I'll have the horses saddled and ready."

With the sublime timing of a duchess, Claire rose from her place at the far end of the immense dining table, a hush falling over the company. "Ladies," she announced. "I believe the gentlemen are ready for their port and cigars. Let us repair to the drawing room, where we can enjoy sherry, tea and unpolluted air."

Everyone chuckled, the gentlemen rising to their feet to assist the ladies from their chairs.

Adam leaned over Mallory's shoulder as she stood. "In the morning," he whispered in her ear.

"Until tomorrow."

With relief, Mallory made her way out of the dining room, and after employing a small bit of stealth, upstairs to the sanctuary of her bedchamber.

At ten minutes after seven the following morning, Adam tapped his quirt against the side of one of his polished black Hessians while he waited just outside the stable for Mallory to arrive.

As promised, the horses were saddled and ready, his roan stallion huffing air through his nose and occasionally tossing his head with an impatience to be off. For Mallory, he'd selected a spirited mare, knowing she wouldn't enjoy riding an animal with too placid a disposition. Pansy, the grooms had assured him, was an excellent choice despite her uninspiring name.

One of the barn cats sauntered past, pausing to give him a haughty inspection before continuing on her way with a flick of her slender brown tail.

He was beginning to wonder if he'd have to go knock on Mallory's door again when suddenly she was there, slightly breathless as though she'd been rushing. She came to an abrupt halt, her breasts rising and falling beneath the military-style braid and gold buttons that adorned her bodice, the long skirt of her navy blue riding habit gathered heavily over her arm. On her head she wore a tall shako-style hat with a length of white gauze tied around the crown, its ends left to trail down her back.

"My pardon for being late," she said. "And before you remark on the somber color of my attire, this was the only riding habit Penny could make ready on such short notice. I haven't been riding in ages, and she did what she could."

He smiled and walked forward. "Then you may extend my compliments to your maid since she's turned you out splendidly. As for your slight tardiness, I'm just glad you are here and didn't change your mind about going on our outing."

"I assumed if I failed to show up, you'd come after me."

He laughed, knowing himself fairly caught.

She drew another deep breath, her breasts rising and falling again in a display of femininity he couldn't help but admire, particularly when a pair of the buttons gleamed in rather strategic locations.

"You slept well, I hope," he said, forcing his thoughts away from her ample charms.

"Well enough."

"Bad dreams?" he asked, knowing her too well not to hear faint undertone in her voice.

A pair of tiny creases lined her forehead. "Nothing out of the ordinary." Swinging around, she gazed toward their waiting mounts. "The horses are ready, I see, and look eager to be off. Shall we go, my lord?"

Briefly, he considered pressing the matter of her bad dreams but decided to let her keep her secrets—for now. "Yes, let's be off before some of the others awaken and decide to wander our way."

Needing no further prompting, Mallory went to the mare, taking a minute to rub the animal's forehead. The horse chuffed with obvious affection.

"I take it the two of you are acquainted," he said.

"Pansy and I are old friends. Ned bought her for me not long after my first Season, and I rode her often that summer and fall. We tried taking her to Town the next spring, but she started nipping at some of the other horses, so we decided she'd feel more comfortable in the country."

"Well, she'd better not try nipping Eric, or she might find herself nipped back."

"Eric?"

Adam grinned, the stallion stamping a hoof in acknowledgment of his name. "That's right. He's a big, powerful brute, rather like a Viking, so I thought Eric seemed fitting. Plus he has a reddish coat, thus, Eric the Red."

Light gleamed in her jewel-toned eyes, and for a fraction of an instant, he thought she might smile. But she didn't, her mouth remaining set as she moved to lead Pansy toward the mounting block.

"Allow me," Adam said, stopping her.

Before she had time to protest, he settled his hands around her waist and lifted her effortlessly upward. Instinctively, she laid her palms against his shoulders, clinging to him as he set her slowly onto the sidesaddle. Propriety demanded he release her the moment she regained her balance. Instead, he left one hand curved against the softness of her hip, relishing the sensation of womanly flesh and rich cloth rubbing against his skin as she worked to hook one knee into the saddle and the other foot into its stirrup. If possible, he would have managed the whole procedure for her, sliding his palm beneath her skirt to fit her knee around the pommel, then stroking her bare calf as he eased away.

But it was far too soon for such bold moves, and considering her current emotional state, he was a cad even to think such things. Then again, he was a man, a sexually healthy adult male who was denying himself the pleasure of a willing bed partner for the duration of this fall season—and quite probably for some long while after. But much as it might pain him, he wanted no one now but Mallory.

She'll be mine, he swore to himself. *She has to be mine.*

With her securely settled and arranged, he handed her the reins, then turned away to stride to his horse. Swinging up easily into the saddle, he wheeled his stallion around and met Mallory's gaze. "Ready?" he demanded.

She nodded. "Shall we ride toward Snowshill?"

He nodded back. With a cluck of his tongue, he set Eric in motion, Mallory catching up fast to ride confidently at his side.

The yards flew past at a comfortable gait, the countryside stretching before them in a collage of shape, color and texture. The loamy scent of earth and grass mingled with pastoral aromas of grazing sheep and ripening fields of barley and wheat. Thick areas of woodland dotted the landscape in variegated shades of brown and green, while yellow, pink and white flowers nestled beneath the sheltering branches of a forest so ancient only the trees knew their true age.

Still within the boundaries of Braebourne, they forded a small stream, then rode up the other side to a lush hill that had splendid views of the valley and a small village beyond. To the east stood Braebourne herself, the stately home rising in a splendor of golden Cotswold stone, shimmering glass and hand-cut marble. The grounds were some of the finest in England, Adam agreed, and contained majestic landscaped gardens, a pair of artificial lakes complete with follies and a small, private chapel that was nothing short of an artistic masterpiece.

Reining in their mounts near a graceful stand of beech and oak trees, he and Mallory paused to appreciate the natural beauty around them. Early-morning sunlight shone from above, the rays warm against her face as she closed her eyes to drink in sensation.

"Why don't we stop here for a little while before turning back?" Adam suggested. Without waiting for her agreement, he leapt to the ground and came around to help her dismount.

After the briefest hesitation, she leaned forward to clutch his wide shoulders and let him swing her to the ground. The clean fragrance of shaving soap, starch, warm leather and man teased her nose at his closeness.

Releasing her, Adam returned to his horse to gather a blanket and a small wicker hamper. "I had Cook pack us a light repast. I assume you didn't have time for much of a breakfast this morning."

"Only tea," she admitted, remembering the toast she'd left untouched on the tray Penny had brought to her room. Her stomach gave a painful squeeze, now clearly regretting that decision.

By mutual agreement, she and Adam chose a comfortable grassy spot with a light dappling of shade that was cast by one of the nearby trees. After helping spread out the blanket, she took a seat, reaching out briefly to arrange the long skirt of her riding habit so it didn't take up too much room.

Adam joined her seconds later, dropping down near her side. "Let's see what Cook sent along," he said, opening the hamper. Reaching in, he began laying out the items. "Cheese, a soft sheep's milk from the look of it, and biscuits. Scones with butter and honey. Two wedges of beef pie. A quarter of a cold chicken and . . ." He paused, digging into a far corner of the basket. " . . . two fresh peaches and pears. Oh, and there's a flagon of small beer and a tin of milk as well."

"Heavens. I thought you said it was a 'light repast'!"

He grinned and passed her a linen napkin. "I believe Cook is concerned about you and may have overdone."

Beneath her breath, she gave a light grumble.

His smile widened. "Eat what you want. There's no requirement we finish all of this. So, how would you care to begin? Cheese on a biscuit or a wedge of this pie? It smells so good, it's making my mouth water."

"Cheese, I think, and maybe one of the scones," she said. "And the ale is all yours by the way. I don't care for it in the least."

"That's why we get on so well, Mal, since the idea of drinking milk for breakfast fairly curdles my stomach." Closing his eyes, he stuck out his tongue and gave a mock shudder.

Without realizing, her lips started to curve upward with humor, then abruptly she stopped. With a scowl, she glanced away, biting into the crisp, cheese-covered biscuit she held in order to cover her discomfort. If Adam noticed her brief inner turmoil, he didn't comment, apparently content to begin his own meal.

They ate in companionable silence, listening to the birds chirp in the trees and the occasional buzz of a honeybee as it droned from flower to flower in search of pollen. The sun was full now in the sky, the temperature rising as the hour progressed. Luckily a light breeze was blowing that kept the air from turning too hot, the weather just right for an alfresco meal.

To her surprise, she ate far more than she intended, finishing her biscuit and cheese, half a buttered scone, one of the peaches and two mouthfuls of chicken that Adam pressed her to try. She was more than well satisfied by the time she stopped, glad for the exercise the ride home would provide.

While Adam polished off the second wedge of beef pie and the last of the small beer, she began repacking the wicker hamper. As she did, a yawn caught her, one that was sharp enough to draw tears.

"Stars, I'm sleepy all of a sudden," she confessed. "Too much breakfast."

He cast her a knowing look. "Not enough sleep, I suspect." Wiping his hands clean on a napkin, he placed a last couple of items she'd missed back in the hamper, then closed the top and set it aside. "Why don't you lie down for a few minutes?"

"Oh, I'll be all right," she said, then just as quickly had to lift a hand to cover another sudden yawn.

Adam chuckled and shook his head. "Stretch out and close your eyes. It's quiet here and comfortable."

"We should be getting back."

"There's no rush. Besides, in your current state, you might fall asleep on Pansy and topple off."

Hearing her name, the horse's head came up. She gave a whinny and tossed her head up and down.

Adam laughed. "See? Pansy agrees. She thinks you should take a nap rather than taking the risk of injuring yourself on the ride home."

"She thinks no such thing, and I wouldn't topple off."

Nod off, perhaps, Mallory admitted to herself, as she fought a deep wave of weariness.

Lie down, Adam had said. How incredibly tempting his suggestion was. And how incredibly easy too. All she had to do was stretch out on the blanket and close her eyes. Of course, doing so would be completely improper. Ladies didn't go to sleep in the presence of gentlemen to whom they were not related. Then again, if she was concerned about the proprieties, she wouldn't have ridden out alone with Adam at all. Or eaten breakfast with him out of doors with no one around for miles.

Realizing she was being foolish, she covered another yawn with her hand, then nodded, scooting lower on the blanket so she could lie back and still have room to rest her head on the blanket.

"Hold there," he said, stopping her gently. "You'll never get any rest wearing that hat."

"Oh, I guess you're right." Blinking against her sleepiness, she reached up to tug free the pins that anchored the bonnet in place. But he stopped her again, setting her hands into her lap before reaching up to ease the pins from her hair.

Despite her tiredness, her heart pumped faster, blood beating in thick pulses as her eyes slid closed. She swayed, her body tingling, as his large hands moved tenderly around her head. His fingers brushed lightly over her temples and cheeks and the back of her head as he pulled out the pins. After lifting the hat away, he reached up to smooth her tresses.

"Sleep now, Mallory," he murmured, cradling her against him as he eased both of them down to lie side by side on their backs.

She made some faint demur when he tucked her closer, angling her so that her head was pillowed on his shoulder. But she was too sleepy and wonderfully relaxed to care, knowing she was safe and secure in his arms. Letting go, she drifted into a deep slumber.

At her side, Adam was awake, his pulse pounding out a heavy, satisfying beat at the sheer pleasure of holding her so close. He was aroused as well, his shaft hard, his body throbbing with a gnawing, visceral ache. But the sexual need was a mere distraction compared to the sheer joy of lying with her as she slept. He smiled, reveling in the knowledge that she trusted him enough to let down her guard and forget her pain, even if only for a brief while.

Closing his eyes, he breathed in the sweet jasmine scent of her skin, wishing he could pull the rest of the pins from her hair so the thick mass would tumble like waves of dark silk over his chest. Not for the first time, he wondered what her hair looked like when it was down. Did the strands trail to the middle of her back or lower still?

Images flashed in his mind of her rising above him, her tresses falling forward to surround their faces while she kissed him and he kissed her back. They would be long and passionate, those kisses, sultry and seductive in a way neither of them would be able to resist or forget.

A sudden, intense throb in his groin brought him abruptly back to reality. Stifling a groan, he struggled to force the fantasy away. Once he had himself firmly under control, he angled his head to study her, smiling again to see her so deeply asleep. Unable to resist, he brushed his mouth against her cheek and forehead, her skin as smooth as satin beneath his lips.

With a sigh, she burrowed closer against him.

Swallowing a fresh groan, he stared up at the sky and let her sleep.

Chapter 5

E ver so slowly, Mallory came awake.

At first she didn't move, far too warm and contented to do more than float in that deliciously drowsy state that was halfway between wakefulness and sleep. Snuggling closer against her pillow, she let her mind drift, aware that she couldn't recall the last time she'd slept so well or so peacefully.

Months, it seemed, or was it years?

She frowned at the question, then frowned again harder when she realized that her pillow was firmer than usual, nothing the least bit goose-feathery about it. Even odder was the sound it was making, a steady, rhythmic beat that was almost like a heart.

But a pillow doesn't have a heart.

Nor were any of the pillows on her bed scented with a heady combination of clean perspiration and masculine warmth, with hints of horse, leather and shaving soap mixed in. Inhaling deeper, she detected another scent, faint but reassuringly familiar.

Inviting.

Delicious.

Adam.

Her eyelids popped open, and she sat straight up, her gaze locking on the watchful chocolate brown eyes of the man lying beside her. One hand flew to her chest, her fingers encountering the hard buttons and smooth braids that decorated the front of her riding habit. Memories of the morning came tumbling back—their early-morning ride, their out of doors breakfast and the sudden bout of weariness that had swept through her just as the time had arrived for them to ride home.

"Gracious," she said on a breathy rush. "I guess I fell asleep."

His mouth curved up at the corners. "You certainly did."

"How long was I out?"

He leaned up on an elbow but made no further effort to rise. "Without consulting my watch, I can't do more than hazard a guess, but I'd say about two hours."

Her lips parted. "Two hours! Oh, you should never have let me sleep so long."

"Why not? Clearly, you were tired, exhausted even, considering the fact that you slept like a stone."

"Maybe so, but you ought to have awakened me regardless. It must be coming on eleven o'clock by now."

This time he sat up, taking a moment to withdraw his pocket watch from his waistcoat. "It's eleven twenty-four, so you weren't too far off the mark." Snapping the case closed again, he returned the gold watch to its pocket.

"We need to get back," she said, rising to her knees so she could stand up, only to find her legs bound inside a mass of cloth. "I didn't tell anyone but Penny that I was riding out with you this morning, and we'll have been missed by now for sure."

Before she could untangle herself from her voluminous skirts, he was on his feet and reaching a hand down to her. Deciding it would be faster and easier simply to accept his assistance, she laid her palm in his and let him pull her up. Once she was steady, she beat at a pair of wrinkles in her riding habit. "We should leave," she said.

"Not without this," he reminded, leaning down to retrieve her forgotten hat. "Truly, there's no need for worry. Claire is fully aware that you're with me."

She froze. "Claire knows? You told her? When?"

"Last night after you retired for the evening. I'm certain Edward knows as well. If there had been any objection, he would have been in the stables at first light."

"Oh! Oh," she said again, tension sliding out of her shoulders as she realized he was right. Still, there were a few of the guests, Claire's parents, for one, who might not approve. Then again, the earl and countess probably assumed she was spending the morning in her room. And even if they did not, she had every right to be with Adam if she wished. She'd known him since she was a child; he was as much a constant in her life as her family.

"So," he said, reaching out to smooth a couple of stray locks of hair into place, tucking one behind her ear as if she were still that child. "You'll come riding with me again tomorrow?"

"Tomorrow? Early again, do you mean?"

"If you don't mind leaving the house before everyone else is stirring."

"But won't your absence be noted? I'm sure Ned must have some hunting excursions planned for the gentlemen.

It's grouse season, after all. You've probably missed the first outing already."

"I'd much rather come riding with you than shoot a brace of birds. The rest of the men can claim my share. Believe me, I won't mind since I've never been all that keen for blood sports, even if I am ruthless enough to dine on the results."

"You're not ruthless, only practical."

He gave her a wry look. "There are many who would not agree. But since you believe me to be practical, I must tell you that it only makes sense for you to ride out with me again on the morrow. After all," he continued in a persuasive tone, "your reasons for coming along today remain unchanged. The party continues on, in tandem with all the activities and entertainments planned for the guests. Who knows, mayhap your cousin Wilhelmina will decide to direct the company in a play. As I recall, she adores theatricals. I'm sure she would delight in finding a part for you."

Mallory folded her arms over her chest. "Then she will have to offer that part to another lady. I have no interest in stage acting at the moment."

"I'm sure you do not. But only think how much easier it will be to avoid all such entanglements if you are out of the house with me?"

She scowled, thinking of all the additional hours that remained in each day. "Unfortunately, we cannot be gone from dawn till dusk."

"No," he agreed, "but long enough to put you out of sight and hopefully out of mind when it comes to any schemes that may arise."

She narrowed her eyes, noting the ever-present twinkle in his gaze. "Why do I have the feeling you are manipulating me again?" she said.

He laid a palm against his chest. "Why, you wound me, sweetheart. I am merely attempting to help."

And so he was.

"So you'll come, then?" he said.

She hesitated only a moment before she nodded. "I'll come."

"Good." He smiled. "Oh, and Mallory."

"Yes?"

"You've my permission to fall asleep in my arms anytime you like. I rather enjoyed acting as your pillow today."

Warmth rose in her cheeks. "Then I shall be sure to stay awake tomorrow."

"Here now, don't make promises you may not be able to keep." Giving her a wink, he set her hat on her head, then began the careful task of pinning it into place.

He and Mallory rode back, left their horses at the stable, then walked to the house, all without encountering any of the guests. Once inside, they met Croft, who informed them that the gentlemen were indeed out hunting, while the ladies had settled on the idea of picking wildflowers in one of the nearby woods. Everyone would be returning sometime in the next hour in order to rest and change their attire for nuncheon.

"I'd best be off to my room then," Mallory told Adam as soon as they were alone again. "If I time things right, perhaps I can plead a headache and skip the meal."

"You'll do nothing of the sort. Have your maid help you into an afternoon gown, and I'll see you in the dining room."

Her strawberry pink lips parted in clear surprise. "In the dining room! But I don't want to join the others. We agreed."

"We did no such thing."

"Of course we did. You promised." Her brow furrowed. "Whose side are you on anyway?"

"Your stomach's, that's whose," he retorted, taking her arm to lead her up the stairs. "I may be helping you avoid wildflower expeditions and the like, but you need to eat." She opened her mouth again to utter a retort, but he stopped her. "Now, no more arguing. Go on and enjoy a couple of hours' rest and solitude. I shall see you for the midday meal."

Hurt shimmered in her gaze, as she shook off his hold. "I thought you understood."

"I do," he said, his tone gentling. "Better than you might realize."

Casting him another look that was a mixture of anger and betrayal, she spun on her heels and hurried away, her dark blue skirts trailing behind her. He watched until she reached the end of the corridor and disappeared from view.

"You're dealing with her surprisingly well," Edward Byron, Duke of Clybourne, commented as he stepped out of a nearby room. "Better than the rest of us have this past year, I'll confess."

"Your Grace," Adam said, turning toward Mallory's tall, powerful, dark-haired brother. "I didn't realize you were home. I assumed you were out hunting with the others."

Edward shook his head. "I let Cade and Jack do the honors for me today. There were several matters on the estate I deemed more important than playing host this morning."

"Estate matters should take precedence, particularly since there'll still be plenty of game birds left to catch tomorrow," Adam agreed.

The corners of the duke's mouth turned up in clear

agreement. "Exactly. From what I understand, you're doing quite a bit of estate work yourself these days. How are the improvements coming on Gresham Park?"

"They've really just begun in earnest, but so far, every-thing is going well."

Edward studied him for a moment. "You'll have to tell me more of the details. I would be most interested to hear."

Adam inclined his head, knowing he would enjoy the discussion with a man of the duke's insight, experience and intelligence.

"Are you certain, however, that you can afford to be away from home just now considering the improvements you're undertaking at Gresham Park?" Edward asked. "Like the game birds, there'll be other years and other parties for you to attend here at Braebourne."

He met the duke's keen blue gaze. "Much as I appreci-ate your and the duchess's hospitality, it's not the party that's drawn me here."

Edward gave a sage nod. "No, I didn't think it was. She's still fragile yet, but then you know that."

"I do."

"My sister's been through a lot. I won't have her hurt any further."

Adam's jaw tightened. "She won't be. Believe me, I would kill anyone who ever hurt Mallory."

"Yes, I rather expect you would. She thinks of you as a friend, though, so you would do well to have a care."

"Where she's concerned, I am always careful. And though I see no reason why I should have to say it, my intentions toward her are strictly honorable."

"I know that. If they weren't, you'd never have gotten within ten yards of her."

Adam squared his shoulders, he and Clybourne fully

aware that if he'd decided to pursue Mallory years ago, nothing—not even her powerful family—could have stopped him from having her.

The duke gave a wry smile. "Truth is, I like you, Gresham. We all do, the entire family. As for Mallory, she's always held you in particular esteem, in many ways I believe she sees you as her seventh brother."

The reminder rankled. "I am *not* her brother."

"No, you aren't."

"Are you warning me off?"

"Not at all. Only suggesting you go slowly."

Adam barked out a laugh. "Considering the number of years I've known her, I don't think I could go any more slowly."

Edward narrowed his eyes as if a missing puzzle piece had just clicked into place.

"I'm taking her riding again tomorrow," Adam stated. "I trust you have no objection."

The duke sighed. "Actually, I think it's an excellent plan. I've seen more life in her these past two days since you arrived than I have in the last fourteen months. She's been like a ghost up till now, floating around this house as if she were invisible, or as though she wished she were."

Pausing, Edward twisted the emerald signet ring around on his little finger. "That little disagreement I overheard between the pair of you . . . for a moment she seemed like the old Mallory again. She had a spark, a fire that's been absent too long. Do what you will to bring her all the way back. Just have a care while you're about it."

"As I said, I am always careful with Mallory. She means the world to me."

"As she does to me." Taking out his pocket watch, Edward flipped open the gold case. "I think there's enough time for a drink before nuncheon. Come have a glass of wine, and you can tell me about Gresham Park and your plans for it."

Relaxing suddenly, Adam smiled. "Now that would be my pleasure."

Closing her bedchamber door on a near slam, Mallory stalked toward her dressing room, unbuttoning the front fastenings on the bodice of her riding habit as she went. Yanking off the close-fitting jacket, she tossed the garment onto a nearby chair, then went to work on the skirt. The tiny mother-of-pearl buttons at her waist presented a far more difficult task since they were located at the small of her back. Unwilling to wait for her maid's assistance, she reached behind herself and stretched, twisted and contorted until the buttons finally came free. The heavy skirt billowed past her hips to land in a dark blue puddle on the floor.

Stepping clear, she walked toward the washstand. Only then did she catch a glimpse of herself in the mirror and note the irritating fact that her hat was still pinned to her head.

Blast it all!

Reaching up, she began ripping out the pins Adam had done such an excellent job of applying, heat rising in her cheeks at the memory.

How dare he order me about, she thought. Telling her to rest and change and come down to nuncheon like a good girl. From the way he talked, she was the veriest child, fomenting some immature rebellion instead of mourning a loss of the most grievous kind.

Michael would never have behaved like such an insensitive, overbearing bully, she thought. *He wouldn't have made me do things I do not wish to do, then use the excuse of its being for my own good. He—"*

Abruptly she stopped, a sheen of moisture gathering in her eyes. Laying down the pins in her hand, she slowly pulled off her hat, the dyed dark feathers bobbing in a way that reminded her of those worn by the horses in a funeral cortege.

How could she have forgotten him for even an instant? she wondered as she sank into a nearby chair. How could Michael have been so far from her thoughts today when he was with her constantly? But for the first time since his death, hours had passed without Michael in them. Instead, she'd thought only of Adam today, the strength of his personality and the diversion provided by their outing driving everything else away.

Lord, she'd even slept curled against Adam's side. And not just any sleep, but a deep, dreamless, refreshing sleep that left her feeling better than she had in ages.

On a soft moan, she covered her face with her hands.

Not long after, a light tap sounded at the dressing-room door, starched skirts whispering as someone entered the room.

"You're back," said Penny. "I just heard tell, or I'd 'ave been here sooner to help you out of your clothes. Did you have a good time on your ride?"

More tears filled Mallory's eyes since that was precisely the problem. She had enjoyed herself all those minutes, all those hours, when she hadn't been thinking about Michael.

"Oh, miss, what is it? What's wrong?"

Lowering her hands, Mallory shook her head, unable to speak.

"Do you have a headache? Why don't I draw you a nice hot bath, then you can lie down for a while."

Sniffing, Mallory wiped at her tears. "Please draw the bath," she whispered, her voice rough. "But I won't have time to lie down. I am to attend nuncheon with the others."

Penny made a clucking noise under her breath. "I'm sure everyone will understand if you don't feel up to it."

Everyone but Adam!

A little spurt of anger returned since she knew he would likely come upstairs after her if she didn't appear at the appointed time. And she certainly wasn't going to send down a note trying to explain her feelings. It would be impossible—as impossible as Adam Gresham himself.

No, she had no choice. She had to go. But that didn't mean she had to like it.

"I'll need an afternoon gown," she told her maid. "Something appropriate for nuncheon and not too somber."

"Are you certain, miss? You look so pale. Maybe you took too much air today, and you're coming down sick. Perhaps I should call your mother."

"No. I am not sick, and you are not to call Mama."

Penny's mouth grew pinched. "One of the other ladies then? They just arrived back. I could send for Her Grace or Lady John or your cousin. Or Lady Cade, though I hate disturbing her seein' how big she is with child. If it weren't fer his lordship's bad leg, I think he'd just have done with her slow gait and carry her around the house instead."

"I rather suspect he would," Mallory agreed, thinking about her brother, the wounds he'd suffered in the war and limp that would plague him for the rest of his days.

For a moment, she considered Penny's suggestion, knowing it would be nice to talk to one of her sisters-in-law. She loved them all—Claire, Grace and Meg. Then there was her cousin India and her old London friends as well, Jessica and Daphne, whom she'd once whispered with about almost everything—beaux and gowns and any interesting piece of gossip that came their way.

But every time she considered expressing her sorrow over Michael's passing and how lost and adrift she'd felt in the months since, she retreated deeper inside herself instead. She could barely express her grief to herself, let alone articulate it to someone else. She wanted to bury the pain, not dredge it all up again.

And she certainly didn't want to tell them about Adam. Although what there was to say about him she really didn't know other than the fact that he seemed to be infuriating her at every turn lately. Besides, given the family's collective opinion on the subject of her mourning, they would probably support his every move!

"Just draw my bath and pick out a gown, any color but white."

Penny opened her mouth as if she had more to say, but she closed it instead and gave a nod. "Yes, miss."

Eyes dry again, Mallory drew a deep breath and wondered how she was going to get through the remainder of the day.

Chapter 6

erhaps I'm not dealing with Mallory as well as Edward believes, Adam decided on a doleful note as he waited outside the stables the next morning.

She was fifteen minutes late already, and he wondered if she would show up at all despite her promise to ride with him again today. Prodding her out of her blue devils had seemed like the right thing to do, only now he wasn't so sure.

After their exchange of words yesterday on their return to the house, a renewed sadness seemed to have swept over her. She'd appeared for nuncheon at the appropriate time, attired in a lovely gown of apricot silk that lent an attractive glow to her raven tresses and creamy porcelain skin. And though she'd responded to any question or remark put to her by the others, she was otherwise silent, her eyes and humor downcast.

To his frustration, she'd picked at her meal in spite of

his gentle admonitions to eat, then disappeared upstairs the instant the meal concluded. Dinner was a repetition of the same, with her attending the event in body but not in spirit.

In his mind, he went over everything they'd said and done, and for the life of him he couldn't fathom why she would turn so despondent again. All he'd insisted on was that she put in an appearance at meals. Surely that wasn't enough to send her into a decline? But last night, when he'd gently tried to draw her out on the subject, she'd rebuffed his efforts with a silence that was stygian in its impenetrability. If they hadn't been surrounded by nearly two dozen of her family and friends, he would have taken her by the shoulders and given her a rousing shake.

Then again, as he'd wondered once before, perhaps his instincts were leading him down the wrong path, and his attempts to revive her spirits were doing naught but driving her deeper into her gloom.

Sighing aloud, he gave his stallion a soothing pat on the neck. The horse was restive and anxious to be off. Mallory's mare was as well, the animal tossing her head and pawing the ground in hopes of putting the saddle on her back to good use. Maybe he should tell the grooms to exercise the horses since Mallory obviously wasn't coming. If he hurried, he supposed he could join the men for the hunt—a notion that seemed as dismal as his mood. Swinging around, he started back toward the stable when a flash of emerald caught his eye.

"I'm here. Let us ride," Mallory declared, her blue-green eyes glinting as if they contained a tempest. And perhaps they did. Her expression was set, her shoulders and spine taut beneath her riding habit, long skirts swirling around her kid leather boots as though propelled by a wind. Obviously Penny had discovered another riding habit in Mallory's wardrobe. He waited to see if she would use that as her reason for being delayed once again.

Instead, she gave no explanation at all as she strode past him. Going to her mount, she took the reins in hand and began leading Pansy to the mounting block.

Adam stopped her with a touch. "I'll assist you up."

She fixed him with a look but did not refuse. Looping the reins back over her horse's neck, she positioned herself so he could lift her into the saddle.

"I didn't think you were coming," he said, moving around in front of her.

A brief silence followed. "I very nearly did not."

"Mallory, I'm not sure what—"

"Forgive me," she interrupted in a hard voice, "but I don't want to talk. All I want to do is ride. If that's a problem, then perhaps I should ask a groom to accompany me."

His jaw flexed. "You have no need of a groom. I shall ride with you."

Imperious as a queen, she lifted her chin and waited for him to help her onto her horse.

Studying her face, he noticed the faint shadows beneath her eyes. "More bad dreams?" he asked.

Her mouth tightened, and she reached again for the reins.

He stopped her, wrapping a hand around her arm. "Fine. You want to ride, and *only* ride, then that's what we'll do. I won't say another word."

Rather than waiting for her to place her foot inside his cupped palms, he caught her around the waist and tossed her up into the saddle. But unlike yesterday, he didn't wait to make sure she was comfortably settled. Instead, he strode to his horse and swung up, thrusting his booted feet firmly into the stirrups. Gathering the reins in his gloved palms, he cast a glance over his shoulder to make sure she was ready, then squeezed his knees into the stallion's flanks to set him into a run.

Quickly, Mallory drew abreast, horses' hooves thundering across the verdant fields with enough force to startle an occasional rabbit or bird. Neither of them spoke, the world flying past as they rode side by side. Without conscious agreement, they retraced their path from the day before, crossing the grassy acres, fording the stream and pounding up the hill in record time.

At the top, Adam reined his stallion in, not willing to push the animal harder or farther than he could go. Mallory slowed as well, falling into an easy walk at his side. At length, he stopped. Moving her horse into place beside his, she did the same.

Birdsong and the gentle susurration of the wind filled the silence, Pansy's bridle jangling in a bell-like tone as she lowered her head to clip the grass.

"Better?" Adam demanded in a quiet tone, as he gazed across the picturesque valley.

A soft sigh flowed from Mallory's lips. "A bit, I suppose."

He said nothing further, having already broken his pledge not to speak.

"Adam, I'm sorry," she said. "About earlier, I . . ."

He leaned forward in the saddle and waited for her to continue.

"I don't want us to be at odds."

He turned his head. "I didn't realize we were."

An expression of relief crossed her face before crumbling again with renewed sadness. "Everything is just so very difficult right now. Sometimes, I just . . . oh, I don't know."

Dismounting, he walked to her and reached up. "Come. Why don't we walk?"

Her eyes were bright as gemstones in her face, her cheeks stained pink from the vigorous exertion of their ride. Accepting his aid, she let him swing her to the ground.

He took a moment to secure the horses to the branch of a nearby tree, where they seemed content to resume their grazing. Folding Mallory's hand over his arm, Adam led her in an easy stroll.

One minute lapsed into another, silence reigning between them again, only this time it was a quiet of companionship rather than conflict. His boots crunched on a twig, the trees overhead laden with a bounty of succulent green that mirrored the tender grass below.

"You know, Mal, I actually do understand a bit about what you're going through," he stated in a low tone.

Her fingers tightened against the sleeve of his fawn riding coat. Otherwise, she gave no outward response.

"It's not quite the same, I realize," he continued, "since I didn't lose someone I planned to wed. And yet, love is love, isn't it, whatever its form or relationship?"

He waited, wondering if she would respond. Instead, she kept strolling at his side.

Part of him hesitated, wishing he hadn't initiated the conversation. Yet loving Mallory as he did, he was willing to do whatever he could to alleviate her misery, even if it might reawaken old feelings he'd rather not nudge back to life.

"Have I ever told you about my sister?" he asked with a bleakness he couldn't entirely conceal.

Her gaze flashed to meet his. "No, not really. She died many years ago, did she not?"

He nodded. "When she was sixteen. I'd just started my first year of university when I learned of Delia's death."

"It was an accident, was it not?"

His mouth curved in a cynical slant. "That's right. An *accident*. A terrible, untimely accident."

"Why do you say it like that?" she questioned as she drew to a halt. "Is it not true?"

Stopping as well, he turned to face her. "According to my late father and the physician who examined her body at the time, she was the victim of an accidental drowning. They found her one morning floating in a lake near Gresham Park, said she'd swum out too far and was too tired to make it back to shore. But how could a girl who'd been swimming in that lake from the time she was a young child misjudge badly enough to drown?"

Mallory laid a hand against his chest. "Accidents do happen."

"You're right. And I might have believed that's exactly what it was if not for her letter." He paused, swallowing against the knot that still had the power to tighten in his throat, even after all these years. "She drowned herself, Mallory. She took her own life."

"Oh!"

"It isn't necessary for me to tell you all the sordid details. Let me just say that she was desperate enough, despondent enough that she couldn't bear to go on living. She told me why she'd made her choice and begged me to forgive her. By the time her letter arrived, it was already too late. She was gone."

"Adam, I'm so sorry." A tear traced down her cheek.

Reaching up, he brushed it away with a thumb. "I didn't tell you all this to make you sad or to gain your sympathy. I just want you to realize that I know how hard this past year has been for you and how you're feeling. I've felt it too. The pain and loss, the anger and confusion, and most especially, the guilt."

Her eyes widened, her lips trembling on a quiet gasp.

"It's what everyone goes through when they lose someone they truly love. But I overcame it, and you'll do the same. You're strong, Mallory, and it will get better."

"But I'm not strong," she whispered, more tears sliding from her eyes. "And I keep waiting for it to get better, but it doesn't."

Withdrawing a handkerchief, he tenderly wiped her wet cheeks. "Maybe it would if you'd let it."

She frowned. "What do you mean? Are you saying I *want* to be unhappy?"

"No, I know you don't. But I do think you're afraid to let yourself take pleasure again from your life. For a long while, I blamed myself for Delia's death, and whenever I did something I enjoyed, I felt terrible afterward."

He paused, deciding not to tell her how, in the months right after his sister's suicide, he'd tried to escape his grief by indulging in a spate of wild behavior. He'd bedded countless women, gotten drunk, landed himself in more than one brawl and had even begun gambling heavily.

Then one morning he'd awakened in a squalid room, his head pounding like a set of drums and his pockets emptied of all his cash. He'd been robbed and what was worse, he didn't even remember the event. It occurred to him then that if he continued on the same path, he was in very real danger of turning into his father.

That sudden realization proved more sobering than a week in gaol. Determined not to shame Delia's memory, or squander the small legacy his mother had left him— money his father couldn't legally touch and the only reason he was able to attend Oxford at all—he'd set about curbing the worst of his excesses. Reapplying himself to his studies, he'd kept mostly out of trouble, and by eighteen, had matured into a man.

Drawing a breath, he stroked a hand along Mallory's arm and met her sorrowful, sea-colored gaze. "It took some time," he said, "but I finally realized that my suffering would never bring Delia back; nor would it have made her happy. She was a kind, generous person, and she would never have wished to see me sad. I can tell you without hesitation that Michael Hargreaves wouldn't want you to be sad either. He would want you to live and have a happy life. He's found his own peace. Give yourself the right to find yours."

Mallory trembled, something shattering on her face. "But I'm afraid I'll forget him," she confessed on a whisper, as more tears slid free. "We had such a short time together before he was sent away to fight. I worry if I go back to my old life that it will be as if he never existed. As if I've abandoned him somehow."

Adam curved an arm around her back and drew her close. "You haven't abandoned him, and you will never forget. You loved him. Real love never fades." He pressed a handkerchief into her hand and offered what comfort he could, as she buried her face against his chest and cried.

He didn't speak as he held her, fighting the jealousy that twisted inside him while she sobbed out her love and grief for another man. It was an emotion unworthy of him and one he knew he should not feel. Still, he wasn't a saint, far from it. He was only human, only a man. And despite his best efforts to be noble and self-sacrificing, a small, selfish part of him couldn't help but resent the hold Hargreaves had on Mallory—even from beyond the grave.

At length, her tears ceased, her sobs turning to shaky inhalations and weary sighs, as she leaned against him. Using the damp silk handkerchief she held balled up inside her fist, she blew her nose and blotted her tear-stained eyes.

Reaching into his pocket, he produced a fresh handkerchief. "Here, have another."

She drew a hiccupping breath, and tried, but didn't quite manage to smile. "You're right, I have rather used this first one up, haven't I?" Accepting the second square of white silk, she pressed the dry cloth to her eyes and cheeks and nose, pausing at his gentle urging to give "one more good blow" despite the inelegance of such behavior.

But he and Mallory had known each other for far too many years to stand on formality at this point. If they had, she would never have cried in his arms today at all, he realized.

"Gracious," she declared, straightening slightly inside his embrace. "I must look a sight."

But she didn't, she looked beautiful, he thought. Her lashes framed her luminous aquamarine eyes in dark, spiky rings, while her cheeks were burnished as red as crisp fall apples. As for her lips, they were swollen from her crying—plump and full and lusciously moist.

Sweet as candy, he thought. *And every bit as delicious,* he was sure.

"No," he murmured in answer to her query. "You look lovely as always." Then, before he even knew what he was doing, he bent and touched his mouth to hers, desperate for a taste, however brief it might be.

But a taste couldn't begin to be enough, yearning roaring to life inside him, burning in his veins as blood beat between his temples and pooled lower in his belly and between his thighs.

She gave a clearly startled whimper, but didn't try to push him away. If she had, perhaps he would have stopped. Instead, desire urged him on, encouraging him to take more. He'd waited years to hold her like this and kiss her. He'd dreamt countless times of how her lips would feel against his and the way her small, supple body would curve into his own much taller one. Yet his imagination was as insipid as water to wine when compared with reality—the sensations, scents and flavors more divine than anything his mind could create.

Mallory, my love, he whispered in his head, as he gave in to what he craved and deepened the kiss. Parting her mouth, he claimed her with a long, slow, sultry ease that was just this side of heaven.

She whimpered again, this time with confused hesitation, the relative inexperience of her touch impressing itself upon him as nothing else could have done. She might have been kissed before, he realized, but she was still a novice when it came to sex and the sensual arts. He, on the other hand, was experienced—extremely experienced—with a knowledge of things that would have set her blushing from the roots of her hair to the tips of her toes. Compared to him, Mallory was a dewy-eyed lamb wandering unaware in a peaceful meadow, while he was the hungry, ravening wolf lying in wait just over the nearest rise.

Suddenly aware of exactly what he was doing, he broke their kiss. She swayed slightly in his grasp, her eyes closed as breath puffed in tiny gusts from her mouth.

"Oh," she sighed.

"Oh" didn't begin to describe it.

Taking a step back, he made sure she was steady on her feet, then he let her go.

Her eyes popped open and immediately fixed on his. "W-what was that?"

Rather than responding, he lifted a brow, schooling his features into a calmness that hid the violent need still coursing through his body.

"I-I mean I know what it was," she went on in a breathless voice that made shivers run down his spine. "But why? Why did you k-kiss me?"

She looked utterly and completely bewildered.

"Because, my sweet," he drawled in a smooth tone, "you looked as if you needed to be."

Mallory stared, her heart racing frantically in her chest.

Stars and garters, she thought, *Adam just kissed me.* And not a peck either but a full-blown, passionate claiming that was unlike any kiss she'd ever had before. Even Michael had never kissed her like that, and he'd been her fiancé.

She paused suddenly at the thought of Michael, yet she was so dazed, so bemused, that the usual melancholy she felt when she thought of him didn't appear. All she could do was stand there, her entire body tingling with heat and pleasure.

For years, she'd been aware of the rumors about Adam's prowess and reports of all the women who secretly—and not so secretly—clamored to share his bed. Once at a party in London, she'd accidentally overheard a pair of women—one a widow and another who wished she were—comparing a list of their lovers. None of them, the widow told her friend, came close to the ecstasy she'd found in Adam Gresham's arms. Then she'd gone on to bemoan the fact that she'd only been with him once and that despite her best efforts to win him back, he wasn't interested.

Apparently, Adam had a habit of never staying with any one woman for long, his elusive behavior seeming only to enhance his already formidable appeal among the fairer sex. And now that she'd experienced his kiss, she could see that his reputation for pleasuring women was in no way an exaggeration. Fully two minutes had passed since he'd ended their own kiss, and she was still worried the top of her head might blow off, her riding hat along with it.

"Are you hungry?" he inquired, jarring her out of her musings. "I had Cook pack us a little something again just in case."

Hungry? How could he possibly think of food at a moment like this? Then she recalled why he said he'd kissed her.

Because, sweetheart, you looked as if you needed to be.

So it had been a sympathy kiss, had it? His embrace driven not out of any real sense of desire for her but rather from a need to distract and cheer her.

What a lowering realization.

And yet, she knew he'd meant it in a kindly way and was only acting as her friend. Obviously, he was willing to do whatever it might take to rally her spirits, even if the effort required him to shock her out of her gloom with an unexpected embrace.

One that had clearly dazzled her more than Adam.

All she had to do was look at him to confirm that fact, since he seemed his usual calm, sophisticated self, un-ruffled and apparently unaffected as well. Considering all the women he must have kissed in his two-and-thirty years, why should she be surprised? She was just one among many, she supposed, memorable only by virtue of the fact that she was his longtime friend.

No wonder he was so unfazed.

For all she knew, maybe he hadn't enjoyed their kiss at all. And if that were true, what must his touch be like when he really wanted a woman?

Her brows drew into a frown.

Adam cocked his head. "Shall we stay and eat, or would you rather ride home?"

A mere half an hour ago, she would have opted to ride straight home. But a strange restfulness seemed to have invaded her system, along with a sense of shared understanding. Adam knew what it was to grieve. He'd experienced loss and come out the other side. As for his rather high-handed kiss, she supposed she couldn't hold it against him, not when she knew his intentions had been good.

Besides, she'd left the house again this morning without eating breakfast, and quite suddenly she realized she was starving.

"A light meal wouldn't go amiss," she admitted. "But don't think we're going to make a habit of riding together and sharing a meal in this spot every morning."

"Of course not," he said solemnly. Then he ruined the effect by smiling, his face so handsome her breath caught at the sight.

It's only the kiss, she told herself, and she would forget it in a trice. She and Adam were friends, no more, no less, and he was only devoting himself to her at present because of that friendship.

For now, she would let herself take advantage of his kindness and hope it helped her heal. Beyond that, she didn't know. She would deal with each day as it came, she decided, and care naught for the future.

While he returned to the horses, she waited as he retrieved a blanket and the small hamper Cook had packed. After seeing to their seating arrangements, he helped her settle comfortably across from him on the blanket, then he opened the basket.

"Sausage links or ham biscuits?"

Her stomach rumbled at the savory scents. "One of each please. I'm utterly famished."

Grinning in clear approval, he filled her plate.

Chapter 7

In spite of Mallory's statement that she and Adam
wouldn't make a habit of riding out together
every morning, that's precisely what they ended
up doing over the course of the next ten days.

Each morning Mallory met Adam at the stables, where
they would mount their horses and make the ride to what
she now thought of as "their" hill. Once there, they would
laze away the next few hours, seated on a lawn blanket
while they ate whatever delicacies Cook had packed for
them. Their conversations ranged from intense to sublime,
as they explored any number of subjects and opinions.

After that emotionally charged day when she'd sobbed
out her grief in Adam's arms, she knew she could talk
to him about anything. Yet neither of them spoke again
about the loved ones they'd lost, perhaps because they'd
already said everything that needed to be said.

And then there were the times when they didn't say
anything at all, content in the quiet as they enjoyed the

simple pleasure and peacefulness of being in each other's company.

But as Mallory stood gazing out her bedroom window on the morning of the house party's thirteenth day, she knew there would be no outing with Adam today.

Lumbering grey clouds with sinister black underbellies crowded the sky, rain already beginning to pour in a way that heralded a full day of heavy precipitation. Soon, the ground would be saturated, the mud puddles and sodden grass that squished underfoot sure to keep everyone else inside as well.

Briefly, she considered climbing back into bed but crossed to ring for Penny instead.

Less than a minute later, a light rap came at the door.

"Come in," she called, surprised her maid had made it upstairs so quickly.

But it wasn't Penny who entered the room, as a pair of silvery blue eyes peered around the doorjamb. "I'm not disturbing you, am I?" Meg inquired, opening the door wider so she could fit her rounded figure past the threshold. She wore a royal purple silk dressing gown that looked beautiful against her fair skin and ash-blond hair.

"No, not at all," Mallory said.

"It's so gloomy outside, I thought I noticed candlelight under the door and hoped you were awake."

"You did, and I am. But what are you doing up so early? I would have thought you'd still be abed."

Moving farther into the room, Meg stopped and rested a hand on her protruding belly, rubbing her palm in an easy circle. "I would be if it weren't for this little one. He's been kicking half the night and keeping me and Cade awake. I finally decided to get up and see if walking around might calm him."

"Has it?"

Meg gave a rueful smile. "*No.* He's just as active as ever. I expect it won't be long now before he arrives. Maximillian was the same way that last month, constantly turning over and pummeling me under the ribs. I told Cade then that he wouldn't need to enroll him at Gentleman Jackson's since he's already proficient at the science of boxing."

The corner of Mallory's lips twitched at the image, thinking of her little nephew, who was already a scamp and a handsome, green-eyed charmer at the young age of two. No doubt this new baby would follow in his footsteps.

"But come and have a seat," Mallory said, gesturing toward the sofa. "Penny should be along any minute now."

"Are you sure? You probably want to go back to bed yourself, what with this rain."

"No, I'm up for the day, and since I can't go riding, I was thinking about having breakfast here in my room. Would you care to join me?"

Meg's face lit up. "Well, I could use a bite. Then again, I'm always ready to eat these days. I swear no matter how much I consume, I'm still starving."

"Sit then, and I'll order us a feast."

"Ooh, a feast," Meg said as she carefully eased herself onto the sofa. "I like the sound of that. Neville does too."

Mallory lifted a brow. "Neville?"

Meg grinned. "The baby. It's what I've taken to calling him lately."

Mallory took a seat next to her sister-in-law, tucking the edges of her own apricot silk dressing gown closer around her legs. "Are you calling him Neville then?"

A laugh rippled from Meg's lips. "No, but don't tell Cade. He can't abide the name and bristles up every time I use it. I know it's terrible of me, but I cannot resist teasing him. Before Neville, it was Orson and Filbert. He doesn't like any of them."

"I can't say I do either."

Meg laughed again. "You don't think we should add an Orson Byron to the family?"

A tap sounded at the door, and Penny came in, interrupting the frivolity.

Mallory had just asked her maid to send down to the kitchen for breakfast when another blond head peered around the door.

"I couldn't help but hear you talking," Claire said. "What are you two doing up?"

"What are *you* doing up?" Meg said, as Claire strolled deeper into the room.

"Early-morning feeding in the nursery, you should know all about those, Meg. I just got the baby down again and was on my way back to bed when I heard the commotion."

"We're hardly making enough noise for a commotion," Meg declared. "But we are having a nice visit. Oh!" She jumped faintly, bracing for a moment before rubbing a hand over her stomach again. "Definitely another boxer on the way and not a little angel like your Hannah, no matter if Cade is hoping for a daughter."

Claire smiled, her gaze alive with warmth and love. "Hannah is a sweetheart. I have to admit I've never seen a sunnier, more contented baby. Well, except for Nicola maybe."

"What's this about Nicola?" said Grace, who moved into the room. "My mother's hearing improves whenever anyone mentions my little girl's name."

"I was saying what wonderful babies she and Hannah are," Claire stated.

Grace's mouth turned up. "They are. Jack says God doesn't make them any sweeter than Byron girls."

"Jack is right," Claire agreed.

"If we could table this baby admiration society for a moment," Meg interjected, "I believe Penny was on her way downstairs to get us some breakfast."

"Oh, that's where I was headed when I heard all of you," Grace said.

"To the kitchen at this hour? Why are you awake and so hungry you can't wait until breakfast is served in the morning room?"

"Jack had me up, and I couldn't go back to sleep." A faint dusting of color crept into Grace's cheek.

"Had you up, did he?" Claire waggled her pale brows and gave a naughty grin that no proper duchess should wear. "Edward often has me up at dawn too, but somehow I never seem to mind."

"Cade does the same, not lately though," Meg offered. "With all my tossing and turning, he's so tired by dawn, the poor dear takes advantage of every minute of sleep he can manage."

The ladies laughed.

Everyone, that is, but Mallory, who found herself wondering if she ought to have covered her ears. Ordinarily, she wouldn't mind being privy to a bit of spicy conversation, but not about her brothers!

As if aware of her reaction, Grace sent her a look of apology. "Sorry, Mallory. We'll try to behave."

"You're right, Grace," Claire agreed. "We're probably shocking Mallory to pieces, not to mention poor Penny, who's turned at least three shades of pink since we began this conversation."

Turning to her hovering maid, Mallory nodded for her to be on her way. "Breakfast for four, if you please."

"Five actually," Grace piped. "That's the other reason I'm so hungry this morning. I'm expecting again."

Cheers and exclamations went up, everyone rushing to hug Grace—everyone, that is, except Meg, who maintained her spot on the sofa as she reached up her arms for an embrace, which Grace returned with alacrity.

Mallory brushed a kiss against Grace's cheek. "I'm so happy for you!"

"Maybe a boy this time." Grace grinned, her blue-grey eyes sparkling with unconcealed joy. "Though a second girl would be wonderful too. Oh, just listen to me carry on."

Mallory swallowed down the sudden lump that rose in her throat before nodding again toward Penny. "Five breakfasts then, or shall we make it six for Neville?" she added with a glance at Meg.

Meg hooted with laughter and patted her stomach. The others demanded to know who this Neville was, to which she jovially began to explain.

"What's all this?" India asked as she came through the doorway. Her dressing gown swirled around her ankles, her long black hair pulled back into a tie at her nape. "Are you having a party?"

"A celebration actually," Claire stated, going on to share Grace's good news.

Mallory threw up her hands in surrender. "Just tell Cook to prepare a lot of food, Penny. And you'd better run on quickly before the rest of the household arrives."

Grinning, the servant bobbed her head and hurried from the room.

"Well then, India," Claire demanded. "Why are *you* awake? Baby or husband?"

With his usual ride with Mallory out of the question because of the rainstorm, Adam took his time bathing, shaving and getting dressed. Standing in shirtsleeves and waistcoat, he sat down at the polished walnut writing desk to pen a brief missive to Mallory. Halfway through, however, he abandoned the effort and shrugged into his coat instead.

If Mallory was still abed, he would leave word with her maid to have her join him when she was ready. At least he hoped she would join him rather than spend the day alone in her room. Even now she still tended to avoid the house-party gatherings except for meals, which she attended with solemn aplomb.

Leaving his room, he strode down the wide corridors, his boots soundless on the soft Aubusson carpets. As he walked, he passed an impressive collection of paintings done by masters both old and new, including one Caravaggio, a Rembrandt and a Turner. On the air drifted the rich scents of polished wood, beeswax candles, hothouse roses and hydrangeas—large urns and vases full of the fresh flowers arranged throughout the house.

A colorful display of pink and white zinnias stood on a small table across from Mallory's bedchamber. He was considering taking one to give to her when he heard feminine laughter coming from her room—lots of feminine laughter.

Curious, he crossed to the half-open door and gave a light rap.

"Oh, I do hope that's the housemaid with more crumpets," said a voice that he recognized as belonging to Meg Byron. "The first basket wasn't nearly enough."

He pushed the door wider and entered the room. "Sorry to disappoint you, your ladyship, but I arrive empty-handed. Though had I known you were in dire want of crumpets, I would have nipped down to the kitchen first and brought you up a fresh basket or two."

Exclamations erupted from the five ladies present as he stepped inside to find the group arranged around the room, some seated in chairs and others on the sofa, including Mallory, who sat next to Meg.

"Adam Gresham!" Claire said. "Count on finding you lurking outside a lady's bedchamber so early in the morning."

He sent her a carefree smile. "Oh, you'll find that I enjoy lurking outside ladies' bedchambers at all hours of the day—and night."

Feminine chuckles floated in the air, although he noticed that Mallory didn't join in. Outside, the rain continued to pour, thunder crashing in loud bursts, while a rough wind rattled the windowpanes. But the women all looked relaxed and cozy in spite of the inclement weather.

"As you can see, we've descended on Mallory and are having breakfast in her room," Claire continued with a good-natured smile. "I suppose it would be highly improper to ask you to join us, my lord, particularly since none of us are dressed for the day."

"You appear sufficiently clothed to my way of thinking, and looking as lovely as a rose garden in full bloom. But alas, you are right about the impropriety of my remaining, not to mention the challenges I would likely receive from your husbands. Were one of them to find me with you, they might think I was trying to form a harem."

All of the women gasped, even Mallory, before releasing a fresh burst of laughter.

"I believe it is that other Byron, the poet, who is interested in harems, my lord," India remarked, once she had recovered sufficient breath. "Surely you do not subscribe to such goings-on?"

"No, indeed. Such notions are far, far too shocking,"

he said with great seriousness, then ruined the effect by winking.

They laughed again.

"I'm afraid, dear ladies, that I must withdraw and leave you to your repast," he said. "Ah, and just in time since the maid is here with your extra crumpets."

While the others began dividing up their new bounty, Adam turned to Mallory, lowering his voice. "If you aren't too famished and can tear yourself away, might I have a word?"

"Of course," Mallory agreed.

Grace and Meg were playfully fighting over the last of the strawberry preserves as Adam stepped aside to let Mallory lead the way from the room. He couldn't help but admire the view as he followed her out, her slim hips swaying in a most enticing fashion beneath the skirts of her dressing gown. Of equal fascination was her hair, which hung in thick, raven-dark waves all the way to her hips.

So now I know just how long it is, he mused with a wolfish inner smile. He flexed his fingers at his sides, wishing he could stop her so that he might caress the shining strands. He'd pet her like a cat and make her purr. Then he would bury his hands in the lush, silken depths, kiss her wildly and make her purr some more.

Mallory drew to a halt in the corridor just outside her bedroom door and turned to face him.

Luckily, he had a great deal of practice at controlling his features; otherwise, his expression would surely have given away his libidinous musings.

"Why don't we walk on a little farther?" he suggested in an even tone. "The ladies may be busy with their tea and crumpets and conversation, but their ears are still in excellent working order."

Her aquamarine eyes sparkled at his remark. Nodding,

she continued down the hallway, pausing only when she reached an alcove near the end. "Will this do?"

He glanced at the recessed window seat, then nodded. "It should do nicely. Shall we sit?"

Gathering her skirts, she lowered herself onto the padded blue damask cushion. Adam joined her, angling himself so he could gaze into her beautiful face and watch the parade of emotions that never lay too far below the surface.

Unwittingly, Mallory had chosen an intimate spot, the dark sky outside casting them in shadows and seclusion. He supposed this wasn't the best place to sit and one he probably shouldn't have encouraged. And yet, he couldn't resist, no more than he could resist Mallory herself.

"So, what is it you have to tell me that the others oughtn't hear?" she asked, leaning toward him with an old eagerness that pleased and relieved him to see. Perhaps her spirits were slowly beginning to improve.

"Nothing. I just wanted to wish you a good morning without our having an audience," he told her.

"Oh." Her shoulders drooped with obvious dismay.

He hid a smile. "You were expecting something else?"

"No." Her brows knitted above her eyes. "Yes. Oh, I don't know. It's just that you took such pains to prize me from the others that I thought . . . well, that it must be something a bit more important."

"Saying good morning to you *is* important. And I never mind prizing you away from anyone, since you are nothing less than a prize. A perfect, wonderful prize that, like a greedy child, I would prefer never being made to share."

She stared at him for a pronounced moment before the corners of her mouth edged up, and she shook her head with amusement. "Adam, the things you say sometimes.

If I didn't know better, I would think you were flirting with me."

His heart gave a sharp squeeze since that's exactly what he had been doing—although perhaps not deliberately. The words had just sort of rolled off his tongue with unconscious ease. But rather than admit the truth and confess to feelings he knew she wasn't yet ready to hear, he sent her an insouciant grin.

"Don't be absurd," he said, letting his eyelids slant low to conceal his expression. "I am only trying to divert your attention from this plaguing rainstorm and the disappointment of our being trapped inside today. Is it working?"

He sensed, rather than saw, her smile. "Yes, my lord, I believe it is."

Having steadied his emotions, he met her gaze once again. "Good, since I was sorely put out that we were forced to cancel our usual morning ride."

"As was I," she agreed in soft tones. "Our rides have become the highlight of my days lately."

His heart gave another heavy beat. "Mine as well." Realizing he was rapidly sliding back into dangerous territory, he redirected the conversation. "Which is another reason why I decided to stop by your rooms this morning."

"Oh?" She cocked her head, the movement causing a thick length of her dark hair to slide forward over one shoulder.

He couldn't help but notice the way the strands curved over her breast, then lower to gather in a silky pool in her lap. He flexed his fingers again, yearning to touch.

"I didn't want you spending the day alone and putting in an appearance at meals only," he said, quietly clearing his throat.

"As you can tell, I have been far from alone this morning."

"Not by design though," he pointed out, "or am I mistaken?"

"They all quite took me by surprise, even if their companionship has turned out to be most pleasant."

"And after your sisters-in-law finish breakfast and depart, what were you planning to do then?" He paused, silence falling between them. "Precisely as I thought," he continued. "You're going to sit in your room and watch the gloomy weather."

"Of course I am not," she denied.

"Then you're going to sit in some *other* room and watch the gloomy weather."

She made a face. "Ha-ha, very funny."

"It might be if it weren't the truth. Which is why I wanted to invite you to join me in the library for a game of chess. Or cards, if you would prefer. Jack isn't the only one in the Byron family who has an affinity for knowing when to hold a hand or toss it aside."

"Thank you for the compliment," she said with a tip of her head. "And, if you'd asked me an hour ago, I would have said yes."

He lifted an inquiring eyebrow. "But?"

A rueful sigh escaped her lips. "I don't know how it happened, but they've cozened me into joining them all in the drawing room today. We're to have rainy-day fun and games."

He couldn't help but grin at her alarmed expression. "Maybe it won't be so bad."

"Why is it I can never think of a useful excuse to escape?"

"Maybe you shouldn't. Maybe it's time you started

joining in again. But only for this afternoon, if it proves not to be to your liking."

A slight frown creased the smooth skin of her forehead.

"And if Claire and your mother set up card tables, as I suspect they will," he went on, "you and I can play, after all. I stake an early claim to have you as my partner."

Her gaze warmed. "To that I shall gladly consent."

"Excellent." Grinning, he caught her hand and raised it to his lips.

He meant to brush a quick kiss over the top, but instead turned her hand over at the last moment and buried his mouth against the satiny flesh of her palm. Instantly, he knew he'd made a mistake, his eyelids sinking down, as the honeyed scent of her skin swam like a drug in his head. Need coursed through him, an intensity of longing that was growing harder to control by the day.

If she hadn't still been in a fragile state, if she weren't only just beginning to emerge from the shattering pain of her mourning, he knew he would have done far more than kiss her hand. How easy it would be to tug her across the brief space that separated them. What bliss to pull her onto his lap and kiss her until neither of them could breathe.

She wasn't even dressed, not really, seated here across from him in nothing more than her nightrail and dressing gown. How easy it would be to tunnel his hand underneath, to reach beneath those thin skirts and explore all the delicious flesh they concealed.

Damnation, she's driving me mad.

As though her palm had suddenly turned hot as a fireplace poker, he released her. Turning his head, he stared out at the storm, using the seconds to collect his senses.

"Adam?" she questioned, clearly puzzled.

"I wouldn't be surprised if this storm goes on into the night," he said, his voice sounding strained even to his own ears. "Hopefully it will be over by tomorrow, and the sun will be shining again."

"I certainly hope it is."

He slid the gold chain of his watch fob between his fingers. "I suppose I ought to return you to the ladies now. They're probably about to send out an emissary."

"I doubt that since they know I'm completely safe with you."

Safe with me, are you?

She made him sound like one of Esme's tame pussy-cats, who spent their days lounging in idle splendor on all the best chairs in the house. If she were privy to his thoughts, she wouldn't be nearly so complaisant. Still, he supposed her virtue was in no imminent danger from him—for now anyway.

"Nevertheless," he remarked, "you're in your dressing gown. What would the other guests think if they found us together?"

Her eyes widened with sudden self-consciousness, her hands reaching up to check the buttons at her neck and smooth back her tresses. "Oh, you're right. Only imagine the reaction if Claire's parents happened along, especially with my hair down. I suppose I ought to have pinned it up before I came out here, but it's just so irritatingly heavy and long. Remember how Claire cut hers two Seasons ago? Mayhap I ought to follow her example and crop it off as short as a boy's. After all, *La Marsden* was all the rage at the time."

"No," he choked out, making no effort to conceal his outrage.

She stilled, her gaze locking with his. "Don't you like cropped locks on women?"

"No, I do not," he said again, hard and uncompromising. "And you are *never* to cut your hair, do you hear me? The very idea is an affront. Swear to me you won't."

"Well, I hardly think it would be all that dire—"

"Swear, Mallory. I will have your word. Your hair is far too beautiful to ever consider cutting it."

She stared at him for a significant moment, then shrugged. "All right, if it means so much to you. I reserve the right, though, to trim the ends every once in a while. An occasional session with the shears makes it healthier and much easier to manage."

Relaxing, he shot her a smile. "An inch or two won't hurt, I expect." He climbed to his feet, knowing he should leave before he said or did something he regretted. "Allow me to escort you back."

"No need. I believe I know the way to my own bed-chamber."

He nearly insisted, then decided to relent and bowed instead. "And so you do. I shall see you soon for whatever entertainment their Graces have in store."

"I cannot wait," she replied with a sad resignation in her voice.

He smiled. "It's just cards, Mal. But if matters become too overwhelming, we'll sneak off to the library for chess or to the orangery for a stroll."

"I may hold you to that, my lord."

"And I may try to make you." Sending her another smile, he forced himself to turn and walk away.

Mallory watched Adam stride down the hall, knowing she ought to follow his example and make her way back to her bedroom and the impromptu breakfast party still taking place inside.

Instead, she settled deeper against the window-seat

cushions and gazed out at the steadily falling rain. As she did, she thought about her conversation with Adam, relieved to know he would be with her today, ready to lend a sturdy shoulder should she find herself in need of one.

He'd been so good to her since his arrival, putting up with her moods and tempers and tears. But then Adam had always been good to her. He was good *for* her as well, forcing her to emerge from the worst of her gloom, even if his methods might offend and infuriate her at times. And as much as she loved her family—and heaven knew she did—it was Adam to whom she turned, Adam in whom she found comfort and the ability to confide.

Perhaps it was because he was like family, and yet not family, that made her feel so at ease in his company. That and the fact that out of all her friends, he was one of the dearest. It was true that weeks, even months, might sometimes pass when she would not see him, the two of them exchanging only the occasional letter or small gift. And yet he was never far away. She had only to send word, and he would be there as fast as horses could run. She had but to ask, and he was ready to offer his aid, his counsel and his friendship.

There were even times such as this past year when she hadn't needed to ask him anything at all. He'd just known what she required, whether it be solitude or a little judicious nudge in the right direction. The pain of Michael's death was still with her, hovering always in the background. Yet, since Adam had come to Braebourne, she didn't feel quite so numb any longer. For the first time in over a year, she could actually make her mouth turn up in a smile—even if the emotion behind it wasn't always entirely genuine.

She supposed some might say she was leaning too much on Adam, that she was taking advantage of him when he was neither her relation nor her beau. But he didn't seem to mind. He'd sought her out, after all. Inviting her to ride and walk with him, to sit by his side at dinner, and to have private early-morning tête-à-têtes that would have scandalized a girl in possession of more delicate sensibilities.

She paused at the thought, her lips tingling at the memory of his brazen kiss that day on their hill, a kiss she couldn't seem to put out of her mind.

She'd been right, of course, that he'd done it to shock her from her emotional stupor rather than out of any true desire for her. He was a rake, after all, and knew all the best ways to seduce a woman if he chose. But obviously he didn't choose, at least not with her, since he'd made absolutely no effort to repeat the interlude this week and more, despite any number of opportunities.

Not that she wanted him to, because she didn't.

Still, he'd had the most peculiar expression on his face this morning. If she hadn't known better, she would have thought he really *did* want to kiss her—that he'd been dying to do so, in point of fact.

But she was just being absurd. Adam didn't feel that way about her, nor she for him. How could she when her heart belonged to Michael?

Grimacing against the sudden jab of pain, she curled a fist against her chest. As she did, she caught the sound of feminine laughter drifting from her bedchamber.

She needed to get back, she reminded herself, needed to bathe and dress and find some way to go on with what was sure to be a very long day.

Fixing a purposely cheerful smile on her face, she stood and marched along the corridor. Greetings rang out as she entered her room, all the women volubly happy to see her. To her surprise, another family member had joined them—her brother Jack, who was relaxing in casual splendor on the sofa, his arm curled snugly around his wife.

"I came to find Grace and discovered a party going on instead," he told her. "Where's Adam, by the way? I hear the pair of you went off to talk."

Her brows drew tight. "We did, then he continued on his way."

Jack studied her for a long moment before nodding. "Do you want this last crumpet? None of these heartless wenches would let me eat it until you returned."

Grace gave him a nudge with her elbow. "Heartless wenches indeed."

He chuckled and bussed Grace on the lips despite the impropriety.

"So, about that crumpet?" he asked Mallory.

"It's all yours," she told him.

Taking a seat, she listened to everyone talk as the last of breakfast continued.

Chapter 8

A few hours later, Mallory rose from the card table, she and Adam victorious in the game of whist they'd just finished playing. They'd been partnered against her brother, Drake, and her friend, Jessica Milbank, who'd spent her time trying to flirt with Drake rather than paying attention to which suit she ought to lay down.

For Drake's part, Mallory had been able to tell by the stiff set of his mouth that he'd been both exasperated by Jessica's poor play and uncomfortable at having to fend off her undisguised advances.

Mallory had always considered Jessica a lovely person at heart, but with her third Season now past, she was obviously growing anxious in her quest to find a husband. Though why she'd decided to throw her cap at Drake was anyone's guess.

All of Society, and most particularly the Byron family, knew he had no interest in taking a wife. And from what

Mallory had overheard, he had little reason to change his mind given the mistress he kept in Town. Apparently, she gave him complete freedom, never complaining about his odd hours, his unpredictable, often distracted moods, or the obsessive nature of his mathematical and scientific endeavors.

Had she asked, Mallory could have told Jessica she didn't have a chance with Drake, especially after Jessica committed the unpardonable sin—in Drake's eyes anyway—of admitting that she'd never heard of Sir Isaac Newton, gravity or the laws of physics.

And she'd driven the nail even deeper when she'd laughed outright at the idea of people ever being able to harness the power of electricity for any practical purposes, such as the creation of artificial light. "Only a madman would try doing something so incredibly dangerous," she'd stated as a bolt of lightning from the storm flashed in the sky. "And for what, when we already have candles?"

Twin arcs of lightning had flashed in Drake's eyes at that heresy, and for a moment Mallory thought he was going to fling down his cards and leave the table. Too much of a gentleman, though, he'd held his temper and finished the game. The instant it was over, however, he'd stalked across the room, where he stood now having a drink.

Still oblivious, Jessica had followed.

Adam chuckled low in his throat. "She reminds me of a puppy who doesn't know when to quit."

"Hush," Mallory scolded. "Jessica is a very nice person."

"Indeed she is," he said in a far more serious tone. "I have always found Miss Milbank to be a most pleasant young lady, as well as an excellent dancer. However, she and Drake go together nearly as well as oil and water."

"I was thinking eggs and anchovies—a really foul combination, do you not agree?"

He laughed, tossing back his head in a way that drew a few gazes. But his outburst was forgotten an instant later as a roar went up from a table at the other end of the drawing room. Glancing over, she saw Claire chortling as she scraped a small pile of winnings to her side of the table, Jack clearly surprised, while Edward and Quentin both looked on with amused approbation.

"Claire must have taken a game from Jack," Mallory said. "I think she's one of the only people in the family who enjoys playing against him, given the fact he always wins."

"Not always. It would appear he has found a worthy opponent in our new duchess." He glanced back at Mallory. "If you've had enough of cards for now, would you care for a beverage?"

"A glass of lemonade would not go amiss."

Executing a clipped bow, he departed to procure her drink.

Espying a sofa in the far corner of the room that offered an enticing measure of privacy, Mallory strolled that way.

She'd just taken a seat and was straightening the skirt of her pale rose afternoon dress when Lady Damson appeared, dropping down beside her.

"At last!" Daphne declared, as she leaned over to give Mallory a quick kiss on the cheek. "I've been longing to visit with you for ages, but we never seem to have a chance."

"Hallo, Daphne. How are you today?"

"Fat," she said, patting her exceptionally trim stomach. "Your brother and sister-in-law serve the most delicious fare. If I'm not careful, Harold will decide I've grown too wide and toss me out."

"I rather doubt that," Mallory said, glancing toward the innocuous, bespectacled Lord Damson, where he stood talking with Lord Edgewater and Mr. Hughes. As if noticing he was under scrutiny, he turned his head and gazed over, his eyes alighting on his wife.

Surreptitiously, he waggled his fingers at her. Daphne waggled hers back.

"I don't believe you have anything to worry about," Mallory said. "He clearly dotes on you."

Daphne giggled. "He does, does he not? Foolish old thing. But that's marriage for you. If only you and the major had been able to tie the knot before—" She broke off, eyes wide with distress over her remark. "Forgive me. I didn't mean to . . . you know . . . upset you."

Mallory drew a breath and forced a smile. "It's quite all right. Michael is dead, and there's no reason to gloss over the fact. And you're right that it would have been lovely if we'd been able to marry before he died."

But he'd wanted to wait until he returned from the fighting before they wed. He'd wanted to beat Boney, then come home and resign his commission for good, so they could start their family. Instead, there'd been no marriage, and, as for the Little General, he was still waging war across the Continent. Why couldn't Michael have been a little less altruistic? Why couldn't he have put her needs first for once instead of England's?

Frowning over the disloyal thought, she returned her attention to Daphne.

Reaching over, the other young woman patted the top of her hand. "You poor dear, everyone knows how deeply you've grieved his loss. It's most admirable of you, but I have to say that I'm relieved to see you out and about today. Not that I blame you for not joining in more before. No, no one could blame you, no one at all."

Mallory folded her hands in her lap, wondering why it sounded as if Daphne was doing that very thing.

"But now you're here," her old friend continued, "and this dreary day gives us the perfect excuse to stay inside and catch up on all the news."

"What news might that be?" Mallory asked, little caring about the answer.

"Oh, all the doings with our old crowd. You don't know since you missed the Season, but Harcourt Mason is being received at Veronica Lancaster's country home this summer. You know how those two got on, so imagine my astonishment . . ."

Nodding at what she hoped were appropriate intervals, Mallory let Daphne talk. The other woman barely paused for breath as she rattled on, apparently happy to carry the whole of the conversation. As she did, Mallory found herself wondering if she'd ever really enjoyed such mindless chatter and idle gossip. She guessed she must have . . . before. But now it all seemed like a rather meaningless waste of time although admittedly one in which many members of Society frequently indulged. Daphne, she realized, was the same as she'd ever been—pretty, effervescent and unapologetically spoiled. She hadn't changed.

Instead I am the one who's changed, Mallory thought. *I am the one who no longer fits in.*

"So you'll come then?" Daphne was saying. "For you simply must visit. Harold and I would love to have you over to the estate, and while you're there, I can introduce you to any number of eligible men. I know it might seem too soon, but it has been more than a year already, and by next Season . . . well, the new crop of debutantes always crowds the field. Just look at our poor Jessica. She'll be three-and-twenty next year. I hesitate to say this, but if she doesn't make a match soon, she may find herself on the shelf for good."

Leaning over, she patted the top of Mallory's hand again. "There's no rush for you, of course, not yet anyway. But I would hate to see you delay too long before you start circulating again. If you do, all the really choice gentlemen may be taken, and you'll end up having to choose someone who is well . . . how should I put this . . . not worthy of your level of refinement and beauty."

Mallory's spine drew straight as a post, her mouth tightening.

"Unless there's something—or rather *someone*—about whom you're not telling me." Daphne shot her an encouraging smile.

"Whatever do you mean?"

"Gresham, of course. You've been thick as thieves with him ever since he arrived."

"Adam and I are friends, you know that," Mallory said, her voice stiff.

"Well, yes, but that was *before*."

"Before what?"

"Before he came into funds, goose. Now that he has a feather to fly with—or rather a great many feathers—he's one of the most eligible bachelors in Society. Every Mama from Dover to Dundee will be lining up to catch him for her daughter. Unless you snag him first."

"Well, I won't," Mallory shot back, her skin literally prickling with anger. "Nor am I interested in *snagging* any man when I'm barely out of mourning. I think it's incredibly unfeeling of you to even suggest such an idea. And here you claim to understand how I feel about Michael's death. Well you don't, but then how could you when you've never lost anyone or anything you ever truly loved."

Daphne sputtered, a hand going to her throat.

Mallory jumped to her feet. "I'll hear no more about

this, and I expect you not to mention the subject to anyone else either. Now, if you'll excuse me, I believe I am wanted across the room."

She wasn't, of course, but she couldn't bear to remain anywhere near Daphne at the moment. Turning a deaf ear to her friend's pleading, she marched away. Tears stung her eyes, and she moved without direction, wanting only to escape. Then, suddenly, Adam was there, his tall frame blocking her path.

"What has happened?" he demanded in a low tone, bending briefly in order to set down the drinks he'd procured for each of them.

"N-nothing, it's nothing. I just have a headache of a sudden."

Gently, he led her toward a corner where they wouldn't be overheard. "Balderdash. You don't have a headache. I saw you talking with Lady Damson. What has she said to distress you so?"

She sniffed and wiped her eyes. "The details aren't important, and I'd prefer not to say."

His shoulders squared. "It was about Hargreaves, I suppose."

And you, she thought. But she wasn't about to tell him that. "He was mentioned," she said.

Adam didn't respond, his body visibly on edge. Abruptly though, he relaxed and laid a comforting hand on her shoulder. "Do you want to leave? I'm sure we could find a way to escape without too much notice. We could even play that game of chess in the library, if you'd like, or stroll in the orangery. Unless you want to return to your room."

I would like nothing else, she realized. Yet despite what Adam said, people would notice her retreat, including a few who had probably noticed her exchanging words with Daphne. Her family would be worried and the others curious to know what had been said. She'd caused enough talk since the house party started. She didn't want to cause any more.

She shook her head. "No, I shall stay."

"You're certain?"

Her eyes now dry, she drew herself up and met Adam's gaze. "Yes, it's time I stopped hiding in my room like a coward. No matter what was said, I shall be fine."

He skimmed a finger over her cheek. "That's my girl."

She trembled, an odd wave of guilt washing through her at his tenderness, guilt and something more that she didn't want to acknowledge.

Stepping free of his touch, she nodded toward their abandoned beverages. "I'll try some of that lemonade now."

"Of course." Retrieving the drinks, he handed her a tall, cool glass. For himself, he'd chosen red wine. "More cards?" he asked, taking a swallow from his goblet.

She shook her head. "I was thinking it might be more entertaining to see what the children are up to. I believe Esme and the others are engaged in a rousing match of jackstraws and marbles."

In deference to the gloomy weather, the adults had agreed that the young people should be invited down from the schoolroom for the afternoon so they might partake in the drawing-room festivities. Even the babies had been brought downstairs for a while before growing too tired and fussy to remain.

"Unless child's play is beneath your dignity, my lord?" she said.

His eyebrows arched high. "Come now, when have you ever known me to be too high in the instep for a bit of lighthearted fun? Although I suspect I may need a refresher in the finer points of both games, since I don't think I've played jackstraws or marbles since I was eight or nine years old."

"Then it is time you learned anew." Slipping her hand over his arm, she led him forward, hoping the game proved to be just the distraction she needed.

Mallory wasn't sure how, but she managed to endure the remainder of the day. She even enjoyed herself on occasion, especially as she listened to Adam tease and jolly the Byron and Marsden girls until they were convulsed with uncontrollable laughter.

Hearing their merriment, Leo, Lawrence and Spencer Byron lowered their own dignity enough to join the group. Unable to control their nature, the twins began flirting with seventeen-year-old Ella Marsden, who was soon blushing to the roots of her blond hair.

Their antics earned them several severe frowns from Mallory, which only seemed to increase their efforts. Once Adam noticed, however, all it took was a few quiet words, and they grew circumspect as a pair of clergymen.

As evening approached, the festivities came to a temporary halt so everyone could retire upstairs to rest and change their attire for dinner. After a brief nap, Mallory selected an evening gown of figured copper silk that lent her skin an extra glow of vitality.

Seated between Adam and Cade, she found that the dinner went easily. Then it was time for the ladies to withdraw. Determined to follow through on her pledge not to hide away—or at least to make the attempt not to—Mallory ignored the impulse to go upstairs to her room and followed the others into the drawing room instead.

Sticking close to Claire, Grace and Meg, she was able to avoid any further conversations with Daphne, who tried once or twice to gain her attention. And then, the gentlemen arrived, strolling in with the last of their brandy in hand and the lingering aroma of cheroots on their clothes.

With the rain still drumming against the windowpanes, there was no possibility of taking an evening stroll in the gardens or engaging in any other outdoor entertainments. With an eager smile, Jessica Milbank stepped up to the pianoforte and gave a lively, well-executed performance. When she finished, someone suggested the idea of dancing, which was greeted with great enthusiasm. And to Jessica's obvious relief, cousin Wilhelmina graciously offered to take her place at the pianoforte—the widowed Mrs. Byron declaring it was the young people who had the energy for such activities.

While several of the others in the room began arranging themselves for a cotillion, Mallory settled on the sofa next to Meg and sipped her tea.

Suddenly Niall Faversham appeared before her and bowed, his pale hair brushed back from his attractive face with casual disregard. "Lady Mallory, would you care to take a turn with me? I promise I shall be especially careful and not step on your toes."

"I'm sure there's no danger of that, Mr. Faversham," she said, well aware of what an excellent dancer he was. "I thank you for your invitation, but I'm afraid I am not dancing tonight."

"What's this about not dancing?" declared Lord Howland, who stepped forward to join their small circle. "But you must dance, my dear Lady Mallory. With *me*!"

"I beg to differ, Howland," Faversham complained. "I asked her first."

"Yes, but she has refused you." Howland grinned, displaying his teeth with their crooked upper incisors. "Obviously she was waiting until I arrived so I could ask her."

"The devil you say," Faversham retorted. "She only needs a moment more to reconsider her decision and say she will stand up with *me*."

"I'm sure she'd sooner take to the floor with an orangutan."

"Which is exactly why she'll have no interest in you, what with that thatch of red on your head that you call hair."

If Mallory hadn't known they were friends, she might have been alarmed. Instead, she couldn't help but smile over their bickering. "Gentlemen, you are both very kind to ask, but I simply must say—"

"Yes," Meg interrupted. "Oh, do go on, Mallory, and choose one of them. If I didn't have Oswald on board here," she said, patting her mounded stomach, "I assure you I'd be dancing."

"I thought you were calling the baby Neville?" Mallory observed.

"I was, but it's Oswald now." Meg shared a saucy wink with her that went completely over the heads of the two men.

"Listen to the wise counsel of your sister-in-law, my lady," Lord Howland said. "Come say you will dance."

"Yes, choose one of us as Lady Cade so eloquently suggested," Mr. Faversham said. "Choose me."

Mallory hesitated, wondering how she had come to such an unanticipated pass. Glancing out into the room, she searched for Adam. Her lips parted when she discovered him making his way onto the makeshift dance floor with Jessica Milbank on his arm.

Apparently, Jessica had given up on Drake—who'd taken convenient refuge on the far side of the room with Lord Edgewater and Lord Damson—and had transferred her interests elsewhere. That in itself didn't surprise Mallory. What did was the fact that Adam had accepted her overtures.

Mallory's brows lowered, her earlier conversation with Daphne replaying itself in her head. Had Daphne said something to Jessica about Adam? Had she mentioned perhaps that Mallory had renounced any claims to him, leaving Jessica free to invite his attentions. Which, she was, of course. But still, Adam and Jessica . . . it was almost unfathomable.

Mallory forced herself not to grimace, wishing now that she *had* gone upstairs after all. But she'd promised she would make more of an effort to join in, and what better way to do so than participating in the activity at hand.

"Very well," Mallory said. "You have convinced me, and I shall dance."

Faversham and Howland straightened to their tallest heights and squared their shoulders, each clearly vying to cut the most appealing figure.

"So, which one of us will you choose, Lady Mallory?" Lord Howland asked.

She shot another glance toward Adam and Jessica, her fingers curling into a fist when she saw Jessica playfully tap her fan against Adam's chest, then toss back her head on a laugh.

"I'll dance with you both," Mallory declared, turning her attention back to her two admirers. "Mr. Faversham shall partner me first, since he made the earliest claim, and then you, Lord Howland."

Although not wholly satisfied at having to share her favors, the two men nodded in agreement.

Mr. Faversham extended his arm. Rising from the sofa, Mallory let him lead her forward.

*   *   *

Pity has a lot to answer for, Adam thought, as he affixed a polite expression to his face and listened to Jessica Milbank regale him with a list of all her favorite haunts in London—most of which happened to be millinery shops.

After she'd been excused from the duty of playing piano for the assembled company, Jessica had walked out into the center of the room and waited, clearly expecting one of the gentlemen to ask her to dance. He'd watched as she cast a hopeful glance toward Drake, noticing his very determined interest in whatever Lord Edgewater was saying—despite the fact that he knew Drake couldn't stand the other man's Tory politics. Realizing that her first choice of partner wasn't going to solicit her hand, she'd begun casting about for someone else. During her visual sweep of the room, her gaze had landed on Adam, and she'd sent him a painfully hopeful smile.

Aware that Mallory was settled comfortably on the sofa next to Meg, he decided to take pity and act the gallant toward her friend. After all, it was only one dance.

Unfortunately, Miss Milbank lit up as brightly as a small sun at his invitation, giggling and mincing and flirting with all her might, as they made their way to the floor. He was silently repeating his bit of optimistic rationalization regarding the promised dance with Miss Milbank when he glanced toward Mallory and felt his eyes go wide.

Flanking her on either side were Howland and Faversham, the pair obviously attempting to work their wiles on her. *Poor fellows,* he thought with amused sympathy, since he knew Mallory would refuse them, given that this was her first full evening back among company.

But then, not less than a minute later, she stood and accepted Faversham's arm.

Adam's mouth tightened, his eyebrows drawing into a severe downward slant. *Surely she hasn't said yes.*

He watched as the pair strolled forward to join the couples assembled for the dancing. *Sweet Jesu, it looks as if she has said yes!*

"Is something amiss, my lord?" Jessica Milbank asked in a quiet voice, a small vee of concern wrinkling the bridge of her petite pug nose.

Glancing down, he realized he'd completely forgotten the young woman waiting at his side. Recovering immediately, he fashioned a smile. "Of course not, Miss Milbank. I am merely anxious for the dancing to begin."

Her confidence returned. "Oh, it shouldn't be long now, I expect. Only look at everyone who is taking part."

And she was right, a full eight couples were gathered to partake in the lively entertainment. In addition to himself and Miss Milbank, there were Jack and Grace, Edward and Claire, Quentin and India, Lady Damson and Mr. Hughes—and Mallory and Faversham, of course. Some of the even younger set were joining in as well, since earlier Ava Byron and Claire had both agreed that there could be no real harm in letting the older girls escape the schoolroom for the evening. This left Leo to partner Ella Marsden, while Lawrence did the same for his cousin Anna.

Given the war injury that had left Cade with a limp, he no longer danced. But he didn't seem to mind, especially since he'd slipped into Mallory's abandoned spot on the sofa next to Meg. The couple sat murmuring to each other, their heads bent close, as if they were courting rather than starting the third year of their marriage.

"Is everyone ready to begin?" Cousin Wilhelmina called in a happy voice from her place at the pianoforte.

"We are indeed, cousin," Leo replied. "Play us something rollicking."

Chuckles rose at his exuberance as everyone arranged themselves into the proper positions. To Adam's frustration, he found himself at one end of the room, while Mallory stood at the other. Briefly, he met her gaze. Then the music began and, seconds after, the first steps of the dance.

Miss Milbank resumed her patter, politeness forcing him to evince enough interest that she wouldn't realize that his real thoughts lay elsewhere. When he could, he glanced toward Mallory, watching as Faversham skillfully led her in the lively movements, ones that soon added a pretty pink to her cheeks.

By the time the first dance concluded, Mallory's eyes were bright, a hint of a smile hovering on her lips. *She has always loved to dance,* Adam thought as he bowed to Jessica Milbank and she curtseyed back.

With skillful finesse, he soon managed to detach himself from Miss Milbank in a friendly way, putting her in the hands of Mr. Hughes for the next dance. The duke's young secretary looked a tad dazed by the introduction, but as Adam strode away, Hughes seemed genuinely pleased with Miss Milbank's companionship. And, if Adam guessed right, she with his.

Crossing to where Mallory stood, still conversing with Mr. Faversham, Adam made her a bow. "Lady Mallory. Would you care to stand up with me for the next set, assuming it hasn't already been claimed?"

"Actually, it has," Lord Howland said, inserting himself into their group. "The lady is promised to me. Is that not so, Lady Mallory?"

She met Adam's gaze, the truth of Howland's statement plain in her ocean-hued eyes. "Thank you for asking, but Lord Howland is right. The next dance is his."

"So, be off with you, Gresham," Howland said with a

toothy smile. "I've already had to battle Faversham to-night for the lady's favors. Don't need you sniffing around her as well."

"I'm not *sniffing* around anyone, and I'll thank you to keep a civil tongue in your head," Adam retorted. "There may be a great many canines in residence here at Brae-bourne, but Lady Mallory isn't one of them."

"Well, of course, she ain't," Howland blustered. "Never meant to imply such a thing. Lady Mallory, surely you don't think that I would ever—"

"No, I know you would not," she said, her eyes glinting as she shot Adam a look.

He gazed back, refusing to glance away. Crowding out the other men, including Howland, who was still sputtering over his remark, Adam stepped close to her. "I shall return once the next dance is done," he murmured into her ear. "So don't make any further promises to anyone but me."

Her lips parted, surprise plain on her face.

Adam turned, Howland still mouthing assurances about Mallory's beauty, grace and style. Cousin Wil-helmina began playing the next song soon after as couples paired up once again for the dance.

Rather than seek out a new partner, Adam went to the far side of the room. Taking up a spot with a good view of the dancing, he leaned his shoulder against the carved marble surround of the room's massive fireplace. He couldn't help but smile when he noticed Henry, and one of the other dogs—Handel, he thought—sleeping nearby on a comfortable bit of rug.

Quietly patient, Adam waited. As he did, Howland botched a step that made Mallory leap back to save her toes. Her gaze found Adam's, and she hid a rueful grin before continuing the dance.

Finally, the tune ended, the dancers drawing to a halt once more. Straightening away from the mantel, Adam sauntered toward Mallory.

"Howland," he said. "I believe it's your turn now to go away. So, shoo."

Howland ruffled up but offered no further challenge. Making Mallory a gracious bow, he turned his back on Adam and left the makeshift dance floor.

"I don't think Lord Howland is terribly pleased with you at the moment," Mallory said. "And here I thought the two of you were friends. Don't you socialize with him at your club?"

"Quite frequently. Which is why I know he'll bluster and glare at me for a day or two, then, like this weather we're having, his mood will clear and all will be well again."

She shook her head. "Men. I shall never understand the species even if I do have six brothers."

"Men are easy to fathom. It's women who are the true mystery." Pausing, he cocked his head to one side. "But listen, if I am not mistaken, your cousin is practicing the opening strains to a waltz."

"That's not likely, considering she thinks the waltz is a scheme being perpetrated by the French in order to erode the moral fiber of the English population."

Adam smiled. "Someone must have talked her into loosening her strictures."

He watched as Mallory glanced toward her brother Leo, who was grinning like Lucifer himself, as he whispered something into Ella Marsden's ear. The girl's cheeks fired up, as if she'd been shoved into a kiln before a giggle flowed from her lips.

Mallory rolled her eyes heavenward. "Yes, let's guess who."

Before they had a chance to discuss the matter further,

Cousin Wilhelmina played an opening flourish that signaled the beginning of a new set.

Taking Mallory into his arms, Adam swept her into the dance.

To his intense gratification, her cousin was indeed playing a waltz, which afforded him the opportunity to hold Mallory far closer than he would have been able to do otherwise. That's why the new dance, which had only recently been imported from France, was causing such a stir. Pulling her another inch closer, he whirled her in a tight circle that drew an exhilarated gasp from her lips.

"Delightful, is it not?" he said.

She nodded and followed his lead, her skirts billowing outward in a coppery swirl, her aquamarine eyes alive with undisguised pleasure.

Adam guided her into one graceful turn after the next as they moved across the floor amid the rest of the dancers. But he was barely aware of the others, all his thoughts, all his emotions focused on the beautiful, wonderful woman in his arms.

Gazing again into her eyes, he saw a happiness rising on Mallory's countenance that he hadn't glimpsed in such a very long time. She might think she could no longer enjoy herself, but with each new day she came a step closer to breaking free of the sorrow that had imprisoned her for so many dark months. She might still grieve in the days and weeks to come, but she would find happiness as well.

Wanting to give her that happiness and more, he spun her faster, guiding her into a series of quick, thrilling turns that made his pulse beat faster. And suddenly she smiled, laughter bursting from her throat with a sound of carefree abandon that made his own heart sing.

The old Mallory was back. Now, he only had to find the means to keep her here.

Chapter 9

Mallory was still humming the melody of the waltz under her breath as she crawled between the cool linen sheets on her bed. A single candle burned in a holder on her bedside table, Penny having snuffed out the rest before departing for the evening. Plumping the pillows, Mallory settled back against the feathery mounds, the mattress enveloping her in a pleasant softness as she sank backward. Curled in the shadows at the foot of the bed lay Charlemagne, the black cat regarding her through observant green eyes.

"It was lovely tonight," she murmured to the animal. "I would never have dreamed a dance could be so intoxicating."

Her first waltz.

No wonder it was all the rage among the most daring of the fashionable set. No wonder as well how scandalous many found it, especially the older generation, who believed there was entirely too much indiscreet touching involved. That was why she was glad Adam had been her partner. She would have been self-conscious with someone else. But with Adam, she'd been able to relax, confident and secure in his embrace.

Closing her eyes, she let herself remember, reliving the sensation of whirling across the floor held in his powerful arms. In those few brief moments, she'd felt as though she were flying, her feet quick and light enough to skip across the clouds.

Heavenly.

Charlemagne inched closer, curling himself tight against her ankles where he lay atop the thin summer coverlet. His gentle purrs drifted to her ears, lulling her to sleep. Still dreaming of waltzing in Adam's embrace, slumber carried her away . . .

She spun in a dizzying circle, the air sweet in her lungs, the grass soft beneath her slippered feet. Adam was whirling her, leading her to the strains of the most beautiful music. He murmured in her ear, his warm breath sending a shiver over her skin as he said something that made her laugh.

It felt good to laugh. So good. So right. And yet it shouldn't, though she couldn't precisely remember why.

The music played on, growing louder with deep bass notes that were jarring rather than harmonious. They pounded, the earth trembling beneath her feet. An acrid scent burned the lining of her nostrils, as an odd, warm wetness seeped into the satin of her dancing slippers. The shoes were white and pretty like her gown, but suddenly she wasn't on a dance floor anymore.

Opening her eyes, she stared and found not white, but red, her shoes drenched in sticky scarlet. And rather than new spring grass, she stood in a rough field, the earth torn asunder in deep troughs and gouges. And everywhere there were bodies, so many bodies, draped in red wool and awash with blood the color of claret wine. Moans rose up around her, mixing with the rumble of cannon fire.

Mallory.

Somehow, she heard her name from amid the chaos, smoke obscuring her vision as she hurried forward.

Mallory.

I'm coming, she called, though she didn't know to whom she spoke, only that she had to find him and soon.

Hands reached out to her as she walked, plucking at her skirts, begging for her aid, her comfort. But she couldn't stop, she had to find him now, before it was too late.

Mallory.

She rushed faster, searching every crumpled body, peering at every devastated face. Her dress turned red as she went, her hands stained with blood that she couldn't seem to wipe away no matter how hard she tried.

And then, finally, he was there, slumped in the mud with his back half-turned toward the sky, his uniform ripped and blackened. She ran to him, tears of joy streaming over her cheeks as she sank to her knees at his side.

He was here, he was hers and she had found him.

Shaking him, she waited for him to wake, to call her name one more time. Without thought, she reached out and pulled him onto his back so he would see it was she.

Michael, she said, meeting his beautiful grey eyes.

Only then did she notice how they stared in a way that no longer saw. Only in that moment did her gaze move lower and stop, widening in shock at the bloody hole that once had been his chest. Horror rolled through her, burning her throat as she screamed and screamed and screamed.

On a shuddering gasp, Mallory sat bolt upright in bed, her heart thundering like the booming cannons that had been in her dream. Clammy sweat beaded her forehead, her skin flushed hot and cold as shivers racked her body. Nothing seemed quite real, flashes of the nightmare still playing in her head while she huddled beneath the rumpled sheets.

Gradually, she became aware of the bedside candle, burned down to a guttering nub in its silver holder. And the shadowy outline of Charlemagne, who now lay on the far corner of the bed, safe from her restless movements while she'd been asleep.

He blinked at her and gave a quiet meow.

Something inside her crumbled at his gentle entreaty, breath hitching inside her lungs as she struggled against the overwhelming rush of despair.

Curling herself against her drawn-up knees, she began to cry.

The rain stopped during the night, dawn bringing with it a return of warm golden sunshine and clear blue skies. The ground, however, was still wet, the fields turned easily to mud by both foot and hoof.

For this reason, Adam dispatched his valet with a note for Mallory rather than make the assumption that she would meet him at the stables at the usual time. After yesterday's interruption of their morning rides, they'd made no new plans. Although she had told him in a glad voice when they'd parted last night that she looked forward to seeing him on the morrow.

Freshly bathed and shaven, he was fastening the silver buttons on his grey waistcoat when his valet returned.

"I left the note, your lordship," the servant said with polite precision. "However, Lady Mallory's maid informs me that her mistress is still abed and wishes not to be disturbed."

Adam paused, stifling the scowl that rose to his forehead. Instead, he gave a quick, two-fisted tug to the hem
of his waistcoat, then reached out for the dark blue coat
that matched his trousers. "Thank you, Finley. That will
be all for now."

With a familiar grimace of disapproval at not being
allowed to help his master don the coat, the servant gathered up Adam's cold shaving water and a pair of damp
towels, then withdrew.

It wasn't until the other man closed the door behind
him, that Adam allowed his emotions to show, a heavy
frown settling across his brow.

Still abed is she?

He wondered at the news, since over the past two
weeks she'd become a dedicated early riser. Then again,
he reasoned, as he shrugged into the tight-fitted coat and
adjusted the cuffs, maybe she was just tired. What with
last night's dancing and the late hour at which everyone
had retired to bed, it was entirely understandable. And
based on her buoyant mood, there should be no reason for
a return of her melancholy humor. And yet . . .

Deciding he was overthinking the issue, and that she
just wanted an extra couple of hours of rest, he left his
room and went to the library. Once there, he contented
himself with a cup of coffee while he waited for breakfast
to be served.

To no one's great surprise, including his own, Mallory
did not attend the morning meal. At its conclusion, he
decided to join the gentlemen for a few rounds of target
practice, as the ground was too wet for actual hunting. He
and Cade took two rounds apiece before Edward rallied at
the last and succeeded in beating them both.

They were all in a fine humor by the time they returned
to the house, ready for a libation and something to satisfy

their hunger. Now afternoon, he expected to find Mallory awake and downstairs with the ladies. His mouth drew into a line when he saw she was not.

"Have you seen Mallory?" he asked in a low aside to Claire not long after he entered the drawing room.

The duchess nodded. "Her maid sent down her excuses only a few minutes past. A headache she says. Ava and I went to look in on her, but she's sleeping, and the drapes are still drawn."

He scowled. As a rule, Mallory didn't get headaches, not unless she was ill with a cold or the ague. She could be laid low with a summer ailment, he supposed. Then again, it didn't seem likely given her energetic dancing last night. His natural instinct was to look in on her himself; but if she really was unwell, he supposed he ought to let her rest instead.

And so he decided to wait and hope that her health improved again soon. But nuncheon passed, then dinner, with no sign of Mallory.

"How is she?" he asked the dowager duchess once everyone had assembled in the drawing room after dinner.

Ava Byron set her flower-covered Meissen teacup back onto its saucer. "Much the same as earlier. She says her head pains her, but . . ."

"But?" he prompted.

Ava sighed. "But I fear it may be her heart again, since her spirits seem sadly blue deviled. I don't understand, when only last night she was laughing and dancing in this very room. She hasn't done either since the major was killed, and it warmed me to see her enjoying herself again." Reaching over, she gave his hand a quick squeeze. "You've done her so much good since you arrived, Adam."

"Apparently not enough if her spirits are flagging again."

"Don't worry. I am sure she shall rally by tomorrow and be back among us all."

But Mallory did not rally and spent the next day in her room. He went to see her in the morning and again that afternoon, but found the way to her bedchamber firmly barred by her maid.

"I am sorry, your lordship," Penny told him in a low, stern voice. "But Lady Mallory is indisposed and cannot be disturbed. I will let her know you stopped by."

He sent her his most charming smile. "Come now, surely a quick visit won't do any harm? Ten minutes. Five, if you insist. I only want to make sure she is all right."

"She is resting and will be fine," she said, refusing to meet his gaze. "I will tell her you called." In clear dismissal, she shut the door with a decisive click.

He considered marching inside regardless—after all, it wasn't as if he hadn't done so before—but even as he started reaching for the knob, he stopped. If he forced his way inside now, he would only cause a scene, one that might prove troublesome for both Mallory and himself. He would wait to see if she put in an appearance at dinner and, if not, he would decide then what to do.

Mallory tossed on her bed, kicking back the covers in the overly warm room. She'd heard the clock strike two not long ago, and yet she could not sleep. Or rather she was afraid to sleep, worried what dreams might arrive once she closed her eyes. Ever since the old nightmare had returned two nights ago, she'd been sunk in misery, and worse than that—guilt.

Guilt for enjoying herself.

Guilt for forgetting Michael.

Guilt for secretly wishing the past year had never happened and that she could wake to discover that everything she'd suffered was nothing more than another terrible dream.

She hadn't been lying when she'd complained of a headache. Her head had throbbed from crying, lack of sleep, and despondency. And so she'd hidden herself away again, unable to face anyone, not even Adam. Maybe most particularly Adam since she knew she would never be able to hide the truth from him. He saw through her far too easily.

Needing a distraction, she reached for the book on her bedside table. But she had trouble concentrating, the words swimming in and out of her thoughts. She was about to start over from the beginning when the soft click of her door opening and closing brought her head up.

"Penny? Is that you?" she called, peering into the shadows beyond her bed.

A long beat of silence followed before she heard a soft footfall. "Don't be alarmed," said a low, silvery voice. "It's only me."

The book in her lap slid to the floor with a thud that made her jump. "Adam?"

He stepped into the pool of candlelight that surrounded her bed, revealing himself fully. Despite the hour, he was still attired in his evening clothes—or the majority of them anyway since he'd already removed his coat and loosened his cravat.

"What are you doing here?" she asked, giving a hasty tug at the sheets to pull them high.

"I saw your light and thought I would see how you are doing."

"At two o'clock in the morning?"

He leaned one shoulder against the carved walnut post

at the foot of her bed and crossed his arms. "Seemed as good a time as any, better actually considering the fact that your gatekeeper isn't on duty."

She didn't pretend to misunderstand his reference to Penny. "No, she's asleep, along with everyone else in the house. Which is where you ought to be too. In your room. Asleep."

"You're not, asleep that is. How are you by the way? Any better? Claire and your mother said you've had a headache."

She stared down at the summer-weight counterpane, plucking absently at the material. "I have."

Before she really even heard him move, he was standing beside her, his large hand covering her forehead.

"What are you doing?" she asked.

"Checking for fever." He touched her cheeks next—one, then the other. "You don't seem too warm."

"I'm not ill, at least not in the way you mean." She jerked away. "It's a headache, not a contagion."

He gave a gentle smile. "I am grateful to hear that, for both of our sakes."

"Now that you have assured yourself I am not at death's door, you can go back to your bed," she told him.

"Not yet. Not until you tell me what has you so distressed again."

"I am not distressed."

"Don't lie. Not to me, Mallory."

"It's nothing." She shrugged. "I am only tired."

"And yet oddly, you are awake in the middle of the night, reading a book rather than sleeping. Why is that?"

"Go away," she entreated.

He shook his head. "You ought to know that you can't get rid of me so easily." Without waiting for permission, he took a seat next to her on the bed, their hips touching through the sheet and coverlet. Reaching out, he smoothed his hand over her hair. "Now, tell me what has happened."

"It doesn't signify," she murmured, rubbing her fingertips over the counterpane.

"Obviously it does since it has made you so sad. I thought we had agreed not to keep secrets?"

He was right, they had agreed. And considering all the things she'd shared with him already, what did one more confidence matter? "I had the nightmare again," she said on a tremulous breath.

"Ah."

Her head came up, her gaze meeting his. "*Ah?* What is that supposed to mean?"

"Just 'ah,'" he explained with a slight smile. "And the fact that I am not all that surprised. So what's this nightmare about? And don't try to put me off with excuses and denials this time. I think it will do you good to talk of it."

"I don't know if I can," she whispered, as pieces of the dream flashed inside her mind. "I've never told anyone."

"Then it's time you did."

Needing the comfort of his strength, she leaned her head against his shoulder and closed her eyes. Drawing a bracing inhalation, she swallowed against the knot in her throat, then forced herself to begin.

"I'm on a battlefield," she whispered. "I'm dressed all in white, but my gown is red, stained and wet with blood. And everywhere I look there are dying and dead men."

In quiet, halting sentences, she described it all, down to the last detail. He let her speak, attempting no interruptions and asking no questions as she spoke. When it was done, she fell still and silent, aware of a curious lassitude that had spread through her body, easing the tight muscles in her neck and back.

"It's no wonder you're troubled," he said, low and rough. "That is a dream that would keep grown men awake."

"Even you?" she couldn't help but ask.

He nodded, rubbing his hand over her back in a soothing motion. "Yes, even me. I suspect it would leave me trembling and in need of a good stiff drink."

"You wouldn't tremble. As for the drink . . . I wish I'd thought of that. Maybe if I'd liberated one of Edward's bottles of brandy, I could have managed more than a couple of hours' sleep over the past two days."

"A small dram wouldn't hurt, but only in the short term. Spirits aren't the answer. In fact, they might give you an entirely new set of bad dreams."

She sighed and eased back so she could look into his face. "Then what is the answer? Because I'm . . ."

Lines of concern gathered on his forehead. "You're what, Mal? Go on. Tell me."

"A-Afraid. I'm afraid to go to sleep. Afraid I'll have the nightmare again, and it will sink me so deep I'll never climb out again."

"It won't."

She sent him a look of doubt.

"I don't mean you'll never have the nightmare again," he amended, "but you won't go under because of it. What have I told you before? You're strong. You'll get through this. And there's something you're forgetting."

"Oh? And what is that?"

His eyes shone a rich, reassuring brown. "It isn't real. As vivid and realistic as your nightmare may be, as terrifying and heartbreaking as it undoubtedly seems, it's still only make-believe."

"But he did die on a battlefield."

"Yes, but not the one in your imagination. It's not real,

and if you have the dream again, I want you to remember that. *It's only a dream.*"

"You make it all sound so simple."

"I don't mean to imply that it's easy, but in time the nightmare will go away. Trust in that, Mal, and believe in a future when you'll sleep peacefully again."

She nodded, knowing intellectually that he was right. Yet in her heart the worry and fear remained. Truly, when she considered the matter, the only time she'd slept peacefully since Michael died was the morning when she'd lain in Adam's arms. When he was with her, she was safe. When Adam was near, the world didn't seem quite so bleak.

"I'm glad you came here tonight," she confessed. "Even if it is highly improper."

A slow grin spread over his mouth. "As you are well aware, I rarely do anything that *isn't* improper. I mean, where's the spice in life if one must always be worrying over such tedious trivialities as following the rules?"

She smiled back, finding it impossible to resist. As she did, a measure of the desolate fog that had been blanketing her spirits lifted away, leaving her lighter and less weary than she had been these past two days.

"That's my girl," he said in clear approval. "You ought to have told Penny to let me in earlier, you know. You could have saved yourself a great deal of worry and woe."

"But we would never have been able to talk like this," she said, rubbing a fingertip over one of the buttons on his waistcoat. "I would never have told you about my nightmare, not with an audience in the room. And quite likely, I would be just as troubled now as ever."

"On that score, you may be right. I'm glad it's just us tonight too." He covered her hand and pressed it flat against his chest, idly stroking her fingers. A quiver traced over her skin, a heightened tingle that made her wonder if there was too much electricity in the air.

Apparently Adam felt it as well, a dark gleam flaring to life in his seductive brown eyes, his lids sliding lower as if he'd suddenly grown sleepy. But she knew there was nothing genuinely sleepy about him, his instincts keen and razor-sharp in his watchful gaze.

Abruptly she became aware of her dishabille, realizing that she wasn't wearing anything more substantial than a thin cotton nightgown. True, it was a demure garment with buttons that fastened all the way up to her neck. But still, it was nothing more than a slight bit of cloth that separated her bare skin from his gaze and touch. Worse yet, they were on her bed, and he was only partially clothed himself; the two of them seated so close that she could see the pulse beating powerfully in his neck.

Oddly weak and without the will to move, she sat mute, her heart thundering in her ears as he slid his fingers into her hair and cradled the back of her head. He angled her face slightly, then tipped his own head in the opposite direction.

Mercy, is he going to kiss me?

What's more, do I want him to?

Lost to his gaze, she had her answer seconds later, her mind and body abandoned to the moment and the man as he narrowed the distance between them and covered her mouth with his own.

Bliss swept through her, a rising tide of pleasure that she was helpless to resist. She'd trembled before beneath his caress, but that sensation was nothing compared to the quake he was evoking now. One long, powerful arm curved around her back to draw her flush against him, his kiss turning deeper and more demanding.

Feathering the tip of his tongue across her lower lip,

he left a trail of fire behind that made her gasp out loud. The instant her mouth opened, his tongue glided in, teasing around the contours of her soft flesh with sultry dips and swirls that made her quiver all the more. Her blood sizzled, the heat in the room rising to a steamy haze that made even her thin nightgown seem too much.

Maybe I should pull it off.

Maybe he should help me.

Her eyelids popped open at the startling notion, breath panting from her lips as she pulled away.

What am I thinking?

What is he?

Despite her having broken their kiss, he didn't release her, his arms locked securely around her back, his fingers still tangled in her hair.

"W-why did you do that?" she asked in a breathless voice, her senses spinning in a crazy jumble around her. "D-did you th-think I looked like I needed to be kissed again?"

Something feral burned in his eyes, a look that was both raging and wild. "No. This time I'm the one who does."

Chapter 10

*A*dam knew he should let her go.

He was in too deep already and on the brink of entangling himself further still if the ache in his groin had anything to do with the matter. And yet, in spite of all the very excellent reasons why he knew he should release her—primary among them the fact that he was in her bedchamber in the middle of the night with all six of her brothers sleeping just down the corridor—he couldn't seem to make himself turn her loose.

Nor could he stop himself from wanting to take another heady draught from her ripe, honeyed lips. Plump and red and tender, her lips were more succulent than the finest fruit nature could grow. No wonder men buzzed around her like bees, even when she didn't notice their existence.

And then there were her eyes, their aquamarine depths as pure and translucent as a tropical sea. If he could swim in them, he wouldn't hesitate to dive in. As he watched, her pupils dilated, guileless desire reflected back in a way that made his blood burn hot and thick.

Maybe it was the blood draining out of his brain—and clearly the sense as well—but before he recognized his intentions, he bent again and crushed her mouth to his.

Jesu, she tastes sweet. And the way she smells . . . like roses and champagne. It was an intoxicating blend that made him delirious with pleasure and hard and hungry with need.

He kissed her again, coaxing her lips wide so he could plunder the rich softness he found inside. She mewled, adorable as a kitten, as she arched in his embrace, her hands lifting to clasp his shoulders and shift through the hair at the back of his neck.

An answering groan rumbled low in his throat, then another as she kissed him back, her tongue sliding over his in an untutored repetition of the moves he'd been showing her. But delicious as he found her kiss, it soon wasn't enough. He needed more, his senses clamoring for a fuller portion of the rapture he knew awaited them both.

Without breaking their kiss, he leaned her back so she lay on the bed, her long, raven hair cascading over the pillows like a dark river. Tracing the delicate length of her throat, his fingers glided lower, pausing to unfasten each button he encountered along the way. He retraced the path he'd forged by brushing kisses over her satiny flesh one slow, tormenting inch at a time.

She arched as he delved beneath the open placket of her nightgown to cup her naked breast. Her eyes flew open in surprise before drifting closed again in bliss, as breath came in rapid gusts from between her lips.

He'd dreamed of touching her like this, but the experience was far better, far more intense and satisfying than anything his imagination had ever created. Her flesh was velvety soft, warm and pliant and a perfect handful for him to fondle.

Her nipples beaded into taut peaks that begged to be caressed, and he was more than delighted to indulge them. She moaned as he stroked her, the sound turning him harder as his erection strained against his trousers. Desire beat in heavy pulses through his body, then even more intensely as he bent lower and opened his mouth over her.

A strangled moan issued from her throat, her fingers sliding into his hair to clutch his head as if she meant to pull him away. Undaunted, he flicked his tongue over her in a way that drew forth a wild shudder. Her fingers relaxed, urging him closer as she offered herself to his ministrations.

He smiled and suckled more deeply, loving the sleek softness of her fragrant skin, the decadent feel of her wet flesh against his tongue. Her head rolled on the pillow as he finished with one breast and moved to pleasure the other. One of her hands was still tangled in his hair. He trembled as she lifted the other and began caressing his neck and shoulders.

Nearly blinded with passion, he drew on her breast even as he reached low, his fingers frantic as they grasped the hem of her nightgown to tug it high. She whimpered, her bare legs shifting as he explored the shape of one beautifully curved thigh. But when he came to the soft thicket of curls at the apex, her legs locked tight, her instinctive reaction barring his way.

He knew he only needed to calm her innocent response, as he continued rousing her natural desires. He was skilled at lovemaking and confident that it would take little more than a few enthralling touches before she was quivering beneath him again, eager to welcome him inside.

But even as he began caressing her with renewed purpose, some faint sliver of conscience burrowed its way into his brain, and he stopped.

What am I doing? he wondered, giving himself a brutal mental shake. *This is Mallory. The woman I love. The woman I know isn't ready yet to take the irrevocable step of surrendering her virginity.*

He could seduce her, true, but at what cost? For as much as her body might crave the passion and pleasure he was giving her now, as much as she might want the release he could bring her, she wouldn't feel the same once their coupling was done.

In the cold light of day, she would despise him for leading her down this path, for taking advantage of her in a weak moment and stealing what was hers alone to give. She would see his passion and her own as a betrayal of everything they had ever shared, most particularly their friendship. Worse yet, she might come to hate him, and her enmity was the one thing he knew he could never bear.

Aching as if he'd taken a blow to the vitals, he gave a wrenching groan and flung himself away to sit at the end of the bed. Gripping the heavy carved post so hard he was surprised it didn't snap in two, he fought the desire still coursing through his veins like a raging fever.

"Adam?" she murmured. "What is it? W-why are you sitting down there?"

He said nothing as he watched her through slitted eyes. Slowly, she sat up, her eyebrows furrowing as she noticed the open placket of her nightgown. Reaching up, her fingers brushed one of her exposed breasts and she flinched, as if only then realizing she was half-naked. Trembling, she plucked the two sides of her bodice closed while simultaneously struggling to yank the skirt of her nightgown over her bare legs. Her skin turned pink as a summer sunset, and no matter how much it might be killing him, he knew he'd been right to stop.

"I should go," he said, his words clipped and gravelly.

Her head came up, fingers clutching her bodice. "Go? But—"

"It's late, and I've stayed longer than I ought."

"Yes, but—"

"You should sleep." Standing, he took a step away. "I shall see you tomorrow, at nuncheon, I trust. Good night, Mallory."

Her fingers clenched harder. "G-good night, Adam."

A note in her voice stopped him, a forlorn little catch that made his chest squeeze tight. He knew he should ignore it and stride to the door as fast as his feet would take him. Instead, he waited. "What?"

She looked up, not pretending to misunderstand. "I'm afraid."

He swallowed. "You'll be fine."

"But what if I have the nightmare again? What if I can't sleep at all? Don't go."

"Mal," he groaned, closing his eyes.

"Please. Just for a little while. I know you can't stay all night, but maybe a few minutes more. I don't want to be alone."

Reaching out, he grabbed hold of the bedpost again and fought the longing still burning inside him.

"Please, Adam."

Say no, his conscience warned him. *Tell her good night again and get the hell out.*

"I'll sit in the chair," he said.

"B-but that's so far away. Could you not sit on the bed? On the far side? It's a large bed. You'll barely know I'm here."

Who is she kidding? he thought.

On the bed? Was she insane? Especially considering what they'd been doing on that very bed only a couple of minutes ago? But then he looked at her, noticing how the flush had drained out of her cheeks and the worry that gleamed in her vivid eyes. Fear was a powerful motivator, he knew, almost as powerful as desire.

"Half an hour," he said between his teeth. "I can't stay any longer than that."

Now who's the insane one?

"Button your nightgown and get under the covers."

She turned a little pink again, then quickly did as she was told, tucking herself in tight. When she was swathed up to her chin, he walked around to the opposite side of the bed and took a seat at the bottom. Leaning back, he rested his shoulder against the bedpost.

A minute of silence passed.

"You can't be comfortable," she said in a small voice.

"I am," he lied. Angling his hip, he searched for a better spot.

Silence fell again.

"There's plenty of room," she whispered. "Why don't you stretch out?"

"Why don't you go to sleep?"

"I can't, not with you all the way down there."

"I'm only a few feet away. Close your eyes and relax."

He could almost count the seconds in the next pause.

"I'm sorry, but I can't," she said. "Don't be angry."

He closed his eyes again. "I'm not."

"But—"

"Fine. I'll lie down if it will help you doze off."

Hell and damnation, she really is going to kill me, he thought as he stood and moved to stretch out on the empty side of her bed.

"Shoes," she reminded.

He gave a little growl low in his throat, then toed off his dress leathers. Swinging his legs up, he leaned his back against the pillows, refusing to fully recline on the bed. He folded his arms over his chest. "Close enough now?"

She met his gaze and gave a little nod. "Thank you, Adam."

His anger melted away, even if his erotic frustration did not. "Go to sleep, sweetheart."

Nodding again, she closed her eyes.

I'll leave as soon as she drifts off, he told himself.

Five minutes passed, then ten.

He began to ease away when she woke, murmuring his name under her breath. With a groan, he relaxed back again, letting himself slide lower on the pillows. Clearly drowsy, Mallory rolled onto her side, facing him. Half-asleep, she reached out and laid her fingers against his arm. Calling himself a dozen times a fool, he covered her hand with his own. A happy sigh escaped her lips as she burrowed deeper into her pillow.

Another five minutes, and she would be fast asleep. Another ten, and the half hour would be up.

A yawn caught him as he waited, the candle burning lower in its holder, the room nearly dark. Mallory's breathing grew even. His breathing slowed as well, his eyelids beginning to droop.

Not much longer, and I'll leave, he thought. *Only a couple of minutes more.*

Then, without his full awareness, he fell asleep.

Mallory snuggled deeper into the pillows, blissfully relaxed and contented. Adam was sleeping at her side, his large body offering her a perfect haven of peace and serenity. She'd asked him to stay, and he had. Smiling, she rolled over and tucked her cheek against his shoulder, the material of his shirt warm and fragrant with the boldly masculine scent of his skin. He shifted beneath her, his long arm curving across her back to hold her close. Reassured by his presence, she let herself sink into a gentle, refreshing slumber where she knew no nightmares would intrude.

Some while later, she awakened to the sound of Adam cursing softly under his breath. "Damnation," he muttered, as he slowly eased away from her.

"What is it? What's wrong?" she murmured sleepily.

"I didn't mean to wake you," he said in a hushed tone. "Go back to sleep."

Still groggy, the urgency in his tone made no sense. "What time is it?"

"Nearly dawn, and I've got to leave before the servants begin their day. I would have left ages ago if I hadn't fallen asleep. Damn, where are my shoes?"

Lying in the dark, she listened to him search for his missing footwear. When he had no initial luck, he resumed his seat on the bed and reached out to light a candle. He'd just struck the flint when a soft knock came at the door.

She and Adam both froze and looked at each other over the flickering light. Immediately, he blew out the flame.

"Don't answer," he whispered. "Maybe they'll go away."

Instead, the door opened on silent hinges, a new pool of golden candlelight proceeding whoever it was coming into the room. Mallory's heart knocked against her ribs, the last of her sleepiness dropping away in an instant.

Adam can't be found here, she realized, wishing there was someplace he could hide. But he was too big to fit under the bed, and tossing the covers over him wouldn't do any good at all—only imagine the great lump he would leave.

"Mallory?" called a gentle voice. "It's me, Grace. I'm sorry to wake you, but I have news that couldn't wait. Meg's in labor, and I thought you would want to know—*Oh!*"

Tall, red-haired Grace Byron, still attired in her night wrapper, came to an abrupt halt at the foot of the bed. The light from her candle was near enough now to cast a circle of illumination over the bed—and the two of them on it.

Grace stared, her blue-grey eyes round as an owl's.

Mallory and Adam stared back.

Adam was the first to break the tension. "Lady Cade's having the baby, is she?" he repeated with aplomb. As though aware of the futility of struggling against the situation, he leaned back against the pillows and crossed his arms.

For her part, Mallory couldn't move at all.

"Y-yes," Grace said. "Her pains began a short while ago and she . . . she . . . what are you two doing together?" She waved a palm in the air. "No, don't answer that. It's rather obvious what you're . . . that is . . . oh, good heavens!"

"It's not what you think," Mallory said, finding her voice.

"Not what who thinks?" asked a new voice as Jack strode into the room. "Did you tell her about Meg? Mama's in with her now, and Cade says he's not so sure he should have given up drinking since he could do with a dram about now—*Bloody hell! Adam? Is that you?*"

"Good morning, Jack," Adam greeted calmly, as if they were meeting over the buffet in the breakfast room rather than inside Mallory's bedchamber.

"What in the blazes are you doing in here?" Jack demanded. "At this hour of the morning? And in my sister's bed no less!"

A heavy silence descended, the usually soft ticking of

the mantel clock growing loud as a gong, or so it seemed to Mallory.

With a casual style she could only admire, Adam crossed his stocking feet at the ankles. "Would you believe I was comforting her?" he said.

Jack's gaze shot from one to the other of them. "*Comforting her!* Is that what you call it? Why *you*—"

"Adam *was* comforting me," Mallory interrupted. "I couldn't sleep, and he came to help."

Mallory shivered as her brother's eyes narrowed. "Help, is it? Well, I don't much care for his kind of *help*." Jack's palms bunched into fists at his sides as he glared at Adam. "Did you touch her?"

Adam met his friend's look, clearly unfazed. "Whatever your sister and I did, or did not do, is none of your business. It's between her and me, and it's private."

Jack bristled. "Private! By God, it's not private, not when it has to do with my little sister. So, did you?"

When Adam refused to answer, Jack's gaze shot to Mallory. "You can tell me, Pell-Mell," he said, using her old nickname in an understanding voice. "I promise I won't be angry. Did he touch you?"

She opened her mouth to say no, but before the word had a chance to form, memories of the heated kisses and passionate caresses she'd shared with Adam raced through her mind. Her nipples peaked, aching anew as she thought of Adam touching her breasts and the enthralling sensation of his mouth drawing pleasurably upon her. Before she could prevent the reaction, her skin grew hot, her cheeks burning like fireplace coals.

"Why you underhanded bastard!" Jack roared. "And to think I trusted you with her. To think all of us, the whole family, let you go off alone with her these past couple of weeks. Here we were imagining her safe in your company, when all the while you were working your schemes on her. I thought you were her friend. Instead, you wanted nothing more than to seduce her into your bed."

"Actually, I believe this is *her* bed," Adam replied smoothly.

A muscle ticked near Jack's eye. "Don't be flippant."

"And don't you be a hypocrite."

Grace sent her husband a rueful glance. "I suppose he does have a bit of a point, darling."

To Mallory's surprise, a faint flush spread up Jack's throat, the muscle in his cheek giving another tic. "No, he doesn't, since this isn't about me. And don't try changing the subject."

"Is that what I was doing?" Adam drawled.

"Sometimes, Gresham . . ." Jack pounded a fist into his palm, looking like he'd rather be pounding it into something—or rather someone—else.

"Look, Jack," Adam said with a sigh, "before you burst a vein in that hard head of yours, why don't you give me a chance to explain—"

"Explain! Explain what?" Jack tossed back. "I believe I've heard more than enough already, especially with the evidence staring me right in the eyes."

"Now, Jack," Grace said, reaching out to wrap a hand around his arm. "Perhaps you should give Adam a chance—"

"I don't need to give him anything except an opportunity to name his seconds. I ought to call you out for this, you know. I ought to put a bloody bullet in you since it's no more than you deserve."

Adam sat up on the bed, his jaw tilted at a pugnacious angle. "You're certainly welcome to try."

"Stop it! Both of you," Mallory cried, flinging out an

arm toward Adam as if to protect him. "There will be no talk of duels or bloodshed."

Obviously aware how upset she was, Adam leaned toward her. "He's just angry, Mal. He's not really serious."

"Speak for yourself, Gresham," Jack retorted.

"Jack!" Grace admonished.

Tears sprang into Mallory's eyes, a knot of misery lodging in her chest. "Hasn't there been enough violence and death already with this horrible war? I l-l-lost Michael. I won't lose either of you, certainly not over something as stupid as a duel of honor. Don't you dare say such dreadful things to each other. D-don't you d-dare let any of this come between you when you've always been such good friends. I won't have it. I won't be the cause . . ."

She broke off, crying now in earnest. Adam's arms came around her and pulled her against his chest.

"Now, look what you've done," Adam accused, hugging her closer. "Get out, Byron, before you upset her any more."

"I believe you're the one who should leave," Jack shot back.

"I'm not going anywhere, not with Mallory in tears. If you want words, we can have them later when—"

"God's nightgown, what is all this racket going on?" demanded a deep, authoritative voice, which clearly belonged to Edward. "Some of the guests are beginning to gather outside in the corridor."

Hearing her eldest brother's words, Mallory cried harder.

"And I thought Meg's giving birth was enough of an uproar for one morning." Edward paused. "Gresham, is that you?"

"Good morning, Clybourne," Adam replied. "I wondered when you might happen along."

Well imagining the expression that must be on Ned's face, she half expected Adam to set her aside. Instead, he continued holding her within the comforting circle of his arms. Drawing a shuddering breath, she tried to stop weeping, but the tears flowed freely in spite of her best efforts.

"Given the circumstances," Edward said, "I don't believe I need to ask the cause of the dispute. However, this is neither the time nor place to resolve the situation—"

"I'll resolve it," Jack interrupted. "With my fists."

Adam tensed, as more tears leaked down Mallory's cheeks. "What did I say about upsetting her," he warned.

"And what did *I* say about taking your damned hands off her—"

"Gentlemen, that is quite enough—" Edward declared in an icy tone.

"Jiminy!" a new voice piped from the doorway.

"And Jehoshaphat!" echoed another that sounded remarkably like the first.

Oh mercy, Mallory thought. *Now the twins are here. Is the whole family going to end up in my bedchamber?*

She had her answer a second later when she heard more footsteps enter the room, including one set that was slightly uneven. "What are you all doing in here?" Cade asked. "The doctor just arrived for Meg and—why the deuce is Gresham in bed with Mallory?"

"I believe that is what's known as a rhetorical question," Drake observed.

Mortified that all six of her brothers were now in the room, Mallory wished she could sink into the floor—or pull the covers over her head at least. Instead, she accepted the monogrammed handkerchief Adam pressed into her palm and buried her face in the silk.

"That's two kerchiefs you owe me now, or is it three?"

he whispered so only she could hear. "Don't worry, Mal. Everything will be fine."

But how could anything be fine, she wondered, *when they'd landed so deep in the suds?*

"Do you know that half the houseguests are standing in the hall?" Claire asked, as she joined the gathering. "What in heaven's name are you all doing in here when Meg is—*Oh!*"

Mallory didn't need to lift her head to know she and Adam had been spotted.

"Exactly," Edward said. "Now we've all seen enough, and clearly the guests have heard enough, so it's time everyone moved along."

"But, Ned, you can't just let this go," Jack complained, rejoining the conversation.

"Certainly not. Honor demands Gresham do the proper thing by our girl," Cade said.

The twins and Drake gave murmurs of agreement.

"I am sure he will," Edward stated in a calm-yet-uncompromising tone. "Later. For now, Meg and the new baby should be everyone's main focus. And breakfast for those of you who have the stomach to eat, which I don't believe includes Cade given his present coloring. Coffee for him, I think. Black, no sugar. Drake, Jack, go with your brother."

Mallory lowered the handkerchief enough to see the men cast severe, this-isn't-over-yet looks at Adam. Jack brushed a kiss across Grace's cheek and murmured something to her before he left with his brothers.

"As for you two," Edward said to the twins, "I'm sure you can find some other means of occupying yourselves." Her younger brothers shared conspiratorial grins, obviously already planning some mischief she hoped wouldn't land them in trouble too.

"My dear," Edward said to Claire, "perhaps you could ring for Mallory's maid so she might dress, then all of you ladies can join Meg."

Claire nodded, while Grace slipped out so she could change her attire as well.

"Gresham, I shall see you in my study after breakfast," Edward stated. "Nine o'clock, shall we say?"

"Of course, Your Grace," Adam replied with ease. "Nine it is."

Turning on his heel, Edward strode into the now-empty corridor—the guests apparently having had the good sense to disperse as well.

Then it was just Mallory and Adam once more, Claire being kind enough to give them a moment of privacy by strolling across to stand in front of the windows at the far end of the bedroom.

"Adam, I'm sorry—" Mallory began, her voice husky with tears.

"Shh," he said, brushing a few strands of hair from her face. "You have no need to be sorry. I told you it's going to be all right."

"But—"

He laid a finger across her lips. "I'll take care of it. Don't worry." Despite Claire's presence in the room, he removed his finger and leaned forward to place a gentle kiss on her mouth. "Get dressed, have something to eat, then go see Meg. We shall talk later."

"Oh, Adam—"

"Look, here's Penny now," he said, as her maid crossed into the room, a surprised expression on the servant's face. Casually, as if he spent every night in Mallory's bed, he stood and looked for his shoes, which he found easily given all the sunlight now creeping through the windows. As dressed as he was going to be with no cravat or jacket, he bent again and pressed his lips to hers for a tender, reassuring kiss.

Ears buzzing, she barely heard her maid's gasp of astonishment.

Then Adam was gone.

Clutching his dampened handkerchief in her fist, she stared across at Claire.

"Black coffee for us both, Penny," the duchess said. "I think we're all going to need it."

Chapter 11

Zachary George Byron made his entrance into the world just after six o'clock that evening, unleashing a healthy wail that echoed throughout the house. Having helped attend Meg through the long hours of labor and birth, Mallory was weary, but satisfied, unable to feel anything other than joy at having witnessed the arrival of her newest nephew.

Across the room, Meg now lay dozing, Cade seated beside the bed, his wife's hand clasped securely inside his own. On his face was an expression of relief and happiness as he watched her sleep.

Poor Cade had looked pale as a ghost during the height of Meg's labor, Mallory recalled, her brother arriving at the bedroom door to see if his wife was dying. Claire, Grace and Mama had been trying to reassure him that all was well when Meg let loose a string of curses that would have made even her late father, the Admiral, blush. Ten minutes later, with Cade at her side, their second son was born.

While the new parents were celebrating, Mallory had gone into the hallway to share the good news with her brothers. To her surprise, she found Adam with them, seemingly at ease despite that morning's explosive row in her bedchamber.

It was the first time since then that she'd seen Adam. Apparently his talk with Edward must have gone well, she thought. Or well enough anyway that her brothers had called a truce rather than decide to lock him up in the medieval dungeon that lay beneath the house. She didn't know if that boded good or ill, and with all the excitement over the baby, she didn't have the opportunity to speak alone with Adam to find out.

After a few brief, admiring peeks at little Zachary— who, Meg admitted, would not be called Neville, Orson or Oswald—the men dragged Cade downstairs to drink a congratulatory toast and smoke cheroots. Ravenously hungry, the ladies repaired to the family dining room for a late dinner, Ava remaining behind with Meg.

Now at nearly eleven o'clock, Mallory returned to look in on Meg and the baby. After a quiet knock, she went inside the bedroom and found her sister-in-law asleep. Cade sat in a chair beside her holding Meg's hand, the baby swaddled safely in dreams where he lay inside his great, hand-carved mahogany cradle.

Tiptoeing back out, she closed the door soundlessly behind her, turned and jumped. "Adam! Gracious, where did you come from?"

"Sorry, I didn't mean to scare you," he said in a quiet voice before sending a nod toward the door. "Everyone doing well?"

"Quite well," she said. "I won't be surprised if Meg is up tomorrow and introducing Max to his little brother."

"At only two years of age, I suspect he won't be nearly as impressed with the new baby as all the rest of us."

"No, I don't suppose he will be." Linking her hands in front of her, she studied the pattern in the hall carpeting. "Adam, about this morning—"

He halted her with a touch, her gaze lifting to meet his. "It's been a long day, and you're tired," he said. "Let's talk about everything tomorrow."

"But what did Edward say? And what about Jack? Earlier, it seemed as if the two of you were back on speaking terms, but he was so angry this morning." Reaching out, her fingers closed over the fabric of his coat sleeve. "He has rescinded his challenge against you, has he not? The two of you aren't going to duel—because if that's how you're resolving the matter, you can find some other way. I won't have you fighting. I won't stand aside and see you injured, either of you."

"Calm yourself," he hushed. "There will be no duel and no fisticuffs either. I had a chat with Jack today, and we've reached an understanding."

"What kind of *understanding*?"

"The kind that you and I will talk about tomorrow." Covering her hand where it lay on his arm, he drew her into a walk, turning her in the direction of her bedchamber. "Now, I want you to go to your room, put all of this from your mind and sleep."

"But what if I can't?" she asked, strolling at his side. "What if I lie awake or . . ." *What if I have the nightmare? The cause of so much trouble.*

She swallowed sharply at the thought.

"If you can't sleep," he said, "I want you to ring for Penny and have her make you a hot milk posset. And if that still doesn't suffice, ask her to send for Jack and me, and we three shall sit in the drawing room and play a round of cards."

"But Adam—"

"What have I said before about 'buts'? Now, here we are," he said, drawing them to a halt in front of her bedroom door. Turning, he faced her, reaching to skim a finger across her cheek.

She trembled, her pulse hammering out an erratic beat. "What is it you're not telling me?"

Something flickered deep in his gaze before he leaned down and pressed his lips to her forehead. "Sleep well, Mallory. Promise you'll call your maid and drink that posset if the need arises."

"All right, I promise."

He stepped away. "Good. I'm sure Penny's inside waiting for you now. Until tomorrow."

"Good night."

He strode away.

Resisting the urge to call him back, she forced herself to enter her room.

Mallory awakened the next morning, surprised to discover that she'd not only slept, but that she had done so deeply and without dreams. She'd been so sure she wouldn't be able to rest, but only moments after climbing beneath the sheets, she'd been out like one of the candles Penny had snuffed before departing for the evening.

Obviously, I was exhausted, she mused, so much so that even the nightmare hadn't possessed the power to intrude on her slumber.

Tossing back the covers, she padded barefoot across the Aubusson carpet and rang for her maid. Dressed half an hour later in an ecru muslin day dress spotted with tiny green leaves, she took a seat at the small table in her sitting room. Sipping from a cup of tea, she opened the note that had arrived from Adam.

> *Meet me in the music room at half past ten.*
> *I shall await you there.*
>
>   *Your Servant,*
>   *Adam*

A quick glance at the clock showed that only twenty minutes remained before the appointed time. Swallowing against the nerves that suddenly jangled in her stomach, she pushed aside her uneaten plate of toast and eggs. As she did, she found herself wondering exactly what Adam was going to have to say about his talk with Edward. She supposed she would find out soon enough.

Adam plucked a string on the harp in the music room, listening to the ethereal note vibrate on the air as he waited for Mallory to arrive.

She must have slept, he decided, since she hadn't sent Penny to find him last night. For Mallory's sake, he was glad. Then again, he wouldn't have minded a late-night card game nor a reason to roust Jack out of his comfortable bed and his wife's adoring arms.

Under the circumstances, it would have served Jack right.

Even now, his friend's attitude stung a bit, along with Jack's instant assumption that he'd seduced Mallory and thoughtlessly stolen her innocence. The fact that he'd stopped just short of doing that very thing didn't lessen the injury to his pride or his affront at knowing Jack thought him little more than an unscrupulous cad. He might have a wicked reputation, which was admittedly well deserved, but then so had Jack prior to his marriage.

Still, Adam supposed that he might have reacted the same had he found his sister in bed with his best friend. He'd have done anything to protect Delia, when she was alive, just as Jack did now for Mallory. As all her brothers did, the whole lot of them, standing together in her defense like the Queen's personal guard.

He expected no less, of course, which was one of the main reasons he'd done his best to conceal his feelings for Mallory all these years. But those feelings were out in the open now, or enough of them at least that the Byron brothers had decided there was no need to tar and feather him or see him bloodied on the field of honor.

Given Mallory's alarm at even the mention of a physical confrontation, he was glad her brothers had been willing to listen to reason. All of them—even intellectually minded Drake—were formidable fighters, their skills impressive with all manner of weaponry, including fists, pistols and swords. He too was considered lethal and he wasn't afraid to fight. When it came to defending himself, he knew he could hold his own against any man, even the Byrons.

But emotionally he would be hard-pressed to battle his friends. Even more, Mallory would never forgive him if he harmed one of her brothers, leaving him doubly glad that words, rather than blows, had been sufficient to resolve the situation.

He was running his fingertips over another harp string when the door opened with a soft click. Glancing up, he watched Mallory slip inside. His arm fell to his side. "Good morning."

She gave him a shy smile and moved a few steps farther into the room. "Good morning."

He took a moment to note how beautiful she looked despite the pale hue to her skin and the uncertain glitter in her aquamarine eyes. Approaching, he took her hand and brushed a kiss across the top. She gave him a quizzical look before he released her again and crossed to shut the door.

"Are you sure you ought to do that?" she asked. "I don't want Jack descending on us again, complaining we're alone and challenging you to another duel."

He sent her a reassuring smile. "There's little chance of that. Besides, we're in the music room today—a far-less-incendiary location than your bedchamber."

"Very true." She skimmed her fingers over her skirt in a nervous gesture. "So what did Ned have to say? Does he understand what happened and why you stayed with me the other night? Surely he doesn't think . . . well, you know—"

"Come," he said, gesturing toward a comfortable pair of chairs that stood near a sunny window. "Let us sit over here and talk."

She paused at the delay before doing as he suggested. Only after she was settled did he seat himself in the chair opposite. "As you're aware, His Grace and I met yesterday morning to discuss the events that transpired between you and me, and the uproar that followed. I explained why I came to your room, as well as the reason I remained."

"You told him about my nightmares?"

"I did, and that you were too worried and frightened to be left alone."

"So he *does* understand," she said, tension sliding from her shoulders with clear relief. "I shall have to talk to Ned myself, of course, but I'm glad he realizes that nothing of any real consequence occurred."

One of his eyebrows swept high. "I wouldn't say that exactly."

Color washed into her pale cheeks. "But surely you didn't tell him about kissing me? That has nothing to do with our being found together, so there's no reason why he needs to know."

His mouth twisted into a wry smile, amused by her elaborate rationalization.

"Besides," she went on, "I heard you tell Jack that what you and I did together was private and none of his business. I should think the same would apply to all my brothers, most especially Ned."

Adam laughed, unable to restrain the impulse. "Don't worry. I didn't tell him I kissed you—or indulged in any of the other very pleasurable things we did. Then again, I had no need to do so."

Her eyebrows drew close. "What do you mean?"

"I mean that Edward isn't stupid, nor is Jack, who saw you blush red as a Maharajah's ruby when he asked if I'd touched you. But even if I hadn't laid so much as a finger on you, it would make no difference."

"Any difference to what?"

"Surely you must realize?" he said in a gentle voice.

But as she gazed at him, he knew she didn't. Despite her knowledge of Society's strictures that forbade an unwed young woman from being alone with a man, Mallory had obviously convinced herself there would be no lasting consequences to their having been discovered together.

Part of him wished there weren't any repercussions. Certainly, he hadn't planned on getting caught in her bed, and were it not for the fact that he'd fallen asleep, he would have been in his own room long before Grace paid her unexpected early-morning visit.

But he had fallen asleep.

He had gotten caught.

And there was no going back.

His intention, of course, had been to court Mallory, slowly and with patience in order to give her the time she needed to recover from her loss and see him as far more than a friend. For in spite of her passionate response to his kisses, he knew she wasn't ready yet to accept everything he wanted to give.

But there was nothing for it now, and she would have to adapt to the reality of their situation. As for himself, he couldn't feel entirely sorry.

He wanted her.

He loved her.

And he would take her by any means possible.

Meeting her interested gaze, he realized that she was waiting for him to explain. "What is it then that I'm supposed to know?" she asked.

"The fact that there is only one possible solution to this situation."

Moving from his chair, he went down on one knee, then reached out and gathered her hand into his.

"Mallory Byron, will you marry me?"

Chapter 12

*M*allory stared, aware that her eyes must have grown large as a pair of planets. "D-did you say *marry*?"

Adam fixed her with a steady gaze, his words low and firm. "I did."

"B-but Adam, surely you don't want to marry me. Nor should you need to do so."

His eyebrows arched upward with a sardonic sweep.

Her own brows arrowed down. "Is that what you and Ned talked about? And why my brothers aren't trying to maim you any longer? Because you've agreed to wed me and do the honorable thing?"

"I rather doubt I would be here with you now were it otherwise."

She huffed out a breath. "Oh, but this is terrible, ridiculous and completely unnecessary. Did you tell Edward that I am untouched? That I am still a maid and that nothing happened which requires the two of us to take such a drastic step?"

"Your brother and I didn't discuss any intimate details, remember? Besides, there was no need."

"No need!" she returned, nerves squeezing like a fist under her breastbone. "Of course there's a need. Oh, and please do get up. How can I have a reasonable discussion with you while you're kneeling in front of me?"

"The same way you're having an *unreasonable* discussion," he said in a calm tone. Moments later, however, he stood and resumed his seat. "Mallory, marriage is the only option."

She sprang to her feet. "Not if we explain the situation to Ned and Jack and the rest of the family. They'll see no harm has been done, and in a few days, everyone will have forgotten all about the matter."

"And what about the throng of inquisitive guests who stood in the hallway listening to every word that was spoken? Do you think they'll forget about Jack's calling me out after having accused me of ravishing you?"

"But you didn't ravish me."

"No, I only kissed you and touched you, then fell asleep in your bed. Admit it, Mal," he said. "You're good and compromised. There's no getting around that fact."

She paced several steps. "But you said yourself once that we're all friends here. Maybe if I explained it to them—"

He shot her a pitying look.

"Surely they would see reason and not say anything," she argued.

"Can you imagine Daphne Damson not saying anything? That woman couldn't keep a secret if she knew her tongue would be cut out the moment she finished talking." Standing once more, he crossed and took her hands inside his own. "We must wed, it's the only way. If I don't marry you, I'll be branded an unprincipled scoundrel. Far worse, you'll be ruined beyond redemption. I doubt even your lineage and dowry would be enough to gain you a respectable offer from another man."

But she didn't want another man.

She didn't want *any* man.

Not now at least.

Staring at Adam's cravat, she swallowed against the sinking feeling lodged in her stomach. Adam was right, of course. There was no other way, not unless she was willing to accept the shame of being a disgraced female, an outcast in Society. If she refused him, it was no exaggeration that she would indeed be ruined forever.

"Is the idea of marrying me really so dreadful?" Adam asked. "I've been told of late that I'm not such a bad catch."

Glancing up, she met his gaze and caught a glimmer of raw emotion lurking deep in his dark brown eyes. She paused. Surely she hadn't hurt him? Then he blinked, and the expression was gone.

No, she decided, *I am only imagining things. Adam's skin is as tough as oxhide. He must realize this has naught to do with him personally.*

Still, when she spoke again, it was with care and complete honesty. "Of course marrying you wouldn't be dreadful. It's not that, it's just . . ."

"Just what?"

Her lashes swept down, her voice a near whisper. "I'm just not ready to marry anyone. Not now. Perhaps never."

He slid a finger beneath her chin, lifting her face so she had no choice but to meet his gaze. "But you forget. I'm not just anyone. I'm Adam. Your friend, who knows you and will always be there to protect you and to make you smile."

"But it isn't right. For me or for you. You deserve better than a forced union. You ought to have the right to find a woman you love and be free to marry her. I don't want to take that from you because of a single, impetuous act that happened one night."

Trembling, she drew an unsteady breath. "If only I hadn't asked you to stay, none of this would have happened. If only I hadn't been afraid after my nightmare, we wouldn't be standing here talking about having to wed."

"If you want to talk about if-onlys," he said, "then we ought to mention the biggest one of all. If only I hadn't come to your bedchamber the other night. But I did, and it was my decision and mine alone. Just as it was my decision to remain when you asked me to. I did nothing that wasn't of my own accord, and I am more than ready to accept the consequences of my actions."

Letting go of her hands, he set his palms at her waist. "As for your wish not to bind me in marriage, it is a sweet gesture, but truly, I have no desire to be set free. To be honest, it's time I married. Now that I am restoring Gresham Park and making it livable again, it needs a mistress. Even more, the house needs a family. It deserves a bit of laughter ringing through the hallways again and inside all those rooms that have stood silent for far too long. You think I'm trapped, but I'm not. This situation isn't ideal, I agree, but I know you will make me an excellent bride."

"You say that now, but what if you come to regret your decision? What if you meet someone else and wish you were able to be with her?"

"I won't," he said, his eyelids sweeping down, concealing his expression. "Believe me, I've had plenty of time to become acquainted with all the eligible ladies of the Ton, and I have no interest in any of them. Nor would I want some chit just out of the schoolroom who would make me feel as if I'm already halfway to my dotage." Glancing up again, he met her gaze. "Trust me, Mallory, marrying you will be no sacrifice, not on my part at least."

She said nothing, too conflicted to speak.

"I know you're still healing, and this isn't what you wish right now, but think of the benefits. We've known each other for ages, and I am confident that we shall suit."

Yes, she realized, they would suit. How could they not when they knew so much about each other? When they'd shared so many things together over the years? Living day to day with Adam would be pleasant, even easy.

"Then too is the freedom you would enjoy," he continued. "As my countess, you would have your own house and be able to establish your own rules and ways of doing things. I would give you free rein to redecorate and refurbish the house however you like, the choices would be entirely up to you. And frankly, I think a change of scenery might be exactly what you need."

"In what way?" she asked.

"You are comfortable here at Braebourne. Maybe too comfortable, with a lifetime of memories, including a few that I suspect still bring you pain."

A lump settled in her throat as she thought of Michael and the misery of the past fifteen months.

"A new place, a new home, would give you an entirely clean slate," Adam said. "There would be no past there, only a future, the one that you and I choose to make. Which leads me to another benefit."

She tipped her head. "Oh? What might that be?"

"Children."

A new knot formed, this time in her chest.

"If ever there was a woman who ought to have children, it's you, Mal. I've seen you with the little ones, and you're wonderful. They love you, and you love them back. Only yesterday, you held little Zachary in your arms, and a more perfect picture I've never seen. I cannot imagine you not having babies of your own."

"I still may, in time," she said.

But as she considered the idea, she wasn't so sure. After losing Michael, she couldn't imagine putting herself back in the marriage market, going through the bother of flirting and courting and trying to find a man she wanted to wed. Yet without a husband, there would be no children.

Once again, Adam was right. She did want babies. It would break her heart all over again never to have that chance.

But reentering the ranks of eligible ladies during some future Season was a moot point, was it not? With her reputation in shreds, Adam was her only hope for a husband and family. If she didn't wed him, there was little chance she would marry at all. She would become a spinster, and there would be no babies.

Ever.

Her nieces and nephews would be her "children." But would they be enough? Would they fill the empty space she knew would exist inside her heart?

"Which leads me to the last, and perhaps most persuasive benefit of all," Adam said, as he played a hand over her hip.

"What?"

"This." Reaching up, he cupped her cheek in his palm and pressed his mouth to hers.

Her heart leapt wildly beneath her breasts, blood instantly rushing to places it had no business going. She couldn't help herself, her body responding, even as her mind struggled to catch up with the tumult Adam was provoking. Her eyelids grew heavy, then slid closed as pleasure swept through her with the inexorable force of a tide. Brain muzzy, her muscles grew lax, knees weak and unsteady as he drew her deeper beneath his spell.

Thank God, he'd locked an arm behind her back; otherwise, she would surely have crumpled to the floor in a heap. Yielding to his command, she parted her lips and let him inside, dazed by the lush, sultry decadence that threatened to burn her inch by delectable inch.

He stroked a hand over her hip again, then lower to pull her tighter against him. "I don't think we need to worry about whether or not we're physically compatible," he murmured against her lips.

Her eyelids opened, a quiver chasing over her nerve endings.

"Count this as a mere taste, sweetheart, of all the pleasure I can give you. Marry me and let me show you more. Be mine, and I'll take you on a journey the likes of which you've ever only imagined."

She gasped as he crushed her lips beneath his again, desire spinning her in a crazy dance that left her utterly undone. She could barely think, her senses too overwhelmed for rational thought.

And yet, he wanted an answer.

"Say yes, Mallory," he urged, punctuating his words with tiny plucking kisses. "Tell me you will be my bride."

Fighting to collect her scattered wits, she stared into his dark, melting eyes.

Eyes she knew.

Eyes she trusted.

This was Adam. Her friend and confidant. The man she turned to more than any other in the world. He would take care of her. He would be good to her. With him, she would never need to fear. For in spite of his reputation, she knew without asking that he would be faithful, making sure he never broke the sacred vows that would bind them together.

But more, if they married, she might be able to laugh again the way he wanted, filling his home with glad sounds rather than silence. In his arms, she might be able to forget her pain, smothering it beneath the rapture of his touch and the promise of carnal pleasures she knew were no exaggeration or lie.

All she had to do was answer him.

All she had to say was yes.

"Are you sure this is what you wish?" she whispered, her heart beating in her chest as fast as hummingbird wings. "I don't want you to be sorry."

Something hot and violent flashed in his gaze, an undisguised longing that made her tremble. "I will never be sorry," he said on a rasp. "I want this. I want you."

Seconds slid past as she stood inside his arms. "Then yes, Adam, I will marry you."

A fierce elation burst like fireworks inside Adam, happiness vying with passion as he bent to claim her mouth once more. He knew he was showing his true feelings, perhaps a bit too enthusiastically, but he couldn't help himself.

She's mine, he thought. *Never again will I let her go.*

Forgetting himself completely, he ran his fingers over the buttons on the back of her dress, slipping the first one free of its loop.

Without warning, a knock came at the door, the knob turning before he had a chance to realize what was going on.

"Wedding bells had better be ringing," Jack said as he stepped over the threshold. "Or I really will call you out this time, old chum."

Mallory gave a squeak of surprise and tried to step away. Adam kept her where she was, turning her so she stood tucked close against his side, his arm looped over her shoulder. "You're certainly making a habit of barging in on people these days," Adam remarked.

Jack arched a sardonic brow as he strode farther into the room. "I knocked, which would have been sufficient if you two hadn't been busy dallying together."

"Jack!" Mallory complained, cheeks coloring.

Her brother ignored her, his attention focused on Adam. "And considering that you've been in here for the better part of an hour, I assumed you must surely have gotten around to settling matters with Mallory. You have, have you not?"

Adam nodded. "You may indeed wish us happy, since your sister has done me the great honor of consenting to be my wife."

Jack glanced between the pair of them before his face split into a wide smile. Striding forward, he pulled Mallory out of Adam's embrace and into his own, hugging her as he bussed her on the cheek. "Every happiness, Pell-Mell."

"Thank you, Jack," she said, returning his hug.

"You're to tell me straightaway if he doesn't treat you as you deserve." Jack released her and took a step back. "I'll be there in an instant to bully him back into shape and give him a thorough thrashing besides." Turning, he faced Adam. "Count this as your only warning, Gresham."

"Warning duly received, Byron."

From the corner of his eye, Adam saw Mallory scowl with concern, obviously concerned that he and her brother were about to come to blows again.

But Adam knew she had no need for worry, Jack cuffing him on the arm a moment later before pulling him into a hearty, backslapping hug that Adam returned with equal enthusiasm.

"Congratulations and welcome to the family!" Jack said with a laugh, as they broke apart. "It'll be good making it official since we've been brothers in all but name for years. Now we will be in truth as well."

"My thanks. And let me just say that I couldn't wish for better relations if I'd chosen them myself."

He and Jack laughed, all their prior animosity gone.

"Men!" Mallory declared in an exasperated voice. "Since you two obviously have a great deal of celebrating to do, I believe I shall return upstairs to my room."

She turned on her heel to leave, but before she got more than a couple of steps, Adam reached out and caught her hand. "Just a moment there, my dear."

"Yes, what is it?"

"First," he said, tugging her gently forward, "that I look forward to seeing you for nuncheon. You will be there, will you not?"

Her expression softened, her voice dropping low. "Yes. I shall be there."

He smiled and leaned down to brush a kiss over her forehead. "Second," he continued, "there is this."

"What?"

Gently, he spun her around so her back was to him. He didn't say a word as he fastened the single open button on the neck of her gown with quick efficiency. Cradling her close so they were turned away from Jack's gaze, he kissed her neck. "There," he whispered in her ear, "you're presentable again. Although I rather wish I'd had time to open a few more of these buttons rather than having to do this one up again."

Her skin warmed, color rising on her neck and ears.

"Be good, and I shall see you soon." Straightening, he released her.

Her own back straight, she marched toward the door, clearly not trusting herself to give him another glance.

"We should tell the others," Jack said, as soon as Mallory left the room. "Everyone will be waiting to hear, assuming Mallory doesn't tell them first."

"I suspect she means it about returning to her room. I doubt anyone will see much of her again until the midday meal."

Jack nodded, then thrust his hands into his pockets. "One last word, if I might."

Adam resisted the urge to cross his arms. "Yes?"

"This marriage between you and my sister—I know it isn't what either of you planned. I know too that she's in a bit of shock, everything rushed as it's been."

"Forced, you mean."

"I wouldn't put it quite that way considering the kiss I happened upon when I came in here, not to mention finding the pair of you in her bed." Briefly, Jack's jaw grew taut at the reminder. "Look, what I'm trying to say is—"

"You want to know if I care for her?" Adam interrupted. "Or if it's only physical."

Jack met his gaze, creases gathered on his forehead. "Something like that."

"I love her, Jack. I would give my life for Mallory, she means that much to me."

For a long moment, Jack studied him. Suddenly he relaxed. "You really do, don't you? Grace told me as much. I guess I ought to have simply taken her word. She has a deuced inconvenient way of being right, don't you know."

One corner of Adam's mouth turned up. "Your wife is a very wise and observant woman."

Jack smiled, his mind's eye clearly turning inward on some pleasant thought. "Grace is a marvel. I thank heaven for her every day."

"I feel the same about Mallory. I'll do everything in my power to make her happy."

Jack met his gaze again. "I can see that you will."

"I would appreciate it, however," Adam said in a serious voice, "if you didn't say anything to Mallory about our conversation, you or Grace. Mal's been through a rough patch and needs a bit more time to adjust without my acting the swain."

"So you haven't told her how you feel?"

"Not yet. I will when the time is right."

Jack looked as if he was going to disagree, then changed his mind. "I'll leave it up to you to decide." Pausing, Jack offered his hand. "Sorry I was so angry, by the way. I just didn't expect to find you in her bed."

"I'd have done the same if I were you. Don't bother yourself about it again." Relieved that he and Jack were in accord once again, he shook his friend's hand.

"Shall we go celebrate then?" Jack asked.

Adam grinned. "Most definitely."

Chapter 13

*M*allory spent the rest of the day wondering exactly what it was she'd done.

I'm engaged to Adam, was the refrain she couldn't get out of her head. *I'm engaged to Adam, when I'm not ready to be engaged to anyone.*

But she and Adam had already been over this, and there was no going back—especially not after the congratulations began pouring in.

Her mother sought her out first, giving a soft rap on Mallory's bedroom door. "Hello, dear, may I come in?"

"Of course, Mama," she called from where she sat in a chair near the window, Charlemagne curled contentedly in her lap.

"I've just had the news from Edward," Ava said as she closed the door behind her and crossed to take a seat in the chair opposite. "So Adam's doing the right thing? He's proposed?"

"Yes, he has."

"And you've accepted?"

Mallory's hand slowed as she petted the cat's black fur. "Yes, I have."

Her mother paused, a gentle expression in her clear green eyes. "It is the only thing to be done, of course. Considering what occurred, you cannot remain unwed. I am sorry though that we did not have a chance to talk before now. The house was in such flux yesterday, what with Meg having the baby, and all of us so tired afterward. I just thought it would be best to let you sleep last night rather than insisting we converse."

"It's all right, Mama. As you say, it wouldn't change anything."

"I know, but still, we ought to have talked earlier."

Mallory rubbed Charlemagne's chin and earned an appreciative purr. "I'm sorry for the scandal. Are you terribly cross with me?"

"Cross? Why no, darling. Surprised perhaps that Lord Gresham was here in your bedchamber, but Ned explained the matter. He says you've been having nightmares."

A lump rose in Mallory's throat, and she nodded.

"If you were troubled, you ought to have come to me, or one of your brothers or sisters-in-law. The fact that you did not, and that you preferred to unburden yourself to Adam, reveals a very great deal."

Yes, Mallory realized, she supposed it did. For no matter how close she was to her family, Adam was the one in whom she always felt she could confide.

"Which is why," her mother continued, "I am not at all distressed that you and Adam shall marry. I suspect you feel you need more time to recover from your mourning, but this turn of events strikes me as a good thing. You and Adam have always gotten on famously, and a change of scenery will do you good. Managing your own house shall as well. It will keep you occupied and leave you little time to dwell upon memories best put aside."

"That's what Adam says."

"And he is right." Reaching over, her mother caught her hand and gave it a squeeze. "It's hard losing people we love, but it's part of life. Your major is gone, and it's time for you to let him go."

In that moment, she realized she hadn't let Michael go. Not really. She might have watched them lower his casket into the ground, but she'd never truly buried him. Instead, she'd been clinging to his memory as if his death were all some great mistake and that one day he would walk through the door again.

But he never would.

Michael was dead.

But Adam wasn't.

Adam was very much alive; memories of his kisses tingled on her skin even now. Kisses she wanted to repeat, touches she longed to explore in greater depth and detail.

She blinked, forcing the warmth not to rise in her cheeks over having such thoughts while she sat across from her mother.

"You and Adam will be good for each other," Ava said. "If you let him, I believe he'll make you happy. If I thought any differently, I'd keep you here at home with me and plague take the scandal."

Mallory smiled, then she laughed. "I love you, Mama."

Ava stood and leaned down to give her a hug, a disgruntled Charlemagne leaping off Mallory's lap just in time not to be squeezed in the middle.

"I love you too, Mallory," Ava said, kissing her cheek.

When her mother straightened, Ava's eyes were moist with tears. She blinked them away, while Mallory did the same.

"Well now," her mother declared. "We have important arrangements to plan."

"Arrangements? What arrangements?"

"Why your wedding, of course! I always thought I'd have a year or more to plan your nuptials, but I suppose two weeks will have to suffice under the circumstances."

"Two weeks, but—"

"Wait any longer, and we'll have another scandal on our hands, what with people speculating about whether Adam is really going to marry you or not."

"Of course he will. But two weeks, that's not enough time to arrange a wedding." And most definitely not long enough for her to wrap her mind around the idea of actually being his wife.

"It shall have to suffice," her mother insisted. "Otherwise, the house party will be over, and tattlers like Daphne Damson will be on their way home, eager to spread word of your supposed impending ruin."

Mama resumed her seat. "No, much as it pains me—and believe me it does, since you children are *always* putting me to the trouble of planning impromptu weddings—you and I shall have to whip something together posthaste. But I am certain it can be done."

Lacing her fingers together, Ava began considering ideas aloud. "You'll marry in the chapel here at Braebourne since that's the most reasonable location. Meanwhile, Adam can procure a special license so the banns need not be read. As for your gown, we shall send word to Madame Morelle in London. She has all your measurements, although she'll have to take them in as you've lost weight since you were last in her shop."

"But she and her seamstresses will be in a panic with so little time to complete a new gown," Mallory said.

"Mayhap we should look through my wardrobe. Surely we can find something suitable."

Her mother shook her head. "No, that won't do at all. We may not have time to plan an elaborate wedding, but you shall have a proper wedding dress nonetheless. Rest assured that for the right price, Madame will move heaven and earth to create something truly special for you."

"But what about the fittings?"

"She and her girls can come here to Braebourne. It shall be a treat none of them will wish to miss."

No, Mallory conceded, she didn't suppose Madame or her assistants would pass up an opportunity to see the principal residence of the Duke and Duchess of Clybourne. The visit would likely keep them sharing remembrances for the next year to come.

"As you wish then, Mama."

"Come now, don't look so harried." Her mother leaned across again and patted her hand reassuringly. "It shall all come together and splendidly too. You've always loved planning events, just think of the fun. As for your dress, what better excuse for spending money than on one's own wedding gown?"

It was true. Before Michael died, Mallory had taken great pleasure in her wardrobe, never appearing in anything that wasn't the first stare of fashion. While she'd been in mourning, however, clothes had been the last thing on her mind. After more than a year, she realized that her wardrobe must be dreadfully passé.

"It would be nice to have a new gown, I suppose," Mallory admitted.

"Of course it will. You haven't bought anything since you were last in London. You're sadly overdue, my dear."

A slow smile curved Mallory's lips. "When you put it that way, it seems almost an obligation."

"Exactly. Edward will be delighted to buy you whatever you like, I am certain."

Particularly since it would be the last time he was obliged to do so. Once married, Adam would assume responsibility for her, financially and otherwise. She knew that he had come into a great deal of money recently. Fleetingly, she wondered how much it was. She supposed the vast majority of the funds were being used to repair his estate, precisely as they should be. And of course there was her dowry, which would not be an insubstantial sum. But whatever amount remained, she vowed she would live within their means. Despite what he said about wanting to marry her, she never wished to be a burden to Adam. She never wanted him to have regrets.

"Now," her mother said, interrupting Mallory's thoughts. "About the guest list. Whom shall we invite? Not too many more than the guests already in residence, but a few additional, don't you think? Here, let me find a pen and paper, and we will decide."

Inviting Charlemagne back onto her lap, Mallory relaxed in her chair and began helping her mother plan.

After dinner that night, Mallory strolled into the drawing room, her head still spinning with talk of wedding preparations—not to mention all the hugs and best wishes she'd received from friends and family throughout the day.

Accepting a cup of tea from Claire, she located what she hoped would be a quiet spot on the sofa. She'd just taken her first sip when Daphne sat down next to her.

"Well, aren't you the sly boots?" Daphne said with a twinkle in her eyes. "As I distinctly recall, you said you didn't have any interest in Lord Gresham, and now here you are engaged to him. What happened to the two of you being nothing more than friends?"

Mallory set her cup back onto its saucer. "We are friends. But circumstances have changed."

"They most certainly have. Only imagine my amazement when I heard all the shouting the other morning and learned that Adam Gresham was in your bed! You certainly are the clever minx, aren't you?"

"There was nothing clever about it," Mallory defended with a frown. "Surely you aren't implying that I orchestrated the matter?"

"Not a bit. I'm only saying that fate conspired to toss you together, and you took advantage of the situation. You'd have been a fool not to do so considering how elusive Gresham has always been. And now that he has money, well, it makes him that much more tempting, does it not?"

"His money is of no consequence to me," Mallory retorted. "I would esteem him just the same were he as poor as the village ragman."

"That's reassuring to know, sweetheart," Adam said, appearing suddenly behind the sofa. "Although no matter the circumstances, I believe I could do better than selling rags."

"Well, of course, you could." Mallory set her cup and saucer on a nearby table, having very nearly spilled tea on her dress as a result of his abrupt arrival. "It was only a metaphor. To use another, you really are as silent as a cat, my lord, sneaking up on people without warning."

"Then it's a good thing you like felines." Walking around the sofa, he eased onto the seat next to her and leaned close. "*Meow*," he murmured, his breath warm against her ear.

Her pulse quickened to a frantic pace, her nipples tightening into peaks as a delicious shudder chased over her skin. Only through sheer force of will did she keep from crossing her arms over her chest. Striving to compose herself, she cast a glance upward from beneath her lashes and noticed that he was plainly unconcerned whether or not his remark had been overheard. If anything, he seemed to be enjoying himself.

"Lady Damson, forgive me," Adam drawled as if he had only just noticed the other woman. "You were saying something to Lady Mallory before I interrupted. Pray continue."

Daphne stared for a long, silent moment. "I was only saying that . . . well, that is . . . I was just wishing Mallory happy in her coming marriage."

"Is that what you were doing? I couldn't tell from the tone of the conversation, but then I try never to eavesdrop."

A flush rose on Daphne's cheeks. "I truly do wish nothing but happiness for Mallory, my lord. She deserves no less after everything she's suffered."

Reaching over, Adam took Mallory's hand and brought it to his lips. "You are right. She deserves to be cherished. I am only grateful that I will be the man lucky enough to do so."

Daphne glanced between the two of them, her expression softening at whatever it was she saw. "So it really is a love match then? Mallory, you should have told me. You ought not to have been so shy."

Mallory opened her mouth to contradict the remark, but Adam spoke before she could form the first word. "We were trying to keep things quiet, but circumstances conspired against us. You understand."

"Oh, of course," Daphne said, a hand fluttering to her chest. "True love cannot be contained, nor can real passion. It's so dreadfully romantic. Just wait until I tell Jessica. You don't mind if I tell Jessica, do you? Considering we're all such bosom beaux."

Without waiting for Mallory's answer, Daphne sprang to her feet, bid them a quick farewell, then hurried across the room.

Adam waited until she was out of earshot before leaning close again. "No one will imagine I was compelled to marry you now. You may rest assured your reputation is back on its old solid foundation."

"But Adam, she thinks we were having a passionate love affair when that isn't the case. Well, not actually," she amended, remembering what had happened between them that night in her bed.

"What she believes is that I had already proposed and just couldn't wait for the wedding night," Adam stated. "As she said, everyone will think it's romantic. Even Society's most rigid sticklers will unbend and forgive you. You'll probably get twice the presents for the wedding."

"I don't want twice the presents, not if that's the reason."

"So you'd prefer to be thought of as a ruined woman whose family made sure your groom was forced to the altar?"

"No, and do not be obtuse, my lord."

He laughed. "Is that what I'm being? I thought I was being gallant."

"Now you really *are* being obtuse." Their gazes met, and suddenly she smiled, tension she hadn't realized she felt easing from her shoulders. "Thank you."

"For what?"

"For everything. I shall do my best to make you a good wife."

His expression sobered, a gleam shining deep in his eyes. "I know you will, Mallory."

He looked as if he was going to say more, when from across the room, Edward tapped a spoon against a wineglass in order to gain everyone's attention.

"If I might have a moment of your time," the duke said, smiling as he looked around the room. "As you all know, my sister has agreed to marry Adam Gresham, a fine man and a longtime friend of our family. I want to welcome him to the fold and propose a toast to the couple."

"Hear, hear!" piped Jack and Cade and several others.

"So please join me in wishing them every health and happiness." He raised his glass. "To Adam and Mallory!"

All those in the room lifted their glasses, a few of the ladies hoisting teacups instead. "To Adam and Mallory!"

Huzzahs filled the room, and a fresh flood of congratulations came her and Adam's way. She didn't have time to talk to him alone again the rest of the evening.

It was only as she was climbing into bed hours later that she wondered again what he'd been on the verge of saying. Deciding he would tell her later if it was important, she curled under the sheets and went to sleep.

Chapter 14

The next two weeks sped past in a flurry of preparations, the entire household buzzing with anticipation and excitement over the coming nuptials. All of the house-party guests had elected to remain for the ceremony, while neighbors from near and far began to pay impromptu calls in hopes of eliciting an invitation.

For Mallory it seemed as if she'd been tossed into the eye of a storm, the world spinning around her at a whirlwind pace while she did her best to keep up. At least the burst of activity kept her occupied from morning to night, leaving her so weary by day's end that she fell asleep almost instantly.

At first she'd worried about having more nightmares, but to her relief none arrived, her dreams filled instead with seating charts and invitation cards, color schemes, table settings and menus.

At the beginning of the second week, Madame Morelle and her assistants arrived to complete her wedding dress. Mallory dreamed of that as well—imagining herself drowning in yards of silk and being prodded by a thousand and one fitting pins.

But no dreams caught her attention like the ones she had of Adam. Perhaps that, more than any other, was the reason the nightmares did not return.

In her imaginings, he held her in his arms, kissed and caressed her with a slow pleasure that sent her pulse racing in fantasy as well as fact. More than once she awakened to find herself clutching her pillow to her chest, disappointed to realize it was made of feathers instead of flesh and blood.

As for any real kisses from Adam, there had only been a few, always stolen and far too brief to be truly satisfying. For although she saw him every day, they spent little time alone. The wedding plans kept her busy during the day, while the guests monopolized both of their evenings. And with everyone scrutinizing her and Adam, the two of them agreed that he shouldn't come to her room again before they wed.

Not that she was sure she was ready for him to do so. For in spite of their engagement and the undeniable passion she experienced in his arms, as well as her dreams, she was still getting used to the changes in their relationship. After years of friendship, it sometimes seemed odd to think of him as her fiancé.

As she stood in her sitting room, being fitted for her wedding gown, it was even more astonishing to realize that in only one day's time, he would be her husband. A mere twenty-four hours from now, Adam would be sanctioned by God and man to come to her bed, and more, to have complete carnal knowledge of her body.

"Ow!" Mallory cried, a jab of pain rousing her from her woolgathering.

"Forgive me, my lady," Madame Morelle said, a length of pins set in paper draped around her neck, "but it is difficult to fit you properly if you will not hold still."

"O-of course. My apologies," Mallory said, promising herself that she wouldn't let her mind wander again, especially not onto the dangerous subject of Adam. "I shall endeavor to be as still as a statue."

"You may certainly continue to breathe," the modiste said as she pinched a length of fabric underneath Mallory's raised arm. "When I say you can, that is. Breathe and hold, please."

Doing as she was ordered, Mallory inhaled and waited, the mantua maker securing a pin with a quick pair of thrusts.

"There, all done," Madame said. "You may lower your arm again, my lady."

Mallory did so gratefully, wondering how much longer the fitting was going to take.

As if Madame had heard her—or perhaps it was the heavens taking pity instead—the seamstress stepped back and reviewed her work with an appraising eye. "*Et voilà! Fini!*" With an elaborate sweep of her arm, she motioned toward Mallory. "Your Graces, your ladyships, may I present you with the bride."

The five Byron women, who were arranged in a semicircle of chairs, looked up and gave collective sighs of approval.

"Oh, you look exquisite," Ava declared.

"Beautiful," Grace agreed.

"Perfection." India smiled.

Claire clasped her hands against her chest. "Only wait

until Adam sees you coming down the aisle. He'll be dazzled."

"He won't be able to tear his eyes away." Meg shifted baby Zachary to her opposite arm, then redraped the shawl around her shoulders so he could continue nursing.

Esme, who was the only Byron female not seated in a chair, looked up from where she sat in the window seat, a sketch pad in hand. "You look lovelier than a princess."

"A duke's daughter shall have to suffice, but thank you, dear heart," Mallory said, sending her younger sister a smile. "Thank you everyone, especially you, Madame."

The modiste gave a Gallic shrug, clearly confident in her own talent. "But come, you have not seen the dress." Striding forward on a swish of poplin skirts, Madame turned Mallory so that she faced the floor-length mirror, two of Madame's assistants scurrying to adjust the angle.

Mallory stared, not quite recognizing herself for a moment. It had been so long since she'd done more than cast a quick glance in a mirror that it was as if she were gazing at a stranger. But a very fashionable stranger, she had to admit, the gown made in a style Madame assured her would be all the rage come the new Season.

Made of snowy white silk organza, the dress billowed around her like a gossamer breeze. The sheer, almost transparent half sleeves were stitched with tiny seed pearls that caught the light to cast a creamy glow. Encircling her torso just beneath her breasts was a satin ribbon adorned with small, delicate white silk rosebuds. The ribbon was tied in a bow at her back, the ends left to trail down amid two sweeping double lines of white leaves that cascaded to the hem. Matching leaves swept around the hem, where they intermingled with another scattering of seed pearls.

To complete the ensemble, her dark hair would be pinned high and twined with a double strand of round pearls. She would wear a pair of long white kid gloves, and delicate creamy satin pumps would grace her feet.

"So? What do you think, Mallory?" Ava said, coming to stand at her side.

"I think Madame has outdone herself once again. My appreciation for making me a beautiful bride and with so little time in which to accomplish it."

The modiste bustled forward. "You would be a beautiful bride no matter what you chose to wear, Lady Mallory, but I am most gratified that you approve. And that you selected my establishment to create your gown."

"I would go nowhere else."

Madame beamed. Then, turning abruptly, she clapped her hands. "Hurry, girls! Let us help Lady Mallory out of her gown so that we may work. There is much yet to be done before tomorrow."

Taking care not to stab her with any of the pins that held the dress together, Madame's assistants extracted Mallory from the garment. Left standing in her shift and a single petticoat, she stood mute as the women departed in a swirl of energy and skirts.

Her maid, who had been keeping a quiet watch from the nearby dressing room, came forward, a peach day dress draped over her arm. Lifting her arms, Mallory let Penny help her into the gown.

After her maid departed again, Mallory joined the others. As was generally the case these days, they were reviewing plans for the ceremony and the elaborate wedding breakfast that would follow. Rather than join the debate about whether to substitute local apples for a variety of hothouse fruits being transported from London, Mallory slid into an empty chair next to Meg.

"Is he asleep?" Mallory asked in a soft voice as she regarded the infant held in her friend's arms.

Meg nodded. "With his tummy full, he dozed straight off. I'm thinking about taking him up to the nursery, but the instant I lay him in his cradle, he'll probably wake again. On the other hand, I need to be going up soon anyway. I promised Maximillian that I would read him a story before his afternoon nap. If I plan things correctly, they'll both be asleep by the time I need to come downstairs for a nap of my own before dinner."

"May I hold him?"

"Of course. Careful now, or he'll take exception to being passed about and make all of us sorry." She shared a smile with Meg as her sister-in-law leaned across so they could make the transfer. For a moment the baby scrunched his face tight at the disturbance, but as soon as he settled against Mallory's warm bosom, he quieted.

"He's lovely," Mallory said, stroking a finger lightly over the paper-thin skin of one of his rosy cheeks.

"Just wait until you have your own. Who knows, mayhap we'll be sitting here together next year admiring your new baby."

Warmth spread through Mallory like a rising sun, a shy smile playing over her lips at the notion. "Yes, mayhap."

She held Zachary for several minutes as the others continued to review the arrangements for the next day. She made no comment, content merely to listen. Then it was time for Meg to take the baby up to the nursery, time as well for Mallory to go downstairs to greet the latest influx of guests and family members who had arrived for the wedding.

What had begun as a modest list of forty had swelled to more than a hundred, with another seventy-five invited for the wedding breakfast. As things now stood, she would much rather be married with only her family and a few of Adam's closest friends in attendance. With his father and sister deceased, he had few relations—only an elderly aunt too frail to travel and a few cousins with whom he exchanged letters at Christmas and little else.

At one time, Mallory knew she would have adored the hullabaloo of a large Society wedding. Now, she rather envied Ned and Claire, who'd run off to marry in a small parish church with only the vicar's wife and daughter there to serve as witnesses. How exquisitely peaceful that must have been, how beautifully romantic.

But as tempting as an elopement might be, everyone was counting on tomorrow's ceremony. The entire household had put so much work into the preparations—cleaning, cooking and arranging the various rooms that would be used for the festivities. Madame Morelle and her assistants had been sewing, often long into the night, in order to complete her wedding gown and a couple of new dresses for her honeymoon. Her family and friends had helped wherever they could. And then there was Mama, who had done everything possible to make sure tomorrow would be the most special event in Mallory's life.

She couldn't let them down, any of them, even if she might have talked Adam into running away. Besides, tomorrow was only one day out of her life—not so very much to ask for all that she had been given.

A single day that would forever after change her life.

Swallowing against a fresh fluttering of nerves, she stood and was about to follow the others from the room when Esme appeared at her side.

"I've been working on this," Esme said, a piece of drawing paper in her hand. "I thought you might like it, as a memento of your old home after you've moved into your new one."

Carefully, Mallory took hold of the drawing, struck by the fine details and how beautifully the scene was rendered. It was a view of the grounds from her bedchamber window, a vista as familiar to her as her own name. In the foreground lay a portion of Braebourne's vast formal gardens, trimmed and maintained with elaborate precision by a small army of gardeners. The trees still carried a full complement of green leaves, the late-summer flowers providing a final burst of color before the coming cooler temperatures would take them away until spring.

A pretty folly with a small lake stood off to the east, an array of birds always gathered 'round. While to the west lay an area of fallow earth not at all in keeping with the rest of the landscape. Ned had installed the garden plot for Claire not long after their marriage. He called it her "mole patch"—a term that never failed to elicit an embarrassed laugh from Claire, even if none of the rest of the family was allowed in on the joke.

In the distance beyond was a wilder landscape that flowed into rolling hills and lush stands of old-growth trees, shady spots where she'd spent many an idle hour lounging with a book or lost in daydreams during her childhood days.

The vista was so very dear, and Esme had captured it perfectly.

Blinking away a tear, she pulled her sister close for a warm hug. "You could not have given me anything better. Thank you, love."

Esme smiled, showing her pretty white teeth, as her arms wrapped tightly around Mallory's waist for a long moment.

"I shall have it framed and hung in my room at Gresham Park," Mallory said, after they eased apart. "That way, I shall be able to see the views from both of my homes every morning."

"There's something else I should like you to have,"

Esme told her, her smile falling away to be replaced by a serious look. "I've given it a great deal of thought, and I want you to take Charlemagne with you."

"But he's your cat."

Esme shook her head. "He likes me, but he loves you, and I think he will pine with sadness when you leave. I shall miss him, of course, but I have lots of other pets. Besides, you and Adam will need a cat, and he's a good one. Tell me you'll take him, Mallory. I won't feel right otherwise."

Tears sprang to her eyes, her throat squeezed as if it had been tightened by a bowstring. "If you're sure, then yes, I would love to have him. He and I have become old friends these many months."

"I know, that's why he belongs with you."

Wrapping her arm around Esme's waist again, she drew her near. "Has anyone told you what a wonderful sister you are?"

Esme ducked her head, her lips curving upward. "Just you, but that's because you're my only sister."

"Well, if you had more, they would all sing your praises." Turning away, Mallory daubed at her eyes with her sleeve. "Everyone must be wondering where I am. And you as well. You've probably been missed in the schoolroom despite your reprieve for the fitting."

Esme made a face. "I'm supposed to be reading history today."

"Then you had best get on with it." Crossing to her escritoire, Mallory laid down the drawing, admiring it once more.

"Mallory?"

She turned and met her sister's gaze. "Yes, dear?"

"I think you'll be happy with Lord Gresham."

"Do you?"

"He loves you, you know, a very great deal."

Loves me? Yes, of course, as a friend, the same way I love him. As for anything else . . .

An odd sensation formed in her stomach, a funny tingling that made her wonder what it would be like to be truly, passionately, violently loved by Adam Gresham. To be wanted with the full force of his personality, the great depths of his heart and soul.

But she was only being foolish, and Esme was reading far too much into her unexpected nuptials. Her and Adam's marriage was a union of circumstance, a joining of like minds and willing spirits. They would do well together, she knew. But passionate, romantic love . . . she'd had that once for far too brief a time, and she didn't want to have it again. Never more did she want to experience the giddy highs and desolate lows that came with such intense emotions.

Being friends was better.

Being friends and lovers was even better still.

Smiling, she gestured toward the door. "Off we go then before they send someone to find us. There is still so much to do before tomorrow."

Chapter 15

The next morning, Adam stood at the altar of the Byron family chapel, attired in his best dark blue coat and fawn trousers. His waistcoat was cream with a reserved gold key pattern, his shirt snowy white, his cravat tied in an intricate trone d'Amour. On his feet, he wore black dress shoes that were polished to an almost blinding gleam, courtesy of his valet.

He'd pleased and surprised Finley by permitting the man to assist him today, initially by letting the servant hand him one pressed neckcloth after another until Adam finally achieved the look he wanted. Next, he allowed the valet to help him into his tight-fitting coat, then stood still while the man ran a brush over his back and shoulders to remove any stray specks of lint.

But this was his wedding day, and the minor intrusion on his privacy seemed a small price to pay. For Mallory's sake, he wanted to look his best. When she saw him standing in the chapel, he wished her to be proud, to be pleased, that he was the man she was marrying.

He resisted the temptation to check his pocket watch, knowing the hour must be nearly at hand. Conversation from the dozens of seated guests reverberated inside the elegant chamber, echoing off the high, domed ceiling, with its beautifully painted angels, cerulean blue skies and pristine pale clouds, before dropping low to skim across the smooth white marble floors.

Drawing a deep breath, he caught the sweet scents of flowers from the large vases filled to overflowing with sprays of white jasmine and pale apricot musk roses.

Next to him, he saw Jack check his watch, his best man obviously sharing his own earlier impulse. On Jack's far side, also serving as his groomsmen, stood Cade, Drake, and Niall Faversham, who had apparently recovered from his brief infatuation with Mallory.

A good thing, too, Adam thought, *since Mallory belongs to me.* No other man would ever possess her. After the wedding night, she would irrevocably be his.

"Five minutes," Jack said. "Nervous?"

"No," he answered, realizing it was the truth. If anything, he was impatient to proceed. Unlike most men, he happened to be eager to marry. Mallory Byron was the woman he loved above all others, and he could barely wait to join his life with hers. "You have the ring, I presume?"

Jack grinned and patted a pocket in his waistcoat. "Right here, safe and sound."

Adam nodded and stared down at his shoes, doing his utmost not to think again about tonight and the pleasure he knew he would find with Mallory in his bed. With very little prompting, he could imagine the scene—Mallory lying warm and naked against the sheets, her hair rippling in a dark wave over the pillows, her lips red and swollen from the kisses he'd given her as she beckoned him closer for more . . .

Abruptly returning to his senses, he stopped and shook the fantasy clear. As he well knew, there'd been enough scandal already without his causing more. Only imagine the reaction were he to become visibly aroused in front of more than a hundred guests, and at his own wedding to boot.

His lips quirked at the notion, and he glanced up.

Suddenly there stood Mallory, framed by the chapel's wide, oak double doors. For an instant, he forgot to breathe, forgot *how* to breathe, his senses overwhelmed by her sheer beauty, an ethereal loveliness that quite put the angels overhead to shame. Dressed all in white, she was stunning.

Pure.

Perfect.

Absolutely innocent.

With her attendants, Grace, India, Meg, and Claire beginning their procession up the aisle, Edward stepped to Mallory's side and bent to whisper something in her ear. She smiled slightly, then took his arm. Soon, they began the traditional march, moving gradually forward.

As they did, Adam became aware of his heart beating in deep, powerful strokes as though it were trying to escape from his chest. Inhaling as fully as he was able, he strove to calm himself, to clear his mind so he could make it through the next few minutes of the ceremony.

Her gaze met his as she drew to a halt at his side, nerves and some other indefinable emotion shimmering in the ocean-hued depths of her eyes. Edward released her into his care, but Adam barely noticed the duke, his every thought centered on Mallory as the two of them turned to face Vicar Thoms.

Dearly beloved . . .

As if from a distance, he heard the clergyman begin the ceremony, the solemn words resonating inside the chapel that had grown quiet save for an occasional cough or rustling of fabric as someone shifted in their seat.

Adam tried to concentrate, aware that he needed to follow along so he would know when it was time for him to say his vows. But it wasn't easy, not with Mallory standing barely two inches away, not when he wanted to touch her and kiss her and tell her how very much he adored her.

Instead, he kept his hands loose at his sides, his shoulders straight, his gaze focused ahead. From the corner of his eye, he could see her, noticing the way her fingers were clasped, white and strained, around her bouquet of apricot roses.

He sent her a look, wanting to reassure her that she needn't be so nervous. Before he could catch her gaze, the vicar was asking him to take the first of his vows.

In a strong, clear voice he said the words that would bind him to Mallory, knowing as he did that he meant each and every one. Then it was Mallory's turn, her own iteration soft and low, her gaze cast down beneath her lashes.

When the clergyman asked *who so giveth this woman* . . . Edward stepped forward to respond, laying her hand in Adam's in a final affirmation of his blessing and consent. Claire took Mallory's bouquet, then it was just he and Mallory, the rest of the wedding party and the guests seeming to fade away.

Her fingers were cool and trembled ever so slightly within his own warm grasp. Holding them tighter, he silently urged her to look up. But her eyes moved no higher than his cravat as he spoke the next of his vows, then she hers.

Then it was time for the rings, Jack passing him the oval cut aquamarine he'd purchased when he'd made the quick trip to London in order to procure the special license. He'd chosen the gemstone, set in gold with a surround of small diamonds, because the color reminded him of Mallory's eyes. Now, if only she would glance up, he would be able to judge again how well it matched.

Her fingers shook once more as he slid the ring in place, a sensation of wonder sweeping through him at the realization that Mallory was now truly his wife.

Until death us do part, he thought with another fierce beat of his heart.

Moments later, she fit a wide gold band on his finger, an act not required by the ceremony but a visible commitment he wished to accept nonetheless. Then, the vicar spoke the final words that pronounced them husband and wife, and the ceremony was over.

Or nearly.

Smiling, Adam curved his palms around her arms in a gentle clasp and pulled her close. She glanced up, her eyes wide and glazed with nerves.

Bending near, he brushed his lips against her cheek. "Don't worry, sweetheart," he whispered for her ears alone. "It's only me, Adam, whom you've known since you were a girl."

She gave an almost imperceptible nod, a measure of the anxiety fading from her gaze.

"You're mine to cherish and protect now, and as long as we're together, there is nothing you will ever need fear again."

Then, ignoring the dictates of convention and the gazes of all of the people watching, he folded her close and sealed his vows with a kiss.

* * *

At the first touch of Adam's lips, Mallory thought she heard church bells ringing. But the chapel had no bells, so she supposed she must be hearing the wild rhythm of her heart clamoring between her ears. As for the chill that had permeated her skin from the time she'd awakened this morning, it melted like so much ice under a warm summer sun—Adam's strong arms holding her too close not to absorb the heat from his robust body.

She knew the two of them were being watched as though they were players on a stage, and yet beneath the sweet pressure of his kiss, everyone else ceased to matter, ceased even to exist.

This was Adam, who had always been her friend.

This was Adam, who was as familiar to her as breathing.

So why had she been so nervous?

Why had the idea of marriage left her so afraid?

Trembling beneath the intoxicating delight of his mouth moving over hers, she no longer had the faintest idea. Then, just as she was about to slide her arms around his neck to pull him even closer, he broke their kiss.

The world returned in a blinding rush—the scent of roses drifting on the air, shafts of golden September sunlight gleaming through the chapel windows, the press of over a hundred pair of eyes watching with avid, open-mouthed interest.

Heat and color burst to life in her cheeks as she dipped her head, a smattering of laughter breaking out among the assembled company. Peering up through her lashes, she met Adam's rich, chocolate brown gaze and read the boyish pleasure there and in his wide, white-toothed grin.

A laugh escaped her own mouth, and without entirely realizing how, she found herself smiling. After planting another quick kiss on her lips, Adam drew her arm through his and led her back down the aisle.

The wedding breakfast came next, a far more elaborate affair than she had originally envisioned. With so many people in attendance, the formal dining room had been arrayed with dozens of chairs and tables, each spread with a crisp white cloth and flowered Meissen china edged in gold.

She and Adam took their places at the head table with her family and his groomsmen on either side. The meal had barely started when she was handed a glass of champagne. She took a sip, the wine tasting sweet and cool on her tongue, frothy bubbles tickling her nose.

The servants brought forth a sumptuous variety of food, platters arranged with a selection designed to tempt any palate. There were coddled eggs with buttered toast points, tiny pancakes drizzled with sweet treacle and whipped cream, smoked salmon, rare roast beef, ham, pasties, puddings, cheese, juicy hothouse berries, succulent golden peaches and crisp red apples.

Adam made sure she ate, tempting her with one delicious morsel after another that he offered to her on his fork. Meanwhile, the champagne continued to flow, the servants so efficient that the level in her glass never seemed to grow lower no matter how much she drank.

"Open up," Adam said, holding out a plump, sugar-dipped strawberry that sparkled like a jewel beneath its sweet coating.

Obediently, she parted her lips and sank her teeth into the berry, flavor bursting in her mouth as a tiny drop of juice trickled toward her chin. She giggled and reached for her napkin.

"Allow me." Using the edge of his thumb, he wiped away the errant drop. Instead of drying his fingers on his own napkin, though, he licked away the drop. Then, without losing eye contact, he slowly ate the rest of the strawberry.

A shiver ran like an invisible caress along her spine.

Mercy, I hope no one is watching us, she thought, *since Adam looks as if it's me he'd rather be nibbling on instead of that strawberry.*

Taking up her champagne, she hid her reaction to the astonishing thought in a long, cool swallow. The room gave a slight spin, and her glass bobbled in her hand, wine sloshing dangerously near the rim. Ever so carefully, she returned the drink to the table, another giggle escaping her throat as she did.

"If I don't mistake the matter, I believe you're just this side of being foxed, Lady Gresham."

She peered at him, lines wrinkling her forehead. "Lady who?"

"Gresham," he repeated.

"Who's that?"

He sent her an amused glance. "Why you are, sweetheart."

She puzzled over the matter for a moment, then laughed. "La, and so I am. I'd quite forgot; I'm a countess now. How very singular."

Lifting her hand, he kissed her palm, stroking a fingertip over her wedding ring as he did. "How very delightful, my dear Mallory Gresham."

"Oh, heavens, that's right. I'm not a Byron any longer."

"No. Now you're mine."

Her stomach gave a flip at the intense expression in his eyes, a look she decided must be the alcohol talking. "I suppose I oughtn't have anything else to drink."

"Very likely not," he agreed. "But go ahead anyway."

"Really? Why?"

A slow smile moved over his sensual lips. "Because I like you like this."

"Foxed, you mean?" She hiccuped, then covered her

mouth with a hand, as a fresh giggle rose up like the champagne bubbles in her glass.

He shook his head. "No, happy. I like hearing you laugh."

Before she had time to consider the truth of his statement, he plucked another sugar-coated piece of fruit off her plate—a blackberry this time—and popped it into her mouth. She chewed and swallowed, then took another imprudent sip of wine.

Mallory was still floating on a surfeit of food, wine and wedding cake as she let Penny finish helping her into her traveling dress three hours later.

The gown—another of Madame's last-minute creations—was fashioned of buttercup yellow sarcenet with a matching, short-sleeved pelisse. An adorable cottage bonnet of pale chip straw, that was shaped rather like an inverted bucket, curved along her cheekbones, its ribbons tied in a saucy bow beneath her chin.

Charlemagne regarded her from a nearby chair, his ears angled as if he knew something unusual was afoot. Crossing to the cat, she stroked his velvety head. "You shall be fine here with Esme until I return from my honeymoon next month. Then you're coming with me to Gresham Park. It shall be an adventure for us both."

The cat purred.

An adventure.

That's how she had decided to regard her marriage. Anything else was . . . well, she wasn't sure what it was. Which was why sometime between her first glass of champagne and the laughter she'd elicited among the guests as she'd playfully crammed wedding cake into Adam's mouth, she'd chosen to regard her marriage as an interesting new escapade on which she was embarking.

Rather like launching a ship and setting off as an explorer into the unknown. And her new life was indeed unknown even if her new husband was not.

A knock sounded at the door, diverting her attention.

In trooped all the Byron ladies, who announced they were there to make sure Mallory had everything she needed before she went on her way. She received a wealth of hugs and kisses, as well as some good-natured teasing about her mildly inebriated state.

With all her luggage packed and in the hands of several able-bodied footmen, she was escorted downstairs, where the process began again. This time it was her brothers who did the hugging, kissing, and well-wishing.

Adam joined her, saying a round of good-byes before he took her arm and led her to the coach. Guests poured from the house, her mother waving tearfully with a handkerchief clutched in her hand, as the coach doors were closed and the horses set in motion.

And then they were away, Braebourne growing smaller and less distinct as one yard melted into the next. Soon, the house vanished altogether. Leaning back against the comfortably upholstered seat, she stopped watching the vista and gazed at Adam instead.

"Are you all right?" he asked from where he'd propped himself in the far corner.

She nodded, her throat thick with a sudden swell of emotion.

Opening his arms, he gestured for her to come to him. Sliding across the seat, she did, burying her cheek against his shoulder. "Where is it we are going again?"

"North."

"So you still won't tell me our destination?"

He shook his head. "It's a surprise. One I believe you'll like."

"I'm not sure I care to be surprised, my lord," she said, leaning far enough back to meet his gaze.

He gave her nose a quick, playful tweak. "You love surprises, and you know it. Now, why don't you close your eyes and rest. We have a good distance to travel today."

"I couldn't possibly sleep," she said, far too wound up to relax, even with all the champagne she'd imbibed. "How many miles is it?"

He gave her an enigmatic smile. "A great many."

"Are there mountains?"

"Perhaps."

"Lakes?"

"Possibly."

"What about heather? Is there any of that?"

He arched a dark brow. "If you're trying to catch me out, it will do no good. And no, we're not going to my hunting box in Scotland. It's a perfectly good accommodation for men but no place to take a lady for her honeymoon."

"Why? What's amiss with it? Or are you worried there are too many animal heads mounted on the walls, and that all the dead staring eyes will give me a fright?" she inquired with a mock shudder.

He barked out a laugh. "There are no animal heads on any of the walls. I don't care for such ghastly mementos, as you are well aware."

"That's a relief," she said. "After we arrive at Gresham Park, it will save me the trouble of having them removed and stored in some dark corner of the attic."

He shot her a smile. "You'll be doing far more buying than storing once we are in residence. But I can safely assure you there are no hunting trophies for you to sequester in the nether regions of the house."

At the mention of Gresham Park, she realized she knew little more about his principal estate than she did his hunting box. To her knowledge, none of the family had ever visited his ancestral residence, a place she'd once heard him describe as a "moldering pile of bricks." But as she knew, he was actively making improvements now, and she supposed no matter its condition, the two of them would turn it into a gracious home.

"So, what else is wrong with your hunting box?" she asked, resuming their earlier conversation.

"Nothing is wrong with my hunting box. But it's small and rather spartan when it comes to creature comforts. You deserve a better, far more elegant establishment than a rough bachelor's hideaway."

"I'm sure I could have managed."

Tightening his hold, he urged her closer. "I don't want you to manage. I want you pampered and cared for and thoroughly indulged."

"You make me sound horribly spoiled," she said, reprimanding him with a light tap on the shoulder.

"As well you should be, madam wife." Capturing her hand, he placed a kiss on the center of her palm. "Anything you want, you have only to say."

"What I *want* at the moment is to know where we're going?"

"But I've already told you. North."

She stuck out her tongue and drew a fresh laugh, his broad chest reverberating against her side. Slowly, his humor faded, his gaze roaming over her face, only to pause when it lowered to her lips. She'd seen that look before and knew what it meant.

He was thinking about kissing her.

Her heart hammered beneath her breasts, the last of the alcohol in her system turning to vapors in her brain that left her weak and shivery. Part of her ached for his touch, but another part hesitated. She'd been alone with Adam countless times before, but now that they were wed, none of the old strictures applied.

He could do anything to her.

Anything at all.

Still, he surely wouldn't indulge in the sorts of liberties he'd taken that night in her bedchamber, not while they were in their coach with the servants just outside?

Or would he?

Inwardly awash with a combination of nerves and anticipation, she watched as he bent his head to take her lips.

Without warning, a yawn caught her.

She covered her mouth with a hand, as moisture pooled in the corners of her eyes. "I'm sorry," she mumbled around her palm.

Pausing, he gave her a rueful look. "I thought you weren't tired."

"I'm not," she denied.

But to her consternation, she realized that quite abruptly, she was powerfully, almost painfully, tired.

"It's been a long, eventful day," he said with clear understanding.

Reaching up, he untied the bow beneath her chin and pulled off her hat, carefully tossed it onto the seat opposite. Smoothing his fingers over her cheek, he placed gentle kisses on her forehead and mouth, then tucked her close. "Sleep."

"B-but I'll be fine. Just give me a minute."

"Sleep, Mallory. There'll be time enough for everything later."

Later.

He meant tonight.

In bed.

At his urging, she lowered her head to his shoulder, finding it amazingly comfortable. And before she quite knew what was happening, she fell asleep.

Adam silenced a groan, knowing this was going to be one of the most trying excursions of his life. Just the thought of kissing her had turned him randy as a goat, his shaft stiff and aching between his legs.

It's what happened, he supposed, from going without sex for the past several weeks. But he'd decided to put aside his own need and wait for Mallory, knowing she was the only woman he truly craved.

Equally his fault was encouraging her to have a bit too much wine at the wedding breakfast. Not that he'd been planning to take her here in the coach—certainly not given that it would be her first time. Still a few kisses, an intimate touch or two, wouldn't have gone amiss. Now, to his express consternation, he was in the mood to dally, while she was clearly in need of sleep.

Then again maybe it was better he hadn't started anything between them. Why torture himself by tossing extra kindling on the fire? This evening, once she was rested, would be soon enough.

Now, he only had to get through the next few hours.

At least he could console himself by holding her.

The woman he loved.

The woman who was finally his wife.

Adjusting her slightly so that she was lying more comfortably in his arms, he leaned back and watched through the window as the forests and fields passed by.

A few hours later, Mallory tied the ribbons beneath her chin to secure her hat in place, glancing out the window as the coach rolled along a narrow country road lined with low, ancient-looking stone walls.

Dusky, early-evening sunshine turned the sky the color of newly minted gold, hints of pink, red and copper creeping along the edge as nature gave one final burst of light before its inevitable surrender to the night. Around them rose hills of green, vegetation thriving in an untamed panoply of texture and hue. In the distance lay a winding stream that coiled like a slumbering serpent, its bed strewn with dark grey boulders, brown rocks and pebbles the color of wet sand.

Before she had time to study the landscape any further, the coach turned onto a forested lane, springs bouncing as the vehicle continued upward. The conveyance drove along another curve, then out into an open area where a massive structure dominated the hillside.

"A castle," she declared, admiring the wide stone façade, complete with towers, turrets and crenellations that were covered in a profusion of ivy. There was even a drawbridge and moat.

"Like it?"

She nodded. "It's wonderful."

Adam smiled. "Good. Then welcome to your home for the next month."

"You mean we're staying here? In a castle?"

"Surprised?"

"Yes." And she was, since she'd never imagined spending her honeymoon in an actual medieval castle.

"Pleased?"

"Very. But where are we? Assuming I'm finally allowed to know."

"Wales."

"What made you think to come here?" she asked. "For

that matter, who owns this property? Unless it's yours, and you've just never happened to mention owning a castle in Wales."

Adam grinned, his eyes twinkling. "I believe the subject would have come up by now if I did. No, this belongs to Weybridge. It's not his principal residence, of course, but it's an old family holding. I believe he said a Marlowe ancestor built it sometime in the ninth century—or maybe it was eighth? After a thousand years though, what's a hundred years give or take?"

Mallory arched an eyebrow. "So it's Quentin and India's?"

"They thought a stay here would make a nice wedding present. I hope you agree."

She looked again at the massive stone structure as the coach moved over the drawbridge and into the bailey. Meeting Adam's gaze, she smiled. "I do. This is . . . splendid."

Closing her eyes for a moment, she concentrated on a new sound and scent. "Are we near the sea?"

"On the northern coast. If you look hard enough, Weybridge says you can almost see Ireland."

Sliding her arms around his waist, she gave him a fierce hug. "Thank you."

"Don't thank me yet, not until you've seen the inside," he teased. "The duke assures me it's been modernized, but maybe that just means they tacked coverings made from something more substantial than waxed animal hides over the windows."

She laughed. "I think I see glass in the windows, so I suspect we won't freeze."

"No matter," he said, cupping her cheek in his palm. "Either way, I'm sure I'll think of some method for keeping you warm at night."

Her pulse thumped, then thumped again as Adam pressed his mouth to hers for a slow, gentle kiss. At length, he raised his head. "Shall we go inside, Lady Gresham?"

Breathlessly, she stared into his eyes, then nodded. "Yes, my lord."

Chapter 16

In spite of Adam's warning, Mallory found the inside of the castle even more pleasing than its exterior. True to Quentin's word, he and India had appointed the rooms with modern furnishings, plush Aubusson carpets and an array of luxurious amenities. And yet the castle retained elements of its ancient past, including suits of medieval armor, displays of ancient battle-axes, swords and other vicious-looking weaponry, and an array of intricate, hand-stitched tapestries that told stories of both valor and defeat.

Bidding a temporary farewell to Adam, Mallory allowed the friendly, bespectacled housekeeper to escort her upstairs to her bedchamber, where she discovered Penny already inside, busy unpacking her mistress's belongings. The room was striking, with an immense royal blue tapestry that dominated one wall, a stone fireplace so large she suspected she could stand inside, and a massive, dark cherrywood tester bed with elegant gold silk hangings.

She had scant time to look around before Penny came to help her out of her traveling attire. In the adjoining bathing chamber that had likely once been a withdrawing room, a pair of footmen filled a wide copper tub with hot water.

Once they departed, she pinned her heavy hair atop her head, then disrobed. Stepping into the bath, she relaxed, steam rising pleasantly around her. Luckily, she'd washed her hair only last night in preparation for the wedding—a wise decision considering she would never have been able to dry the long strands in time for dinner tonight.

After soaking a few minutes more, she rose from the tepid bathwater and toweled herself dry.

Then it was time to dress for the evening meal.

With Penny's assistance, she donned a simple, yet elegant, evening dress of violet shot silk. Around her neck, she added a small pearl drop pendant, then stepped into a pair of matching violet silk slippers.

Soon, a clock chimed the hour and it was time to descend.

Until today, she'd never been anxious about being with Adam, but tonight she was. The earlier effects of the champagne were long gone, nerves whizzing like fireworks in her stomach as she walked down the stairs. At the base, one of the footmen directed her to the dining room, where she discovered Adam already waiting.

He stood at her entrance, smiling as he came forward to take her hand. "You look beautiful."

He looked beautiful as well, she judged, admiring the stark black-and-white evening attire that accentuated his dark eyes and swarthy complexion. Of course, she would never tell him that, since "handsome" was the accepted term for a man who was as powerfully, starkly masculine as Adam.

Yet that's what he was—beautiful.

The kind of man who made women swoon. The sort females chased in hopes of earning even a sliver of his attention.

Now he was her husband.

Suddenly she wondered if she would be enough to satisfy him. She was innocent and knew almost nothing of the marriage act. What if she disappointed him? What if she failed as a wife when, until now, all she'd ever known was how to be his friend?

She gulped at the thought, aware that she and Adam had been pushed into this marriage. That they'd been hurried to the altar before either of them had time to truly consider their feelings or what it would really mean to their lives.

All her earlier worries rushed back upon her, magnified by the realization that this was her wedding night, whether she was ready or not.

Giving her a quizzical look, Adam drew her toward the table, her legs stiff as she walked.

"Have a seat," he suggested, pulling out her chair.

Gratefully, she sank down onto it, busying herself with her napkin while he settled into the seat on her right.

"Wine," he said, signaling the footman, who was waiting to begin service.

"N-no, I couldn't. I shouldn't," she said, laying a hand over the top of her glass, "Not after all that I consumed this morning at the reception."

Adam gave her another probing look. "One glass will do no harm."

Gently easing the goblet clear, he positioned it so the servant could pour.

Once the man withdrew, she reached out and took a sip, the rich, red claret smooth against her tongue. "If you aren't careful, you'll turn me into a lush."

He grinned. "There's little chance of that, I suspect." Pausing, he drank a mouthful from his own glass. "However, should it become a problem, I'll see to it your beverages are watered."

"Watered! Why I—I . . ."

Chuckling, he took another swallow from his glass before returning it to the table. Meeting her gaze, he gave her a wink.

Pursing her lips, she glanced away.

"And here is the first course," he said. "Soup. Excellent."

Despite the delicious scent and flavor, she found herself unable to eat more than a couple of spoonfuls, her bowl of seafood bisque going mostly to waste.

Adam made no comment as the dishes were removed and the next course was served—a lovely selection of delicately braised root vegetables in a buttered wine sauce.

Fish and meat offerings followed, along with an array of accompaniments. With each one, Mallory did her best to eat a bite—or at least pretend to do so—as she followed Adam's lead by chatting about ordinary, unassuming subjects.

Throughout the meal, she kept expecting him to remark on her lack of appetite, to say something about her rather falsely animated conversation. He knew her too well not to see through her façade. But he made no comment, offered no reproof, as if he understood her reticence and was content to let her be.

Finishing her one glass of wine with a gulp, she stared down at her dessert of apple tart with sweet whipped cream and knew she couldn't bear to so much as try it. On any other occasion, she would have been digging in with gusto since she loved both apples and whipped cream.

But not this evening.

Not when her single glass of wine had done nothing to alleviate her anxiety. She might have been tipsy this morning, but she was sober as a stone tonight. Sober and unaccountably nervous over what was soon to transpire between her and Adam.

Oddly, she didn't know quite why she was so worried since she enjoyed Adam's kisses. Loved them, truth be known. Yet there would be more tonight than kisses, more even than the knee-weakening caresses he'd given her that one night in her bed.

What if I'm not enough? she thought again. *What if we cross a line tonight that can't be undone? What if I wake in the morning, and he's suddenly no longer my friend?*

"Why don't you leave that," he said, indicating her untouched dessert, "and go up to bed. I'll be there in a little while."

She paused, both of them expecting her to make her excuses and leave the room. Instead, she ran the tip of a fingernail over the weave in the tablecloth, thoughts tumbling wildly over themselves.

"Adam, would you m-mind terribly . . . that is, would it be all right if you didn't come to my room tonight? It's been such a long day and I'm . . . sorry but I'm tired."

From the corner of her eye, she saw his hand still, tightening briefly before it relaxed again. "Are you sure you're just not nervous? That will pass, you know, if you let it."

She drew a breath. "I'm sure you are right. Even so, I'd rather not. At least not tonight, that is. Tomorrow we can—"

"Very well, if that's what you want," he said in an emotionless voice.

A lump formed in her stomach, knowing immediately that she'd done the wrong thing and wishing she could retract her words. Glancing over, she saw the taut line of his jaw and the shuddered look in his eyes that would no longer meet her own.

"Maybe we could—"

"Go to bed, Mallory," he interrupted thickly. "Go to sleep. I won't trouble you further this evening."

Shoulders sinking, she pushed back her chair and stood. He didn't look at her, just picked up his wineglass and drank what remained as she walked from the room.

Adam's fingers tightened around his now-empty wine goblet, so forcefully he was surprised the glass didn't shatter in his hand.

So, she doesn't want me in her bed tonight, he thought. *She's tired and wishes to sleep.*

Perhaps she *was* tired in spite of her nap in the coach. The past two weeks had been exhausting, he conceded, and today especially so. Still, he knew weariness had nothing to do with her wish not to consummate their marriage. Ever since she'd come downstairs for dinner, she'd been on edge, nervous and awkward in a way he'd never known her to be. But he sensed that her reserve came from more than simple bridal nerves and a woman's natural concern about making love for the first time.

That he could have handled.

That he could have soothed away with patience and a gentle, assured touch.

Nor was it a lack of passion on her part, for in spite of her innocence, he'd felt her response each time he held her in his arms. He knew women, understood what gave them pleasure, and he was in no doubt that Mallory desired him. When he had his hands on her, she burned, and it wasn't mere conceit that made him think so.

No, if it was as he suspected, her reticence stemmed

from a sense of misplaced loyalty and guilt. Before taking her vows with him today, she'd sworn herself to Hargreaves. Now his rival was holding her to her promise— even from beyond the grave.

For all Adam knew, she might not consciously recognize the reason for her behavior. Perhaps she was feeling a sense of doubt and hesitation about their relationship and thought it would be easier to remain his friend rather than become his lover. That way she wouldn't have to accept a new level of intimacy between them. That way she wouldn't have to stop clinging to her memory of Michael Hargreaves—or her love for the other man.

For therein lay the problem.

She might be his wife, but she hadn't chosen him. They might be married, but regardless of what the law recognized, Mallory could only obey what was in her heart— and for her, it wasn't him.

Oh, she loved him in her way, he knew, but she wasn't *in love* with him. She desired him, but it was with a kind of guilty pleasure unworthy of the pure, peerless love she'd shared with "her major."

Bloody perfect Hargreaves, he cursed, as he clenched his hands against the arms of his chair. *The honorable selfless hero whose memory can't be sullied or disdained.*

Were he competing against a flesh-and-blood rival, he would have stood a fair chance. But how did a man battle a ghost? How could he hope to win her love when she idolized the recollection of a dead man that would never be changed?

Thank heavens he hadn't told her how he felt, that he hadn't offered his heart to her on a silver salver, then given her the knife with which to slice it in two. He'd spared himself that particular indignity, at least. Left that small sliver of pride mercifully intact.

For all the good it did him.

For all the satisfaction he received, knowing he would be spending his wedding night alone.

Because she was tired.

Because she would rather be alone, left in solitude to think and dream of someone else.

Pain spread like a poison through his veins. With trembling hands, he reached for the brandy decanter the servant had set on the table during the last course. Pulling out the crystal stopper, he poured himself a hefty draught and tossed it back in a long, burning swallow. He coughed, then poured another, downing the second with another punishing gulp.

Taking up the glass and bottle, he surged to his feet, his every thought filled with Mallory. He imagined her upstairs, attired in some frothy nightgown as she relaxed against the sheets. She would be soft and sweet, her hair flowing around her in rippling, raven-hued waves.

At only the idea of her, his hunger returned, need clawing at him like a beast that had been denied the very air it breathed, the food and water it ate and drank.

And he had been denied, robbed of what he'd wanted for such a very long time. If he couldn't have her love, then, at the very least, he ought to be able to enjoy her body. But that too was denied him.

Of course, he could always go to her room and seduce her. He possessed the skill. After years of practice, he was well-versed in all the tricks and techniques necessary to rouse a woman to completion. With the right words, the right touches, he could have her writhing beneath him as she begged to be taken. Even given her maiden state, he felt certain he could give her profound pleasure.

Oblivious to the glances of the servants, he strode out into the hallway. Taking the stairs in a forceful stride, he walked toward her bedchamber. Entering her private quarters would be easy given the fact that their two master suites were connected by a door in their respective dressing rooms. He didn't know if she'd noticed the passageway, but he had, having planned to use it when he came to claim his marital rights.

Continuing on to his bedchamber, he stalked inside, startling his waiting valet as he pounded across the carpet-covered stone floors.

"My lord, I trust you had a good repast," Finley said.

Adam mumbled something that resembled a growl. Prowling across to a nearby table, he set down the purloined brandy decanter and glass with a marked lack of care.

"I've laid out your sleeping attire and have hot water with which you may bathe. Shall I assist you to shave and disrobe?"

Adam fixed him with a dark look. "No."

The valet hesitated. "I know this is a special evening, and I thought perhaps—"

"I'll shift for myself. Good night, Finley."

For a moment, the other man looked as if he might make another attempt to be of service. Instead, he paused, then inclined his head. "As you wish, my lord. Ring, should you have any need of me."

"I won't. Not tonight."

The only one I have need of tonight is Mallory.

With a slight bow, the servant let himself out of the room.

Kicking off his shoes, Adam went to the washstand and splashed warm water into the basin. Stripping off his cravat, he flung it aside, followed by his shirt, which he shucked off over his head in a single pull.

Leaning over, he rinsed his face, chest, and under his arms. Toweling himself dry, he poured a fresh bowl of water and reached for his toothbrush and tooth powder. Teeth clean, he tossed the brush aside and went across to gather his robe. Divesting himself of his trousers, he slid into the brown silk garment and yanked the belt tight around his waist.

Ready, he turned and stalked across to the connecting door, his hand closing over the knob. But even as he began to turn it, he thought again of Mallory's words.

Would you mind terribly if you didn't come to my room tonight?

Suddenly he stopped.

Hell and damnation, what am I doing?

He'd promised he would honor her request, that he would let her sleep and not trouble her again this evening. Was he really going to barge into her room and wake her? Was he truly going to seduce her and, by doing so, run the risk of his need turning to something more—something dark and wrong that he would never be able to take back?

No matter his longing, he would never, ever, do anything to hurt her. Regardless of his pain, he loved her far too much.

Squeezing his eyes shut, he bit out a curse and released the handle. He turned away, running his fingers through his hair as if he feared he'd gone just a little mad.

Walking back into his bedchamber, he bent to pick up the glass and decanter, carrying them across to a large chair by the fire. Pouring a dram, he sat and stared into the flames, wondering how long it would be before he too could sleep.

Mallory sighed and beat a fist against her pillow before rolling onto her side. Eyes wide, she stared into the darkness, then sighed again.

I can't sleep, she thought.

No matter how she tried, she was finding it impossible to relax, impossible to rest. After the day she'd had—not to mention the past few weeks—she should have dropped off the moment she pulled the sheets over herself.

Instead, she'd spent the past two hours lying awake, her mind running in circles as she thought again and again about what she'd said to Adam at dinner. Seeing over and over the taut, withdrawn expression on his face, the blank glaze in his eyes that she knew he'd used to mask his hurt over her rejection.

Because even if she hadn't meant it as such, she had rejected him. After all, this was their wedding night, and she'd told him she wanted to be alone. Told him she didn't want him, when it wasn't actually true.

She did want Adam.

She was just so confused, her emotions too over-wrought to be intimate with him tonight, to let him claim her virginity. And yet, perhaps his touch was exactly what she needed, his kisses the oblivion she ultimately craved.

Still, she was scared, afraid in ways even she didn't fully understand. Her fear was the reason she'd refused him tonight. Her worry the cause of this rift she'd caused between them.

If she had the chance to do it all over again, she would never have said a word. She would simply have done as Adam suggested and come upstairs. Penny could have helped her change into the same shockingly diaphanous pink silk nightgown she was wearing now—an addition Madame and Mama had obviously slipped into her traveling case without her knowledge—and left her to wait for Adam.

But she hadn't, and now he was angry.

She hadn't and now, worst of all, he was hurt.

Adam was a proud man, and she'd spurned him on their

very first night as husband and wife. How long would it be before he forgave her? If he forgave her at all?

Sighing again, she rolled onto her back and thumped her hands against the covers. If only she could sleep, she wouldn't be having this uncomfortable inner debate. She would be lost in dreams—or perhaps nightmares, and heaven knows she didn't want to contemplate that. Luckily, she hadn't had another nightmare since the evening she'd asked Adam to stay with her.

The night that had landed them both in holy wedlock.

Yet Adam hadn't complained or struggled against the situation. He'd merely accepted and tried to make the best of being forced to take her as his wife. Swallowing against the lump in her throat, she sat up, wondering suddenly if perhaps that's what she should do as well. Stop struggling and simply be his wife, regardless of her qualms or reservations.

Was he asleep? she wondered. Was it possible he was having as much difficulty resting as she?

She knew he was in his bedchamber, since she'd heard him come upstairs some while ago. The door had opened and closed, a low rumble of masculine voices drifting briefly down the hallway as he'd exchanged a few words with his valet. The servant had left soon after, presumably to seek his own bed, then the house had fallen quiet.

Swinging her legs off the side of the bed, she reached for the tinder on the nearby table, then lighted a candle. A golden glow drove away the surrounding shadows, providing her with enough illumination that she was able to locate her robe.

Before she gave herself more time to consider, she slipped her arms into the garment, then returned for the candlestick.

The flame flickered as she carried it before her. Crossing the suite, she wondered if the connecting door Penny had mentioned would be easy to find, and more importantly, unlocked.

She located it with little difficulty; the door was made of ordinary, painted wood set into the wall on the far side of the dressing room. Approaching on bare feet, she reached for the handle. The metal was cool against her fingers, her heart thundering inside her chest, as she hesitated one last moment.

What if he was asleep?

What if he wasn't?

Knowing there was only one way to find out, she forced herself to turn the knob. To her relief, the hinges were well oiled, so there was no squeak to announce her presence. Although her candle unfortunately acted as a beacon in the darkness.

Making her way through his dressing room, she paused at the edge of his bedchamber and glanced toward his bed.

Empty.

So he is awake.

Her heart pounded violently again—although whether it was with relief or disappointment she wasn't sure. Then she saw him seated in a large chair near the fireplace, his face hidden in the shadows, his long legs stretched out beneath his robe.

Had he seen her?

What should she say?

Before she had time to decide, he leaned slightly forward and met her gaze. "What are you doing here?" he asked, deep and rough.

"I . . . um . . . I couldn't sleep."

A long pause followed. "Another nightmare?" His tone sounded faintly bitter this time and less than sympathetic.

"No. I came to talk."

He gave a humorless laugh. "Talk, is it? If that's why you've come, then you can save it for later. I'm not in the mood at the moment, rather like you weren't earlier."

She cringed, never having seen him in such a foul temper. Clearly the situation was every bit as bad as she'd imagined. She'd known he might be angry, but not like this.

Leaning back in his chair, he swirled the contents of the glass in his hand, ignoring her as if she'd already departed.

She gripped the candle tighter, a leaden sensation plummeting to the bottom of her stomach. Obviously, he'd been drinking, but he was notoriously good at holding his liquor, and if he was inebriated, she couldn't tell.

"Still here?" he demanded, startling her. "I thought you were tired."

"I was."

"Well then, run along, why don't you?" Suddenly he sighed, the sound filled with woeful resignation. "Go to bed, Mallory."

She hesitated, tremors chasing over her skin. "As you wish, my lord."

He gave a derisive grunt, plainly expecting her to turn and leave. Instead, she walked deeper into the room, not knowing where she found the nerve.

"What are you doing now?" he asked, brows drawn into a fearsome scowl.

Without meeting his gaze, she crossed to the far side of the chamber where the mahogany tester bed stood, one that appeared to be even more enormous than her own. Pulling back the covers, she climbed in.

Chapter 17

A dam stared, his eyes growing wide as he peered around the side of his chair at the bed and the woman who now lay upon it.

His mind must be playing tricks on him, he decided, or else it was the liquor—though in actual fact he hadn't imbibed that much, certainly not enough to get him so foxed he would be seeing things. Studying her, he watched as she stretched out against the sheets, her long hair spilling over the pillows as he'd earlier fantasized.

His eyes narrowed, wondering why she'd changed her mind.

He'd never known Mallory to be untruthful, yet he wondered if she had been dissembling when she'd said she hadn't had another nightmare.

Was she scared and in want of company, but knew he was in too dreadful a mood to comfort her right now?

Had she been dreaming of Hargreaves again, yet hesitated to mention it for fear of upsetting him further? Well, if that was the case, she could get out of his bed right now and return to hers.

She was sadly mistaken if she thought he would act like some damned eunuch and lie there next to her without claiming his husbandly rights. If it's sleep she wanted, she could do it in her own bed. As for company, she could call Penny. Let her maidservant stay up all night with her. Of course if she did call Penny, there would be talk of a different kind.

Plague take it, he didn't care. Let the servants chatter and spread rumors. Everyone except her immediate family thought he'd taken her innocence already. As for gossip of trouble between them, it was no more than what half the Ton expected, despite word that theirs was a love match. Which he supposed was half-true given that one of them was in love.

Whatever her motivation, he decided, he would have the truth out of her soon enough.

Then they would see.

Setting down his glass with a thump, he surged to his feet. The edges of his robe flapped around his calves as he crossed the distance between them in a few long-legged strides. Stopping beside the bed, he gazed down, detecting fresh anxiety in her eyes.

"So, you've had a change of heart, have you?" he said, not worrying if he loomed over her. "I thought you were tired and didn't want to be with me tonight."

"I *was* tired, but I couldn't sleep."

"Yes, so you said. Shall I climb in with you then?"

"If that's what you want," she said in a tremulous voice.

Placing his hands on either side of her, he leaned down. "Oh, I want a great many things, Mallory Gresham, and if you stay here in this bed, you'll find out exactly what they are. So, you're ready to be my wife now, are you?"

"Y-yes," she whispered.

"Then why haven't you taken off your robe? I'm sure you don't generally sleep in that particular garment."

A flush crept up her neck and into her cheeks, a becoming pink that made her even prettier than she was already. "B-because of my nightgown."

"What about your nightgown?"

"It's . . . it's sheer."

He stilled, his pulse beat faster as blood pooled low. "How sheer?"

"Could we not just blow out the candles?"

Abruptly curious, he shook his head. "No, we could not."

"Adam—"

"I assure you, I'll be seeing a great deal more of you than this nightgown." He paused. "Unless you're not actually planning to stay, after all."

Lines formed on her brow. "Of course I am."

"So you didn't have another nightmare?"

Her eyes turned round. "No."

"You didn't wake up and feel afraid?"

"I never went to sleep. I told you, I couldn't rest." She studied him with a questioning gaze. "Is that what you think? That I came here because I was too frightened to be by myself?"

"Are you?" he charged.

"No!"

"Then why are you here," he demanded, "since you sure as Hades didn't want to be earlier?"

"Because I'm sorry."

"Sorry, are you?"

"Yes. I didn't mean what I said at dinner. I was just nervous and scared, and I feel terrible for ruining our wedding night. I know I hurt you, and that's the last thing

I would ever want to do. Don't be angry with me, Adam. Please."

"I'm not angry," he denied, his heart twisting at her words.

"Yes, you are, and you have every right to be." Reaching up, she urged him to sit down next to her on the bed. When he did, she sat up and locked her arms around his chest, leaning her face against his shoulder. "I'm your wife. I should be with you."

"So, it's guilt then, is it? You're here to do your duty?"

"No, I . . . no, I want you as well."

But in spite of her words, he could tell there was indeed a measure of guilt involved, as well as a desire for them not to be at odds. She wanted to be friends again, and she was willing to be intimate with him if it would soothe his wounded feelings. He realized she was being honest about being scared, which he had to admit was only natural given the fact that she'd never made love before.

Part of him knew he ought to be offended that she was offering herself for reasons of obligation and guilt.

Another part urged him not to be a fool.

She's in your bed. What more do you want?

Love?

But he would take whatever he could get for the moment and worry about the rest at another time. She was his wife, after all. He had days and months and years to woo her. Somehow, he would make her love him. If it took his whole life, he would find a way.

Deciding he'd wasted enough of their wedding night already, he slid his hand into her hair and gently tipped her head back. Without giving her time to say another word, he took her mouth, parting her lips so he could delve inside.

She shuddered, yielding to his demand, answering

his claim with a willing response of her own. Tongues tangling, he drew on her with the hunger of a starving man, losing himself in her flavor and scent, roses and warm, womanly flesh that filled his senses and clouded his thoughts.

At length, he broke their kiss, gazing into her vivid jewel-colored eyes as he eased her slowly back onto the bed.

"Well, now," he said on a husky rasp. "Let's take a look at this nightgown."

Mallory quivered, her pulse throbbing wildly in her veins.

He'd forgiven her, she realized with relief—his anger now turned to passion. So too had her worries, as if his touch carried some magical property that had the power to drive away all doubt and fear and replace it with desire. So long as she was in his arms, nothing else seemed to matter. When she was with him, everything felt right. If only she'd reminded herself of that earlier, this evening's trouble could have been avoided. As for what the morning might bring, she would deal with it then, whatever it might be.

Despite her newfound confidence, however, she tensed when he opened her robe, her natural modesty asserting itself as he peeled the thin fabric away from her body. Closing her eyes, she waited, imagining his gaze roaming over the nearly transparent confection of silk and lace and the way her flesh was scarcely hidden beneath it.

"Beautiful," he said in a reverent tone. His fingers curved against her neck, caressing her in a slow, sleek glide that went from throat to collarbone, then down the length between her breasts. Her lips parted on a silent in-halation, a fine tremor radiating outward to the tips of her fingers and the ends of her toes, nerve endings sparking wherever he roamed.

He went lower, taking his time as he skimmed his fingers over the flat plane of her stomach, pausing to circle around her navel before continuing on.

Her eyes flashed wide when he stopped, gasping as he placed his palm just above the triangle of curls that lay at the juncture of her legs.

"I approve your choice of attire," he said. "It leaves just enough to the imagination to be interesting. A shame you'll have so little opportunity to wear it."

"I won't?" she asked breathlessly.

"No." His fingers glided upward again, slowing as they reached her breast. "Since I have every intention of taking it off you." He flicked a thumb over one nipple. "And keeping it off you."

A fresh gasp filled her lungs, along with a shudder that was as shocking as it was exciting.

Rather than reaching immediately for the hem of her nightgown though, he leaned forward and crushed his mouth to hers again, kissing her with an intensity that was hot and lush and voluptuous. He was tender yet demanding, patient yet rash, eliciting a range of sensations that sent her spinning.

All the while, his hands were far from idle, strumming in languorous caresses over her breasts and belly, her hips and thighs. The thin layer of silk that separated them created a tantalizing friction, one she was helpless to resist as her body turned aching and pliant.

The room faded, shrinking down so that it seemed as if no one and nothing else existed except Adam and the bed on which the two of them lay.

Abandoning her mouth, he dappled her skin with a line of kisses, his lips moving over her cheeks and eyelids, her temples and chin and neck. Locating a particularly sensitive area behind her ear, he drew the edge of his tongue over the spot in a slow glide before blowing against it. His warm breath sent concussive shivers racing deep inside her veins, then again as he kissed his way downward until he reached her breasts.

She arched in a delirious haze as he drew one of her nipples into his mouth, suckling her through its lace covering. Her senses caught fire, wet heat pooling between her thighs as if the two spots were somehow connected. She ought to have been mortified, she supposed, or at least faintly stunned. Instead she found herself wanting more—craving his kiss, his touch, his possession, whatever it might entail.

As though he were attuned to her thoughts, one of his wandering hands eased beneath her hem, the material gathering against his wrist as his fingers glided upward. From calf to knee to thigh, he crept higher, her flesh burning everywhere he touched. When he reached her inner thigh, he paused, fanning his thumb in a wide arc that made her flesh yearn and quiver as it turned weak as jelly.

Breath soughed from her parted lips, as she resisted the contrary urge to draw her legs closed, feeling suddenly and inexplicably shy. But she needn't have worried as he continued upward, his hand retracing the path he'd already forged once through the opposite side of the silk.

Reaching the breast on which he'd been feasting, he raised his head and replaced his mouth with his hand, cupping her fully inside his wide, capable palm. Meeting her gaze, he fondled her with a lavish caress that made her moan. "Touch me," he murmured.

For a moment, she wasn't sure she could speak, too awash with emotion to respond.

Leaning over, he kissed her again, his mouth uncompromising against her own. "Touch me," he ordered.

"W-where?" she panted.

"Anywhere," he said, punctuating his words with sultry, drugging kisses. "Everywhere. I have to have your hands on me."

Wanting to please him, to pleasure him as he was pleasuring her, she laid trembling fingers against his cheek. His skin was faintly rough with an evening's growth of whiskers, mildly abrasive in a way that only added enjoyment to his kiss.

As she watched, he closed his eyes, clearly approving the contact despite the innocence of the location. Trailing her fingers lower, she slid them over his bottom lip, finding it silky and warm.

She jumped when he opened his mouth and drew one of her fingers inside, her body throbbing as he swirled his tongue around it as if he were enjoying a sugar stick.

After giving her a teasing, painless bite, he let her go. "Continue," he said. "Touch me more."

But how could she when he did such wicked things? When his fingers continued playing against her breast in ways that were driving her half-mad?

Somehow though, she did as he asked, sliding her hand along his throat to his chest where the edges of his robe parted to reveal a section of his taut, hair-roughened muscles. With a boldness that surprised her, she eased her hand beneath the lapel and traced his form, intrigued by the contrasts in textures as well as the warmth, finding him delectably toasty.

In response, Adam pulled in a breath, clearly enraptured by her tentative exploration, the look on his face encouraging her to proceed. Without intending to, she flicked her fingertip over his flat male nipple, causing the nub to draw even tighter.

He gave her nipple an answering pinch, using just enough pressure to send a sharp, throbbing ache straight to the place between her thighs. Her legs shifted restlessly, her body afire.

With an ease that astonished her, he stripped off her robe, then just as quickly cast her nightgown onto the floor after it. She barely had an instant to acknowledge her nakedness, or for her shyness to return, before he deftly parted her thighs and slid a long finger inside her.

Her eyes flew open, a gasp issuing from her throat that turned instantly to a moan, as a flood of the most extraordinary pleasure burst inside her.

Laying her back against the sheets, he fastened his lips to one of her breasts again, drawing upon her with a wet suction that was just this side of heaven. And all the while, he stroked her, his finger moving inside in a steady, soul-stealing rhythm.

When he added a second finger, her mind grew dim, senses caught in a torrent of pleasure from which there could be no escape. Nor did she wish there to be, all inhibition seemingly erased as his two fingers worked her slick center to devastating purpose.

He eased her thighs farther apart and caressed her even more intimately, moans she couldn't hold back issuing from her mouth in short, staccato bursts. Her hands curled against the bedclothes, nails digging into the linens with a grip that threatened to leave rips. Then suddenly he pressed her with the heel of his palm, rubbing her in a way that made stars explode behind her eyelids.

The room spun, her body caught in a maelstrom of delight that had her hips arching upward as if to capture more. Pleasure rippled through her in waves as reality shifted on its axis.

Sighing, she sank back.

Floating.

Smiling.

But if she imagined she'd reached the heights of bliss, she was quickly disabused of the notion as he slid down her body and settled himself between her legs. Dazed, she couldn't speak as he hooked one of her legs over his shoulder, then slid his hands beneath her buttocks to angle her toward him.

This is it. He's going to have me now, she thought. Yet if that was the case, why was he still wearing his robe? And why had he stretched himself across the mattress in a way that didn't seem quite right?

Their gazes met over the length of her naked form, his large hands gripping her, controlling her. "You're small and I could cause you a lot of pain," he said in a gravelly voice. "I plan to make sure you're good and ready when I take you. Don't be shocked, sweetheart. I promise you'll like this."

Like what?

The question barely formed in her mind before Adam leaned low and kissed her in a place that made her eyes open wide and every last bit of air whoosh from her lungs.

She shuddered, hips twisting in his hands. But he held her steady, forcing her to accept the possession of his mouth, as his tongue darted in and out to lick and suckle in the most overwhelming way.

He'd told her not to be shocked, but she was.

He'd promised she would like the things he was doing to her body, and he was right. More than right, pleasure sizzling through her veins and sinew, all the way to her bones.

A low, keening cry warbled from her lips—hot, violent need pounding inside her as his touch erased some last lingering bit of maidenly reserve. She rolled her head against the pillow, writhing in his grasp, wanting more, wanting him.

Reaching down, she threaded her fingers into his hair and pressed him closer. She thought she heard him chuckle before he renewed his efforts in a way that soon had her soaring with rapture.

He drove her up, pushing her over her peak, only to start again seconds after. She climaxed, how many times she didn't know, her mind and body utterly saturated in intense sensual gratification. By the time he stopped, she was nearly insensate, limp and lax and exhausted.

She watched out of dazed eyes as he sat up and stripped off his robe, revealing his large, powerful body, and the big, heavy arousal that jutted from his hips. She thought she saw his shaft pulse, a drop of moisture appearing at the tip.

Under different circumstances, she might have experienced a few qualms, but she was too relaxed to be anxious, too satiated to do more than admire his impressive physique—and the first male member she'd ever glimpsed.

Stretching out beside her, he took her in his arms.

"Adam, I don't think I can, you know . . . again," she whispered.

"Come?"

She nodded. "But I'm ready now. I want you to take your ease."

He smiled. "Oh, I will. And you will too. I'll make sure of it."

Pulling her tighter, he crushed her mouth beneath his, abruptly impatient, suddenly wild. He kissed her as if he couldn't get enough, as if they'd passed some point from which there was no return. And there was no going back, she realized, their intimacy forging a bond that could never be undone. Nor did she want it to be, suddenly reveling in their closeness.

Wanting to please him, she answered his passion, kissing him back with every ounce of energy that remained in her body. He'd given her such pleasure already. He deserved to find his own.

Yet, to her complete amazement, her desire soon began to reawaken, Adam stroking her with a clear master's touch.

Aching and needy, she clung, running her palms over the warm, smooth length of his back and shoulders, then lower along his spine in a move that made his muscles ripple with clear approval.

Senses awash, she drank in his delectable, brandy-tinged taste, breathed in the heady musk of his skin, which turned her hot and giddy. Delirious with passion, she tangled her fingers in his hair and held him closer, angling her mouth and tongue so that she could return his kisses with the same fervid ardor as he displayed.

With the sound of her unsteady breath ringing in her ears and her desire heightened once more to a fever pitch, she made no demur when he parted her thighs and settled himself over her.

Without further preliminaries, he thrust inside, sheathing himself so that he only went as deep as her body could accept. Pausing, he held himself steady and leaned down to brush soothing, tender kisses over her trembling mouth. Then he thrust again, causing a sharp burst of pain to twist inside her.

She cried out, unable to think or breathe as she struggled to adjust to the sensation of having him inside her—his shaft so large that it seemed a miracle they fit together at all.

Yet, inexplicably, the pain began to recede, the ravenous hunger he'd awakened earlier returning to lay siege to both her body and her mind.

As if aware of the change, he eased back, then thrust again, lodging himself even deeper, her channel growing hotter and wetter than before, leaving her so slick that his powerful penetration seemed exactly right.

Absolutely perfect.

Murmuring endearments into her ear, he coaxed her to wrap her legs around his waist. Then he began to move, setting up a rhythm that made her toes curl with delight and her heart hammer at a mad pace inside her chest.

Moaning, she clutched her arms around his wide shoulders and closed her eyes, abandoned to the ecstasy rippling through her like a rising tide. He leaned low and took her mouth, using his tongue to ravish her with the same thoroughness he was using to claim her below. The double penetration was nearly her undoing, her senses all but overwhelmed as a new rush of longing burned bonfire hot. She quaked, wondering if she might go insane from the force of the sensations rippling through her, and from the hard, raw, yearning demand that pounded like a gale.

Sliding his palm down, he cupped one of her breasts and caressed the peak, making her groan and thrust her hips up to meet his own relentless demand.

She shuddered, needing release so badly she thought she might cry. Seeming to understand her frustration, her yearning, he slipped his hands beneath her bottom and angled her, shifting so that on his next stroke, she had no choice but to take his full and complete penetration.

Her head arched back, a wail echoing from her lips as the world split wide, darkness threatening to engulf her as she plunged into a maelstrom of ecstasy. Quivering, she let pleasure sweep through her in an explosion of light and heat and joy. She didn't know what heaven was like, but she suspected this must be close.

Above her, Adam continued thrusting, quickening his movements to a frenzied pace until he gave a hoarse shout, his hand clenched in the pillow beside her head as he claimed his own satisfaction.

For long moments, their ragged breathing was the only sound in the room, his body lying heavily on top of hers. But she didn't mind, nestling her face against his shoulder to savor his scent and warmth.

After less than a minute, he eased away, rolling onto his back. But he wasn't abandoning her, quite the opposite, Adam reaching out to tug her gently against his chest to cradle her in his arms.

"Get some rest," he murmured, kissing her temple and cheek.

"Hmm," she agreed, still floating on a haze of bliss.

"I plan to wear you out again soon, so you'll need the sleep."

"Oh. All right."

Chuckling, he ran his hand over her back and along her arm in a sweeping caress. Half-asleep already, she turned and burrowed even closer.

Not long after, she heard him whisper something against her hair, words sounding curiously of devotion, oddly of love. But she was too drowsy to concentrate, too replete to pay them any heed as she drifted on the brink of sleep.

Vaguely, she sensed him reaching down to pull the covers over them both, brushing her hair back from her face as he kissed her forehead again.

Then darkness swept over her, and she knew no more.

Chapter 18

Mallory opened her eyes several hours later to find Adam awake and watching her, his head propped on his bent arm as he lay beside her in bed. Sunlight edged past the curtains, revealing all the corners that had lain in darkness the evening before. A tiny frown marred her forehead as she took a moment to remember the night just past, a faint warmth creeping over her skin when she did.

He grinned, obviously reading her thoughts. "Good morning."

"Good morning."

Becoming aware that she was lying naked from the waist up, she reached for the covers.

Adam stopped her with a hand. "No need for that," he said, his gaze moving over her breasts. "I assure you the view is exquisite." Eyes twinkling, he flicked a fingertip over her nipple and watched her flesh draw tight. "As I said, exquisite."

Pleasurable shivers chased over her skin before gathering with a yearning ache between her legs. She shifted against the bedclothes, wondering how she could already want him again after the night he'd just given her. A glimpse at the tented shape of the sheet draped over his hips showed he felt the same. Smiling again, he leaned down and kissed her, his mouth moving in a tender, yet thorough claiming.

"Shall we remain abed this morning?" he asked in a husky drawl. "Or might you be a tad too sore to indulge in any more love play at present?"

Shifting her legs again, she realized she was sore, a pang of discomfort making itself known. And no wonder, she thought, recalling the stunning force and rapture of his possession. Just the memory of it was enough to make her tremble. Theirs truly had been a wedding night to remember.

"From your silence, I can tell I shall have to restrain myself, until tonight at least," he said. "For now, I think a hot bath is in order. Shall I ring for Penny?"

She nodded, pleased by the suggestion.

"While you're getting ready, think about what you'd like to do today."

"Do?"

"Of course. If I can't spend the day tupping you, as I'd prefer, then we shall be forced to resort to some other means of amusing ourselves. A ride is likely out, so I suggest either a visit down to the beach or else a jaunt into town. I understand there's a rather decent village less than a mile away." Kissing her again, he slid his lips across to her ear. "I hear they have shops."

"Shops, do they?"

"Hmm. Shall I take you on a raid?"

A laugh burst from her lips, a playful sound that left

a comfortable glow in its wake. It was a sensation she hadn't experienced in a very long while—not since Michael . . . She stilled, waiting for the usual chill to sweep over her. But it didn't, the warmth of Adam's gaze, the reassurance of his touch, too strong to let anything ruin the harmony of her mood.

Actually, as she considered the idea, a day spent strolling and shopping with Adam sounded quite pleasant—more than pleasant really. The excursion sounded wonderful. "Well, if you insist," she told him in a jaunty tone, "who am I to refuse?"

Laughing himself this time, he pressed his mouth to hers for another exuberant joining, kissing her until her thoughts turned hazy, scattering like feathers cast into a swirling breeze.

By the time he eased away, her pulse was thudding madly, her senses energized by a delicious layer of need.

Perhaps they should stay in bed, after all, she thought with a lazy smile. Then she slid a leg upward over his and decided once again that they shouldn't.

Having apparently noticed her slight wince, he leaned away. "I'll ring for your maid. Go on, and she'll be with you directly."

Dropping another kiss on her lips, he rose from the bed. Tossing back the covers, she reluctantly did the same.

Shrugging into his robe, Adam watched Mallory make her way through the connecting door. For a moment he nearly called her back, wanting to suggest they scandalize the servants and take a bath together. But he stopped himself, knowing he'd never be able to keep his hands off her if he did. Not now, not after he'd experienced the breathless, soul-stealing heaven of her embrace.

He'd known it would be good between them, he just

hadn't realized how good. And to think last night had been her first time. Just imagine what it would be like once he'd had a chance to teach her how to tap into the core of her sensuality. Just imagine the pleasure they would share in each other's arms, with each other's bodies.

As for more, she would love him in time, he assured himself. Already, she was laughing and smiling. Only one day of marriage, and she was more like the joyous, playful Mallory he'd once known so well.

Of course there'd been that moment, he remembered as he crossed to ring for his own hot bath, the instant when he'd seen that look in her eyes—the one she got whenever she thought of Hargreaves. But it hadn't remained long, especially after he'd kissed her, determined to pleasure her until she couldn't think of anyone or anything but him.

Her husband.

The man with whom she would spend her life, raise her children, grow more and more contented until both of them were old and wrinkled and grey. With each sunrise, the memory of Michael Hargreaves would lessen and grow more indistinct. And with each sunset, the only man who consumed her heart and mind would be Adam.

A knock sounded at the door. Calling permission for the servant to enter, he stood and began to get ready for the day.

"Oh, I cannot decide," Mallory declared later that afternoon as she stood trying on hats in the local millinery shop. Adam waited patiently nearby, the milliner herself standing at the ready to assist Mallory as she studied her reflection in the mirror.

"The trim on this one is such a lovely color," Mallory said, turning her head to get a glimpse of the chip-straw bonnet from all angles.

"Seafoam blue, your ladyship," the milliner told her with a proud smile. "I dyed it meself to match the ocean here on our very shores."

Mallory smiled at the woman's description, the air inside the shop tinged with the pleasant scents of sea brine, woven straw, silk and ostrich feathers. "Yet the one with the apple blossoms is very sweet as well," Mallory continued, once again inspecting the selection of hats. "Then there's the shape of that adorable carriage bonnet. Oh, mercy, I just don't see how I can possibly choose between them?"

"Nor should you have to. She'll take them all," Adam stated, addressing the milliner as he strolled forward. "See to it they are boxed up and sent 'round to the castle."

"But Adam, that's six hats!" Mallory protested.

"Which all look beautiful on you," he told her before turning again to the milliner. "She'll wear the one she has on now since it reminds me of her eyes. Pray have the bonnet in which she arrived boxed and sent along with the others."

"Of course, yer lordship," the shop owner said, smiling as wide as her mouth would stretch. "It will be my express pleasure. I'll see 'em wrapped m'self and have my son drive 'em over in the dog cart this very afternoon."

"Adam," Mallory said in a low voice, as the other woman collected a pair of the hats and stepped away to pack them. "What are you thinking? One, or even two, would have sufficed."

"Mayhap. But you like them all, so why not indulge? I warned you we'd be raiding the shops."

Lines of concern formed on her forehead. "Well, yes, but still–"

"Your frugality is appreciated, sweetheart, but entirely unnecessary." Bending down, he stole a quick kiss that made her lips tingle. "Besides, I don't believe you ever worried about overspending when your brother was paying the bills."

"No, but that's because Ned has more money than most small countries. I suspect he's as wealthy as the royals."

Adam sent her a look. "Wealthier, I think. But not to worry, I believe I can still afford to buy you a few bonnets here and there."

"I'm sorry," she amended, realizing she might have wounded his pride. "I didn't mean to imply—"

"I know you didn't, but you are not to be concerned. I have lots of money these days, and it's my pleasure to spend some of it on you. Just be glad we're not at a jewelers, or you'd likely have six new baubles by now," he teased.

She relaxed, a slow smile curving across her mouth. "Six, is it? Why not seven? One for each day of the week. If you aren't careful, you know, I just might take you up on that offer."

"When next we're in London, it's off to Rundell and Bridge we'll go."

"Adam—"

"*Mallory.*" Meeting her gaze, he waggled his eyebrows.

A laugh burst from her, loud enough that she clapped a gloved palm over her mouth to muffle the sound. But Adam tugged her hand down to hold inside his own.

"Isn't there something you'd like to say to me?" he asked.

She knew exactly what he meant, but decided to tease him back a bit. "No," she replied with mock innocence. "I cannot think of a thing."

"Can you not?" he growled, clearly aware of her ploy. "If you don't watch yourself, madam, I may tell the shopkeeper not to box up those bonnets after all."

"But you'd ruin her day."

"Most probably her week, since my guess is that it usually takes her that long to sell six bonnets."

"We can't have that," Mallory murmured.

He stepped closer. "No indeed."

She inched nearer as well. "Thank you, Adam."

"You are most welcome. Now, what other ways have you thought of to express your gratitude?" he asked, giving her hand a light squeeze.

Her eyes widened. "Nothing I can do here."

"She's in the back, packing everything away. We're entirely alone."

"But we might not remain that way." Her heart began to race as memories of their night together flashed in her mind. She met his gaze and saw an answering gleam, suddenly aware that he'd read her thoughts again—a most annoying ability. "I never fully realized before, but you are a wicked man."

A grin spread across his mouth. "And you are absolutely enchanting. Now give me a kiss before she returns."

"We ought to simply be on our way. A nice stroll along the beach would be lovely."

"It would, *after* you kiss me. Come on, wife, and don't spare the tongue."

"Adam!"

"Hurry up. Tick-tock, time's a wasting."

"I ought to box your ears, is what I ought to do."

He took hold of her other hand and pulled her against him. "But you won't."

No, she conceded silently. He was in no danger from her. Quite the opposite, in fact, since she was the one whose emotional equilibrium seemed at risk.

Kiss him here in a millinery shop! What other outrageous things will he want me to do?

But as she considered the question, she realized chances were good she wouldn't refuse him anything, whether they were in public or private, in bed or out.

Flushing over the thought, she cast a glance toward the curtains that separated the front of the shop from the back, then arched up on her toes. "Well, come down here so I can reach you."

Chuckling, he did as she asked.

She closed her eyes a moment after their lips touched, pressing against him so she could find a good angle. One of his arms curved around her waist, holding her steady as her mouth moved against his with a soft, sweet pressure. Pulse hammering, she pulled away—or tried to since he wouldn't let her go.

"Where was my tongue?" he asked.

"Where it always is," she retorted, "in your mouth!"

He grinned. "One more, with lots of feeling."

"You want feeling, do you?"

"Definitely."

Glancing behind her again to make sure they were still alone, she arched against him and crushed her lips to his, opening her mouth so she could slide her tongue inside his. She intended to keep this second kiss brief as well, but he tasted too good, felt too intoxicating to stop.

Another few seconds, she mused, *what can it hurt?*

But a few seconds turned to a minute and before she realized it, she was kissing him as if they were the only two people in the world.

"Ahem," came a soft voice. "Pardon me for intruding, but your purchases are ready."

Mallory broke the kiss and tried to step away. Adam refused to let her, though, using the arm he'd looped around her waist to hold her close.

Far from appearing scandalized, the milliner sent them

another wide smile. "I heard tell there were honeymooners up at the castle. It does my heart good to see young love in such full bloom if you don't mind me saying so."

In love? Is that how we look? Mallory wondered.

She supposed it was, given the fact that she and Adam had just been caught kissing. But looks could be deceiving, as she well knew, since Adam didn't love her—not in the romantic sense anyway.

And despite her worries last night, their friendship seemed as solid as ever. Adam still liked her, and after last night, he clearly liked having her in his bed, as well. As for any stronger emotions than friendship or passion, she had no illusions. She'd gone into this marriage with her eyes wide open. She knew why he'd married her, and it wasn't for love.

Rather than disabuse the shopkeeper of her romantic fancies, however, Mallory merely smiled.

"Blessings to ye both on yer marriage," the milliner continued. "May ye always be as happy together as ye are today." The older woman gave them another one of her expansive smiles. "Now, is there any other way I can assist ye both?"

"Actually, there is," Adam said, his words taking Mallory by surprise. "I was wondering if you might direct me to a reputable jeweler here in town. I believe I'm going to buy my wife a new bauble."

Three hours and two baubles later, he and Mallory returned to the castle. In spite of her assurance that she had no need of jewelry, he insisted, selecting a very fine gold-and-sapphire necklace and a brooch made of emeralds, pearls and yellow diamonds that had been fashioned to look like a basket of daffodils—the national flower of Wales.

Perhaps it was a case of pride on his part, but he wanted

to lavish her with more gifts. As he'd told her, he was well able to bear the expense now, and he planned to pamper and keep her in the style to which she had always been accustomed.

"A keepsake of our honeymoon," he said as he pinned the brooch on her gown. "That way you'll never forget this day."

She smiled, eyes twinkling in a way that let him know she was pleased. Unable to resist, he kissed her again, delighting as he watched her cheeks turn pink.

Purchases in hand, he led her outside for their promised stroll along the harbor, then it was time for the carriage ride home.

Dinner that night was the complete opposite of the evening before, the meal one of relaxed conversation and frequent laughter. Rather than picking at her food, Mallory ate with enthusiasm, clearly enjoying the various courses that were laid before them. While they dined, he couldn't keep himself from touching her, reaching over to cradle her hand or stroke a finger across her cheek.

Rather than remaining behind to indulge in the traditional after-dinner glass of port, he accompanied Mallory to the music room, where he spent an hour listening to her play the pianoforte. It was an experience he found both enthralling and frustrating—enthralling because she played so beautifully, frustrating because he couldn't stop thinking about stripping her naked and taking her to bed. But rather than seducing her then and there, he let her go upstairs alone, forcing himself to wait a few minutes before doing the same.

Inside his bedchamber, he washed and shaved, then drew on his robe. Impatient, he went to the connecting door, gave a quick rap on the panel, then walked inside.

Attired in her nightclothes, Mallory sat at the dressing table, her maid behind her, brushing her hair.

"Good evening to you both. Penny, I'll finish this, so why don't you run along to bed." He walked deeper into the room.

The servant paused, then set aside the brush and dipped a respectful curtsey. "As you wish, your lordship. Good night, my lady."

"Good night," Mallory said.

Moments later, he and Mallory were alone.

"She was nearly done," Mallory said. "It wouldn't have taken more than another minute or two."

Strolling over to the dressing table, he picked up the brush. "I'm sure it would not, but now the pleasure is mine."

Moving behind her, he stroked the soft boar's-head bristles through her long tresses, smoothing his hand in its wake. Rich and luxuriant as the finest Chinese silk, her hair flowed over her shoulders and down her back in a thick, raven-dark curtain, shining with vitality.

In the mirror, he watched her eyes slide closed, a sensual glow of enjoyment rising on her skin with each slow, methodical stroke. Taking a heavy length of her hair in one hand, he brushed it all the way to the end, then released it. He did the same with another section, then the next, until each strand was smooth and tangle-free. After a last few sweeps of the brush, he set it on her dressing table.

Moving her hair to one side, he leaned down and buried his face against her neck. "You smell wonderful," he said, breathing in the lush fragrance of her skin.

"It's only soap."

"No, it's you," he murmured as he nuzzled a particularly sensitive area behind her ear. "You're sweet as honey and twice as delicious. I ought to know, having had the exquisite satisfaction of tasting you."

A shudder rippled through her, a tiny moan issuing from between her lips.

Kissing his way along her throat, he slipped his hands around her body and drew her back against him. He held her for a long moment before covering her breasts with his palms.

Sighing, she arched into his grasp, a fresh moan rising on her lips as he began caressing her. Angling her head back another inch, he crushed his mouth to hers, kissing her with a slow, intoxicating possession that left his blood buzzing and his body aching for more.

Much more.

Suddenly ravenous to touch her bare flesh, he slipped his hands beneath the lacy cups of her bodice and fondled her—skin to skin. Her nipples drew into tight little nubs that begged for his attention. Happy to comply, he played with them in ways that clearly drove her wild, her legs shifting restlessly beneath her nightgown, breath beginning to pant from her lungs.

He was no less immune, his shaft jutting hard against her back, throbbing to have her.

All of her.

Every last wonderful, satiny inch.

Straightening, he pulled her to her feet. She swayed for a moment, an expression of hazy confusion on her face.

"You won't be needing these anymore," he said, reaching for her garments. In a few quick tugs, he unclothed her, tossing the thin scraps of silk aside that they fell to the floor in a filmy puddle.

Her natural modesty asserted itself, her palms coming up to shield herself from his gaze. But he refused to allow it, pulling her hands down and holding her arms out to her sides.

"There's no need for that," he told her. "No reason you

should ever feel ashamed. You're beautiful as a goddess, Mallory Gresham, and like a goddess, you should flaunt what nature has seen fit to bestow. Never try to hide your beauty away and most especially never try hiding it from me."

"If I'm not careful, you'll turn me into a complete wanton, my lord."

"Well then, let's make sure not to be careful."

She made a sound that was somewhere between a laugh and a moan as he swept her into his arms and carried her to the bed. Laying her down on the turned-back sheets, he stripped off his robe and joined her.

Kissing her with a greedy delight, he touched her everywhere he could reach, running his palms over each angle and curve as he roused her hunger higher and hotter.

Dizzy from a surfeit of pleasure, Mallory tried to keep pace, her senses overwhelmed from his touch. When he'd stripped off her clothes, she had felt shy. But with each caress he destroyed her inhibitions, with every kiss he made her burn for his possession. Kissing him wildly, she let him draw her deeper into the fire, into a place where nothing was forbidden, and the pursuit and attainment of pleasure was the only rule.

She wanted him to take her, needing him to claim her as fully as he could. Instead of letting her reach her peak as he had last night, he played with her, tormenting them both, as he drove her half-mad with unsatisfied desire.

Did he think she wasn't ready again? Did he plan to enslave her to the point where she was forced to beg? Realizing she no longer cared, she did exactly that.

"Take me, Adam. Please, I want you."

With a faint laugh, he rolled onto his back. "If you want me, then come and get me."

She met his gaze, confused. "W-what do you mean?"

"I mean there are other sexual postures than the one we used last night. Come over here," he invited. "Let me give you a firsthand demonstration."

Crawling to him, she laid her hands on his chest, still uncertain what he wanted her to do.

"Swing a leg over my hips," he said. "It's your turn to be on top tonight."

On top!

For a moment she stared, first into his dark, sensual eyes, then lower, at the very visible expression of his desire thrusting hard and high above his stomach. As she watched, she thought she saw it twitch, his shaft obviously eager for her touch.

"You'll have to help me," she said, sliding forward to do as he asked.

"Gladly, my sweet." Reaching out, he clasped her hips between his broad palms and settled her over him. "You start."

But she didn't know how. With his assistance, she found just the right angle, taking him inside her with several enthralling little pumps. By the time she paused, her heart was beating in a crazy rhythm, her pulse throbbing violently between her temples and lower as if it were connected to her very core.

But she hadn't gone far enough, she realized. She needed him deeper.

"You do the rest," she said, panting. "I can't."

Teeth clenched with clear longing, he took hold of her, then thrust upward in a powerful stroke, his movement seating him fully.

A gasp left her throat, her inner muscles clenching around him, but without so much as a hint of pain.

Quite the contrary.

She bit her lip against the near agony. "Oh, sweet heaven."

He groaned. "I know just what you mean."

Moving his pelvis again, he set up a rhythm, stroking in and out of her in a way that made her entire body burn hot enough to turn to ash. Mirroring his pace, she pumped against him in return, each sensation better than the last.

Pulling her down, he took her mouth, kissing her with an almost frenzied passion as both of them fought to reach their peak. Kissing him back, she gave herself completely to the moment, his touch so good she could barely think, every nerve ending inflamed, her mind and heart about to explode.

Then, without warning, the pleasure claimed her, shaking her with a fury. Crying aloud, she let the rapture take her, shivering as rivulets of bliss streaked outward to pool in her veins and deep, deep inside her bones.

Adam took his satisfaction as well, pouring himself inside her with a soothing warmth.

Limp, she fell forward across his chest, struggling for air.

How long she lay there, she didn't know, everything floating around her in a lovely haze. Adam stroked her hair, his touch only adding to her pleasure.

At length, once she'd recovered sufficiently to move, she leaned up and looked into his eyes. "That was . . . amazing."

He gave her a slow smile. "I was thinking fabulous."

"That too," she said, smiling back.

Tucking her head against his neck, she let herself float again, drawing invisible lines across his chest. As she did, she remembered something he'd said. Curious, she leaned up again. "You mentioned that there's more than one position. So exactly how many are there?"

To her surprise, she felt his shaft stiffen inside her, her words apparently reawakening his desire.

"An infinite variety if one knows what one is doing," he said in a rough voice. "Although I've never taken the time before to actually count." Bumping their hips together, he drew a gasp from her. "Why don't we give it a try? We're at two now, so we've got a long way to go."

Chapter 19

*O*ver the month that followed, each day slid one into the next, Mallory content to let herself drift from moment to hour to day, taking each as it happened.

Thoughts of Michael came to her on occasion, but with less and less frequency as time moved on. At first, when she realized she wasn't thinking about him, a stab of guilt would assail her, leaving her silently anguished. But then Adam would say or do something to divert her attention, his actions invariably punctuated by his physical attentions as well—a warm touch, a bold kiss, a devastating caress that drove everything else away. Before she knew it, Adam, and the pleasure he brought her, were the only things on her mind.

Later, when she came back to herself long enough to remember her earlier guilt over Michael, she would often find herself feeling guilty for a completely different reason. By thinking about Michael, was she somehow betraying Adam? Adam was her husband now, her lover, and more than ever before, her friend. Did she not owe her loyalty to him? But if that were true, then what about Michael? She couldn't forget him completely since that too would be its own sort of betrayal.

Oh, it was all too confusingly troublesome, she decided, and so, as their honeymoon continued, she did her best not to dwell on such thoughts and emotions. Instead, she allowed the hours to slip past, content to let Adam guide her from one moment to the next, satisfied simply to be with him in this special place and time.

During the day, he kept her occupied with a variety of activities—drives and rides and strolls, visits to neighboring towns, serene churches and ancient ruins. Together they explored the natural beauty that Wales had to offer, marveling at its depth and variety. He even took her fishing one afternoon, persuading her to remove her shoes and stockings and pin up her dress to her knees so she could wade across to stand on a likely-looking rock.

Quite soon she discovered that the fish weren't nibbling, but Adam was, as he led her back to shore so he could nuzzle her neck and a great deal more besides.

Pulling her down onto a blanket he'd earlier spread over the grass, he made love to her, showing her yet another new sexual position that left her both delighted and dazed.

When it came to carnal passions, he never failed to please her and please her often. They made love at least twice a day, in the morning and at night, and sometimes more. In fact, as their honeymoon went on, Adam's appetite for her only seemed to increase, growing ever bolder and more inventive.

There was another afternoon she didn't think she would ever forget when he'd slipped off his shoe at the nuncheon table and proceeded to rub her with his stocking foot and toes. She'd spent the entire meal in complete agony, having no notion of whether she ate or not. She'd been nearly frantic by the time he finally dismissed the footman. But rather than leading her upstairs to their bed, he locked the door and took her there in the dining room instead—first on the table, then again with her seated in his lap, his falls open and her skirts drawn up to her waist.

As she'd lain limp and replete against him, he'd murmured they were up to number thirty-six and promised he'd show her thirty-seven later that night. To her exhausted satisfaction, he more than kept his vow. Adding yet another variation, he left her amazed to find her bones still intact, since she'd thought they must surely have melted from the rapture.

But now the time had finally arrived to leave; their honeymoon was nearly over.

Watching Penny as she packed the last of Mallory's clothes into her trunk, Mallory found herself wishing she and Adam could stay here indefinitely. Mayhap she ought to write Quentin and India and ask for more time? But even though Adam never said a word on the subject, she knew he needed to return to Gresham Park. He'd neglected his business concerns and the improvements being made to the estate for more than a month already.

Like it or not, she knew, it was time to return to the real world.

Concealing a sigh, she reached for her gloves and bonnet—an adorable green velvet yeoman's hat finished in the front with a white ostrich feather that curved just above her eyes. It was one of the six chapeaux Adam had purchased for her from the millinery shop in the local village. To her delight, the hat made an excellent foil for her fawn traveling dress. Had she not known differently, she would have imagined they had been purchased with each other in mind.

"That's the last of yer things, my lady," Penny announced, shutting the case and buckling the leather straps. "Shall I send these down with the men?"

"Yes, of course."

"Have ye seen Gresham Park afore, my lady?" Penny ventured, after she went to call the footmen to come collect the luggage. "I was wondering what it's like."

Mallory shook her head, recalling her earlier musings on that very subject. "I've never been there, but I'm sure it's lovely."

At least she hoped it was lovely.

Aware that Penny had never lived anywhere but Braebourne or Clybourne House in London, she decided it best not to repeat Adam's "moldering pile of bricks" comment regarding the estate; better to arrive and deal with whatever they might find when they found it.

Then again, she trusted Adam. Whatever the condition of the house, she knew he would see to her comfort—and that of the servants as well.

With everything packed, Mallory cast one last glance around the room. As she did, a wealth of memories rushed upon her—most especially of the nights she'd spent here with Adam. She knew she would never forget a single one, not even if she lived to be a hundred. But there were a host of new memories waiting to be made at Gresham Park, she reminded herself, a lifetime of experiences yet to be had.

They would be good ones, she vowed.

Adam hadn't planned to marry her, nor she him, but their marriage was going to work and work well. She would see to it. She would make him a good wife, better even than he expected. And she already knew he would make her a good husband—the very best, if their honeymoon was any indication. Which is why there was no need to be sad about leaving, not when years of satisfying married life lay ahead of her.

Years of happiness as well. For in that moment she realized that's exactly what she'd been this past month.

Happy.

In ways she hadn't been in such a very, very long time.

And who knew, she mused, perhaps she and Adam would come back here someday. Surely Quentin and India wouldn't mind, not unless they planned to be in residence themselves, and even then the four of them could make a party of the visit.

Or not, she amended with a rueful smile, as she remembered all the lovemaking postures she and Adam had tried out—and in more than just the bedrooms. Were they to return, she wasn't sure she'd be able to meet her cousin's gaze without blushing.

Flushing slightly now, she glanced down and adjusted one of her gloves, hoping Penny hadn't noticed.

But her maid was too busy supervising the footmen, who were on their way out of the room with her baggage in hand. Deciding she had better not tarry any longer, Mallory turned and walked downstairs.

She discovered Adam in the front hall, conversing with his valet. Finley bowed moments after he saw her, then took his leave.

Smiling, Adam strolled forward, stretching out a hand to take her own. "All ready?"

After one final glance around the castle's interior, she met Adam's gaze and nodded. "Yes, my lord, let us go home."

They drove by coach all that day, stopping at a hotel in Bristol for the night before continuing on early the next morning. Late-afternoon sun burned high and bright on the horizon by the time they arrived at Gresham Park the following day.

Mallory's first sight of Adam's Buckinghamshire estate was a pleasant one, great stretches of fertile green fields and small, tidy forests spread out everywhere she could see. On closer inspection, she caught sight of several wild, overgrown fields and stretches of fallow farmland; but as she knew, Adam was working hard to reclaim them. He'd told her he had hopes of improving the land and by doing so, bettering the lives of not only himself and his tenants, but the local community as well.

The house, she noted, as the coach drew to a halt at the front door, was indeed fashioned of brick, but the edifice was far from the ramshackle affair Adam had once dubbed it. A two-story Jacobean manor, the residence appeared neat and well maintained, the sprawling façade, with its mullioned windows and openwork parapets gleaming a mellow red in the clear afternoon light.

"It's lovely, Adam," she said on a sigh as he helped her from the coach, the finely crushed stone on the drive crunching beneath her shoes. He gave her an enigmatic look, then drew her arm through his, leaving the coachman to see to their belongings.

She expected a servant to open the door, but Adam did so himself before guiding her into a wide entrance hall paneled in heavy dark oak. The floors were also made of wood, their surfaces clean and neat but bare of carpets and scuffed from long, hard use. Other than a single vestibule table with a cracked marble top, the hall lay empty.

It was also still devoid of servants.

"Where is your butler?" she asked, drawing off her gloves. "Surely he ought to have greeted us by now?"

A curious expression that looked almost sheepish swept

over Adam's face. "I have no butler at present. Haven't had the time yet to hire one."

Mallory stared, momentarily taken aback by the idea of not having a butler or majordomo in residence. She'd been raised surrounded by dozens of staff; Braebourne had at least three hundred servants employed at any one time to take care of the many needs of the building and its residents.

"Ah, well," she said, sending him a smile. "We shall have to rectify that shortly, do you not agree?"

He smiled back. "Most definitely. Now, why don't I show you upstairs to your room." Stretching an arm out behind her, he indicated the staircase made of more dark oak, the heavy square banisters beautifully carved with the shapes of apples, figs, birds and stags.

"I would enjoy freshening up," she admitted, "but first, I'd like to see a bit more of the house."

He frowned, then smiled again. "We've had a long trip. Let's get you settled and in Penny's capable hands. Plenty of time to tour the house once you're rested."

Had she not known Adam since she was a child, she might well have fallen in with his suggestion. But she knew his voice, knew his tones, and could tell there was something he didn't want her to know.

Turning, she met his gaze. "I would rather see the house now, at least a small section of it. Your housekeeper can give me a complete tour tomorrow, I expect."

Thrusting his hands into his pockets, he glanced away for a brief moment. "I'm afraid there's no housekeeper either. You'll need to hire one with the butler."

Scowling, she crossed her arms. "Exactly what staff are in your employ? Just so I'll know who to put on my list."

His jaw firmed. "Sufficient to keep the house maintained. In addition to the coachman and footman, we have a cook, a pair of housemaids, and a gardener. And of course, there are Finley and Penny now that you are in residence."

Mallory paused to consider the small number of servants. Then again, she supposed Adam had been away a great deal of the time and had no need of a large staff. Shrugging, she smiled. "Actually, I expect it will work out brilliantly. This way I can start fresh and hire whomever I like." She paused again. "Assuming you are giving me authority to hire new staff?"

His lips curved upward, his features relaxing. "Of course you have authority. You are mistress of the house, and the household is yours to manage however you see fit."

"Good. Then let's see a bit more of my domain."

His smile faded again. "Mallory, I really think you ought to freshen up first. Let me show you to your bed-chamber, and I'll take you on a tour later."

"Why?" she asked in a lowering tone. "What is there that you don't want me to see?"

"Nothing."

"Obviously there is *something,* so out with it, Adam Gresham."

He gave her a mutinous look, then relented. "Fine. Go on then, if you insist. I believe seeing will be explanation enough."

Suddenly anxious about what she might discover, she went to a nearby set of double doors, then paused. Maybe she ought to do as Adam suggested, she mused, and go upstairs to find Penny. But no, she told herself, she wanted to know what he was trying to delay her seeing.

After all, how dreadful could it be?

Laying a hand on the knob, she pushed open one of the doors.

The room was large and broad, illuminated by a bounty of natural light pouring in through windows that ranged the length of the outside wall. Fashioned from the same dark, elaborately carved wood used in the entry hall, the space spoke powerfully of a bygone century. Possessed of a bold, almost masculine quality, the main features of the room were composed of high ceilings, built-in cupboards and shelves, and a huge marble fireplace. At the far end of the room stood an open second-story gallery where people could observe the goings-on from above. Given the age of the house, she suspected the ladies of the family used to sit there, framed as if in a tableau by delicate carvings and ornate wooden arches.

Ordinarily, she would have found it a most pleasant room were it not for one thing.

It was empty.

And by that, she meant bare, pared down to the wood with only the architecture remaining. There wasn't so much as a stick of furniture, not a rug or a book. The fireplace grate lay bare as well, without a bit of kindling for a fire. No curtains hung over the windows, the embrasures appearing stark and lonely.

Empty.

Whirling around, she turned to find Adam leaning against the wall, his arms crossed over his chest.

"But where is everything?" she asked. "Why are there no furnishings?"

"Because there aren't any," he said, a sardonic expression on his face. "My father sold them off years ago."

She'd heard rumors of the late earl's profligate nature—gambling, drinking, loose women and all manner of other unsavory activities—but she'd never imagined something like this. With Adam's reluctance to show her the house still fresh in her mind, a new thought occurred. "But surely you don't mean that all the rooms are like this?"

"That's exactly what I mean." Adam peeled himself away from the wall and strolled forward. "If it wasn't nailed down or glued in place, my dear old papa made sure it was converted into coin. Sometimes he didn't even bother with that, bartering items instead for whatever it was he wanted at the time. Years ago, one of the servants told me he got drunk and traded all of the bed linens for a dozen eggs. Apparently, he'd already sold off the chickens, and he was hungry. You'd have thought he could at least have held out for more. Two dozen eggs perhaps and a slab of bacon."

Crossing to a window, he gazed out. "Then, too, he gambled away a significant portion of the family heirlooms. I believe the silver service that had been a gift from Queen Elizabeth herself was lost in a game of lanterloo to a merchant, who melted it down for specie. All the family portraits went as well, including the one of my mother painted just after her marriage. But she was dead by that time, so I suppose he saw no harm."

"No harm! But that's monstrous."

"Yes," Adam said in a flat, cold voice. "That's exactly what he was." Suddenly he sighed and turned to face her. "I should never have brought you here. I ought to have taken you straight back to Braebourne and left you in your brother's care until I had an opportunity to set the house to rights. But I suppose I was too selfish to be without you even that long."

Her heart beat at a faster pace, a hand she hadn't even realized she lifted, pressed against her chest.

"If you want to go now, I'll understand," he continued, not quite meeting her gaze. "But lest you imagine you'll be sleeping on the floor, you won't. As soon as I knew we were to be wed, I had the countess's chambers completely refurbished. There's everything you could possibly need, but if there's anything you don't like, you have only to toss it out and start over."

"Adam—"

"There's enough new furniture in the dining room and in one of the small salons that I believe you won't be wholly uncomfortable," he went on. "I even had a writing desk installed so you could keep up your correspondence with your family."

Pausing, he raked his fingers through his hair. "It's nothing to what you're used to, I know, and admittedly a frightful mess, but I've been putting all my energy into seeing to the estate. Rebuilding the tenant cottages, un-blocking neglected streams, dredging ditches, repairing roads and making sure we'll be able to plant a crop in the fields come this spring.

"As for the house, the outside was nearly as derelict as this room, but I've about brought it back to life. I thought I'd tackle the outside first, then concentrate on the inte-rior. I was a bachelor, so what did I care so long as I had a bed and a place to eat a meal? Then we married, and there wasn't time to do it all."

Pausing again, he stared at the floor. "I thought if you saw your bedchamber first, the rest might not come as such a dreadful shock. But I won't blame you in the least if you want to go. Shall I send for the coach again? Have Penny repack your belongings? Or will you stay the night? You can set off at first light, and I can—"

"What you can do is stop talking nonsense," she in-terrupted, crossing the distance between them. "I'm not going anywhere. This is my home now, regardless of its condition at present."

His gaze flew up to meet hers.

"From what you've told me, we shall be perfectly comfortable," she said, reaching out to slip her arms around his waist. "I assume the bed is more than a straw pallet tossed on the floor?"

His eyebrows drew together. "The bedstead is made of cherrywood and has a big mattress stuffed with goose feathers."

"And the dining room has a table and chairs rather than a few shipping crates on which we would need to perch?"

His mouth drew up in a slant. "Indeed, I believe a full complement of chairs was brought inside with the table."

"You've bought china and silverware and linens?"

He slipped his arms around her and tugged her closer. "We could eat with our fingers, but only if you wish. Otherwise, we'll have to do with the cutlery at hand."

"And the salon has a couch, perhaps a tea table so we can enjoy a cup before bedtime? Or perhaps something stronger in your case?"

"I don't need anything stronger, not if I have you. I've discovered that you are my very favorite nightcap."

She laughed and snuggled against him. "Then it sounds as if we have only to settle in. As for the rest of the house, it shall be like a blank canvas to a painter. You did say I would have a free hand?"

"As free as you like. You have my leave to buy anything and everything you want."

"I'd be careful if I were you, or I just might take you up on that offer."

Grinning, he dropped a kiss on her mouth. "I shall count upon it. In fact, I've already asked for some sample books to be sent from London. A few ideas to get you started."

She beamed back at him. "I cannot wait. I knew marrying you would be an adventure."

"An adventure, hmm? I'm not sure how I should take that."

"As a compliment, that's how. Now, why do we not go see the bedroom you've furnished for me? I'm dying to get a glimpse at the decoration."

"I hope you like it. I did my best with the colors and such."

She tightened her hold. "I'll love it. I already know that I shall."

Smiling, he leaned down and pressed his lips to hers, claiming a slow, sweet kiss that made her toes arch against the insides of her half boots.

"I'm going to love trying out the bed tonight," he said. "We'll see just how soft the goose feathers are."

"And how tightly the ropes have been strung."

He tossed back his head on a laugh. "We'll make them sing, just wait and see."

Chapter 20

To Adam's express pleasure and relief, Mallory adored her new rooms, exclaiming over the elegant Chippendale furnishings made of satinwood and maple, the pale cream walls and apricot draperies. She loved the plush divan and chairs in her sitting room, the pieces upholstered in muted gold damask that gave the room an extra richness—or so she informed him.

With his hands thrust inside his pockets, he'd watched as she flitted around the rooms, pausing to admire various pieces here and there, including the rosewood writing desk he'd selected for her. Smiling, he enjoyed the expression of delight on her face as she pulled open the drawers to discover supplies of ink, pens and sheets of crisp stationery that bore the crest of her new title as his countess.

After suggesting that Penny retire to her room to unpack her own belongings, Mallory surprised him by locking the door. Going to the bed, she'd lain back against the vanilla satin coverlet and stretched out a hand toward him. Seeing no reason to resist her invitation, he let her pull him into her embrace, losing no time as they proceeded to christen the bed in the most glorious of fashions.

And so began their residence at Gresham Park, the days rolling easily from one to the other over the next three weeks.

In the mornings, Adam rose early to ride his stallion, Eric, around the estate, the horse having been brought from Braebourne after the wedding together with Mallory's mare, Pansy. On his outings, he visited various tenants to discuss their concerns as well as to oversee the improvements he was making to the land.

Sometimes Mallory joined him on his rides, both of them getting to know their neighbors and the local tenantry, so that soon they were being greeted with friendly hellos and waves as they passed. Having been raised to believe in the virtues of ministering to the sick and the poor, Mallory carried on the tradition at Gresham Park.

With Cook's smiling participation, Mallory saw to it that baskets of food were delivered to those in need. She also secured the assistance of the village doctor, making certain the ill and elderly were receiving the care they required. One old woman, who'd lived on Gresham land her whole life, told Adam that his new lady was nothing less than an angel sent among them. With complete seriousness, Adam agreed.

After sharing nuncheon together, he and Mallory usually parted again for much of the afternoon. During those hours he would retreat to his office to review the estate accounts, answer correspondence and take care of other sundry business. Often, he was joined by his new steward, who'd come highly recommended by Edward. Already, the man was proving his worth in terms of enthusiasm, honesty and a progressive turn of mind. Despite some initial reluctance to hire a steward at all, Adam found himself glad of the extra assistance.

As for Mallory, he was vastly pleased to see how effortlessly she'd taken over running the household. If he hadn't known better, he might have imagined she'd been doing it for years, stepping into the role of mistress of the house with nary a problem or complaint.

In fact, based on the cheerful smiles and happy comments from the servants, he knew they all but worshipped her. Particularly after she hired a butler, Brooke, and a housekeeper, Mrs. Daylily, both of whom immediately set just the right tone in the servants' hall.

Mallory had told Adam over dinner one evening that she planned to take on even more staff—housemaids, footmen, a cook's assistant, and an extra scullery maid or two since there would be additional mouths to feed once all the new staff were in place. Having lived frugally these past several years, he hadn't considered the necessity of hiring additional staff. But he trusted Mallory, and if she thought there was a need for servants, then he decided to leave it all in her clearly capable hands.

There was one other new occupant as well, Charlemagne, the cat, who arrived about a week after Adam and Mallory. He'd looked none too pleased at having been shut inside a wicker hamper for the long coach ride from Braebourne. Emerging with a mutinous gleam in his eyes, he'd thumped his tail warningly. But he calmed the instant Mallory lifted him into her arms, starting to purr when he realized who he was with.

Adam supposed he purred too in his own way when Mallory held him. He certainly couldn't resist her touch, longing for her when they were apart, wanting everything from her when they were together.

And therein lay the only bleak spot in their otherwise excellent marriage. She still didn't love him, at least not the way he wished.

Even so, he couldn't help the way his heart brightened with hope whenever she interrupted his work to share some news that simply couldn't wait. Or when she laughed and teased him as she indulged in a bit of flirtatious conversation. And, of course, there were the nights.

Long, dark hours spent in her sweet arms, sheathed in her soft warmth, knowing that no matter how many times he took her, how many times he slept by her side, it would never be enough.

Only in those quiet moments of intimacy did he feel fully himself. Only then did he give himself permission to show her his love, letting passion express what he knew he dare not say aloud.

Of course he thought of telling her at least a dozen times a day. "Mallory, I love you," he would say, as he took her in his arms. "I've always loved you."

In his fantasies, her face came alive, happiness bursting from her as she kissed him until neither of them could think.

But then he would imagine a different outcome, her expression animated not by pleasure, but by dismay, surprise that turned to pity and guilty regret over the fact that she didn't return his affection.

And so, he said nothing.

He supposed he was being a coward, but everything was so good between them, he didn't want to risk ruining it. They were happy together; it was selfish of him to want more.

Or was it?

Glancing up now from his work, Adam reached out to scratch the cat's velvety black head. Charlemagne blinked his green eyes from where he lay on one side of Adam's desk before glancing longingly toward the doorway. Mallory was inspecting the attics today and had banished the feline from the top floor, much to the animal's displeasure.

"She'll be finished soon, my fine sir," Adam told the cat. "Then you can snuggle with her to your heart's content."

If only he could be as certain as Charlemagne that he was loved, he would be content. Yet content or not, he would never stop saying the words—at least to himself.

Mallory, I love you.

Drawing a deep breath, Adam reapplied himself to the investment statements he'd received from Pendragon, going over the activity and recommendations for future acquisitions.

Ten minutes later, he'd finally managed to focus his thoughts on his work when a light tap came at the door.

"Am I interrupting?" Mallory asked in a quiet tone. "I can come back later if you wish."

Glancing up, he smiled and laid down his pen. "No, not at all. Come in. Charlemagne and I have been wondering how you were faring in your search of the attics. Was it as dismal as I assume?"

How could it not be? he mused, considering the fact that his father must surely have looted the place of anything valuable years ago. The one time Adam had ventured up to the top story after coming into his title, he'd found nothing but an assortment of broken furniture and worthless odds and ends. Sour memories had crowded in upon him at the sight, and he'd left without doing much more than glance around. He hadn't been up there since. But Mallory had wanted to see what might remain before having the servants clear out the lot as trash.

"Who knows?" she'd told him. "There might be a fine old piece of furniture or two that we can still use."

Rather than point out the futility of such a hope, he'd let her do as she wished.

And so this morning, he'd idled in her dressing room for a few extra minutes as Penny helped Mallory don her shabbiest gown. Mallory next wrapped a clean kerchief around her head, then tied a voluminous apron she'd borrowed from Cook around her waist. Sending her on her way with a grin and a warm kiss, he'd gone downstairs while Mallory ascended the stairs to the attics. As he knew, having seen the servants gathered in the hallway, she'd taken a pair of housemaids and a strong footman with her to help in the effort.

He smiled again now as she strolled forward, finding her absolutely adorable in her cleaning attire. A few wild brunette tendrils had escaped her scarf and were peeking out from under the material, her formerly white apron smudged with dust and grime.

Seeing her, Charlemagne leapt to his feet and arched his back in an obvious bid for attention. Leaning down, Mallory stroked a hand over the grateful feline, his adoring purrs filling the air.

"It is rather dismal upstairs," she said in answer to Adam's initial question. "The attics are a horrible mess and in immediate need of cleaning, which I've set the maids to tackling. I shouldn't wonder if it's been twenty years since the rooms were touched."

"Probably more, considering my mother would have been the last one to bother. You've a bit of dirt just there, by the way."

Automatically, she reached up a hand to locate the spot. "Do I? Where?"

"On the side of your nose." Slipping his fingers inside his pocket, he withdrew a handkerchief. "Here, allow me."

Doing as he asked, she bent at the waist so he could

wipe the spot. When the smudge was gone, he tugged her near to steal a kiss, finding her lips as smooth and moist as petals. Her eyes were gleaming with a lambent light by the time he let her go.

"So," he said, grinning as he relaxed back in his chair, "did you manage to find anything worth keeping, or is it all junk?"

"Most of it is junk, but there's something I do want to show you. I had one of the footmen leave it in the hall. Stay here, and I'll bring it in."

Hurrying back across the room, she disappeared for a moment before returning with what looked to be a painting in tow. The front of the canvas was turned away from him so he couldn't see the image.

"One of the maids found this hidden behind some boxes stacked in a very dark corner. I wondered if it might be a relative of yours since I couldn't help but notice a resemblance." Turning the painting around, she revealed the work.

Air whooshed out of his lungs in a gust, his heart thumping hard beneath his breastbone, as he stared at the girl in the portrait.

"Do you recognize her?" Mallory asked.

Gazing raptly at the painting, he nodded. "Yes," he said in a thick voice. "It's Delia. It's my sister. My God, I thought he'd sold it."

Or else destroyed it, just as the old bastard had destroyed her.

"Your father, you mean?"

Throat tight, he nodded.

"She was beautiful. And young," Mallory observed. "How old was she when this was painted?"

"Fifteen," he said, somehow managing to find his voice again. "I remember the summer it was done."

The last summer, as he thought of it now. Those final months before he'd left for university, little knowing the fate that awaited them all the next year.

Silently, he studied her pert features—gentle brown eyes, rounded chin and small, soft mouth that were fixed forever in an innocent, unsuspecting smile rendered in brushstrokes and oil.

Seeing her again made him realize how dull his memory of her countenance had grown over the years. How could he have forgotten for so much as an instant?

If only I'd never left her, he thought. *If only I'd had an inkling what he might do, I'd have taken her away before it was too late.*

"Where shall we hang it?" Mallory said, her tone deliberately cheerful, as if she were aware of his ruminations. "I thought the drawing room might be an excellent location. Or we could work on rebuilding the family portrait gallery, starting with Delia."

For a moment he stared. "You wouldn't mind?"

"Mind? Mind what?" She looked confused.

"Displaying her portrait in the gallery. Considering how she died, I wouldn't blame you if you'd rather choose a less obvious location. I could keep her portrait here in my study, for instance."

Mallory's lips drew into a line. "But why would I object? If you want to hang her painting here, then by all means you should do so. But if you're placing the canvas here in your study merely to hide her away, then I couldn't disagree more. Surely you're not ashamed of showing Delia's painting?"

"Of course I'm not," he said vehemently as he shot to his feet.

With obvious care, she set down the painting. "Then why would you imagine I might be? No matter the circumstances of her death, she's still your sister, whom I know you loved."

Pacing to the window, he stared out, arms folded across his chest.

Mallory followed, halting quietly at his side. After a moment, she laid a hand on his arm. "Tell me about her. Tell me what happened."

"You know what happened," he said, biting off the words.

She shook her head. "I know how she died. I don't know why."

"And you don't want to know. Leave it alone, Mal."

Jesu, why did I say anything? he cursed to himself. *Why didn't I just keep my mouth shut?*

All he would have to have done was tell Mallory that he wanted Delia's portrait hung here in his study. She would have accepted his wishes and left it at that. Now she was curious. Now she wanted to know more, to know everything, all the lurid details he'd never revealed to another living soul. He hadn't even told Jack Byron, and Jack knew more about him than anyone else.

Except Mallory.

She knew him—or at least as much of him as he had shown her over the years.

Could he reveal this secret?

Should he?

And if he did, what would she think?

Plainly deciding to ignore his verbal dismissal, she slid her arms around her waist, then tipped her head back to meet his gaze. "Tell me, Adam," she insisted. "Delia looks so young and lovely in her portrait. Why would a girl with her whole future ahead of her become so despondent that she would take her own life?"

Reaching up, she stroked a palm over his chest. "You

said she wrote you a letter. What did it say? After all these years, you really ought to tell someone, you know."

He arched a sardonic brow. "What makes you think I haven't?"

"If you had, it wouldn't be so hard to talk about it now. Unless you don't trust me."

"Of course I trust you."

She pressed herself closer, letting silence speak for her.

Suddenly he lowered his arms and locked them around Mallory. "I don't want you to think badly of her."

"I shan't. I promise."

Gazing into her eyes, he studied her for another long moment, his throat swollen with suppressed emotion. "You know my father was in debt, that he gambled and drank and caroused with the most unsavory sorts of blackguards."

"Yes, that's why the house is bare. Why he sold all the furnishings and valuables."

He glanced away. "That's not the only thing he sold."

"What do you mean?"

"He sold her, Mal. Once I was out of the house, he started trading her to his gaming cronies in exchange for debts he couldn't pay."

She drew a harsh breath. "Surely you aren't saying—"

"That's exactly what I'm saying," he said, looking at her again. "He turned his innocent daughter into a whore."

"But she was only a child—"

"All the more reason they liked her, disgusting animals that they were. That *he* was. I'm ashamed to admit a man like that was my father. I swear I had no idea. If I'd thought for an instant he was capable of such heinous deeds, I would have moved heaven and earth to take her with me, to keep her away from him. But she didn't tell me, and I wasn't aware of the truth, not until it was too late."

"Oh, Adam—" she said, trembling inside his arms.

"When she found out she was with child, the shame was too great for her to bear, so she drowned herself. After I received her letter, I drove here to Gresham Park intending to kill him. I nearly did. I beat him to within an inch of his life before a pair of the servants pulled me off. Only the thought of Delia and the knowledge that she wouldn't have wanted me to hang for his murder kept me from following through."

He drew a breath, then slowly released it. "She didn't name the men who'd used her, but I had a fair idea who they must be. I tracked them down and confronted them, horse-whipping the ones who were too cowardly to fight me man-to-man. I told them if they ever breathed a word of what they'd done to my sister, I'd kill them and the consequences be damned. Over the years, they've all gone to the grave, taken early by the ravages of one vice or another. If justice be served, they are burning in hell even as we speak."

"They must be. They deserve no less for what they did," she agreed.

"My father most of all. I trust the devil has a special torment set aside just for him." He paused, his thoughts carried back to those terrible times and the anguish that had followed. "I never saw or spoke to him again after I left Gresham Park that day. To me, he was as good as dead, and I wanted nothing more to do with him. From that moment forward, I had no family, I had no home."

She stroked her hand across his chest, her aquamarine eyes glittering with a fierce light. "You've always had a home with us. I don't wonder now that you spent all your summers and holidays with my family. I wish I'd known. I wish I'd done more."

His lips curved. "You did plenty. You and the Byrons were my shelter from the storm, and now you are so much more. Now you're my wife, my new family."

"And this is your home once again," she said. "I promise that we'll drive away the last memories of your father and leave only the good ones behind. If I should happen upon a painting of him tucked away in the attic, I'll order it burned with the rest of the rubbish."

A fierce warmth radiated through him, as a laugh burst from his throat. "And I'll provide the tinder."

"Delia's painting goes in the family hall," she stated in a decisive tone. "She'll be placed right next to you and me once we commission our own portraits. She'll be remembered for the wonderful young woman she was, not for the horrible things your father forced her to do. The world believes she died in an accident, and that is what they will continue to believe. You loved her and esteemed her, and that's all anyone ever needs to know. I only wish I'd had a chance to meet her. I feel certain we would have been friends."

The laughter fell away, leaving behind a new warmth and something more, something deeper that he could no longer entirely conceal. Drawing her closer, he took her lips, losing himself in the heady pleasure and the tender benediction of her touch.

Emotions welled within him, clamoring to escape their bonds. "I must have done something right to have found you," he murmured against her lips. "Sweet heaven, Mallory, I love you."

For a moment he didn't realize he'd spoken aloud, certain he'd simply said the phrase in his head as he had so often before. But then he noticed the way she'd stiffened in his arms and how her mouth was no longer moving beneath his own. Drawing back, he met her gaze, aware that he'd not only uttered the words but that she'd heard them.

She stared, eyes wide.

Rather than let the silence lengthen, he forced out another laugh, ignoring the sudden pain blossoming around his heart. "I love you standing up for what's right rather than what Society deems proper. I can always count on you to buck tradition. Thank you for taking Delia's side—and mine."

"Well . . . um . . . there's no other side *to* take." Pausing, she continued gazing at him, puzzlement in her eyes.

Before she could question him, or give him further cause to repine, he kissed her again. "Speaking of bucking tradition, what do you say to an afternoon tryst? You need to get out of those clothes, and I wouldn't mind helping you."

Her eyes widened again but for a completely different reason this time. Without waiting for permission, he bent and swept her into his arms, cradling her high against his chest.

If he couldn't have her love, he decided, then he'd have her body instead. Perhaps it showed a marked lack of pride on his part, but he'd take whatever portion of her he could get and be glad, since anything else was unthinkable.

Ignoring the curious looks of the servants, he carried her upstairs to her bedroom and kicked the door shut behind them. Standing her on her feet, he reached for the apron strings at her waist and slid the ties free. After tossing the garment aside, he began undoing the fastenings on her dress, one slow button at a time. Claiming her mouth with passionate, possessive kisses that made her shiver and moan, he stripped her to the skin.

Sweeping her once again into his arms, he carried her to the bed, where he joined her, seeing to it he made good on his promise and so very much more.

Some while later, Mallory lay relaxed and replete against the well-rumpled sheets, her body humming from the surfeit of pleasure still pulsating through her system. Adam was sprawled beside her, and from the rhythmic tempo of his breathing, she knew he was asleep. And no wonder, since the intensity of his lovemaking had pushed them both to their limits and beyond. She wasn't sure the exact number of postures she and Adam had tried so far, but they'd certainly added a couple of new ones to the tally today.

Releasing a contented sigh, she closed her eyes and let herself drift, deciding that a bit more afternoon decadence couldn't hurt under the circumstances.

Scarcely a minute passed, however, before her eyelids opened again, his earlier words playing once more in her mind.

Sweet heaven, Mallory, I love you.

At first she'd thought she must not have heard him right.

Love her?

Adam didn't love her.

Or did he?

She'd been so surprised, she hadn't said a word, distracted enough by the phrase that she'd been momentarily jarred out of the delightful haze of their kiss. Before she could respond though, he'd sloughed off the declaration by making some new comment about his sister. Then he'd whisked her up here to her room and hustled her into bed so quickly she hadn't had time to think of anything but the overwhelming rapture of his embrace.

But he was sleeping now, and she was awake. Awake and wondering about his words, his feelings.

And her own.

Quite likely Adam hadn't meant to convey anything deeper than the friendly affection they'd always shared, the phrase slipping imprudently from his lips.

Yet what if he *had* meant more? Was it possible that

he was in love with her? And if he were, how did she feel in return?

She loved him, of course, but was she *in love* with him?

A shiver ran through her at the idea, her fingers tightening into a fist where they lay against her bare stomach. Suddenly she was viscerally aware of him beside her, his large body so warm and strong and familiar now that they were lovers. Now that she was his wife.

But love?

God knows she didn't want to be in love; it hurt too much. And yet . . . and yet she could imagine how sublime it would be to love him, to give herself wholly to the emotion and forget about the uncertainties, the fear.

For therein lay her dilemma—she was afraid.

After Michael's death, she'd never thought she would find a way to escape the pain, unable to do much more than survive each day and pray for an end to her suffering. The thought of going through that again, of risking such profound loss if anything should happen to Adam . . . well, she didn't think she could manage such grief another time.

Still, she hadn't thought she could be happy again either—and she was. She hadn't imagined a new life, new pleasures and a future that stretched bright as a rainbow before her.

And all because of Adam.

He'd led her out of her darkness. He'd shown her how to live again. He'd shown her how to love.

Her soft gasp echoed in the air, her heart thundering suddenly beneath her breasts, pummeling her ribs.

Was it too late? Did she, could she, be in love with him already?

And in that moment, she knew the truth. Without realizing when or how, she had fallen in love with him, the feeling creeping up on her with such stealth that she hadn't even been aware. What delicious irony, what rich surprise, to find herself in love with her husband, her friend.

Smiling, she let out a little laugh. Then she grew still again, as the fear returned. What if some tragedy were to befall Adam? How would she endure his loss?

But Adam wasn't a soldier like Michael, she reassured herself. He didn't put himself in harm's way on a daily basis, literally tempting fate to take his life. He was young and healthy—very healthy if their recent lovemaking was any indication—with years and years ahead of him. Anything could happen, of course, accidents did occur, but she had more chance of dying in childbirth than he did going about his usual routine. If either of them was to be widowed, it was far more likely to be him.

But enough of such maudlin speculation, she thought. She was in love, terrifying as that prospect might be.

Rolling over, she pressed herself against Adam's long, bare frame, glorying in the smooth heat of his skin, the crisp texture of the hair on his chest. Leaning down, she laid her mouth against his shoulder and began kissing a path along his body. He shifted beneath her but didn't wake, turning his head against the pillow, clearly lost in dreams.

Hopefully they are good ones, she thought. But she planned to give him something better than dreams . . . much, much better. Skimming her fingers over the broad planes and taut angles of his muscular form, she let herself play, teasing him with touches, rousing him with kisses both lingering and lavish.

His arousal awakened before he did, his shaft stiffening in a most impressive display. Palming its length, she watched his eyelids slowly lift, a groan rumbling from his throat as he met her gaze. His sleepy brown eyes were night-dark with passion, his features stark from the obvious intensity of his need.

"What are you doing?" he rasped, his hips arching of their own accord beneath her grasp.

She smiled and stroked him harder. "What does it feel like I'm doing?"

A moan tore from him.

"Of course, I could always stop," she murmured teasingly.

"Don't you dare!" His hips arched again, his shaft moving inside her palm.

She chuckled and bent to kiss him again, opening her mouth over one of his flat nipples. Flicking it with her tongue, she smiled when he shuddered, his fingers reaching up to tangle in her hair and cradle her closer. With a sudden daring, she bit him just enough to nip, only hard enough to give pleasure rather than pain. A fresh groan left his mouth, his muscles flexing and bowing as if they'd been shot through with a jolt of electricity.

She could tell he was surprised. She was surprised herself, since she'd never initiated their lovemaking before. Until today, she'd always been content to let him direct their bed play. But today she was the aggressor. Now she was the one taking the lead.

Clearly, Adam was enjoying it, as he shifted in ways that encouraged her caresses, inciting her to be as bold and brazen as she wished.

But his willingness to submit had its limits, and it wasn't long before he turned the tables on her and reasserted his dominance. Once he did, all she could do was surrender as he dragged her up and over him. Before she even had time to draw a new breath, he parted her legs and thrust himself inside, burying his powerful erection as deep as it would go.

A keening cry burst from her as savage delight spread like wildfire through her veins. He pulsed strongly within her and sent her senses whirling away.

In the golden afternoon light, she met his gaze, her body filled with more than longing, her spirit alight with newfound love. The words hovered on her lips, fluttering like butterfly wings anxious to be set free. But a twinge of fear rose abruptly inside her, leaving her too shy to confess. And so she bent to kiss him instead, letting her mouth and body speak to him of her devotion, her adoration.

As though sensing the change, he drew back, studying her as he cradled her face in his hands. "Mal?"

But she only shook her head and closed her eyes to kiss one of his palms.

Then neither of them could wait an instant more, Adam thrusting up at the same moment she arched down. The sound of their moans filled the air, her skin growing slick against his own, their flesh joined in a mating that was as fierce as it was profound.

Suddenly she couldn't think at all, dark waves of need washing over her like the ocean crashing to shore in a storm. She cried out when the tempest broke, senses flying apart only to be put together again in a burst of light and rapturous, unending pleasure. She collapsed against him, unable to speak as he found his own completion.

And then there was silence, and calm, their hearts beating in tandem where they lay locked as one. The words rose inside her again, but she was too weary, too satiated, to speak.

Later, she would tell him. Later there would be time.

Sighing, she buried her face against his neck and slept.

Chapter 21

"What would you say about a trip to London?" Adam inquired a couple of days later as he helped himself to a second helping of eggs and ham from the blue transferware platter on the dining-room table.

Watching him apply his fork with such gusto, Mallory decided he was more than entitled to the additional serving, particularly given the energetic way in which he'd taken her that morning. They'd never tupped against the wall in her bathing chamber before, but she'd discovered she rather quite liked the experience.

Come to think, she decided with a delicious inner shiver, she could do with a bit more sustenance herself.

"Go to London?" she said, reaching for another golden square of toast. "For how long?"

"A few days, maybe a week, even two, if you'd like."

"When would we leave?"

"Tomorrow, I thought. Or the day after if you need

more time to pack." Taking up his cup of coffee, he drank a swallow before returning the china to its saucer. "I have some business to which I need attend, and I rather fancied having you come with me." Reaching over, he picked up her hand and raised it to his lips.

Mallory smiled, her pulse racing pleasurably at the contact, as well as the invitation.

"You can shop," he suggested. "I know you've been working with some of the pattern books here at home, but I'm sure it would be far easier selecting fabrics and furnishings in person. There'll be an array of merchants at your disposal, and you can order to your heart's content."

Her smile widened, her fingers tightening against his own. "You've no need to convince me since I'd be more than delighted to accompany you. And you're right, it would be an excellent opportunity to continue my efforts to redecorate the house. As you say, I can make far more progress if I'm able to see the merchandise with my own two eyes. I'll even have a chance to replace this boring china."

"Is it boring?" he said, letting go of her hand to reapply himself to his meal. "Seems entirely serviceable to me."

"Exactly. It's too serviceable and not at all in keeping with the dignity of your title. A set of Sèvres or Wedgwood will be far better. Mayhap I'll even have a service designed especially for us. A lovely script G for Gresham would be nice."

"Or an M for Mallory. I rather like the idea of that," he said, giving her a wink.

"So," she continued, dismissing his suggestion with a shake of her head. "Where shall we stay while we're in Town? Do you still have your bachelor's quarters?"

"We aren't staying in my old bachelor's quarters," he told her, taking up his coffee cup once more as he leaned back in his chair. "Even if I hadn't already let them go, they're far too small and entirely unsuitable for you. No, I've made other arrangements until we have a chance to find a town house of our own."

"Oh? Claridge's then? I've never stayed in a hotel before," she said, rather intrigued by the idea.

"No, not Claridge's. I wrote to Edward and he has graciously offered us the use of Clybourne House for as long as we might have need. I decided to accept since I thought it would make you feel more comfortable."

Leaning across, she reached for his hand again. "You're so good to me."

The easy smile left his face, replaced by an expression of great intensity. "No more than you deserve." Setting down his cup, he glanced away. "Why don't you tell Penny to start packing. We'll leave in the morning if that suits you."

"Yes, completely."

He released her hand, leaving her to return it to her lap. "Adam—" she began.

His dark velvety gaze met hers, his brows lowered in a scowl. "Yes?"

"I—"

I love you.

But somehow it didn't seem the right time for such a declaration, just as it hadn't on any number of other occasions over the past couple of days. But it would soon, she told herself. Once she didn't feel quite so shy—or uncertain and even now a little afraid.

"I—I'm excited about our trip," she stated instead.

The corners of his mouth turned up, and he stood. Crossing to her, he bent and pressed a gentle kiss to her lips. "I am too." Taking her hand again, he drew her to her feet. "Go on now and start getting ready. I shall see you at nuncheon."

Arching up on her toes, she kissed him again. "Yes. Nuncheon, it is."

* * *

She and Adam arrived in Grosvenor Square late the next day, a pair of footmen hurrying down the front steps of Clybourne House only moments after the coach rolled to a stop. With Croft presently at Braebourne, Denton, the underbutler, was there to greet them—his angular features and wide, familiar smile a welcoming sight.

Despite the fact that she and Adam were the only family members in residence, the house didn't seem empty. The rooms and hallways were filled with a warm atmosphere and a bounty of gracious comforts, including vases full of fresh flowers, polished, lemon-scented floors and woodwork, and fires burning cozily in the grates.

After agreeing to accompany Adam, she'd experienced a few twinges of doubt about the decision, wondering how she would feel to return to the city after such a prolonged absence. The last time she'd been here, she'd been steeped in grief over the sudden news of Michael's death, and all she'd wanted then was to get as far away from London as she could.

Yet the instant she entered the town house, she felt once more at home. In some ways, it was as if she'd never left, years of good memories chasing away the bad.

Still, in other ways, it was as if a lifetime had passed, and she was another person entirely. When she'd lived here before, she'd been a girl—courted and cosseted and indulged over the course of more than one Season. Now she was a woman—tempered by grief, matured by experience, gentled by marriage and love.

Walking up the broad staircase and along the familiar corridors, she resolved to enjoy her stay, to begin afresh and make a wealth of new memories—ones that would be her and Adam's alone to share. With that in mind, she suggested they use one of the many guest suites rather than move into her old bedroom. The pair of connected chambers she chose were larger and would provide a far better accommodation for two people. Additionally, Adam's room had an absolutely massive bed with a plump feather tick that she knew they would put to good use.

"Shall we christen it now?" Adam whispered in her ear, his arms stealing around her from behind in spite of the footmen who still busy bringing up their luggage. Skimming his lips over her cheek, he playfully caressed her nape in a way that never failed to drive her wild. "I could shoo them all out and lock the door. We wouldn't even have to take off our clothes, I could just tumble you down and toss up your skirts. What do you say, wife, shall I tup you now, or would you rather wait until later?"

Her nipples drew into aching peaks, her pulse strumming crazily in her veins.

"I must warn you," he continued, rocking her back ever so subtly against him so she could feel his erection, "if you make me wait, I'll expect no less than a penance for your willfulness. Something designed to make you scream loudly enough to wake the servants."

A shudder raked over her spine, and she nearly ordered the footmen out herself. But then she remembered in whose house they were and what time of day it was.

Wondering where she got the strength or the nerve, she turned in his arms, careful to keep her voice low. "I believe then that I'd prefer to wait." Reaching up, she stroked a fingertip over his lower lip. "And don't assume I'll be the only one of us screaming. I believe I'll be able to oblige you in that area as well."

Desire flared hot in his gaze and for a second she thought he was going to ignore her decision and carry her to the bed regardless. With obvious reluctance, however, he let her go. "You've turned into a siren, my sweet."

Smiling, she leaned up and whispered in his ear. "It's what comes, I suppose, of being married to a satyr. All girls should be so lucky."

Tossing back his head, he laughed. "Have your bath and a change of clothes. I'll be stripping them back off of you soon enough."

"I look forward to it, my lord."

Laughing again, he made his way through the connecting door and into his own bedchamber.

Drawing a shivery breath, she sank down onto a nearby couch, knowing Penny would be along any minute to help her settle in.

Adam more than kept his promise, and to his express delight Mallory did as well, the two of them pleasuring each other long into the night. Whether they woke the servants with the sound of their exuberant bed play, he didn't know, nor did he care, having enjoyed their lovemaking far too thoroughly to worry about being discreet.

Awakening the next morning to rays of crisp November sunshine, he rose silently from the bed. Walking around, he bent to tuck Mallory more securely under the covers. She didn't rouse as he did so, too deeply asleep after the night past to notice. Pressing a kiss to her forehead, he left her to slumber, making a mental note to tell her maid that Mallory was not to be disturbed.

Bathed and dressed, he ate a quick repast, then set out from the house to conduct the first of his Town business. He needed to visit a couple of merchants about seed stores for next spring's planting, discuss new tilling methods with an agricultural specialist with whom he'd been corresponding and stop by a new factory that was manufacturing advanced tools and machinery that he was considering testing on a few of the home farms.

Sometime this week as well he planned to call on Rafe Pendragon to catch up on investment matters. If what he'd heard were true, it would seem congratulations were in order on the financier's own recent marriage. Both of them, it appeared, had lost their bachelor status in the past couple of months. He only hoped Pendragon was enjoying married life as much as he was himself.

Directing his horse down the street, crowded even at this early hour of the morning with pedestrians and conveyances of all descriptions, his thoughts went to Mallory.

He was glad he'd invited her to come with him to London. Already her eyes were alive with the fresh excitement of being in Town once again. Fleetingly, he'd wondered if she might grow melancholy over memories of her last visit, when she'd received the news of Hargreaves's death. But to his relief, she seemed completely at her ease. In fact, she'd surprised him with her provocative banter in their bedchamber—her new boldness something he planned to encourage and enjoy.

He couldn't quite put his finger on it, but he thought he sensed a change, a further deepening of the physical and emotional intimacy between them. Sometimes, when he gazed into her eyes, he could almost believe she loved him—really loved him—passionately and with her whole heart. Of course she never said the words, and maybe he was only imagining what he so earnestly wished to be true. Yet quite abruptly he had hope again that Mallory was indeed coming to love him.

Smiling to himself, he turned his horse south toward the Thames docks, where one of the merchants had a warehouse. If he concluded his business early, perhaps he'd make it home in time to accompany Mallory on her shopping excursion this afternoon. And mayhap tonight she might enjoy taking in a play; something entertaining was sure to be in the offing at Drury Lane.

Yes, he decided, their stay in Town was going to be a good one. And with Christmas approaching next month, their days here would give him a chance to search for a few gifts. At the thought, he remembered his promise on their honeymoon to buy her an array of necklaces from Rundell and Bridge—one for each day of the week. He knew she would balk at such an unnecessary extravagance, but mayhap instead he could have something extraordinary commissioned for her. Something that would take her very breath away.

Mentally adding a jeweler's visit to his list of things to do this week, he continued on his way, humming a light-hearted tune under his breath.

Over the next few days, Mallory visited what seemed like half the stores in London, purchasing an array of items she knew she needed for Gresham Park and a bit more besides. Focusing on one room at a time, she bought furniture, carpets, draperies, vases and wall coverings. She ordered a wealth of necessities including candlesticks and chandeliers, fireplace tools, mirrors, linens, washbasins, dishes and glassware. She purchased paintings and books to replenish the woefully small collection in what had once been the library.

To her immense pleasure, she spent one afternoon visiting the Wedgwood showroom in St. James's Square, where she commissioned the new formal china she'd been looking forward to having designed. After much consideration, she decided on a pattern that incorporated the Gresham crest with its ancient shield and heraldic banner done in gold on a ground of cream and regal blue. She bought a second china service with an elegant floral pattern that she and Adam would use on an everyday basis and on occasions when family came to visit.

Occasionally, when Adam wasn't otherwise occupied with his own business appointments, he accompanied her on her outings. She found him to be an excellent companion, since he tended not to interfere and yet was willing to offer well-considered advice whenever she solicited it. Nor did he seem bored, as so many men were in such situations, or in a hurry to leave. He gave her as much time as she needed to shop, never making her feel rushed.

Once the shopping was done for the day, he would take her to Gunter's Tea Shop for a treat, plying her with hot chocolate and buttered biscuits until she would laughingly tell him she couldn't eat another bite.

With most of the Ton at their country estates, Society was thin this time of year, but Mallory didn't mind. At present, she wasn't much in the mood for parties and lavish entertainments. Instead, she preferred spending quiet evenings with Adam, either dining at home or taking in a play with only the two of them seated in their box.

This morning, before Adam left, he'd asked if she might like to attend the opera. Still abed, she'd managed to say yes in between kisses, the amorous antics that followed very nearly making him late for his meeting.

A smile played on her lips at the memory as she alighted now from the coach, a brisk afternoon breeze ruffling her skirts as she strolled up the steps into the town house. Returning Denton's friendly greeting, she handed one of the footmen her hat, gloves and pelisse, her spirits cheerful after another day's successful round of shopping. "Has his lordship returned yet?" she asked the butler.

"No, my lady, not yet," Denton said. "A caller arrived a short while ago, however. I took the liberty of putting him in the drawing room to wait, since he refused simply to leave his card."

"Did he give his name?"

Denton frowned, an unusually reserved expression on his face. "No, your ladyship. He did say he is acquainted with you however. I can have him escorted out if you wish."

She paused for a moment, wondering who in the world could be calling in such an unorthodox fashion. "No, I shall see him, but do not send down to the kitchen for refreshments quite yet. I will ring when we have need."

Likely the visitor was some old acquaintance who'd just arrived in Town and wanted to offer best wishes on her recent nuptials. Well, she would give him a few minutes, and perhaps Adam would be home by the time their guest was ready to depart. Crossing the wide foyer to the downstairs drawing room, she paused on the threshold, then strode inside.

The man stood gazing out one of the windows, his back turned toward her. Her step slowed as she studied him, finding something oddly familiar about the set of his firm, thin shoulders and the golden wave of his hair.

"Good afternoon," she greeted, suddenly even more curious to know who he was, a peculiar tingle shivering along her spine. "My butler informs me you have been waiting. Not too long, I trust."

Slowly he turned to face her. As he did the floor seemed to drop out from beneath her feet, her heart thundering madly between her ears. Numb with disbelief, she stared, wondering fleetingly if she'd lost her mind. Either that, or she was seeing a ghost.

I must be, she thought, *since he can't be real. Can he?*

"Michael?" she whispered in a voice that didn't sound anything like her own.

"Mallory." He smiled, holding out a hand. "My love, I've come home."

Chapter 22

$\mathcal{M}$allory swayed on her feet, a noise like a thousand bees buzzing in her ears. If she didn't know better, she might think she was on the verge of fainting, which was absurd considering that she never fainted. Although she supposed there was always a first time for just about anything.

Apparently alarmed that she was about to collapse in a heap on the carpet, Michael Hargreaves rushed forward and caught her inside his arms. "Mallory, are you all right? I knew this was going to come as a dreadful shock, but I didn't see any easy way to avoid it. Here now, do you need to sit down? Lie down? Maybe I should get you some smelling salts. Do you have any nearby?"

Pressing quavering fingertips against her brow, she shook her head. "No, nor are you to try administering any." She hated smelling salts.

Pausing, she drew a deep, bracing inhalation before lifting her gaze to his. A jolt went through her at the sight of his eyes, such a pure silvery grey she'd nearly forgotten the vibrant depths of their hue. Or the shape of his pleasing, aristocratic features—proud forehead, narrow cheekbones, long, straight nose and sculpted lips. He was thin though, she noted, much thinner than he'd been the last time she'd seen him. He looked careworn as well, and older, with the faintly gaunt cast of someone who was recovering from a very great illness—or ordeal.

Trembling, she stared again, still not believing what she saw. "Michael," she whispered, "is it really you?"

His mouth turned upward into a smile, and he gave a little nod. "Yes, it really is."

"B-but how? You're d-dead. They told me you'd been killed in battle, that you died alongside dozens of your men."

"Yes, so I've been given to understand," he said in a doleful tone. "I suppose I ought to have died with them, but I was grievously wounded instead. A scavenger came along during the height of the battle and robbed me of my possessions. I was too weak and insensible to stop him, even when he stripped me of my uniform tunic, weapons and the signet ring that had been in my family for generations. I understand that's what the Army used to identify the body."

"But if that's true—"

"Then the man buried in my grave isn't me. I was told there wasn't a great deal left of my remains. Or rather the grave robber's remains, since he's the one who was killed bearing my possessions in a subsequent, distant volley of cannon fire."

A shudder racked her frame. "But if you were injured, why didn't anyone know? What happened to you, Michael? Where have you been all these months? It's been more than a year."

"Most of which I spent locked away in a filthy French prison. Everything was in such a shambles after the battle that I was abandoned and left for dead. There were hundreds of casualties. So many fell, it was—" He broke off, his throat moving as he swallowed down the memories.

"It was barbaric," he continued. "As providence would have it, however, a very kind couple found me and nursed me back to some semblance of health. They kept me hidden, but their farm was later raided, and I was taken prisoner. When I told the blasted Frogs that I was an officer, they laughed and refused to believe me. They thought I was lying, trying to earn parole and an easy way home."

"So all of this time, I've believed you to be dead, and you were being held prisoner instead?"

He nodded, running a consoling hand across her back. "I'd nearly given up hope of being released, when Wellington's men captured the town. When they did, I was finally set free, finally able to explain who I really was. Imagine everyone's shock at learning I wasn't dead after all. Imagine my own in discovering that all my friends and family and loved ones had been laboring under the belief that I wasn't just missing but that I had been killed."

"Oh, Michael." Mouth trembling, a tear slid down her cheek.

Reaching out, he brushed it away with the edge of his thumb. "Shh, don't cry. It's all right now. I'm whole, and I'm back, ready to pick up where I left off, where *we* left off. I came to you as soon as I could. I haven't even been home yet to tell my parents. I wanted you to be the first."

Her chest gave a sharp squeeze, guilt rushing upon her.

"I thought I'd try here in London," he continued before she could speak, "and if you weren't in residence, I'd ride on to Braebourne. I assume the duke is here and your mother most likely. Won't they be surprised as well."

He doesn't know, she realized, her stomach churning with alarm. *He doesn't realize how very much everything has changed.*

"Michael, there's something I have to tell you—"

"Whatever it is, it can wait," he interrupted, drawing her more fully into his arms. "We've talked far too long as it is. All I want to do is hold you, kiss you, love you. Sweet heaven, how I've missed you, Mallory. I don't think any man could have missed a woman more."

Then before she could prevent it, his mouth was on hers, and he was kissing her with a hungry longing that made her want to weep all over again. For a moment she let him have his way, closing her eyes as he claimed his long-awaited homecoming embrace. But then she knew she must end it. Knew as well that his kiss wasn't right anymore.

His kiss wasn't Adam's.

Sliding her palms between them, she prepared herself to push him away.

Suddenly, a footfall sounded behind her.

"What in the bloody hell is this?" demanded Adam's enraged voice. "Get your damned hands off my wife!"

Shoving against Michael's chest, she sprang away and whirled around to face Adam.

Adam's eyes blazed like dark coals, his jaw clenched so tightly it was a wonder it didn't snap.

With her pulse thundering like a drum in her chest, she reached out a hand to him, silently beseeching.

Adam ignored it, his entire attention fixed on the man at her side. Suddenly his eyes widened, some of the color leaving his face as recognition set in. "*Hargreaves?* What in the—aren't you supposed to be dead?"

"Yes, but as you can see, I am clearly not." With lines

of confusion etched on his brow, Michael glanced between her and Adam before coming to rest on her. "What does he mean, Mallory? *His wife*? And what is Gresham doing here anyway, if not to pay a social call?"

"There's nothing social about it," Adam stated. "I *live* here, for the time being at least, while Mallory and I are visiting in Town. And by wife, I mean that she and I are married. We were wed a little over two months ago."

Michael was the one whose complexion paled this time, his eyes boring into hers with a dawning agony. "Is it true, what he says? Have you really married him?"

An aching hole opened up in her chest, and she clasped her hands over the spot as if to keep her heart from spilling out. "Yes. Adam is my husband."

Michael glanced away for a moment, his pain terrible to behold. Then he looked at her again. "Why?" he asked in a thin voice. "Why would you marry him when you were engaged to me?"

"Because she thought you were dead," Adam said, stepping to her side. Sliding a notably possessive arm around her shoulders, he pulled her against him. "And before you accuse her of not grieving properly, she did. She nearly tore herself apart over your loss. But she had a right to move on and she has—with me."

Knees threatening to buckle, she leaned into Adam's strength, not sure if she would have remained standing otherwise. She wanted to bury her face against his chest as well, unable to bear the clear devastation revealed on Michael's face. Somehow, though, she mustered the resilience not to hide.

"Michael, I'm so sorry," she whispered. "I never meant to hurt you."

Adam stiffened against her, his arm suddenly like a steel band around her shoulders.

Sweet mercy, she thought, *how can this be happening?* Not only was Michael back from the dead, but now Adam was clearly angry with her, wounded over having caught her in what he must think of as an illicit embrace.

But surely he would understand once she had a chance to explain? Surely he must realize the untenable vise in which she suddenly found herself? Although truth be told, she could barely understand it all herself.

"I think you should go," Adam told the other man. "There is no point in further explanations."

Michael straightened to his full height, shoulders back and looking suddenly every inch the soldier he was. "I believe that decision should be up to Mallory. Mallory, do you want me to leave?"

Yes.

No.

I don't know. Rather than answer, she said nothing.

"I believe you have your response," Adam said. "Now kindly be on your way."

But Michael made no effort to depart, holding his ground as though he intended to defend the position by force if necessary. "Mallory?" he asked again.

"I . . ." she said, her voice breaking as she met his gaze. "He's right. Y-you should go."

A light went out in Michael's eyes, and a pain slashed her like a knife. "As you wish, my lady," he said. "Pray be of good health."

"You as well," she murmured.

Turning on his heels, he strode from the room.

Neither she nor Adam moved until they heard Denton show Michael out the front door.

"Adam—" she began.

He freed her, releasing her so abruptly that for a moment she nearly lost her balance.

"Not now, Mallory. I cannot speak of this now."

"But—" She stared as he prowled away from her, his hands clenched into hard fists at his sides. A knot wedged inside her chest, making her want to weep.

"Go upstairs to your room," he told her, his words rough and sharp as ground glass. "Tell Penny to pack your belongings. We are leaving for Gresham Park in the morning."

Her lips parted. "*Leaving!* But why?"

He rounded on her. "Because we've been here long enough. You've bought sufficient furnishings and what-nots to fill up the house twice over. My business is nearly concluded, and the little that hasn't can be done by post. Now go on. Go on before I—" Pausing, he turned away, stared out one of the windows. "Just go, Mallory. Please."

A shiver rippled through her, shaking her so hard she crossed her arms over her chest to keep herself steady. If only he would let her explain, give her a chance to reassure him that what he'd seen hadn't meant anything. Instead, he was acting as if she'd betrayed him.

It wasn't her fault Michael was alive.

It wasn't her fault he had sought her out here at the house, or even that he'd kissed her.

Michael had taken her completely unawares. What was she supposed to have done?

Slap him?

Realizing it was useless trying to reason with Adam while he was in such a black mood, she turned and went to the door. Pausing on the threshold, she glanced again at Adam but found his back to her still, clearly shutting her out.

Stifling a wrenching cry, she fled into the hall and up the stairs to her bedchamber.

Chapter 23

Adam spoke barely a word that evening, causing dinner to be a quiet, awkward affair. Nor did the two of them attend the opera as originally planned, the relaxed, frolicsome good mood of the morning now such a distant memory it seemed as if it had happened a lifetime ago. Still, she expected him to come to her bedroom as he always did.

Instead, he bid her good night at her door. "Get some sleep. We'll leave first thing on the morrow." Then, without so much as a peck on the forehead, he turned and strode away, entering his own bedchamber without another glance.

And for the first time since their marriage, Mallory spent the night alone. Cold and restless as she lay in the wide bed, she tried to sleep, her thoughts tumbling over themselves like pebbles cast upon a troubled shore.

Adam was so angry with her. In all the years they'd known one another, she couldn't recall a time when he'd been quite so furious with her. Yet as she considered the events of the day, she couldn't think how she might have acted differently.

She had been utterly shocked to see Michael again.

Even now, it didn't seem possible that he was alive, the astonishment of seeing him again as strange and unreal as the news of his death so many, many months ago. If she hadn't stood in the same room with him, talked with him, touched him, she might not believe his return to be real even now. Yet there he'd been, whole and safe and undeniably alive.

Truly it was a miracle, one that only a short time ago would quite literally have made her weep with joy, cry out with elation.

But now she didn't know how to feel.

Confused?

Sad?

Guilty?

She'd seen the pain on Michael's face and witnessed an equal measure of anguish on Adam's as well—the sight of their combined misery threatening to tear her apart.

For a moment, she thought of going to Adam and trying to explain about the kiss and that it hadn't meant anything—at least not to her. But then she remembered his arctic good night, as well as the unspoken rejection in his eyes.

She swallowed, tears welling until one spilled over and slid down her cheek. Wiping it away with the edge of the sheet, she rolled onto her side and tucked herself in as tightly as she could get. Maybe a good night's sleep would put a new perspective on matters, she told herself. Perhaps tomorrow things wouldn't seem quite so bad.

Nevertheless, many long, dark, unhappy minutes passed before she finally managed to drop into a doze.

Her sleep was fretful, her dreams filled with both men, each alternately beseeching, then angry with her, and one another, as they competed for her love and allegiance.

Bleary-eyed and weary when Penny awakened her not long after dawn, she rose from the bed and let her maid help her bathe and dress.

She was just finishing her ablutions, attired in a pewter grey wool traveling gown that exactly suited her mood, when a housemaid tapped on the door and brought in a well-laden tray. "Good morning, my lady. His lordship said you would be taking breakfast in here today."

Mallory arched a brow at the announcement. "Did he now? How very considerate of his lordship."

Apparently missing the sarcasm in Mallory's tone, the girl laid out the dishes on a nearby table, then withdrew.

So he won't even dine with me now, she thought, a sudden burst of affront burning like coals in her stomach.

Well, he isn't the only one who can be angry. From the way he was acting, one would think she'd committed some unpardonable sin. Yes, Michael had kissed her, but it hadn't been her idea. And she'd been in the process of ending the embrace when Adam happened along. Had he arrived even thirty seconds later, there wouldn't have been anything for him to see.

Briefly, Mallory considered sending back her breakfast along with a note giving Adam a few ideas about exactly what he could do with it. Instead, she forced herself to take a seat at the table and choke down a few bites of eggs and toast and tea.

In spite of their present difficulties, she expected Adam to join her inside the coach. Maybe then he would give her a chance to explain what had really happened yesterday between her and Michael—and more importantly the fact that it had no bearing on her marriage to Adam.

To her dismay, however, Adam did not join her. Instead, she glanced out the coach window and saw that he had decided to ride. As the vehicle rolled out of London, he and his horse, Eric, kept pace a couple of yards ahead, precluding any possibility of a conversation during the journey. With her hands clasped tightly in her lap, she leaned back against the black velvet upholstery and silently fumed.

The remainder of the day proved equally vexatious, with only occasional, quick stops to change teams and a single, hour-long break for nuncheon at a busy coaching inn, where he left her to dine alone in a private parlor.

Thoroughly annoyed by the time they arrived at the estate, she refused to take his hand when he came to assist her from the coach. Instead, she sprang to the ground on her own and swept past him with a rigid posture worthy of the daughter of a duke.

After exchanging a few words of greeting with Brooke, she lifted Charlemagne into her arms—the cat having appeared in the front hall to mill around her ankles—then marched up the stairs to her bedroom.

At least Charlemagne isn't angry with me, she thought, as she lowered herself onto the sofa that was set at a comfortable angle before the fireplace. "At least you don't act like a sullen boor," she confided to the cat. Cradling him on her lap, she stroked his silky black fur. His rumbling purrs provided some small measure of consolation but not nearly enough.

No, not enough at all, she thought, a lump forming in her throat. Swallowing against a sudden rush of tears, she decided that a hot bath and a warm cup of tea might be exactly what she needed to soothe her ragged nerves. Gently placing Charlemagne aside, she stood and rang for Penny.

At precisely two minutes to seven, attired in an evening gown of lustrous primrose satin, she went downstairs to the dining room. She presumed she would be treated to more of Adam's brooding man-silence over the meal—if he showed up for dinner at all, that was. It wouldn't surprise her a bit if he refused to join her again as he had for nuncheon earlier today.

But less than a minute later, Adam appeared, taking his usual seat at the head of the table. In a slightly more amenable humor, he made desultory conversation. Briefly, she considered discussing her side of Michael's visit yesterday but decided against it, far too weary to face any more confrontation at the moment. Instead, she confined herself to ordinary, impersonal subjects, relieved when the meal finally concluded, and she could excuse herself to go upstairs.

Weighted down by exhaustion, she let Penny assist her into her nightgown, the servant blowing out all but a single branch of candles on Mallory's night table before bidding her good night.

Mallory had just settled between the sheets, when the connecting door opened and Adam strode inside. Sitting up, she held the coverlet to her chest as she watched him pad barefoot toward her.

His tall, powerful frame was clad in a black woolen robe, the drape of the fabric doing little to conceal the fact that he was naked underneath. Blending neatly into the room's heavy shadows, his hair gleamed dark as ebony, his saturnine complexion arrogant as a pirate come to claim his bounty.

She bristled, her hurt returning over the way he'd shut her out last night and again today. Even in his anger he ought to have at least listened to her side of things. Yet here he was without so much as a by-your-leave, ready to climb back into her bed as though nothing had happened.

She waited for him to say something, even her name. Instead, he drew to a halt bedside the bed and reached for the tie on his robe.

"So you've decided to join me tonight, have you?" she said. "Well, you can turn right around and go to your own bedroom because you're not sleeping in here tonight."

He paused, his eyes sweeping over her. "That's all right, because sleeping isn't what I have in mind."

"You're not doing *that* either!" Tugging the covers higher, she crossed her arms over the top of them.

"If by *that* you mean tupping you, I most certainly am." Leaning over, he gave the covers a hard yank that pulled them completely free. With a flick of his wrist, he sent them sailing to the foot of the bed, leaving her exposed. "Take off your nightgown."

As if her easy compliance were already assured, he unfastened his belt and shrugged out of his robe. In a leisurely move, he laid the garment across the back of a nearby chair, then climbed into bed—large and naked and clearly aroused.

"You aren't undressed yet," he remarked. "Do you need help?"

"No, because I am not getting undressed." She crossed her arms over her chest again. "You don't scare me, Adam Gresham, and I won't be bullied. You've been absolutely beastly to me ever since yesterday when—"

"—When I caught you kissing another man?"

Some of the color drained from her cheeks. "I wasn't kissing him. He was kissing me."

He glowered, his countenance turning more menacing and piratical than before. "And there's a world of difference in that, is there?"

"Actually there is," she stated, suppressing the need to shiver. "Michael kissed me before I had any idea that he intended to. He assumed the two of us were still engaged and didn't realize that so much had changed while he'd been away. He didn't know that you and I are married."

"And prior to his wrapping himself around you like an eel and kissing you for all he was worth, you never thought to take a moment to enlighten him of that little fact?"

"Of course, I did," she declared, ignoring Adam's razor-edged sarcasm, "but he wouldn't let me finish. He kissed me before I had an opportunity to explain. I was ending it just as you walked in."

"Denton told me he was in there with you for a half hour at least," he said in cold accusation.

Bloody butler, she cursed. Next time she saw Ned and Claire, she might have to tell them to have the man sacked.

She gestured with a palm. "Michael was telling me what happened during the battle and why everyone thought he was dead. How he was held captive by the French these past months, then finally freed by Wellington's troops only a couple of weeks ago."

Adam's brown eyes took on a flinty cast. "I don't care if he was dragged down to Hades by the devil himself and escaped to tell the tale; he didn't have any right to kiss you. And by God, madam, you should never have let him."

"I told you I didn't *let* him," she pleaded, her voice breaking. "It just happened. I'm sorry, Adam. Truly I am."

"Good," he told her in a stern voice. "Then you can start making it up to me. Take off your nightgown."

Her gaze flew to his. "But—"

"Fine. I'll do it." Reaching over, he took hold of the

neck of her garment, then rent it in two, the cloth tearing like a piece of tissue.

A gasp shuddered from her lips. "Adam!"

"That's better," he said, stripping the remnants from her body and tossing them aside. "Now, you're just the way I want you."

Taking hold of one of her ankles, he tugged her down so she lay flat on her back. Leaning over her, he banded her wrists inside his fingers and pulled her hands above her head. His dark gaze met hers—lethal, intense, and so compelling that she had no chance of looking away, even if she'd wanted to do so.

"You're mine, do you hear?" he said on a harsh rumble. "Mine and no one else's." He curved his other hand against her cheek before roving lower, sliding his fingers along her throat and shoulder before curving his palm over one of her quivering breasts. "I don't care if Hargreaves has come back from the grave; I've claimed you now, and it's with me you'll stay. You're my wife, and nothing on the face of this earth will ever change that fact."

Without giving her time to respond, he crushed her mouth beneath his, painting her lower lip with a hot, wet stroke of his tongue before delving inside. She yielded, enthralled, as she always was, by the sheer power and breathless intoxication of his touch.

At length, he broke away to scatter fiery kisses over her face and neck, while lower he flicked his thumb across the most sensitive part of one nipple in a way that caused the tips of both breasts to draw into taut, aching peaks.

Arching upward, she twisted against his hold, yearning to be free so she could kiss him as she willed, so she could run her hands in wild circles over his body.

But he refused to loose her, maintaining his gentle, yet unbreakable bond on her wrists. With kisses and caresses that provoked a delicious, almost desperate kind of torment, he played upon her like a maestro at a symphony, stoking her desire, igniting a hunger she could not contain. She gasped, limbs straining again as his fingers glided downward, shuddering against the scorching passion that threatened to turn her blood and bones to ash.

He captured her mouth again in a series of hard, fervid kisses, plundering with ravenous touches that spoke of a deep, unquenchable need.

"I gave you up to him once," he muttered, as he buried his lips against the curve of her throat, "but never again. This time he's the one who can do without you. He's the one who can step aside."

Something about the words broke through the passionate haze that enveloped her, making her pause. "W-what do you mean, step aside?" she asked, fighting the impulse to forget all about talking and do nothing but feel. "When was it . . . when did you ever give me up?"

He stilled above her, their labored breathing the only sounds that filled the air. Long moments passed, emotions flickering over his face like flashes of lightning in a storm-tossed sky.

"Years ago," he said.

"Years?" Her brows angled low. "But I . . . I don't understand."

Suddenly he released her wrists and glanced away. "I've wanted you for a long time, Mallory, far longer than you know. But that isn't important right now," he told her, meeting her gaze again. "What matters is the fact that nothing is going to change between us just because he's back. I am not going to let anything get in the way of our marriage or our happiness. Nothing."

"And nothing will," she said in an impassioned voice. "Truly. I haven't said so before, but . . . I love you."

Something shattered on his countenance. "Mal. My God." Curving a warm hand against her cheek, he pressed his lips to her temple, her cheek, her mouth, kissing her with an ardor whose devotion could by no means be in doubt. "Do you? *Really?*"

Her mouth turned up in a smile. "Yes, *really.* The feeling has been coming on so gradually these past few weeks that I didn't recognize it at first. But I do now."

Briefly, he closed his eyes. When he opened them again, they were shining with a vivid intensity. "I love you too, so very, very much."

He took her mouth again, kissing her with a sweet, leisurely thoroughness that sent her senses whirling. At length, he let her come up for air. As she recovered, her mind somehow returned to the subject—or rather the person—who had led to this moment.

"So you see," she murmured, "you have no need to worry or to be upset about Michael. Seeing him yesterday was a shock, I admit, one I'm still trying to reconcile after believing him dead for more than a year. Of course, I'm happy he's alive, yet sad to be the source of new grief for him. But we didn't know he would come back, and as you said, his return has nothing to do with us. It doesn't change anything between you and me."

Adam threaded a hand through her hair, letting the strands sift through his fingers. "So you're over him then? You don't have feelings for him anymore?"

She hesitated before answering, her earlier confusion returning along with an undeniable surge of guilt. Before Michael had gone off to join the fight, she'd loved him as deeply as any woman could love a man. Yet so much had changed since then, most particularly her feelings.

She loved Adam now.

She was Adam's wife.

And until Michael's return yesterday, she had been happy—in a way she had never imagined she could ever be again. But now Michael was back and clearly still in love with her. She cringed at the thought—sad and torn and remorseful over the pain she was surely causing him. Pain she knew he had not foreseen and in no way deserved.

Turning away from such disturbing thoughts, she gazed into the comfort of Adam's eyes. "Whatever was between Michael and me, it's over now," she said with utter honesty. "Whatever I may once have felt, you are my husband. You are my life."

His rich brown gaze shone with a new light. "As you are for me. So, you won't mind agreeing, then, never to see him again."

"What?" Involuntarily, she tensed beneath him.

He stroked a palm over her shoulder and along her arm. "I don't want you seeing him again. I know you may think it harsh, but I'd rest easier knowing you weren't continuing to maintain a relationship with a man who used to be your fiancé. Seeing you kissing him yesterday made me insane."

"I told you what happened and that *he* kissed *me*."

"Fine. He kissed you. I never want him doing so again."

"He won't," she reassured.

"No, he won't because you aren't going to see him again," he said, his gaze locking with her own. "I want your pledge, Mallory, as a commitment to our union and our love, that you're done with Michael Hargreaves. If he writes, you'll send back his letters. If he seeks you out, you will make your excuses and go on your way."

"B-but Adam, I owe him some sort of explanation at least. I can't just cut him off completely, not without telling him why."

His hand stilled. "He's a bright boy. Believe me, he'll know why."

Her brows drew close. "Well, I—"

"A clean break is best," he told her in a brisk tone. "You said yourself the relationship is over."

"And it is. But we were engaged once, and I've hurt him, however unintentionally the injury may have been done. He has the right to a proper good-bye."

Adam's jaw flexed with reawakened temper. "He has no rights where you are concerned. Not anymore."

"I realize you're still angry about yesterday, but there's no need to be—"

"Need or not, I want you separated from him. So, will you agree?"

She paused, emotions warring in her breast like a pair of opposing armies. How could he put her in this position? How could he expect her to act in such a cold and irrevocable way? None of them—not she or Adam or Michael—had done anything wrong, and yet she felt as if she were being forced to hurt one man in order to satisfy the other.

Surely Adam knew she loved him. Had she not just said so? Had she not just told him he was everything to her now? That she was his wife and nothing about that would change.

And yet he was insisting she turn her back on Michael in the most callous fashion, not allowing her to offer even a word of explanation or an ounce of sympathy over the love they'd shared and lost.

Still, if Adam needed her reassurance, how could she refuse? He'd lost so many people in his life, she realized— his mother and sister to tragedy, his father to a life of vice and dissipation. Perhaps he feared to lose her as well even if he had no need to be afraid.

"Very well," she said. "If that is what you want, then I shan't see Michael again."

"You swear," he challenged.

She glanced away, silently begging Michael's forgiveness for hurting him again. "Yes, I swear."

Primitive satisfaction lit Adam's face, his eyes glittering with a passion that was almost savage in its intensity. Without giving her time to anticipate, he caught her wrists in his grasp again and stretched them high above her head. Swooping down, he claimed her mouth in a way that left no doubt of his possession.

She shuddered with delight, her eyelids sliding closed. They flashed open again seconds later as he reached low with his other hand to unerringly locate the most vulnerable spots between her legs. Before she could do more than gasp, he began touching her with devastating skill and a seduction that was nothing short of astonishing. Rousing her desire to a feverish pitch, he turned her need back upon her doublefold, bringing her to a stunning climax that shook her all the way to her toes.

She barely had time to catch her breath from the first wave of ecstasy when he began driving her toward another. "*Oh—oh—oh, God*," she wailed, her hips bucking beneath the fearsome assault of pleasure.

Utterly merciless, he brought her to completion yet again, using nothing but the touch of his hand, as he willed her body to accept his dominion and the dark onslaught of need that threatened to cleave her in twain. Gasping, she was helpless to resist, completely enthralled and totally abandoned to the force of his ardor and her own raging needs.

Shaking, her thighs wet from having peaked so many times, she thought he must surely be ready to take her and find his own pleasure.

Instead, he slid down, hooking one of her legs over his shoulder before he placed his lips against her. She moaned as sensation sparked within her again.

"I'm the only lover you've ever known," he said in a voice rough with passion. "I'm the only lover you *will* ever know. By the time I'm through, you won't be able to imagine being touched by any man but me. You're mine, Mallory. *All* mine, now and forever."

Suddenly she understood exactly what he was doing. He was branding her, marking her as his own in a way she would never be able to escape. Already she was bound to him. After tonight, she feared she would be enslaved.

Then he returned to his ministrations, kissing and licking and suckling her with an intensity that brought her not just to the brink but beyond.

Without recognizing that the sound came from her own throat, she wailed, peaking with such force that her mind literally went blank, her body quaking from the violence of her rapture. Her heart thundered out a rapid tattoo, her breath coming in ragged pulls between her lips, as she lay too limp and delirious with pleasure to move.

Rising over her, Adam dropped kisses in a wandering path across her body, paying particular attention to her stomach and breasts, which he paused to suckle with a lascivious and utterly shameless enjoyment. She didn't know how it was possible, but her passion soon awakened again, leaving her yearning for his full possession.

Retaking her lips, he kissed her with a raw, unquenchable hunger that left her nearly frenzied. Her fingers twisted into his hair, pulling him closer so she could have more, her tongue tangling with his in a fervid game of hide-and-seek. Sliding one leg up around his hips, she prepared herself to take him in, his erection hard and ready where it arched between then.

But moments later he eased away, flipping her over onto her stomach so that she bounced lightly against the mattress. Reaching for a pillow, he thrust it under her belly, then grasped her hips and angled her so she was resting on her elbows and knees.

She gasped as he inserted his knees between her thighs and spread her wide, leaving her completely vulnerable and at his mercy. His hands slid up to fondle her breasts, squeezing them in the most delicious way inside his wide, capable palms. He caressed her nipples, evoking a long, low moan from her throat that expressed the new depth of her need. She shuddered and bit her lower lip, her flesh burning as if she'd been tossed into a pool of flame.

Ah, sweet heaven, he's killing me, she thought, his touch driving her to the point where she wondered when she was going to start to beg.

"Tell me what you want," he whispered, curving his large body over hers in a way that made her feel caged. "Tell me what you need."

"I-I need you," she whimpered.

"Tell me what else." He rubbed his cheek against hers, then angled his head to caress her neck, nuzzling her with his lips and tongue. "Where do you need me?"

"I-Inside," she murmured brokenly. "I-Inside me."

"Like this?" he purred, as he thrust into her in a long, deeply penetrating stroke.

"Ah God, yes." Arching back, she leaned her head against his shoulder.

He curved an arm diagonally across her and cinched her tight, bracing her against him as he slid out, then in again. His second stroke claimed her more thoroughly than the first, lodging his shaft so firmly inside she didn't think she'd ever before been so powerfully or viscerally aware of him within her. Her legs trembled, making her grateful for his support as he eased back, then thrust again, establishing a rhythm that began slowly at first, then started to build.

He rocked them together, each new sensation stronger than the last, each throbbing pulse of desire lifting her to greater heights of yearning and delight. Literally suspended in his grasp, she was his to control, his to dictate and demand, as he drove her to places she'd never been, to realms of ecstasy that lay halfway between agony and bliss.

She cried out, past the point of caring about anything but the longing that raked her like a set of razor-tipped claws, that twisted through her vitals with a ravenous hunger that only he could assuage.

"Say my name," he demanded, as he pumped into her at a relentless pace.

"A-Adam," she cried, aware of him in every inch of her body.

"Whom do you love?"

"You . . ."

"Say my name." He thrust hard and fast.

"Adam . . ."

"Adam what? Tell me what I want to hear. Say you love me."

"I love you . . . Adam."

He increased his pace, thrusting inside her as if both their lives depended on it. "Again. Say it again."

"I love you, Adam."

"Again."

"I love you, Adam. Ah, God, I do. I love you. Adam, don't stop. Don't ever stop."

Arching her into him, he penetrated her in the most devastating way, stroking her so that her world turned again to fire. She wailed once more as the ecstasy roared through her, sensation breaking her apart before showering her in a joyous haze that pulled her together once more.

Floating in a warm sea of bliss, she hung in Adam's arms as he found his own release, his hoarse shout proof of his deep and lasting satisfaction.

Slumping down together exhausted, she lay with him pressed over her, her mind drifting as lazy tendrils of pleasure continued to flash and flicker all through her body.

At length, he rolled onto his back, taking her with him. She made no demur as he tucked her tight, his large hand reaching to smooth her hair away from her damp brow. Her eyes slid shut, smiling as his lips brushed over her cheek.

"I love you, too, Mallory," he whispered. "I'll never stop—pleasuring you or loving you. And nothing and no one will ever take you away from me again."

Then, before she could form a response, her need for sleep took over, and she knew no more.

Chapter 24

$\mathcal{A}$dam awakened early the next morning, sliding quietly from Mallory's bed in order to bathe and dress for the day.

She was sleeping soundly, a pretty dusting of warm color gracing her cheeks and lips, no doubt remnants of the blistering passion they'd shared during the night.

His shaft sprang to life at the memories, but he ignored his body's eager demands, knowing Mallory needed to rest after the myriad exertions he'd put her through. Though in spite of the intensity of his lovemaking, he didn't think he'd left her with any reason to complain.

Padding quietly across the carpet, he let himself into his room, careful not to disturb her as he closed the door at his back.

An hour later, attired in an old pair of riding breeches, a coat of tan superfine and polished Hessians, he strode out of the house and across the yard to the stables. The lads greeted him with friendly good mornings, then left

Adam to saddle his mount himself as they knew he preferred.

Eric whickered softly at his arrival, the stallion pawing
the ground with clear anticipation of the ride ahead. In
quick order, the horse was readied, Adam swinging up
onto his back with easy grace.

Then they were away.

Adam gave the stallion his head, the frost-covered
ground flying past under the horse's hooves. A brisk November wind shifted like a set of fingers ruffling Adam's
hair and across his cheeks, slapping his skin with cold.

With a contrary turn of mind, he thought of Mallory
lying warm in her bed and the heat of her flesh as she'd
touched him last night. How her fingers had moved over
his skin in fiery caresses and the velvety sensation of her
mouth—hot, wet and divine.

I love you, Adam.

His pulse beat in hard strokes at the memory of her
words, his spirit thrilling to the knowledge that she finally
cared for him as he'd always dreamed. He might very well
have shouted his joy aloud were it not for one thing.

Hargreaves.

Just the thought of his rival's name made his vitals
tighten into a cruel knot. Considering her assurances last
night, he knew he should no longer be jealous.

But he was.

He oughtn't be worried, yet he couldn't keep a niggling
sliver of doubt from jabbing him like a splinter of wood
caught under a fingernail.

He believed her explanation, that Hargreaves had taken
her by surprise, that *he* had kissed *her*. Even so, Adam
couldn't quite get the memory of her in Hargreaves's arms
out of his mind. He couldn't forget the agony he'd felt at the
sight of her kissing the man she had once loved and whole-

heartedly grieved. Nor could he completely quiet the red haze of rage that had engulfed him when he'd first come upon them, betrayal twisting like a dagger in his gut.

In the past, he'd never considered himself a particularly jealous man. Certainly none of his prior liaisons had ever inspired such passionate extremes. On one or two occasions, his more determined lovers had tried to ignite sparks of jealousy in him in order to better fix his interest. Instead, he'd been bored and amused, aware that it was time to walk away.

Then again, he hadn't loved any of those women. Nor had he cared whether they stayed or went their own way, content to end another affair that had run its inevitable course.

But nothing would be ending with Mallory. As he'd so thoroughly demonstrated last night, she belonged to him and him alone—and he would do whatever it took to keep her.

He shifted in the saddle, considering as he did her concern over hurting the feelings of her old fiancé. Hargreaves would just have to recover from his loss on his own, he decided. The major had had his reunion, and as far as Adam was concerned, it was the only one he and Mallory were going to get.

Perhaps after Adam had gotten her with child three or four times and she had a brood of little Greshams tugging at her skirts, he would let her trade how-do-you-do's with Hargreaves once more—assuming the major was married to another by then. Until that day, however, he planned to keep Mallory and her old flame apart and let time put a permanent distance between them.

Despite her assurances that she would not seek out Hargreaves, Adam didn't trust the other man to abide by such strictures. If Hargreaves could, Adam suspected he might try to lure Mallory away; he knew he would if the tables were turned. Well, he wasn't going to give Hargreaves the chance.

I love her too much to ever risk losing her.

Slowing his stallion to a more moderate gait, Adam surveyed the land before him. *His lands,* which he was making whole and prosperous again. His legacy, which would thrive as never before with Mallory by his side.

The same would hold true in his marriage, which would grow stronger over the years. He and Mallory had been happy before Hargreaves's return, and they would be happy still. He would keep her well pleasured in the bedroom and far too busy with the estate matters to dwell on memories of her old fiancé. And as the days slid into weeks, and weeks to months, her thoughts would be so full of her future with him that she wouldn't have time to dwell upon her past with the major. Hargreaves would fade into memory, while Adam would be with her every day—and all through the countless nights to come.

His shaft thickened at the idea of those nights, leaving him thinking wistfully of Mallory sleeping now in their bed.

Slowing Eric to a walk, he forced himself to continue on with his usual survey of the estate rather than turning for home as his body was urging. Time enough tonight for more lovemaking, he told himself. Room enough for a lifetime of nights—and days—with the woman he loved.

Mallory stretched against the sheets, awakening at a gradual pace as she left sleep behind. Opening her eyes, she blinked into the drowsy sunlight filtering into the room. Relaxed and limber, her body hummed with residual satisfaction from Adam's bold sexual demands of the night just past. But then he was always bold, both in bed and out, always sharing new experiences and leading her to heights she'd never known before.

He loves me, she thought, absorbing the idea with a dreamy smile on her lips. *And he's jealous.* Very jealous and extremely possessive—more so than she would ever have imagined he might be.

Her smile fell away, remembering his edict that she was not allowed to see Michael again.

Ever.

A tiny frown creased her forehead, uncomfortable at the idea of turning her back on Michael and not having an opportunity to say a satisfactory good-bye. She'd made a pledge to Adam, however, and she didn't take her pledges lightly.

Still . . . she thought, as she worried the tip of one fingernail between her teeth, she couldn't help but feel bad for Michael. After everything he'd suffered on the battlefield and later in that dreadful French prison, well, it seemed cruel to dismiss him without offering any explanation at all. She could already imagine his dismay and hurt over the fact that she hadn't waited longer for him.

Only three months, he would say. *Three months more, and I would have been home.*

But how was she to have known he would return when she and everyone else believed him long since in the grave? How was she to have realized that another man had mistakenly taken his place in death? Or that Michael would someday come back to claim her?

Ironic now to realize that the wistful, supposedly unrealistic hopes she'd cherished while she'd been in mourning for him had come to fruition. To think of all the times she'd dreamed he would return, that he would walk through the door and tell her he wasn't dead after all, and that his supposed death had all been a tragic error. Really, it was laughable now to consider that was precisely what had come to pass.

Only three months.

If she'd just waited, how those few short weeks would have changed everything. How her entire world would now be different.

But would it be better?

Even knowing what she did now, she had no regrets about marrying, and loving, Adam. How could she when he brought her joy and laughter and such exquisite delights of the sort they'd shared in this very bed only last night? No, if she had to choose, she realized she would do nothing differently.

In the end, she would still choose Adam.

If only he could see that too. She supposed it was only natural for him to feel a bit threatened over the situation, but she wished he realized how unnecessary such emotions were.

She was his wife.

She loved him.

And he had no need to fear that would ever change.

As for her pledge to him, she'd promised not to see Michael, and she would not. Even so, she couldn't evade the nagging sense of guilt that pinched her like a cruel set of fingers.

With a sigh, she tossed back the covers, then rose and went to ring for Penny.

Over an hour later, bathed and attired in a warm woolen gown of dark blue cashmere, she walked down the stairs. She'd just set foot on the bottom step when Adam strode through the front door, having clearly come from the stables. His black hair lay tousled around his head, a hint of extra healthy color lying just under his swarthy-complexioned cheeks and throat.

He stopped when he saw her, pausing for an instant before striding forward, a smile spreading over his face.

She smiled back. "Good morning."

"Morning," he replied with a low, husky lilt.

Despite Brooke and the pair of footmen, who were standing in the hall, Adam took her hand and drew her forward. Bending, he gave her a warm and far-too-lengthy kiss for public view.

"You slept well, I hope," he murmured for her ears alone.

She nodded. "For what few hours you let me sleep."

With a hearty chuckle, he kissed her again. "I suppose I ought to go upstairs and change out of these riding clothes?"

"Now that you mention it, you are a bit ripe with the scent of horse, so yes, I suppose you ought."

Reaching up, he gave her nose an affectionate tweak. "And what shall you do while I'm occupied?"

"From the look of it," she said, craning her head around as a pair of deliverymen were escorted into the hall by Mrs. Daylily, "I believe I shall be occupied as well since the first of the new furnishings seems to have arrived. Arranging it all will require careful oversight."

"Ah," he said, watching as a huge walnut library table was maneuvered through the doors. "Then I shall leave you to your duties. Will you join me for nuncheon?"

"Of course, with you properly attired and wearing rather less eau de equine cologne," she added with a teasing grin.

Tossing back his head, he laughed again, kissed her once more, then turned and strode up the stairs.

Mallory watched until he disappeared. Only then did she turn and join the housekeeper to take charge of the proceedings.

* * *

The next three weeks were busy ones for Mallory, who was consumed with the task of redecorating and refurbishing the house. From morning until evening the halls rang with the sounds of journeymen and carpenters charged with a variety of tasks—painting and hanging wallpaper; attaching chandeliers in the ceiling and light sconces to the walls; screwing in curtain rods and other decorative bits; unrolling carpets and carrying in furniture and crates.

The housemaids and footmen were occupied as well, cleaning, unpacking and arranging the myriad items that arrived with daily regularity from London. As the rooms came together, the house slowly transformed from a barren shell to a warm, comfortable, tastefully appointed home—one fit for an earl and his countess.

The local gentry soon called upon them, curious to see all the changes and to make Mallory's acquaintance as they did.

"Lady Gresham is the Duke of Clybourne's sister," more than one was overheard to whisper in approving, awestruck tones. "Gresham Park hasn't looked so fine in nearly a quarter of a century," said many of the others, visibly admiring of all the changes Mallory had wrought, as she fed them tea and entertained their curiosity.

For his part, Adam was no less occupied, meeting regularly with tenants, farmers and a few neighboring gentlemen eager to discuss the improvements Adam was setting in motion. Over evening meals, he shared the more interesting details with Mallory, explaining that most of his efforts would begin in earnest with the spring planting. Until then, however, there was still plenty of other work to be done.

As for the issue of Hargreaves, there was no further talk on the subject between them. And though Mallory sometimes found herself dwelling on the lack of a proper farewell to Michael, she kept such concerns to herself. As Adam had pointed out, Michael was a grown man, and he knew she was married.

Surely he understood the reason for her reticence.

Surely he was aware why they could not correspond.

Nonetheless, the unfinished nature of their relationship troubled her, and although she knew she'd done nothing wrong, a part of her felt as if she had. She knew she'd hurt him, and she didn't like it, not when he had once meant so very much to her. And still did if truth be told—just not as a lover anymore but as a friend. Funny that he and Adam should have reversed their roles so thoroughly. Sad that she could no longer have both of them in her life, as once she had so innocently done.

Doing her best to put the matter aside, she kept busy with the house and her duties as its mistress—and with Adam, of course, who was never at a loss for ways to keep her entertained.

December soon arrived, bringing colder temperatures and an occasional, frenzied burst of snowflakes. Rather than remain at Gresham Park, she and Adam decided to spend the holidays at Braebourne, a journey she couldn't help but anticipate.

Dressed now in a smart emerald green traveling dress and a warm, red fox cape that Adam had surprised her with that morning, the two of them set out by coach for Gloucestershire.

The roads proved clear, and the drive was not at all unpleasant. With evening darkness beginning to descend hours later, Mallory watched from the window as the ducal estate came into view.

Home, she thought, *though home no longer. Gresham Park is where I belong now.*

Yet everything was infinitely familiar as she stepped from the coach, the immense house, with its honey-hued stone and warm candlelight that burst in smoothing arcs from dozens upon dozens of windows. Servants hurried forth to assist them, Croft greeting them with dignified warmth as they passed through the open front door.

"Mallory! Adam!" Claire said moments later, gliding toward them across the entry hall. "Oh, I'm so happy you are arrived."

Mallory smiled as she and her sister-in-law shared an enthusiastic hug, Adam repeating the process with the duchess moments later. Ned and Esme quickly appeared, and a fresh round of greetings ensued, a pair of the dogs milling around their heels, tails at full wag.

"Come in, come in," Claire invited, slipping an arm through hers once Mallory had divested herself of her cloak. "I've put dinner back an hour so you would have time to refresh yourselves. The family has been arriving all day long, and everyone is here except Cade and Meg. But then that's only to be expected, what with the long journey they have from Yorkshire. They've sent a note that they will be with us by noon tomorrow."

Claire led her into the drawing room, leaving the others to follow. "You look positively radiant. Marriage must be agreeing with you."

"Yes," Mallory said, aware of Adam where he stood only a few feet away. "It is."

"Unless there's another reason," Claire coaxed in a lowered tone. "You're not with child, are you?"

She shook her head. "No, not yet."

"Well, soon I expect. Forgive me, but I suppose I am rather preoccupied with babies at the moment, considering how many there are in the nursery at present, including my own dear Hannah. Then again, perhaps my curiosity is due to my own exciting news. You see, I *am* with child again."

"Oh, that's wonderful!" Mallory reached out and gave Claire another hug.

Claire beamed. "Edward says he doesn't care about the sex, but I feel sure it's going to be a boy this time. The next Marquis of Hartsfield."

"Ah, so you've shared the happy tidings," Ava Byron said, joining them.

"Mama!" Mallory turned, going into her mother's arms for an exuberant embrace.

As they moved apart, Ava took Mallory's hands in hers, then stepped back to appraise her with a shrewd expression in her clear green gaze. After a moment, she nodded and released her hands, clearly satisfied with whatever it was she saw. "You'll do."

Mallory's lips quirked. "I'm relieved you think so."

"You've good healthy color in your cheeks again, and the old twinkle is back in your eye. Adam is obviously taking good care of you."

"Very good," Mallory agreed, glancing toward Adam, where he stood in conversation with Ned.

Her mother's brows knit. "And this business with your major? I was never so astonished in all my life as when you wrote me with word of his return. How are you faring in that regard, sweetheart?"

How am I faring? she pondered.

Even now it seemed like a strange dream that Michael was alive and well, and that her long months of mourning had been naught but a sad misunderstanding. And yet out of its misery, she knew she'd discovered something wonderful and unexpected with Adam—a love that, no matter her qualms, she could in no way regret.

Glancing over, she met Adam's gaze. He smiled and

raised a quizzical brow, the expression in his beautiful, melting brown eyes sending a shot of warmth through her chest. Smiling back, she shared a moment before turning again to her mother and Claire.

"I am well," she replied. "And Michael Hargreaves is no longer *my* major. He is an eligible bachelor once again."

Ava paused, a slightly arrested look on her face. "You are quite right. You are Adam's wife and a most beloved one at that."

"Yes," she agreed.

For a faintest instant she thought about confiding in them about Adam's jealousy when it came to Michael but decided against it. Such matters were between her and Adam and no one else. Besides, his jealous feelings were no longer an issue now that she'd revealed her love and reaffirmed her unwavering fidelity to Adam.

"Oh, but you must be dying for a few minutes' rest and relaxation," Claire said. "I've put you and Adam in your old bedchamber unless you would prefer one of the connecting suites. I can have the housekeeper make other arrangements."

Mallory shook her head. "My room sounds lovely. And this time no one will huff and bellow when they find Adam in there with me."

Claire and Ava stared for a second, then began to laugh.

"What has you ladies so vastly amused?" Jack inquired, arriving just then with an obviously pregnant Grace on his arm.

The three of them laughed again, Mallory deciding the holiday promised to be a good one.

Over the next two weeks, Mallory more than enjoyed herself, making merry with an entire houseful of Byrons, including brothers and sisters, aunts, uncles, nieces, nephews and an assorted array of cousins, both young and old.

The rooms were fragrant with the scents of freshly cut holly and pine boughs, the hallways ringing with laughter from morning to night. Groups gathered to indulge in a steady stream of amusements and winter activities designed to keep everyone entertained. The meals were large and lavish, the formal dining room crowded to capacity each evening. Afterward, the family would retire to the drawing room to drink cups of sweet syllabub or hot, spicy wassail, play guessing games and sing carols.

At night, she and Adam lay snug in her old bed, consummating what they'd once started in that room with none of the earlier restrictions impeding their enjoyment.

Christmas Day arrived amid much gaiety, everyone returning from church services to tear into a literal bounty of gifts. Mallory wasn't sure who was more astonished at the number of presents piled at her own feet—she or her relations. As she began to unwrap boxes, everyone watched with fascinated smiles as one exquisite piece of jewelry after another was revealed.

"I told you I'd buy you something for every day of the week," Adam murmured in her ear, grinning as she gasped aloud over a lustrous strand of pink pearls fastened with a ruby clasp cut in the shape of an oyster shell.

There were also an emerald bracelet, a sapphire diadem, amethyst earbobs, a diamond-and-peridot brooch, and an opal ring that sparkled mysteriously in the sunlight. But by far her favorite was the simplest piece of all, an oval gold locket engraved with roses that opened to reveal space for two special keepsakes.

"You'll have to give me a snippet of your hair for this," she told him as she held out the locket for him to fasten around her throat.

His lips curved in an indulgent smile before he dropped
a kiss against the nape of her neck. "And what shall you
put inside the other half?"

She paused, rubbing a fingertip over the engraved
cover. "Hmm," she mused, "I believe you will have to
wait and find out."

Chuckling, he tipped back her head and gave her a
sweet, lingering kiss. "Merry Christmas, Mallory."

"Merry Christmas, my love."

The next few days slipped past at a pleasant pace for Mallory, New Year's and Twelfth Night celebrations close at
hand. Along with the festivities came the usual talk of
fresh starts and resolutions, which reawakened thoughts
of Michael.

She wondered how his own holidays had been and if
he'd shared them with his family. She hoped so. She also
worried what he must think of her and whether he de-
spised her now. There'd been no contact between them
at all since that one contentious meeting the day of his
return. Yet in spite of the apparent finality of their parting, she still couldn't help but feel that nothing had been
resolved between them, no true good-byes had been said.

Seated alone now in her bedchamber—Adam having
joined the men in a snowy ride across the estate—she
found her old concerns rising once more. This was the
season when all things began anew, and yet so much old
business remained, she thought.

This was a time for forgiveness and understanding,
and yet none of that existed between her and Michael.
Her conscience plagued her like a crow picking carrion,
guilt looming as if it were a dark shadow stretched across
her soul.

She realized that until she made peace with her feelings

of guilt and with Michael, she would not rest properly. Until she offered some explanation for what he must see as her betrayal, she would never be completely happy.

Of course, there was her promise to Adam. She'd vowed not to see Michael again, and she would keep that vow. And yet, she hadn't said anything in regard to writing to him.

Worrying the edge of a fingernail between her teeth, she considered the idea. She supposed some might argue that she was splitting hairs if she wrote to him. Then again, what harm could one letter do, especially if it was intended merely to put things right, to end matters properly between her and Michael.

She needed her treatment of Michael off her conscience.

She needed to say one last and final good-bye.

Without giving herself more time to consider, she stood and crossed to her rosewood escritoire. Taking out paper, pen and ink, she sat and began to write.

Chapter 25

$\mathcal{M}$allory and Adam returned to Gresham Park soon after Twelfth Night, leaving the family behind with fond farewells and promises to visit again soon.

Once they arrived home, Mallory exited the coach, then stepped over the threshold into the comforting warmth of the newly refurbished front hall with its wide walnut-and-gilt entry table, Sheridan side chairs and delicate cream wallpaper with crystal wall sconces.

After handing her mantle and muff to Brooke, she exchanged greetings with the butler, who showered her and Adam with happy tidings for the New Year and their safe return home. She could tell the servants had been busy in her and Adam's absence. Everything was neat and gleaming, the air redolent with the harmonious scents of beeswax polish, bayberry soap, and sweet ash from the well-tended fireplaces.

"I trust the staff enjoyed a good holiday?" Mallory asked, drawing off her gloves.

"Yes, your ladyship. Quite excellent. Everyone was most appreciative of the fare you provided for the Christmas feast, especially the wild geese and the oysters."

Mallory smiled. "And all was quiet otherwise?"

"Very quiet, save for the usual revelers come to call. A few others paid their respects and left a number of gifts and calling cards. In fact, today's post has just arrived. Shall I sort through now, then bring it up to you in the drawing room?"

"That's all right," Adam said, reaching out a hand. "No need for any bother. I shall take it now."

With a nod, the butler went to retrieve a stack of mail waiting on the sideboard.

Adam accepted the offered missives and began flipping through. Pausing, he drew out a pair of envelopes that looked suspiciously like invitations and a magazine that Mallory recognized as *La Belle Assemblée*. "Yours, I believe," he said, passing the items to her.

She smiled her thanks before the two of them moved away from the butler. "I believe I shall retire upstairs and change out of my traveling clothes," she told Adam. "Are you coming as well?"

He shook his head. "I think I'll stop by my study first and see what has been piling up while we've been away."

"Just don't get too busy and forget the hour."

"Never fear, I'll be along soon." Bending down, he kissed her. "Maybe if I time things right, I'll find you in your bath."

She shot him a saucy look. "Mayhap you shall." Trading another smile with Adam, she walked to the stairs, then made her way up.

*   *   *

Inside his study, Adam retrieved a silver letter opener from his desk and applied it to a missive he'd kept carefully tucked out of Mallory's sight.

After perusing the contents, he crushed it in his hand.

Hargreaves.

The bald-faced nerve of the man. So he wanted to meet with Mallory when she was next in Town, did he? Well, the major could wait and go on waiting, since he was never going to see Mallory again—in Town or out. As for the major's letter, there would be no more of those. He would see to that as well.

In regard to Mallory, he supposed he ought to show her the note and discuss the matter with her. She had given her word she wouldn't contact Hargreaves again and to his knowledge she was honoring her pledge.

Yet he couldn't help but recall her initial concerns about cutting Hargreaves off without an explanation, how she'd wanted to put things "right" between them. She was simply too tenderhearted for her own good, unable to see that matters could never be put right, not given the circumstances. Michael Hargreaves had lost her and despite the major's sterling reputation as an honorable man, Adam's gut warned him that Hargreaves would use every advantage to win her back.

It's what I would do, Adam thought, *were our roles reversed. Marriage vows or not, nothing would keep me from her side.*

No, he decided, it was better if Mallory knew nothing of the major's attempts to contact her. When Hargreaves received no reply, he would cease his efforts—eventually. Until then, Adam would do whatever was required in order to keep the major away from Mallory, including censoring her mail.

Beginning today, Brooke would have explicit instructions to bring all correspondence to him first before passing it along to Mallory. Nor was the butler to discuss this minor epistolary detour with anyone else in the household, most particularly the countess.

A niggling twinge of unease rose inside him, but he ruthlessly pushed it aside. Very probably he was acting like a jealous idiot, but he couldn't take the risk. Nothing seemed too extreme if it meant preserving his marriage.

Crossing to the fireplace, he picked up an iron poker and gave the logs a good, sharp stir, red embers flying upward as white ash crumbled away. Replacing the tool in its holder, he tossed the major's letter onto the fire, watching with silent satisfaction as it curled and blackened in the hungry flames.

Only when the missive was fully consumed did he turn away, walking back to his desk to browse through the post once again.

Tossing the other correspondence aside soon after, he went to the stairs and started up, savoring the notion of not just finding Mallory in her bath but joining her.

Ten days later, Mallory pulled the edges of her green-and-rose-embroidered cashmere shawl closer around her shoulders before snuggling deeper into the comfortable width of a library high-backed armchair. A cheerful fire snapped in the nearby hearth, the room pleasantly warm despite the frigid nature of the late January day.

Concentrating on her novel, a deliciously lurid tale of murder and romance that she'd borrowed from Meg at Christmastide, she paid little heed to the occasional burst of snowflakes swirling in the air beyond the mullioned windows.

With Adam away for an afternoon meeting with one of

the local squires, she'd decided to spend a few quiet hours reading. It was a luxury she rarely enjoyed these days, given the callers who often dropped by and the demands of running the household. But she and Mrs. Daylily had already met this morning to review the accounts and plan the week's menus, and it was unlikely that anyone would be calling on such a raw, inhospitable afternoon.

Nearly twenty minutes later, she'd finished one chapter and was beginning the next when a rap came at the door. Glancing up, she discovered Brooke on the threshold.

"Your pardon, milady, but a gentleman has arrived. May I announce him?"

So much for my quiet afternoon, she thought with an inward sigh.

"Yes, of course, please show him in." Marking her place in the book, she set it aside, then rose to her feet. She brushed her palms over the skirts of her winter white day dress to smooth them into place, wondering as she adjusted her shawl which one of her neighbors had decided to venture out into the cold after all. She hoped whoever the gentleman was, he hadn't come to see Adam, or he would find himself sorely disappointed over a wasted trip.

Then Brooke was at the door again. "Major Hargreaves to see you, my lady," he announced.

Her fingers tightened abruptly against her shawl. "Michael!"

Hargreaves strode into the room, attired in trousers and jacket of dark brown superfine rather than his uniform. His thick blond hair lay tousled around his head, as if he'd run impatient fingers through it while he'd been waiting. His keen grey eyes met hers, suppressed agitation clear in their depths.

"That will be all, thank you, Brooke," she said, dismissing the servant, who withdrew on silent feet.

Leaving a polite distance between them, Michael executed a bow. "Lady Gresham, thank you for receiving me. I was not entirely certain of my welcome."

She paused, remembering the last time they had been in the same room together, remembering as well her promise to Adam not to see Michael again. Yet what was she supposed to do under the circumstances? She couldn't very well have him tossed out of the house, not without allowing him a chance to tell her why he'd come. Though why had he come? Surely her letter had said everything that needed saying.

"Of course you are welcome," she said with a false brightness that masked her concern. "Have a seat, and I will ring for refreshments. The . . . um . . . weather being what it is, I think a cup of hot tea would not go amiss."

With an abrupt nod of agreement, he took a seat while she crossed to the bellpull.

Returning, she resumed her own seat.

Only moments after she did, he sprang to his feet once more to pace the length of the room and back. He stopped, briefly met her gaze, then made another circuit. "You are well?" he asked abruptly.

"Yes, quite well."

She wasn't sure she could say the same for him, his complexion still too pale, his long body far too thin.

"And your family?" he continued.

"Everyone is in excellent health. And your own?"

"Fine. Well. Everyone is well." He raked a set of fingers through his hair, pacing once more before he stopped, his shoulders sinking. "Forgive me, I know I should not have come. I waited until Gresham departed, and even then I hesitated to call on you."

"Why have you called, Michael?" she asked in a soft voice. "Did you not receive my letter?"

"Yes, I received it and read your explanation. And yet I could not help but wonder why you have refused to answer my reply."

A tiny frown creased her brows. *What does he mean? His reply?*

He paced a few more steps. "I suppose you feel I've overstepped coming here today, and yet given everything we once meant to each other, I could not leave things as they stood." Stopping, he locked his gaze with hers, his grey eyes searching, beseeching. "Do you truly wish to sever all future connection between us, or do I recognize the work of someone else's hand in this? Your husband's perhaps?"

She glanced away, unable to deny his charge.

"Just tell me you are happy, Mallory. Convince me that Gresham is truly the man you want above all others."

Above me.

The unspoken words hung in the air between them.

She had hoped to spare him this, spare both of them, but there was no easy way around it, she realized.

"He is the man I want. I love him, Michael. I love Adam."

His eyes blazed with an expression that made her chest twist with pain, with remorse. "I care for you very much," she said. "How could I not when we were once destined to share our lives together? But things have changed since you went away. My feelings are so very different now."

"Are they? Despite your words, I refuse to believe you feel nothing for me any longer, that the love we once had together is over and done."

"It is. It has to be. Michael, I'm married."

Striding to her, he took her hands. "I know, and it's killing me. I realize it's wrong, but by God, I still love you, love you so much that I cannot bear the idea that you are gone from me forever. Tell me you feel something of the love you once bore me. Say you haven't forgotten what we once shared."

"I have forgotten nothing, but don't you see that it's impossible—"

"It's not," he pressed. "Come away with me, Mallory, run away with me. We'll go to Scotland or Wales, or even farther where we'll never be found. Canada or the Americas; I've heard there's land just waiting to be claimed. We could have an estate as large as your brother's, maybe even larger depending on where we go."

"Have you gone insane? I couldn't possibly leave—"

"Of course you could. Just say yes, and we'll depart. Pack a bag, and we'll leave in my carriage today."

But before she could tell him that she had no intention of going anywhere, a thump sounded in the doorway. Glancing up, she saw with a sick flip in the pit of her stomach that it was not the maid with the tea.

Adam wore a dark, almost satanic glower, his brown eyes turned nearly black with fury. "The squire and I finished our business early," he said in an icy monotone. "Fancy returning to find you entertaining company, Lady Gresham."

She'd seen Adam angry before but never *this* angry, especially when his eyes lowered to her hands that were still being held inside Michael's. Hastily, she pulled them away, then took a step back to evade Michael as he made a slight move as if to reclaim her.

"Major Hargreaves dropped by unexpectedly," she said, wishing she hadn't heard the slight quaver in her voice as though she had done something wrong. "I had no idea he planned to pay me a call."

Adam's jaw tensed visibly. "Rather convenient that he happened by on an afternoon while I was away.

Mayhap you had a letter from him and have only failed to recall?"

"No. I had no letter from him," she stated.

Michael shot her a look. "But I wrote. Did you not receive my missive?"

"No, I did not."

Michael frowned. "But I was sure it had been delivered."

"Well, the post is never as reliable as one might wish, particularly this time of year," Adam said in a casual voice.

Ordinarily, she wouldn't have thought anything about his comment, but a warning tingle ran down her spine.

Adam knows something about that letter, she realized. *What has he done?*

But she had no time to speculate further as he strode deeper into the room, the set of his shoulders as pugnacious as a prizefighter's. "Now that we have that little detail out of the way, we can move on to more important matters, such as the major's imminent departure." With a stare worthy of a cobra, he regarded Michael. "I want you out of my house. Now! Unless you'd like to stay for the beating I ought to give you after daring to importune my wife."

"Have at it then," Michael shot back. "You'll find I'm rather handy with my fives."

"No!" Mallory exclaimed. "There will be no fighting!"

Neither man paid her the least heed, the pair of them moving forward across the room, bristling like wolves circling as they looked for the best angle of attack.

"I'm not going anywhere, Gresham," Michael said, "not until I've said my piece. I know you forced her to write that letter."

"What letter!" Adam growled, his gaze shooting suddenly to her, his eyes nearly black with fury. "Did you *write* to him?"

"Only to say good-bye," she exhorted, panic hammering against her ribs. "Only to end things for good."

"Because you made her," Michael continued. "Because you browbeat her just like that day when we were together in London. Since I returned to England, I've heard all about your pernicious attentions toward my fiancée while I was away."

"While you were dead, don't you mean? And she's not your fiancée anymore." Adam took another step forward as Hargreaves circled slowly.

"No, because you coerced and compromised her in spite of her obvious grief over me," Hargreaves said, pressing on undeterred. "You manipulated matters so that she had no alternative but to accept your suit regardless of her real feelings."

"Why you—" Adam began.

Michael turned to meet her gaze. "Did he force you, Mallory? Did he seduce you so that you had no choice but to become his wife?"

She shook her head. "No, you're wrong. It wasn't like that."

"He's always wanted you, you know," Michael continued. "When we were engaged, I suspected his interest but held my tongue because you always liked him, and he was a friend of your family. I watched how you treated him, saw that you regarded him as nothing more than one of your brothers, and so I decided he was manageable enough. But the moment I was out of the way, his true colors showed through. While you were vulnerable, he took advantage of you, insinuating his way into your life, sneaking like a thief into your bed."

"Shut your damned mouth," Adam growled, "or I'll shut it for you!"

"Listen to him, Mallory, cursing like the scoundrel he is, for all that he bears the title of earl. Is he abusive to you? Are you afraid of him?"

"No," she protested, shooting Michael an appalled look. "Adam would never hurt me."

"Would he not? How can you be sure? By his reputation alone, he's less than honorable. A cad and a womanizer, who probably wanted your dowry, as well as your virtue, so he could use the money to repair this debt-ridden estate of his."

"If I'd wanted her money, I'd have married her long before you ever came on the scene," Adam said through clenched teeth. "Remember who you're talking about, Hargreaves, before you say something you'll truly regret."

"You know what I think, Gresham? I think you're full of nothing but bluster and bravado, empty threats and no action. If you weren't, you wouldn't have gone behind my back and stolen my woman from me." Turning his head, Michael met her gaze and stretched out a hand. "Come away with me, Mallory. Come away with me now, and I promise you'll never know anything but happiness again."

Before she could answer, Adam let out a roar and lunged at the other man, landing a solid punch to Michael's jaw. Well accustomed to defending himself, though, Michael shook it off, retreating briefly before countering with a vicious punch that drove the air from Adam's stomach.

Adam sucked in a harsh breath, recoiling as he raised an arm in a clearly instinctive move that kept Michael's next punch from making contact with his face.

Michael's advantage was short-lived, as Adam retaliated, landing a pair of rapid blows that snapped Michael's head back in the most alarming way, blood trickling from his nose.

Mallory covered her mouth with a hand, gasping as she watched the two of them pummel each other. "Stop!" she shouted. "Stop this now!"

But they ignored her, fists flying in a series of jabs and punches that made her cringe to watch. Rushing at each other, they landed more blows before becoming locked in a brutal, rib-crushing hug, as if each one hoped to squeeze the life out of the other. Shoes slipping, they crashed to the floor, Adam getting in another pair of punches when he managed to land on top.

Shouting futilely at them again to stop, she wrung her hands, her chest squeezing with a horrible pressure. *Dear God in heaven, they're going to kill each other!*

Unable to look away, she saw blood drip from the corner of Adam's mouth, a livid bruise spreading across his cheek. As for Michael, one of his eyes was swollen nearly shut, his mouth cut and his knuckles raw and bleeding.

When she saw Adam's hands go for Michael's throat, she knew she had to find some way to end this before one of them really did kill the other.

Just then, an alarmed squeak came from the doorway. Glancing sideways, Mallory saw one of the housemaids standing on the threshold, the tea tray clutched in her hands.

Without pausing, Mallory hurried forward and took hold of a large silver pitcher, grateful she had a standing order to bring water with every service.

Racing across the room to where the men were still grappling with each other, she paused to get the best angle, then poured.

Both men sputtered, cursing and moving apart as each recoiled from having cold water splashed on his head.

"Enough!" she declared, holding the dripping pitcher in one hand. "Stop this now, both of you. There will be no more fighting. I won't be the cause of this enmity."

"Mallory," Hargreaves complained, wiping droplets off his face.

"What in the deuce—" Adam retorted, shaking back his wet hair rather like a great dog.

"I won't abide the two of you fighting in the middle of the library like a pair of common thugs," she continued, letting her emotions pour out of her at will. "I won't have it, do you hear? This fight is over."

"I don't think that's your decision to make," Adam said. "I'll decide when I'm done teaching this wife-stealing blackguard a lesson."

"Oh no you won't, my lord. I'll have the footmen in here to pull you off should you attempt any further mayhem."

"Quite right," Michael said.

She turned on him. "And once they're done with Adam, I'll have them toss you out as well, Major Hargreaves."

"Mallory—" Michael said, clearly surprised and wounded.

Adam glared at his opponent, looking as if he were considering whether or not to punch him again regardless of her threat. Instead, he gave a guttural curse, levered himself to his feet, then reached into his pocket for a handkerchief. Stepping away from Hargreaves, he pressed the cloth to his wet, bloody face.

Shaking, she set down the pitcher. "Major, please go. I am sure Brooke will see to your coat and hat."

"Yes, go before I change my mind about killing you," Adam growled, just like the wolf she'd earlier thought him.

Michael bristled visibly, glaring at Adam. "If it weren't

for Mallory, I'd oblige you to try." Pausing, he turned to her. "Will you be all right?"

"Yes, of course." Her shoulders drooped. "Just go, Michael. Please go before this gets any worse."

Hargreaves opened his mouth as if to argue, his gaze briefly meeting hers before he snapped his jaw closed again. Nodding, he stood. "As you wish, my lady."

Turning on his heels, he strode from the room.

Clasping her hands around her elbows, she forced herself not to shake, a knot of worry aching in her stomach in spite of her assurances to Michael.

Then Adam turned and fixed his fierce, dark gaze upon her.

"Adam—" she began.

"Go to your room."

"What?" Her jaw went slack.

"Go to your room. Now! Get out before I—" He broke off and looked away, one fist clenched around his blood-stained handkerchief.

"Before you what?" she murmured, her heart thudding in a dull, heavy beat as a fresh tremor rippled under her skin.

"Before I say or do something I may regret for the rest of my days," he told her in a low, carefully controlled voice.

She trembled again, her eyes growing moist. "I didn't know he was going to call today. I believed everything was over between us."

"Obviously *he* didn't have that impression. Mayhap because of your letter to him," he added in a scathing tone.

"I couldn't leave things as they were. I didn't want him to think badly of me. I only wrote him to say good-bye—"

"You told me you wouldn't contact him," he grated

from between his teeth. "You swore you'd never see him again."

"And I haven't, not until today—"

"You broke your pledge, and so conveniently too, just when I happened to be out of the house on business. Did your farewell note suggest a visit?"

"No, it wasn't like that—" A tear rolled down her cheek.

"Did you know he was going to ask you to run away with him? Or were you just planning to start an affair the moment you were back in Town? Is that why he wanted to meet? So you could make arrangements?"

"Make what arrangements? What do you mean? I don't know what you're talking about."

"I'm talking about his letter to you."

She blinked. "The one he mentioned? The one that went missing?"

"It didn't go missing," Adam informed her, his words rolling from his tongue with deliberate menace. "I confiscated it, then I *burned* it, and by God, I enjoyed seeing what excellent kindling it made."

She drew in a harsh gasp, blood draining from her cheeks. "Y-You read my mail? You *burned* my letter?"

"That's right, and I'd do it again to keep what's mine."

"What's *yours*?" she repeated in a suddenly dull voice. "You make me sound like a possession."

"You're my wife."

"Yes, and as your wife, you should be willing to hear me out. You should be willing to trust me. But you don't, do you, Adam? You believe the worst of me, when all I did was try to show some kindness to an old friend."

"He's not your friend, nor does he wish to be. He wants to be your lover, and he's willing to run off with you to make that happen. I heard him with my own ears, begging you to go to Scotland or Wales or bloody America! Well, you're not going anywhere."

Something cold and hard settled in her chest where her heart had been, something screamed inside her mind that made her want to cry. But the tears that had been threatening earlier didn't come.

He said he loved her and yet he chose to misconstrue her actions. He told her she meant the world to him, but he refused to listen, letting jealousy rule him rather than trust and what was truly in her heart.

If she'd broken her vow not to contact Michael, it had been for kind and honest reasons.

If she'd seemed to waver, she had done so out of regret over hurting someone she'd once loved rather than a lack of commitment to Adam.

But he had no faith in her honesty, and no matter what she did in the future, there would always be a lingering sense of doubt that haunted him, that tortured and tormented them both.

No matter her love, she knew she couldn't live with his suspicion and disbelief. She couldn't bear the knowledge that he didn't love her enough to trust.

Raising her eyes, she studied his face. Her dear friend, the man she'd known since girlhood, her lover and husband.

So familiar.

So handsome.

So beloved.

Then she took a breath and did what she knew she must. "I'm leaving."

"Going to your room, you mean."

She shook her head and met his rich brown gaze. "No, I'm leaving Gresham Park. I'm leaving you."

Chapter 26

Adam stared, a mix of shock, panic and pain tightening around his ribs like iron bands. "The hell you are! You're not going anywhere, and you're certainly not running off with Hargreaves!"

She gave him a cold stare. "I didn't say anything about Michael. I said I'm leaving. I'm going home."

"This is your home," he told her in a fierce voice.

"No, I don't think it is," she said in a doleful voice. "Not anymore."

"Don't be ridiculous." He slashed a dismissive hand through the air. "You can't leave. I won't let you."

She turned sad eyes upon him. "Shall you not? And how do you propose to stop me?"

"Oh, I'll find a way."

"Perhaps," she replied, with a deadly calm that he found more disturbing than tears or anger would have achieved. "I suppose you could lock me up here at Gresham Park.

Chain me in my room and put bars on the windows, as though I were some kind of prisoner. I suppose it might serve for a time, but not indefinitely. After a while, I believe someone would notice. My brothers, for instance."

He scowled.

"No, Adam," she continued in that calm voice that sent a shiver down his spine. "You cannot keep me here, not if I no longer wish to remain."

And as he thought about it, he realized she was right. He couldn't hold her against her will, not unless he did something cruel, something that might make her hate him—or worse that might break her spirit. If he did such a thing, he would be no better than his father. Nor would he ever be able to live with himself again.

His heart constricted in his chest, threatening to burst from the pressure, blood thundering between his temples as he fought the surge of agony that rose within him.

He wanted to rage, but he didn't.

He wanted to drag her into his arms and never let her go, wanted to put up those bars and secure those locks so she could never escape.

But I can't, he realized. If she wanted to leave him, there was little he could do to prevent it.

"Where shall you go?" he asked, choking out the question.

Please God, don't let her say she's going to Hargreaves. That I could not, would not, be able to bear.

"I told you. I am going home," she said. "I am going to Braebourne."

"Can I not convince you to stay?"

Her mouth turned up in a rueful smile. "Only you can decide that. Have you something new to add?"

Suddenly he understood. She wanted him to say that he was wrong to have acted as he had, wrong to have the feelings he did. But in spite of everything it meant, he couldn't help his jealousy, not when he sensed that she still had feelings for Hargreaves.

If not, why else had she written to him?

If not, why had she agreed to receive the other man today, then listen to his protestations of love and his urgings to run away with him?

Adam had died inside to hear those words, wondering if she felt even the slightest temptation to say yes. She wanted him to trust her completely, but how could he when she'd broken her pledge to him? How could he when he knew how much she'd once loved Michael Hargreaves?

The major was right about one thing—Mallory hadn't chosen to marry Adam of her own accord, she'd been forced into it. She said she loved him, but the emotion had come to her late. What if she regretted it now? What if she wished she were still free to marry her first choice of bridegroom? The possibility made him crazy—with jealousy and love.

And now, here she was, telling him she wanted to leave, to abandon him and their home and their marriage. Yet how could he possibly let her go, when he knew she would take his very heart with her the moment she walked through the door?

Closing his eyes, he fought the urge to beg. Maybe if he pleaded and told her what she wanted to hear, she might change her mind. But he had his pride, and, more importantly, he knew he would be lying if he said he had no lingering bit of doubt.

Stiffening his spine, he forced himself to meet her gaze. "I shall take you."

She frowned. "There is no need. I am sure our coachman will have no difficulty making the journey."

"Perhaps not," he stated between his teeth, "but I shall escort you myself. I will not have you traveling alone, especially in the winter. Nor can you make the journey in the dark. We shall leave at first light."

"But I—"

"First light, and that is the best I can offer." Knowing he dare not remain a moment longer, he stalked to the door, wishing there were a way to turn his heart to stone so it wouldn't hurt so badly.

"In case you are concerned, madam," he said in a harsh rasp that didn't sound like his own voice, "I shall not visit your bed tonight. Rest easy knowing you will remain undisturbed."

Then, before he could change his mind, he walked out into the hall.

The trip to Braebourne the next day was silent and exhausting, with neither her nor Adam so much as looking at the other from where they sat on opposite sides of the coach.

When the vehicle finally drew to a halt before the great house, Adam leapt to the ground, then reached up a gloved palm to assist her down. She accepted, making her way before him to the entrance. The door opened, Croft welcoming them with an expression of surprised pleasure on his dignified features.

Before the butler had time to say more, Adam turned and executed a formal bow. "Madam."

Mallory gazed into his dark eyes, not knowing what to say. Good-bye seemed too final, and yet what more could be said under the circumstances?

He opened his mouth, as if to say something, then closed it again, having obviously changed his mind. With a nod, he turned and strode back to the coach, hesitating only a moment while the last of her luggage was unloaded. Giving a low-voiced command to the driver, he climbed inside, a footman hurrying to close the door behind him.

Then, with the flick of a whip, the coach and team drove away, bowling along the wide drive from which they'd only just come.

A crushing ache fell upon her as she watched him leave, her chest growing tight with a kind of pain she'd experienced only once before. And yet this misery was not the same since this time she had brought the loss upon herself. She was the one who had made the choice to part.

Forcing herself to turn, she made her way into the house.

"Mallory?" her mother said, the dowager sweeping toward her with a glad smile. "Whatever are you doing here so unexpectedly? You ought to have sent word you were coming."

Mallory handed her mantle to a footman.

"But where is Adam?" her mother asked. "Surely he didn't go down to the stables, not in this cold?"

"No, he—" Mallory's throat tightened, a pressure that threatened to drown her rising in her chest. "He—"

Ava's chestnut brows drew together. "What is it, dear? What has happened?"

"Oh, Mama," Mallory said, "I've left him. I've left Adam."

Rushing forward, she flung herself into her mother's understanding arms, taking comfort in the soothing lilac-scented warmth, as she started to weep.

Chapter 27

The weather began to moderate as February
slipped into March, the earth beginning to
give subtle signs that spring was on its way.
Inside the house at Gresham Park, however, the winter
gloom continued, Adam sunk inside the darkness of his
thoughts as surely as if he were encased in ice.

Seated inside his study, he tried to attend to the business of the estate—an endeavor that had once filled him
with anticipation and excitement. Since Mallory left,
though, his heart was no longer in it. When she'd gone
away, so had his joy and enthusiasm.

Without her here, what was the point?

Without her by his side, what did any of it really matter?

He'd heard from her only once since she'd left, an impersonal note that asked him to send some of her clothing
and other effects to Braebourne. He'd considered slipping
a letter begging her to come home in among the items, but
in the end he'd sent them on without it.

At least she hasn't taken the cat, he thought, providing himself with some faint measure of hope that she might still change her mind and come back to him.

As for Charlemagne, without his mistress in residence, he'd taken to keeping Adam company. At night, he slept on Adam's bed, and during the day, he often wandered into his study.

Currently, the animal was curled into a ball atop a stack of correspondence on the corner of Adam's desk. Reaching out, he stroked the cat's velvety black fur. "You miss her too, don't you, my fine fellow?" he said. "You wish she'd come home just like me."

Charlemagne blinked at him, his green eyes surprisingly understanding, even sympathetic. Then with his own feline priorities to maintain, he went back to sleep.

Sighing aloud, Adam returned to the document spread out for his review, his attention wandering after every few words as his thoughts went back to Mallory.

Perhaps he should go to Braebourne? She was his wife, and a wife ought to be with her husband.

Perhaps she had a point about his jealousy and suspicions, but how could he not be jealous under the circumstances?

Even now the thought of her entertaining that underhanded jackal was enough to make his blood boil. That and the fact that she'd written to Hargreaves behind his back . . . he still couldn't entirely shake his sense of betrayal despite believing that her intentions had been driven by compassion and a tender heart rather than duplicity. Yet her actions showed that a part of her was still sympathetic to Hargreaves. And if she was sympathetic, then she was vulnerable as well. With the right persuasion, could Hargreaves manage to rekindle the old feelings she'd once known? Could he reawaken her love?

As for her love for him, if she felt as strongly as she claimed, how could she have left him? And how could she continue to stay away?

Oh, Mallory, why won't you come home?

Gulping down a ragged breath, he forced himself to return to his work, even if he wasn't making the least bit of progress at the task.

Five minutes and four fresh attempts at reading the same page of material later, he was about to concede defeat when a knock sounded at the door.

"Enter," he called.

A footman walked into the room. "A messenger just brought this, milord. It's from Braebourne."

He thrust out his hand. "Give it here."

Without waiting to see if the man departed, he slit open the letter, his pulse pounding at the sight of Mallory's distinctive, feminine writing.

Maybe she'd finally decided she missed him too much to stay away and wanted to come home. If so, he would order the coach and set out for Gloucestershire immediately.

But then he saw that the letter was nothing but an additional list of belongings she wished him to send to her brother's estate. More clothing, a few books, and a set of hair combs she'd left on her dressing table.

His heart gave a violent lurch.

Please send Charlemagne, she'd written. *The weather has turned warm enough now for his safe and comfortable passage.*

Crushing the letter in his fist, he flung it aside.

Well, he had his answer then, did he not? She planned to continue their separation.

Their marriage, as he knew it, was over.

* * *

"Will there be anything else tonight, my lady?" Penny asked as she finished brushing Mallory's hair and laid the brush aside. "I'd be happy to go down to the kitchens and heat up a mug of warm milk for ye. I could even add a nip of brandy if ye'd like, to help you sleep."

As her maid knew, Mallory had not been sleeping well of late. Actually, she hadn't had a good night's rest since the day she'd quarreled with Adam and left Gresham Park. Her sleeplessness had only grown worse as their estrangement continued.

Yet each time she considered returning home to Adam, she remembered his wild jealousy—and more, his lack of trust in her. She'd known he was possessive when it came to her and Michael, but she'd never imagined he might go to the extreme of intercepting her mail and actually burning one of her letters! To some, she supposed his actions seemed understandable, even acceptable, since he was just doing what he felt necessary to protect their marriage. Even so, she couldn't help but wonder what it said about their union that he didn't believe her when she'd told him that she loved him and only him.

Given his reputation with women, *she* ought to be the one who was jealous. At this very moment, she could name over a dozen women who would be only too happy to violate their marriage vows in order to have an affair with Adam. But she trusted him and knew he would not violate that faith.

Yet he wouldn't grant her that same respect, that same belief in her affection and fidelity. He couldn't forgive her for showing a little consideration to a man she felt she had wronged, even if it was through no actual fault of her own.

And in spite of everything, she didn't regret writing to Michael since he'd deserved better than her silence. But she deserved better from him now as well. She deserved his respect for her marriage, her choices.

As for Adam . . . well, she'd heard nothing from him since the day she'd left. Perhaps he was glad she'd gone. Perhaps he didn't love her nearly as much as she'd thought.

And so she could not sleep, her nights plagued with unresolved questions and a jumble of conflicting emotions that left her weary and confused—and alone. For despite the steadfast love and support of her family, she was bereft without Adam.

She hadn't told them a great deal, only enough to explain the circumstances that had led to her leaving Adam. Ever loyal, they'd closed ranks around her. Jack had even written saying he'd go have a talk with Adam to straighten his old friend out. But she refused his offer, telling him that she would deal with her marriage in her own way and time.

As for time, Ned had given her as much as she wanted, informing her that she had a home with him and Claire as long as she liked. His only wish was for her to be happy.

Claire and Mama and Esme had been wonderful as well, doing their best to cheer her, even though they knew her spirits were low. Often she played with baby Hannah, who was just learning to walk and whose laughter never failed to make her smile.

Perhaps if she were expecting a child of her own, everything would have been simple. Her place would then be with Adam, and she suspected she would have returned to him no matter their difficulties. But a couple of weeks after her arrival at Braebourne, she'd known there was no baby and that any choices she made were hers alone to decide.

Shaking off her musings, she turned her attention again

toward her maid. "A warm milk would be most welcome, Penny," she said. "The nip of brandy as well."

Anything, she thought, *that might help me rest.*

With a smile and a curtsey, Penny hurried off to procure the nighttime posset.

Crossing to her bed, Mallory sank down on the mattress and gazed at Charlemagne where he lay watching her. Had she been wrong to send for him? Selfish to need his company when Adam might need it more? Did she see condemnation in his round, feline eyes?

"Should I have left you with him?" she asked. "How was he when you left? Does he miss me?"

But the cat could not answer.

Blinking against the sudden moisture in her eyes, she forced herself to lie back against the sheets. Closing her eyes, she waited for Penny to return.

Cannons pounded, the earth quaking beneath her feet, as acrid smoke burned the lining of her nostrils. She walked, an odd, warm wetness seeping into the satin of her thin white shoes. Fields stretched around her, the earth torn asunder in deep troughs and gouges that glistened with red, her slippers turning sticky and scarlet. Everywhere there were bodies, draped in red wool and awash with blood the color of claret wine. Moans rose up around her, mixing with the rumble of cannon fire.

Mallory.

She heard her name from amid the chaos, more smoke obscuring her vision as she hurried forward.

Mallory.

I'm coming, she called, though she didn't know to whom she spoke, only that she had to find him and soon.

Hands reached out to her as she walked, plucking at her

skirts, begging for her aid, her comfort. But she couldn't stop, she had to find him now, before it was too late.

Mallory.

She rushed faster, searching every crumpled body, peering at every devastated face. Her dress turned red as she went, her hands stained with blood that she couldn't seem to wipe away no matter how hard she tried.

Then, finally, he was there, slumped in the mud with his back half-turned toward the sky. Running fast, she went to him with tears of joy streaming over her cheeks as she sank to her knees at his side.

He was hers and she had found him.

Shaking him, she waited for him to wake, to call her name one more time. Without thought, she reached out and touched him, pulling him onto his back so he would see her.

She met his eyes, dead and dark and staring.

She screamed, her throat burning with horror . . .

On a shuddering gasp, Mallory sat bolt upright in bed, her heart hammering painfully beneath her breasts, tears streaming wetly over her cheeks. A clammy sweat she hadn't felt in ages beaded her forehead, her skin flushed hot and cold as shivers racked her body.

Fumbling on her bedside table, she lighted a candle, shaking so badly it was a wonder she didn't burn herself. As her bedchamber came into focus, her gaze fell upon the empty mug of brandied milk she'd drunk a few hours earlier.

So much for its giving her a good night's sleep.

Shuddering, she sank back against the pillows and drew the sheets over herself, reaching up to brush the edge of one hand against her damp cheeks.

She'd had the old nightmare again.

But why? It made no sense, not now when she knew that Michael hadn't died on that battlefield after all. Why would her mind conjure up that one horrible phantasm after so many months forgotten?

Lying quietly, trying to calm herself, bits and pieces of the dream flickered through her memory. As they did, she gasped, tears flowing afresh.

The man she'd found lying on that battlefield hadn't been Michael.

Instead, he'd had rich brown eyes and a beloved face.

Instead, he'd been Adam.

She went down to breakfast late the next morning, having tossed and turned long after awakening from her nightmare. It wasn't until dawn that she'd finally managed to fall into a restless doze, slumbering for a few brief hours—Adam's imaginary dead eyes seemingly seared into her brain.

Concealing a yawn behind her hand, she took a solitary place at the breakfast table in the morning room, sighing gratefully as she sipped hot tea from a cup one of the footmen laid before her. She had little appetite, but rather than suffer the reproving glances of the servants, she forced herself to eat a few bites of the eggs and toast on her plate. She was taking a last restorative sip of tea when Croft appeared in the doorway.

"Pardon me, your ladyship, but a visitor is here to see you."

Her pulse gave a kick, and for a fleeting moment she wondered if it might be Adam. But if it were, she realized deflated, Croft would surely have said. "Did the caller give a name?"

A curious expression crossed the butler's face, one that looked almost sympathetic. "It is Major Hargreaves, ma'am."

Her pulse kicked again, but not with anticipation this time.

She hadn't seen, nor heard, from Michael since that dreadful day when he'd come to Gresham Park. Now he was here at Braebourne wishing to see her again. Briefly, she considered refusing to see him, then changed her mind. There were matters between them that still needed resolving, she realized, so this might as well be the time.

Returning her cup to its saucer, she pushed the china aside. "Thank you, Croft. Pray inform the major that I shall receive him directly. He is in the drawing room, I presume?"

"Yes, Lady Mallory. I mean, your ladyship. Shall I inform the duchess you have a guest?"

She shook her head. "There is no need to disturb Her Grace or the duke."

Whatever it was Michael had come to say, she was sure it would be for her ears alone.

Nevertheless, she waited nearly five minutes before she stood and brushed her hands over her lilac cashmere morning gown. Only then did she make her way from the room.

Michael stood near the fireplace when she entered, his hands tucked into his pockets, his golden brows knit in an anxious frown. The expression cleared the moment he saw her, a tentative smile curving his mouth. "Mallory."

"Michael." She stopped, her hands linked before her. "What are you doing here? I was not expecting you."

As she waited for his response, she couldn't help but notice the hint of yellowish discoloration that was still visible near one of his eyes—the last remnants of his fist-fight with Adam.

His frown returned. "I suppose I ought to have sent word, but given what happened last time, I decided I would save both of us the trouble of attempting to exchange letters."

"Even so, why have you come?"

He strolled closer. "I had heard—that is I had to know if the rumors are true."

"And what rumors might those be?"

"That you're living here at Braebourne again," he said, unable to disguise the hopeful edge to his voice. "That you've left Gresham?"

She fought the urge to sigh. So rumors were swirling already, were they? She supposed she shouldn't be surprised knowing the Ton's insatiable appetite for gossip. Nevertheless, what with the start of the Season more than a month away and most people still in residence at their country estates, she'd hoped her marital difficulties would not yet be widely known.

Apparently she'd been wrong.

"I am staying here for the present," she said, reluctant to admit that she'd left Adam, even if that's exactly what she'd done.

"The moment I heard you'd left, I had to see you," he said, clearly taking her words as agreement. "I had to know if there could still be something between us. We were interrupted when I asked you before, as you may recall."

"Interrupted or not, my answer remains the same."

"Which is?"

"Michael, I am married. We can be nothing to each other anymore. Surely you must see that."

His jaw tightened. "I don't, and I refuse to believe you no longer care for me. You loved me once, Mallory. I know you did."

Her heart constricted beneath her breasts. "Yes, I did—"

"Then come away with me as I asked you once before," he said in an eager rush. "Just because Gresham trapped you into marriage doesn't mean you have to be miserable the rest of your life. Let me take you away. Let me make you happy."

"But I'm not unhappy."

Or at least she hadn't been until Michael had come back into her life and caused this rift between her and Adam. And yet in some ways, she realized, Michael had always stood between them. His ghost a divide that had been nearly as powerful as his living presence.

No wonder Adam was so jealous.

As for his other accusation, that Adam had trapped her, tricked her into marrying him, she knew now that was untrue as well. Perhaps she'd felt compelled to wed him, and yet, as she considered the circumstances and her feelings at the time, she knew the truth.

"You're wrong," she murmured, as the knowledge fully dawned upon her. "Adam may have compromised me, but I married him because that was my wish. I married him because I love him, even if I didn't have the sense then to realize that I did. I think I've always loved him."

Michael's eyes narrowed. "What are you saying? That you wanted him even when you were with me?"

She read the betrayal in his expression, a wrenching sorrow rippling through her veins. "I loved you, Michael. Truly I did, and I would have made you a good and faithful wife, but—"

"But?" he repeated gravely.

"But I love him more. I'm sorry, since I never meant to hurt you. Please believe that I shall always care for you deeply, but only as a friend. Adam is the man I love. Adam is my life."

And I left him.

God, what have I done?

Sudden desolation filled Michael's eyes, turning them the color of storm clouds. "You're all I thought about, all I dreamed of when I was rotting in that French hell of a prison. Did you know that? Did you know that thoughts of coming home to you, of marrying you, were all that kept me going? That I knew if I could just see you again, all my suffering would be worth it?"

She made a gasping sound and pressed her hands to her stomach. "Michael, don't."

"Now you tell me it was all just a sham, that you loved Gresham instead?"

"No, I did love you. You don't understand."

"I think I understand just fine. If you've fallen out of love with me, you can fall back again. You just have to try. You just have to be given a good enough reason." Before she could stop him, he seized her arms and pulled her against his chest. "You'll love me again. I'll make you."

He took her mouth, kissing her with all the passion and desperation pent up inside him. Rather than struggle, she gave him his moment, letting him use all his talents on her. He was skilled at kissing, his lips moving over hers with a confident finesse that would have made most women swoon with rapture.

Yet his finest moves and most seductive touches did nothing to speed her pulse or rouse her desires. He wasn't Adam, and all she could think of was the fact that she wished he were.

Abruptly, he pulled away, a mask of sadness settling across his features. "It isn't any good, is it?" he said, low and despairing. "There's no spark. Not for you at least."

A tear slid down her cheek.

He wiped the wetness from her skin. Resigned, he stepped back, stepped away. "No wonder he fought like a demon for you. Whatever difficulty is between you, don't let it stand in your way. If your estrangement is because of me, tell him he has no further need to worry."

Executing a correct bow, he started toward the door.

"Michael, will you be all right?" She crossed her arms at her waist.

His eyes took on a flint-hard glint. "Don't worry about me. I came back from the dead, after all. I'm sure I can survive something as simple as a broken heart."

"I never meant to hurt you."

"Nor I you. Be happy, Mallory."

Before she could say more, he turned and strode from the room.

Listening to the silence, she knew he was gone.

Trembling, she wiped the tears from her face, then made her way up the stairs.

Chapter 28

"I've brought your dinner, your lordship," Mrs. Daylily announced as she made her way into Adam's darkened study the following evening. "I'll set the tray up over here near the fire, shall I, so you'll be comfortable while you enjoy your meal."

Adam made no effort to move from where he sat behind his desk, the area swathed in a pool of heavy shadow. "I told you I didn't want dinner. Take it away."

The housekeeper hesitated, clearly marshaling her courage before she continued. "But you've got to eat, my lord. You've barely touched anything in days. Cook made all your favorites tonight. Beef pie, cheddar potatoes, and carrots with fresh dill and new-churned butter. There's even a delicious apple tart with clotted cream. I had a dish of it myself at staff dinner before I brought up your tray. It's quite excellent."

"Then enjoy another helping because I don't want any."

"But your lordship—"

"Enough! Leave me be."

The servant straightened, then gave a resigned sigh. "Very well. I'll just light a few candles then before I go. The room is so dark."

"No. I like it dark."

Dark as the misery in my heart, he thought. *Black as the depth of my despair.*

Abiding by his wishes in spite of her obvious disapproval, the housekeeper retreated from the room.

Once she'd gone, he slouched lower in his chair.

Mrs. Daylily meant well, he knew, just as he realized all the staff meant well, the lot of them whispering and tiptoeing around him as if there had been a death in the house. And he supposed in a way there had been, Mallory's absence casting a pall over everything, as if the sun had gone from the sky.

The light had certainly gone from his life, the present darkness an apt reflection of his mood. Ever since he'd realized Mallory was never coming back, he'd been sunk into a state of absolute desolation. He barely slept and had no appetite for food. As for all his grand plans for the estate, he couldn't seem to muster any enthusiasm. He'd taken to passing all the work off to his steward, letting the other man handle the responsibilities that he just couldn't seem to face.

He'd considered drowning his sorrows in the bottom of a liquor bottle, getting so roaring drunk that he would barely know who he was anymore. But that had been his father's solution—smothering his problems in a selfish and self-destructive world of debauchery and shame. He'd tried that once himself all those years ago after Delia's death and knew firsthand that it wouldn't make the pain go away. Nor would it do anything to bring Mallory back.

Each day he thought about driving to Braebourne and doing whatever it took to bring her home. He'd even be willing to beg, if that was the only way to convince her. But what if she still said no? He didn't quite trust himself not to do something insane, like kidnapping her. And as she'd told him already, he couldn't keep her locked away—not forever at least. If she didn't love him enough to willingly be his wife, there was nothing he could do to make her.

And so he sat in the house, sunk in misery. He supposed he would have to get on with living again one of these times soon, but for now, he simply couldn't muster the will.

Picking up the gold locket he'd found upstairs on her dressing table—the one he'd given her for Christmas—he ran his thumb over the engraving.

Mallory.

A hollow ache swelled beneath his ribs, the smooth metal biting into his skin as he squeezed the necklace hard inside his palm. Closing his eyes, he leaned his head back against the chair and wished for oblivion.

He didn't know how many minutes passed before he heard the door open, sensing someone enter the room. "I said I don't want to be disturbed," he said without opening his eyes. "Whoever it is, go the hell away!"

"I see you haven't lost your predilection for cursing while I've been gone although under the circumstances I suppose I can forgive the lapse."

His eyes flashed open. "*Mallory?*"

She can't be here, he thought, wondering if she was some figment of his imagination. Maybe in his despair, he was beginning to lose his mind. But then she walked farther inside the room, her beloved features swimming into view in the murky light.

"It's dark as a tomb in here," she observed. "I'll light a few tapers, shall I?"

He didn't gainsay her but instead abruptly sat up in his chair. As he did, the locket fell from his hand onto the desk. While she moved around the room tending to the candles, he strove to rectify his disheveled appearance, raking his fingers through his hair, reaching up to straighten his cravat before he remembered he hadn't bothered to put one on that morning.

Well, he would have to do, he decided—unshaven jaw, uncombed hair and all. He ought to stand as decorum prescribed, but he didn't quite trust his legs at the moment.

Watching as she turned to face him once more, he noticed the way the increased light played off her emerald traveling gown, the color a perfect foil for her silky raven hair and delicate, translucent skin. Her lips were red from the cold outside, her blue-green eyes bright with a wealth of emotions he couldn't entirely fathom.

"Heavens, Adam. You look dreadful," she said, as if only then seeing him properly. "Before I came in here, Mrs. Daylily mentioned something about trying to get you to eat dinner. Have you been skipping meals?"

"Mrs. Daylily is an old mother hen who should mind her own business," he retorted, not at all interested in discussing their housekeeper or his recent lack of appetite. "Why have you come, Mallory? I presume one of your brothers brought you."

"No, I traveled alone."

"Alone! Has Ned lost his senses—"

"I was accompanied by two footmen, the coachman, and my maid. I was never in any jeopardy."

He scowled. "Servants or not, you shouldn't have been on the road by yourself, nor should Ned have allowed you to be. Why did you not send word? Why did you not write asking me to come to you?"

She moved closer. "I wasn't entirely sure you would

agree, considering I've heard nothing from you since I left. Then too, I didn't want to wait."

His pulse began to beat in thick, hard strokes. "Wait for what?" he blurted. "What is it that was suddenly so urgent?"

"Michael came to see me yesterday," she said.

His stomach lurched, a burning sensation lodging behind his breastbone and the underside of his jaw. *Is that why she's come back? To tell me she's running off with my rival?* It would be like Mallory to do the decent thing and tell him in person. She would consider a letter far too impersonal a way to end a marriage. Well, impersonal or not, he didn't want to receive her good-bye.

He wanted to shout at her to be silent.

He wanted to drag her into his arms and kiss her until she changed her mind.

He wanted to lock her up and never let her free.

Instead, he forced himself to sit, only the fists he clenched around the arms of his chair betraying his true feelings.

"What did the major want then? Although I suppose I don't really need to ask, do I?" he added, unable to keep the bitterness from creeping into his tone.

Visibly gathering herself, she took another few steps forward. "He wanted to know if there was anything still between him and me. He wanted to know if I still loved him."

He stared blindly at the papers on his desk. "And what did you say?"

She glided even closer, moving so she stood less than a foot distant. "I said that I would always care for him—"

A wrenching stab of agony went through his chest as if she'd leaned over and yanked out his heart. He closed his eyes, his breath growing thin in his lungs.

"—But that there is only one man I truly love," she continued in a tender murmur. "And that man is you."

His eyelids flew open, his thoughts spinning wildly around his brain. Now he knew for certain that he was dreaming. Now he realized he really had lost his mind. Yet there she stood, undeniable love shining vivid as a sea in her eyes.

"I know you think you have reason to mistrust me, but you don't," she said. "I know you've been jealous of Michael, but I understand now why that is. You believe I was forced into our marriage, that I didn't choose you with a free and open heart. But you're wrong, Adam. I did want to marry you."

"You were compromised and even then you needed convincing," he said, only then fully realizing how much doubt he'd been harboring because of the circumstances of their union.

"Only because I was scared, frightened of losing my heart again after so much grief. I loved Michael, but I think deep down I knew I loved you more. That I've always loved you, since I was a girl."

His brows drew low. "What do you mean?"

"I loved you when I was a girl, but you made it clear you didn't want me, and so I put you aside, locked my love for you in a little corner of my heart that was never to be touched again. I settled for friendship, and I told myself it was enough. I let myself love Michael, and I did truly love him. But I've come to understand that I loved you first. I love you best, and even if we were not already wed, I would want to be your wife and no one else's. I would want to spend the rest of my life loving you and being by your side.

"Adam, I'm so sorry," she said, crossing the last bit of space between them. "I know now that I should never have left. I should have stayed and fought for our marriage. Please forgive me. Please tell me you'll take me back."

His lips parted, his heart kicking so hard it was painful. *"Take you back?* Of course I'll take you back. And if anyone needs forgiveness, it's me," he said, his voice breaking. "I should never have let you go."

Reaching out, he pulled her to him and buried his face against her breasts, breathing in her honeyed scent, luxuriating in her feminine softness.

Her fingers came up and slid into his hair to caress his head, her touch sending quivers chasing down his spine.

"What about my keeping his letter from you?" he questioned after a minute. "What about violating your trust?"

She met his gaze. "Being with you means more. Being with you means everything. And I'll teach you to trust me by proving my love, my fidelity, all the rest of my days. Besides, if you can forgive me for leaving you, then I suppose I can forgive you for being crazy with jealousy over me."

"I was crazy," he confessed. "I would have done anything to keep you with me. I *would* do anything even now."

"But don't you see, my love, that you don't have to?" She slid her hands down to cup his cheeks. "I'm yours. I want no other, and I never will."

With a sound that was half groan, half growl, he yanked her down onto his lap and crushed her lips to his. In that moment, the world that had been so dark turned light again, his spirit sprouting wings like those of angels, as his heart began to soar. Arching her close—as close as he could get to her with their clothes still on—he ravished her mouth, pouring all his longing, all of his love into their embrace.

As for Mallory, she reveled in his possession, her heart

brimming as she kissed him back with every ounce of passion and adoration she could devise. In his arms there was no hesitation, inside his touch there was only love and need. The spark that had eluded her with Michael's kiss burst forth in a fiery gust of warmth and desire, leaving her incapable of thinking about anything or anyone but Adam.

This, she knew, was where she belonged.

This love was the only one she would ever want or need.

Closing her eyes, she gave herself over to the moment, kissing him to the point of distraction.

She had no idea how much time passed before the two of them came up for air. Breathless, she smiled.

He smiled back, relief and longing and love in his gaze.

"There's something I want to tell you," she said, knowing she needed to unburden herself so there would be no more secrets between them. "Promise you won't get angry."

"Why would I be angry?"

She played her fingers over the bare skin of his neck. "Just promise."

His brows drew close. "All right, I promise."

"Yesterday when Michael came to see me, he kissed me."

"Why that—!" His arms stiffened around her.

"Remember, you said you wouldn't get angry," she reminded.

"That's before I realized what I was promising. I knew I should have killed him when I had the chance."

"No, you shouldn't have, and I'm only telling you this to prove you have no cause for further worry."

He raised a skeptical brow. "Oh? And why is that?"

"Because I realized that you have more than made good on your threat."

"What threat is that?"

"The one you made when you said you'd ruin me for other men. Michael is an excellent kisser, and he tried his best to inspire my interest, but I felt nothing for him. All I could think of while I was in his arms, was you." Reaching out, she brushed a lock of hair off his forehead. "So you see, you have thoroughly destroyed me for any sort of affair. Even if I wished to engage in one, enjoying it would be hopeless."

"You'd better not have any affairs, madam," he warned with a twinkling glint in his eyes.

"Nor you, my lord, so be warned too. Should I ever find you with another woman, I shall be forced to scratch her eyes out, then maim you in some very painful manner."

"And I thought I was the only jealous one." Laughing softly, he pressed his lips to hers. "I want no other woman, Mallory, only you. You say you've always loved me. Well, I know I've always loved you. Since you were sixteen years old, you've been the only woman for me. Why else do you think I steered you away?"

Her mouth dropped open. "What do you mean that you've loved me since I was sixteen! You did not. I was nothing but Jack and Cade and Edward's little sister. You treated me like a child."

He stroked a hand across her shoulder blades. "You *were* Jack and Cade and Edward's little sister, which was why I couldn't let you know my real feelings. I had nothing to offer you at the time, my pockets were far too empty ever to hope to make you my bride."

"So is that what you meant?" she said, casting her thoughts back. "When you said you once gave me up. Do you mean you loved me even when Michael was courting me? That you stepped aside knowing he meant to make me his wife?"

He nodded, his eyes bright with remembered pain.

"You should have told me."

"I didn't want to look like a fortune hunter, a man unable to provide a decent home for his own wife. If we'd wed then, there would have been talk about my motivations, and I never wanted you to have the slightest doubt about how deeply I love you. And I do, Mallory. I love you so very, very much."

"Oh Adam." She sighed, squeezing her arms tighter around him. "Just think of all the years we've lost."

"No," he murmured. "Think instead of all the years we still have. So much time ahead of us. So much happiness to share, you and I."

Leaning close, she let her passion fly free, plundering his mouth again with love. When she reluctantly eased away, she caught a glint of golden light on Adam's desk. "What's that? Is that my locket?"

A faintly sheepish expression crossed his face. "I . . . um . . . I was looking at it."

She paused. "Carrying it around with you, you mean. Oh, Adam, I knew there was a reason I didn't take it with me."

"Why, so I could act like a lovesick fool?"

"No, so I would have a reason to come back. I love that locket."

He laughed, and she joined him.

"I've also decided what I'm going to put in the other half of the inside," she said.

"And what is that?"

"A miniature of our firstborn child, right there next to the lock of your hair."

He grew still. "Mallory, you're not—"

"No, but I hope to be very soon," she added with a sultry smile. "Perhaps after dinner you can try to do something about that."

He gave her a roguish grin. "Who's waiting for dinner! If you're hungry, you can dine in bed, *after* I've ravished you several times. Come here, wife," he said, standing her on her feet, "you have weeks of lovemaking to make up to me."

Then, before she guessed his intentions, he swept her up into his arms. Moments after, a black cat wandered into the room and hopped onto the desk.

"Charlemagne!" Adam declared. Meeting her gaze, he smiled. "Now, I really know you're home for good. You brought the cat."

Her lips curved upward as she tightened her arms around his neck. "I am home, the only place I want to be. Now, take me upstairs, my lord. We have an heir to make."

*The following is an excerpt from
Tracy Anne Warren's
next captivating romance*

*Available 2011 from
Avon Books*

London, England
April 1813

*L*ord Drake Byron strode briskly into his study, wiping chalk dust off his hands onto a white silk handkerchief. He'd come directly from his workshop, where he'd been deeply immersed in formulating his newest mathematical theorem. But as his butler had interrupted to bluntly remind him, his appointment was waiting—and had been waiting for the good part of the past hour.

He cast a quick glance at the back of the bonnet-clad woman seated before his desk, noting the correct set of her shoulders inside her serviceable dark blue gown. He supposed she had every right to be irritated by the delay. Then again, waiting was a servant's lot in life, was it not?

If he decided to hire her for the housekeeping job, she would simply have to get used to his erratic and unpredictable habits. She would also need to have a strong constitution, enough so that the occasional unintentional explosion from one of his experiments didn't send her into a paroxysm of nervous terror. He'd lost more than one housemaid that way, girls too delicate to abide the bangs, booms and acrid smells that emanated through the town house from time to time.

His mother still worried that he might blow himself up, but over the years, she and the rest of his family had come to accept his interests and eccentricities and given up any further attempts at changing him. At present, however, she had no cause for concern, since he was once again indulging his love of theoretical mathematics rather than his fascination for scientific invention.

Still, he hadn't meant to be late for today's interview. Though come to that, he never *meant* to be late for anything. He just got so involved sometimes, he completely forgot the hour.

"My apologies for keeping you waiting," he said, as he rounded his desk and took a seat. "I was working and could not break away." Without looking up, he rifled through the papers scattered in tall stacks across the polished walnut surface, thumbing through several before pulling a single page free.

"The—um—employment service sent over your credentials, Mrs.—Greenway." He perused the page, still not glancing up. "I haven't had time yet to review your background in depth, so why don't you just tell me about yourself. I assume you brought references?"

"Yes, your lordship," she answered in a gentle, silvery voice that put him in mind of birdsong, summer breezes, and strangely enough, warm sheets tangled after a lusty tumble. "I have them right here."

A shiver slid like the tip of a hot finger down his spine. Looking up, he stared.

He'd expected a middle-aged woman, someone plump

perhaps, and motherly, like his last housekeeper. But this woman was neither plump nor middle-aged and she didn't put him at all in mind of his mother. Nor any mother with whom he'd ever been acquainted, come to that. Quite the opposite, he thought, as he took in her slender figure and youthful countenance.

How the deuced young is she? he thought, studying her features.

Glancing down again, he gave the character in his hand a quick skim.

Name: Mrs. Anne Greenway
Marital Status: Widow
Age: 29

Nine and twenty? How could this young woman seated across from him be a full year older than himself? If he hadn't just read her credentials, he wouldn't have believed it possible for her to be more than a handful of years out of the schoolroom. Then again, he supposed determining a person's actual age was an inexact science. As were looks, for though she wasn't pretty in the classical sense, there was something undeniably appealing about her. She was . . . vibrant, her ivory complexion and high, smooth cheeks dusted the delicate hue of just-picked apricots. Her face was heart-shaped with long-lashed, whiskey-gold eyes, a long, straight nose and full, rosy lips that looked as if they'd been formed for the express purpose of being kissed.

But it was her hair, which she'd braided and ruthlessly pinned into a bun beneath her bonnet, that surprised him the most. From what he could discern, the strands were a lush array of autumnal colors ranging from deepest brown to warm red and pale gold. Yet threaded amongst them were a surprising number of silvery strands that gleamed like the precious metal itself.

She is going gray, he mused.

Maybe she really was nine-and-twenty, after all.

"I believe you'll find everything in order," she ventured in that lyrical voice of hers. Leaning forward, she held out a piece of fine cream-colored vellum, her hand small inside a dark blue glove.

Frowning, he paused for a moment before accepting the characters. Opening one, he gave it a quick scan.

"You appear to come highly recommended. You last worked for the Donald family in Armadale, Scotland, I see. I'm not familiar with the town. Where is it located?"

"In the far north on the Isle of Skye."

"Ah, and why did you leave?"

A faint scowl briefly marred her features. "The . . . family decided to emigrate to America, as so many of the Scots have done in recent years. I had no wish to follow them."

"And you're not Scottish yourself. From your accent, you sound English. The Lake District, if I'm not mistaken."

She raised an eyebrow in surprise. "Yes, that's right."

"And Scotland? How did you come to be employed at such a great distance from your home?"

Her gaze lowered to her hands. "The Donalds advertised, much as you have done, my lord. After my husband died, I found myself in need of a situation. Prior to my marriage, I'd worked in service, first as a housemaid, then as a lady's maid. Employment as a housekeeper seemed a much better prospect."

He nodded, glancing again at her credentials. "You have no children, correct?"

"No, none."

"And you believe London will be to your liking? It's

very different from a village in the north." Briefly, he paused. "There is also the fact that I am a single gentleman with a household that is nothing similar to the one to which I expect you are accustomed. I have no wife, nor any wish to obtain one. I also tend to come and go as I please with no regular routine. I may spend one week locked inside my workroom and the next decide to throw an impromptu gathering for friends. Should you find yourself in my employ you will perforce need to adjust to a continually changing environment."

A curiously wry expression crossed her face. "I believe you will discover that I am quite adaptable to any situation, my lord. As for the running of your household, I expect one domicile is very like another at its heart, so I see no difficulty in its management, however unpredictable your schedule may be."

She drew a breath before continuing. "As for London, city life suits me perfectly at present. I am looking forward to the excitement and change of new things."

"Hmmph," he said, the sound an indecisive exhale beneath his breath.

That is precisely what troubles me, he thought, *new things and the potential excitement and change of having her in my house.*

She was far too attractive, and despite her stated age, much too young-looking for comfort. Were he interested in taking a new mistress, well, that would be a different story entirely. He'd have her installed in her own neat little town house in a trice. But she wasn't here to warm his bed and he wasn't the sort of man who took advantage of his maidservants—or his housekeeper.

Then again, he'd never had cause before to be so sorely tempted by a member of his staff, even a prospective one.

If only his former housekeeper, Mrs. Beatty, hadn't decided to quit so abruptly last month. Entirely without warning, she'd turned in her notice and announced with a nervous urgency that belied her usually steadfast nature that she was leaving for the seaside. "My health isn't what it used to be," she told him, "and my doctor suggests a milder clime."

She'd always appeared in the peak of health, as far as Drake could see, but how was he to argue? And so, with little more than a week's notice, she'd packed her bags and taken a hired coach out of the city as fast as it could go.

Glancing down again now, he studied the papers in his hand.

Mrs. Greenway seemed exceptionally well-qualified, to be sure, and heaven knows he had no interest in being put to the bother of interviewing more candidates, and yet . . .

Laying her credentials aside, he met her lovely golden gaze and prepared to do what he ought.

If only she weren't so dashed appealing.

He's not going to hire me, Sebastianne Dumont realized, her nails flexing deep into the brown cotton twill of the reticule on her lap. Her heart beat like a trapped bird in her chest, alarm squeezing painfully beneath her ribs.

But he has to hire me. Anything else is unthinkable.

The interview had seemed to be going so well at first, the answers she'd practiced with such determined concentration rolling easily off her tongue. She'd thought he seemed impressed, but then he'd grown quiet, contemplative. Her fingers clenched tighter as she mentally reviewed his questions and her responses.

Did I make a mistake?

Has he figured out that nearly every word I've told him is a lie?

But how could he know she was lying when her script had been so well researched, so carefully prepared by those who made a profession of deceiving others?

She knew Napoleon's men had gone to great lengths to arrange this position for her so she could gain entry into Lord Drake Byron's house. They'd made sure his former housekeeper left her long-time situation, using cash and threats to pave the way.

She knew they'd made sure she, Sebastianne Dumont, would be the one sent by the employment service for this interview.

She knew they expected her to not only obtain the housekeeping position but to retrieve the information they wanted as well.

There could be no failure. For if she did not succeed, the price would be beyond redemption and cost her everything she most loved in this world.

As for Drake Byron, he wasn't at all how she'd imagined him.

Over the years, she'd heard her mathematician father mention Lord Drake as one of the world's brightest lights in the fields of science, theoretical physics and mathematics. A prodigy who'd earned advanced degrees from Cambridge and Oxford before his twentieth birthday, he'd won a number of prestigious awards, including the Copley Medal.

Had there not been a war raging in her homeland of France and elsewhere across Europe, she was sure he would have been welcomed on the Continent with open arms. As it was, certain parties coveted his work, particularly the secret work he was presently undertaking for the

British government in the realm of encryption and algorithmic ciphers.

Work she'd been sent here to acquire.

Knowing his background, she'd assumed he would be older, more of a contemporary of her father's, with thinning hair, lined features and a belly that had gone as round and soft as bread dough.

But there was nothing doughy about Lord Drake.

Quite the reverse, since he was young, handsome and extremely fit. Tall and leanly muscled, he sported solid shoulders, a broad chest and a flat stomach that belied any notion of his ever developing a paunch.

As for his features, he would catch any female's eye whatever her age. From his head of thick chestnut brown hair to his aristocratic nose, sculpted lips and square chin, he was everything that was pleasing to behold.

Still it was the intelligence and light of good humor shining in his translucent green eyes that appealed to her the most—eyes she had best be careful never to gaze into too closely for fear of being unmasked. For above all else, she must keep him from realizing who she really was and the wrong she planned to commit against him.

But first she had to convince him to hire her or all the rest would make no difference at all.

"I am a hard worker, your lordship," she told him before he had a chance to say something that would end the interview. "You will not find better, I promise."

His brows gathered close. "I am sure that is true, Mrs. Greenway, still I am not entirely positive that—"

"I understand your former housekeeper was with you for a good many years," she interrupted.

He nodded. "Since I first acquired the house here on Audley Street."

"Then I am sure her departure has been most disruptive to your routine, even one as admittedly irregular as your own."

"It has been, yes," he said, his mouth curving up at the corners.

"Then allow me to put it right. Hire me for the position and I shall have your household running again as smoothly and easily as it ever did. More so, I daresay."

"More so, hmm?" he mused in a mellow baritone that seeped through her like warm brandy.

She forced the unwanted feeling aside.

"You don't lack for confidence, I'll say that." He paused, silence settling between them, as the frown returned to his brow. "You are clearly qualified and yet—"

Her chest squeezed painfully, fingers curled against her reticule to hide their trembling. Without thinking she leaned forward in her chair. "*Please*, your lordship, I need this job. Travel from Scotland is not without expense and my severance shall only last me so long. Let me prove to you what an asset I can be. You won't regret it, I swear."

At least not right away, that is.

Her mouth grew dry, her pulse thudding dully in her veins as she waited for his answer. He simply had to say yes. Otherwise she would have to resort to other measures, desperate ones that frightened her to consider.

Slowly, he met her gaze, those clear green eyes of his boring into her own. Holding steady, she forced herself not to look away, not to flinch or in any manner reveal her duplicity.

Abruptly, he nodded. "Very well, Mrs. Greenway, you've convinced me. Starting tomorrow you are my new housekeeper."

At Avon Books, we know your passion for romance—once you finish one of our novels, you find yourself wanting more.

May we tempt you with . . .

- **Excerpts** from our upcoming releases.

- Entertaining **extras**, including authors' personal photo albums and book lists.

- Behind-the-scenes **scoop** on your favorite characters and series.

- **Sweepstakes** for the chance to win free books, romantic getaways, and other fun prizes.

- Writing **tips** from our authors and editors.

- **Blog** with our authors and find out why they love to write romance.

- **Exclusive content** that's not contained within the pages of our novels.

Join us at
www.avonbooks.com

AVON

*An Imprint of HarperCollins*Publishers
www.avonromance.com

FTH 0708